A HUNDRED HILLS

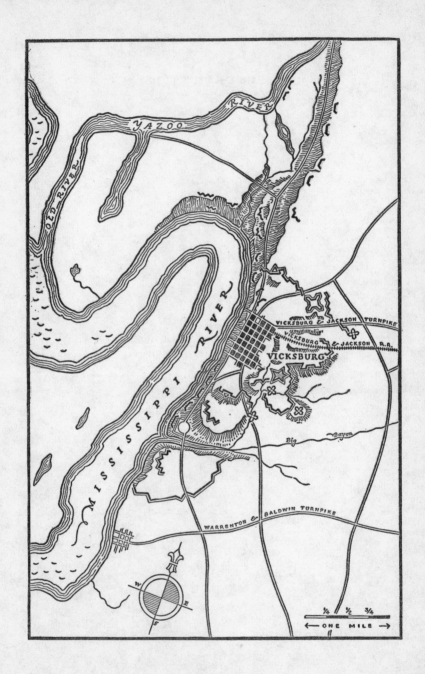

A HUNDRED HILLS

Howard Breslin

THOMAS Y. CROWELL COMPANY

New York • Established 1834

For Pat

And Fran

Vicksburg, the city of a hundred hills, endured the most important siege of the War Between the States. Lincoln, correctly, considered it the key to the Mississippi Valley, but its surrender was overshadowed by the contemporary carnage at Gettysburg. The objective of Grant's most brilliant campaign, these hills and their loss doomed the Confederate cause. All the battles, afloat and ashore, all the officers and units mentioned, are a part of recorded history. The rest is a fictional account of created characters during some days of glory and agony. But neither the heroism nor the suffering on either side, North or South, required any embellishment by the author.

BOOK ONE

The River

THE CANNON atop the bluff roared through the quiet January sunshine with a loud, metallic clang, as if someone had slammed the iron door of a giant oven. Below it, a white target on the mud-brown river, the steamboat whistled shrilly and backed out of range.

Three miles to the south, where the broad Mississippi ran straight again after twisting through the hairpin bend that fronted the battery, was the city of Vicksburg. It was perched high on the yellow-clay rampart of the great stream's east bank, well within earshot of the guns, more accustomed to the high-pitched noise from the steamboat.

On the map Vicksburg was a neat town, a river port, laid out in precise geometric patterns, straight streets, right angles, measured squares of buildings and plots. In reality, because it was built on a billowing series of hills, the little city sprawled across an undulating landscape. Houses and roads were found on many different levels, like flotsam scattered on the crests and hollows of successive waves. Above the rest, on the highest hill, the brand-new courthouse raised its cupola to the sky. It stood in eminent solitude, its fresh-stuccoed pillars ignoring the cannonade that vibrated through the air. Even the bright flag, with its two broad, red stripes hedging the single, white one, hung limply on the pole.

The inhabitants were less indifferent. Along the waterfront, on Levee Street, Negro stevedores stopped work, turned to listen. White overseers forgot to swear, chewed lips or cheroots in silence. Idlers, black or white, stiffened, became suddenly silent. A river pilot in a tavern spilled his drink; a slave girl, marketing, dropped her basket. On the roads drivers and riders tightened fingers on reins. In parlors and dining rooms, backyards, kitchens, and slave quarters, women—both white and black—stared in dismay.

Their city, their state, the new nation known as the Confederacy, had been at war for over eight months, but these were the first cannon shots heard in the vicinity. Indeed, the missiles from the Vicksburg battery at Fort Hill were the first to mar the waters of the Mississippi River.

The distant report was a faint thud by the time it reached the Kittering house on Cherry Street. It disturbed Alexandra Kittering's slumber, penetrated through dreamless sleep. When the sound was repeated she came awake, shaking her head on the pillow, to blink at the brass rods above her bed.

This metal contrivance, complete with handle, held a trolley for mosquito netting, but now in winter it was bare of hangings. The polished brass gleamed as it caught and reflected the sun's rays.

"Mmmm?" asked Alex Kittering in drowsy inquiry.

She shut her eyes again, tightly, trying to concentrate. Something was wrong. Something strange and alien had roused her, but she should be able to recognize it. Once more she heard the dull, far-off noise. Thunder? With the sun streaming through the windows, the room bright, the netting rods asparkle?

"Ridiculous," muttered Alex.

Even as she sat upright Alex remembered. The big, wide bed was a trifle crowded this morning, and the room, as she saw, was strewn with stays, garters, stockings, petticoats and party dresses. A cluttered bed chamber always followed a successful ball.

And it had been a success, Alex thought with triumph. A fitting finish to the holiday season! Not just because it was her seventeenth birthday party either. Naturally, after dancing the night away, her closest friends had stayed behind to share her room and talk things over.

Beside her, Clara Furlong chortled an unintelligible protest at Alex's movement. Beyond Clara's S-shaped form, Emilie Verrier, flat on her back, purred evenly as she slept. But Poll Randall, on the trundle bed near the window, was awake, sitting up, wide-eyed.

"Poll," whispered Alex, "what is it?"

"That was cannon fire, Alex."

Gazing down from her much higher mattress, Alex noted that Poll showed distress in more than her voice tremor. It was evident in her stiff posture, her pallor, her complete disregard of appearance or modesty. Poll's hair, the same brassy sheen as the netting rods, was a tangle; her nightgown had slipped from one shoulder to reveal a rounded white breast.

"Cannon," said Alex, trying not to stare. Far from shocked, she made a quick comparison, glancing from the other girl to her own image in the bureau mirror. The low-cut gowns in the latest fashion made the bosom an important, sometimes daring feature. Of course Poll would never display *that* much, but she was certainly more generously endowed than the slender girl gazing back from the glass. "Are you sure, Poll?"

"Yes. I was awake."

"Those Jackson boys."

"It just must be."

Alex swung her legs from under the covers, slid from the bed, still watching her reflection. She looked, she thought, quite well in spite of the sleep-shine on her face. In the room's brightness her figure was dimly outlined through the thin but voluminous nightgown. Alex was tall without slippers, narrow-waisted without stays; her shoulders were wider than her hips. As she turned in profile to the glass the flimsy fabric molded itself against a curve of thigh and breast.

"The best artillery company in the state," said Alex, happily. The gunners from Jackson, Mississippi's capital, had been a windfall that embellished her birthday party. A full dozen of the sixteen had attended in dress uniforms with fresh faces, soldiers and gentlemen. She had danced with every one. "Weren't they a real addition, Poll?"

"They sound real enough this morning."

Poll Randall's dry tone jerked Alex back to the present. They were old friends and wary rivals. Alex's blue eyes varied in shade with every mood; now they darkened at the implied criticism. Her magnolia skin, the midway bloom between white and brown, flushed as if taking color from the chestnut hair that framed her face.

"You think they're shooting *at* something?"

"I—I don't know."

"They couldn't be!" Alex said, scoffing. She smiled in scorn at the very idea. Then, to ease the sting she twitched her nose at Poll. It was a straight nose, a trifle too *retroussé* for real beauty, and Alex was well aware that the blonde girl cherished that fact.

"It might be practice," Poll said.

"Even if it is, I don't see how they could hit a blessed thing this morning!" Alex's giggle was genuine. "After all that dancing and drinking and gallivanting!"

Clara Furlong's wail was pillow-muffled but plaintive. "Cuddin Alex! Please! I'm trying to sleep!"

"Well, you can stop trying." Alex reached to spank the largest hump of quilt on the bed. "It's full day, and there's cannon shooting on the river!"

"You leave me—" Clara interrupted her squeal as Alex's words made sense. She rose on an elbow, blew tousled brown tresses from dark eyes. "You're funning. I didn't hear anything."

"We did," Poll Randall said, adjusting her gown.

"Sure enough?"

"Certain sure." Barefooted, soundless on the thick pile of the Turkey carpet, Alex strode to the window. She shoved the curtain aside, raised the pane, leaned over the sill.

From this viewpoint she gazed across yard and back buildings, over some treetops and a few roofs, toward a stretch of the river. What she could see of the Mississippi was a tan ribbon of sluggish water. It looked as empty, as placid, as the green Louisiana lowlands beyond the far bank, or the cloudless blue canopy overhead.

"You see anything, Alex?"

"No, Poll. Nothing."

"Emilie!" Clara Furlong prodded with a thumb. *"Emilie!* Wake up! Things are happening!"

Not now, Alex thought, straining to hear any abnormal sound. Without turning from her stooped position, she flapped an impatient hand at the room's occupants.

"Hush, you-all. Listen!"

Obediently, the other girls listened. Clara Furlong was rigid; Emilie Verrier, still drowsy, rolled sleepy eyes toward Alex, and waited. Blonde Poll Randall pouted, but kept silent.

The only sounds that drifted up from outside were the muffled stamp of a horse in the stable, and a soft, unintelligible snatch of song from the slave quarters. Alex, straining her ears, could hear nothing else. Vicksburg seemed almost ominously quiet, as if it dozed uneasily in the pale, heatless, January sunshine.

Waiting, thought Alex. She could not have explained the reason that prompted her feeling. Her slight shiver had nothing to do with the chill breeze from the river, but she straightened, closed the window.

"Well," said Alex, "whatever it was, I guess it's over. Nothing's happening now." She noticed Poll Randall's frown and checked a sigh.

Last night, she recalled, Poll was as gay and frivolous as anyone. Alex conceded the blonde girl's pink-and-white, classic beauty, but the men had flocked around the whole quartet, drawn by charm, light laughter, and skilled dancing. Every well-reared Southern girl worth a nosegay had those virtues; they weren't learned from books.

"Poll," said Alex, "it couldn't be anything serious. There just wouldn't be fighting that near, not way down here." She sounded patient, slightly amused. After a night of dancing the war seemed very far away.

Clara Furlong snorted. "'Course not. That's downright silly!"

"Now, I don't know," Poll said, drawling and serious. "That shooting gave me the strangest feeling. Like—like it marked the end of—of something."

"Sure did," said Clara. "It marked the end of my sleep!"

Emilie Verrier stretched, ran her fingers through her hair, spoke while yawning. "I declare. I hope it did mean the end of all this partying for a while. My feet are a solid ache, my slippers are nearly gone by, and I look like a dead hag!"

Alex saw Poll's mouth tighten in disapproval. Oh, come, she said silently, don't go making mountains. Sure, Emilie was a featherhead, and Clara was as bad, but Poll didn't have to act like a seeress. The fact that Alex shared some of the other girl's uneasiness didn't dilute her resentment.

She keeps trying, decided Alex, to outweigh our advantages with her education. The Furlongs were planter rich; Emilie's family had been conspicuous for wealth and breeding since the days when the French owned the land. Kittering & Son, perhaps the foremost merchant house in Vicksburg, had flourished enough to send Alex to school in New Orleans and on a Grand Tour of Europe. Doctor Randall, Poll's father, was a kindly physician with a small practice and large debts, the remnants of a disastrous speculation in cotton.

Alex slumped on the bed, stroked a thumb along the fluting carved on a mahogany post. She deliberately kept the talk on a light plane.

"It was a real holiday season, wasn't it? First Christmas, then New Year's, then the Anniversary Ball at the Duff Green house—"

"That was biggest," Clara said, "but I liked your party best."

"Well, I'm a sight older than secession, but its first birthday was a lot more important." Alex smiled at them all. "When I saw that crowd celebrating Secession Day I was sure everybody'd be too tired to come to my little old dance the very next night."

"You sound," Poll said, "as if we should have seceded long ago."

Alex caught the slight note of tartness, ignored it. She said: "I can't say that, Poll. Not in this house. You should hear my grandfather. The Ancient stayed in his room all week, drinking and cursing Jeff Davis. Grandfather still doesn't think we should have seceded at all!"

"Cuddin Joab's an old darling," Clara Furlong said, again using the title of kinship to express affection. "But of course he's a New Jerseyite. We just had to secede! We couldn't let that Black Republican baboon of a Lincoln run Mississippi, now could we?"

"I never said we could." Poll sounded defensive. "It's just that I never dreamed the Yankees would fight. All we wanted was to be let alone."

Alex kept her face impassive, remembering her grandfather's remarks about that oft-repeated Southern phrase. Old Joab Kittering was one of Mississippi's earliest settlers, but he had an unbridled tongue, even to a favored granddaughter who was heart-and-soul for the South's cause.

"Shucks," said Emilie, "so the Yankees did fight. They're not all that great shakes at it. We whipped them good at Manassas, and I reckon we can do it again."

Poll shrugged, reached for a wrapper. "We didn't do too well in Missouri and Kentucky."

"For why?" Emilie became more Gallic when she argued. "Because those states are half northern anyway, that's why! Those blue-belly soldiers wouldn't get far in a *real* Southern state!"

Sir Roger de Coverley, thought Alex, was right. There was much to be said on both sides. Manassas, or Bull Run, in far-off Virginia, had been the first and biggest pitched battle of the war, a great Confederate victory. It certainly seemed to bear out Emilie's confidence in the South's military supremacy. But Poll was right about the Border States. She sighed a little for the days when after-the-ball chatter was all about boys and dress and gossip.

Clara Furlong evidently didn't recognize any change. She said, "Maybe Poll likes blue-belly uniforms."

"You mean because of Henri Duchesneau?"

"Of course."

"You two should talk," said Poll. "Or even Alex. In fact I didn't notice that anybody refused to dance with our handsome Creole officer because his coat was blue."

"*Touché,*" cried Emilie. She rolled her eyes, shrugged her shoulders, waved her hands in elaborate gestures. "*Ma chère Mademoiselle Emilie,* may I have the honor? *C'est bon!* And perhaps a stroll in the garden? *Mais, oui!*"

"To me he used English," Clara said with a giggle.

"The Washington Light Artillery," said Alex, imitating Emilie's accent, "from New Orleans wears the blue uniform trimmed in red. It was our somewhat hasty, and unfortunate choice, mam-zell."

Laughing, Poll Randall said, "Oh, come, Alex. No fair. You know Henri has barely any accent."

"Henri, is it?"

"Listen at her!"

"Lieutenant Duchesneau, *s'il vous plaît!*"

Poll blushed, but parried the onslaught. "Go along, Emilie, I heard you call him Henri!"

"You did?" asked Emilie. "Where?"

The quick question brought a burst of laughter from the others. Alex, amused, realized that they had all strolled outside at intervals with the Creole lieutenant. He was a recent asset to Vicksburg's young society, a New Orleans aristocrat detached from his artillery company to teach telegraphy to other officers.

"Don't worry, Emilie," said Poll. "It was right out on the dance floor."

Emilie shrugged, said, "Well, after all, we are both French. One cannot be inhospitable to a fellow descendant of a noble race."

"Golly," Clara said, "how that man can dance!"

"A true gallant," said Alex. She wondered if the others had found Henri Duchesneau as adroit at kissing as dancing. Recalling his swift embrace, the brief, exciting kiss that she'd rebuked only with a light tap of her fan, Alex chuckled. "But beware of brass buttons on that blue coat."

[16]

"Why, Alex, whatever do you mean?" Poll asked innocently.

"They bruise."

"Alex Kittering, how do *you* know?"

"For shame!"

"Brother Bryce should hear you!"

Suddenly, as she gazed at the flushed, laughing trio, Alex knew that they shared a common experience. That was betrayed by the merry reproaches, by the wary flickers as they exchanged glances. She was sure now that Henri Duchesneau had kissed them all. Her own mirth exploded as she saw the same certainty dawn in the other faces.

The room fairly shook with giggles, sputters of unladylike guffaws. Every time one girl looked at another both rocked with renewed glee. It was as infectious as schoolgirl hysteria, and as silly.

Alex recovered first when she remembered Clara's reference to her brother. Bryce Furlong, in Confederate gray, was the handsomest officer in Vicksburg, probably in the entire state. He was tall, blond, broad-shouldered, with a face like a Cavalier's portrait and smoldering hazel eyes. Even Alex, who had known him all her life, had gasped to see him in uniform. He wore it with a bearing that personified the Southern cause.

Bryce had shown jealousy when she returned to the ballroom with the Creole officer. Alex recalled his raised eyebrows, his heightened color. The two men had exchanged only polite sentences, but Alex could still hear the cold voices, testing each other like fencers' foils.

"Telegraphy, Lieutenant Duchesneau?"

"*Oui, mon capitaine.* That is, unfortunately, my present duty."

"You know this—trade?"

"For my sins. My family owned many shares in the New Orleans to Milneburg Railroad."

"Indeed?"

"*Mais, oui.* Summers at Lake Pontchartrain I was encouraged to learn the telegraph. It kept me from underfoot. And, I admit, I had a boy's fascination with the instrument."

"It seems a strange hobby for a gentleman."

"Oh, I race horses, too, Captain Furlong. As you do. We must discuss that another time."

Alex was glad that the music had ended the parley. Bryce, dancing, had been very attentive. Since the war he had changed into a charming beau, a far cry from the lad who had teased her, pulled her hair. Bryce Furlong, of course, was worth ten flibberty-gibbets like Henri Duchesneau.

She was startled to hear Clara Furlong use the same epithet aloud.

"Why, that flibberty-gibbet," Clara said, wiping her eyes. "That Henri! He's as bad as Emilie's Uncle Roger."

"Oh, no," said Emilie. "Uncle Roger is a patter."

Clara chuckled, tapped palm on pillow, deepened her voice. "My daughter, my dear, would have been just your age."

"One hand to the mustache." Poll brushed finger across upper lip. "The other judging your—growth."

"I wonder," Alex said, "what excuse he used on our mothers."

A tap sounded on the door, and it opened. The slave girl who entered was a tall, young woman with an erect, mature figure. She lightly carried a tray of small cups filled with thick, black coffee, the Mississippi eye-opener. Neatly trim in purple dress with white apron and turban, the maid's skin was the color of burnished copper; when she smiled she was very striking.

"Coffee, Miss Alex," she said, smiling around the room. "I heard you-all talking."

"Thank you, Mimosa." Alex waited while the coffee was handed around. Then, as she sipped, knowing the speed of the slave wireless-telegraph, she asked for information. "What was the cannon shooting for?"

"Northern steamboat came down river." Mimosa answered promptly, hiding amusement. The talk she'd overheard had not concerned the cannonade.

"That's all?"

"Yes, ma'am. Jackson gunners drove it away."

"There you are," Emilie said. "No Yankees of any account could get way down here. They'll never reach Vicksburg."

· 2 ·

ALEX KITTERING always considered breakfast the only true family meal. At noon-day dinner or evening supper there were usually guests or absentees. But on a normal morning, when there had been no party the night before, all the Kitterings assembled to face each other and the new day together.

Family meals can be festive, dull or trying. Alex, as she took her place at the linen-draped rectangular table, three days after her birthday, immediately judged that this one would be trying. She could sense the tension; it was almost as tangible as the mixed odors of hot bread and bacon.

Her brothers acknowledged her with stiff nods; her parents with murmured greetings. Old Joab Kittering, her grandfather, at the head of the table, made the mood emphatic and audible.

"Morning, Alex," said Joab, glowering. "You're late. Say your blessing." At eighty-three, he spoke in a rumbling baritone, still strong but rasped rough by years of use and abuse. Joab's voice gave evidence of his New Jersey origin, that he had smoked and drunk much, had the habit of command.

"Sorry, Grandpa." Alex swung her wide skirts aside, slid into the chair on his right. The Ancient, she thought, was on the war-path again. As she bent her head over her plate, the girl gazed furtively at her grandfather.

Joab Kittering, for all his years, was a massive man, solid as a weather-worn tree stump. Wide shoulders stretched his protective knitted shawl; his chest bulged his ruffled shirt front. Joab's shock of silver hair, collar-length and rumpled, reminded Alex of engravings that depicted Andrew Jackson, but this old man's features were pale and sharp, cameo clear even to the grim, thin mouth. The big hands folded around a whisky glass were gnarled and knotty, mottled with brown spots.

Set before Joab was the standard breakfast fare of his latter years—three fingers of Tennessee sour-mash bourbon, a cup of Mississippi-made coffee, a bowl of molasses-sweetened mush. In his younger days he had been a noted trencherman, and he still insisted on his matinal glass of whisky.

He raised it now, using both hands, just as Alex raised her head. Joab sipped, munched, growled at Andrew, the butler.

"Must they keep slamming that window up and down?"

"Sorry, sir," said Andrew, mobile black face expressionless. He spoke with sonorous care, enunciated each syllable precisely, but the result sounded like an oft-repeated recitation. "Missus Epie's orders were to keep it closed, sir."

Hearing her mother's name, Alex stiffened. The noise made at the sideboard where the slaves handed in the cooked dishes from the outside kitchen often annoyed Joab, but his annoyance with his daughter-in-law was a silent, perpetual emotion. Alex, the old man's favorite, knew that, knew, too, that it was something ignored by the entire family.

She watched Joab snort into his whisky, glare down the table. He looked like a stone abbot set into a cathedral niche. The crutches made necessary by his crippling rheumatism hung across the back of his chair; their tips formed a crooked peak above the big head.

Epie Mae Kittering, on her husband's right, glanced up from the hot biscuit she was coating with maypop preserve. She was a tall woman, always poised. The smooth pleats on the bosom of her snuff-colored silk dress might have adorned a breastplate. No wave of her brown hair was out of place, and even the few touches of gray seemed applied by art not nature.

"Did you want something, Father?" asked Epie.

"No."

"Perhaps another log on the fire, Father?"

"Fire's all right."

Alex, spooning grits from the bowl offered by Andrew, hid her amusement at the exchange. The formal term of address, the gruff answers, were familiar weapons in the domestic tug-of-war waged by her mother and grandfather. Epie was the only member of the family to use the title 'Father'; she never called Joab anything else. He reacted with laconic irritation.

The girl watched her mother take a delicate bite of biscuit. Neither her father-in-law's brusqueness nor the mundane business of eating had ever ruffled Epie. Alex glanced at the blaze in the fireplace beneath the Carrara marble mantel, and recalled that Joab had once compared her mother to this high-ceilinged dining room she had decorated.

"She's as polished and solid as the mahogany furniture," the old man had said. "And as brittle, in tinkling crystal, as the big chandelier. She's like the wallpaper, too—a finely drawn pastel, without blood in it."

Gazing around the room Alex understood the comparison. The imported French paper, brought across thousands of miles of ocean, did reflect Epie Mae's cool personality. It was chalk-blue and white, with imitation Fragonard panels, incredibly modish shepherdesses against stylized landscapes. No blustering wind could disturb those painted tresses.

Loving them both, Alex tried, for the hundredth time, to ease the strained relationship.

"Coffee cold, Grandpa?"

"No, Alex." Joab refused to be distracted. He hunched forward, scowled at his son and elder grandson in their gray uniforms. "You both intend to leave Vicksburg, then?"

Stephen Decatur Kittering wiped his mustache with a napkin, and sighed, realizing that his father was going to be difficult. Even though he had lived in the South more than sixty years, made a fortune and owned slaves, the old man refused to accept his proper position as a Southern gentleman.

"I'm afraid so, Pa. As soon as our orders come." Stephen, aware that he sounded too apologetic, glanced at his wife for reassurance.

Joab's scowl deepened as he noted the glance. His son had grown from a polite little boy, shyly afraid of his father, to a polite, fastidious gentleman dominated by his wife. Stephen was going to war the way he

[20]

helped run the firm, rode a horse, danced or drank—correct to the letter, without decision.

"What about the business, Stephen?"

"Grandpa," said Clifton Kittering, "business will have to wait till we whip the Yankees!"

Epie smiled to smooth her son's outburst, but Alex knew it was too late. Joab lowered his head like a baffled bulldog. The girl suddenly saw the resemblance between the three men. Joab was a crude piece of sculpture roughly chiseled; Stephen was the same marble-block reworked in more detail, with deeper cuts; Clifton, at twenty, was the carved-down, finished product of more delicate craftsmanship.

She shook away the thought that just the reverse might be true intellectually. It was tow-headed Clay, the youngest, a precocious sixteen, who displayed Joab's quickness of mind. Ironically, Clay, though a blond stripling, was the image of Epie Mae.

"My boy," Joab said to Clifton, "if Kittering and Son has to wait for Confederate victory, God help us all! It was a damn-fool move to secede in the first place, it was worse to fire on Sumter and start this fracas! But anybody who expects a short, easy war is plumb crazy! War isn't a picnic afternoon, son. It's dirty, and it's miserable, and it—it kills."

Alex felt a prickle of chill at the words. In her first enthusiasm for the South's cause, during those exciting days when state secession followed national election and when war began, she had ignored her grandfather's dire predictions. But she had too much regard for his opinions to sustain that attitude forever.

The other faces at the table congealed into polite disinterest. Young Clay toyed with his fork, boyishly bored. They had all heard Joab too often.

"You went to war once, Father," said Epie.

"To my sorrow."

In his young manhood Joab had followed Andy Jackson to New Orleans. He had hated every minute of it. The ribald, sharp-shooting backwoods riflemen, LaFitte's foul-mouth crew, the scarecrow militia, were still vivid memories. That war in 1812 had been a sorry, slovenly business, without order. The only orderliness Joab Kittering had seen in the whole campaign had been the lined ranks of Pakenham's Redcoat regulars. Gunfire had cut that glittering formation to shreds, won a famous victory, and confirmed Joab's belief that war was a hateful solution to any problem.

"The Yankees wouldn't leave us alone," said Stephen Kittering. "We can't let them invade, Pa."

"We've got to stop them now!" cried Clifton.

"*We* and *them*," Joab said, heavily. "You're speaking of your countrymen."

"Not any more, Grandpa!" Clifton was vehement. "We've had our own country for almost a year, and we've defended it in arms since last April! Those nigger-loving Yankees have been asking for this licking, and they're going to get it!"

"That sounds familiar," said Joab. "That's the way hotheads talked about the Mexicans fifteen years back. 'They asked for it—sic 'em, lick 'em.' Nobody gave peace a chance!"

"But, Grandpa," Alex said, "you didn't vote for Lincoln!" She had clung to that fact whenever Joab's diatribes planted doubts. Nobody in the whole state of Mississippi had voted for Abraham Lincoln. Such unanimity *must* be right!

"No, Alex, I didn't. But I didn't plan on fighting a war just because we—our friends, the South—had lost one election." Joab sounded heartsick and angry. "God Almighty! Couldn't anybody stop to think? The South's had more than its share of Presidents. For years we ran the Senate, the government. All we had to do was hang on! This rail-splitter from Illinois was bound to make mistakes! The country would vote him out the next time 'round!"

"Pa," said Stephen with a placating smile, "I wasn't for secession either. Even Jefferson Davis didn't want it until it became inevitable. But, now it's an established fact. And a man must ride with his own kind."

"A pretty speech out of Walter Scott," said Joab, "signifying nothing. Unless you consider as your own kind the passel of damn fools that got us into this mess!" He waited, but his derision was received with hostile silence. Joab sighed, drained his glass, turned to the butler. "Andrew."

"Sir?"

"Hit me."

"Yes, sir!"

Watching Andrew pour another three fingers of whisky, Alex realized that her grandfather was deeply upset. He almost never took a second glass before starting a work day. But now he spoke to his family with the same mild casualness he had used to the butler.

"I've only one more thing to say. Suppose the South does win this war. It ain't likely but suppose it." Joab was ungrammatical only when he wanted to stress a point. "Suppose we establish the Confederate States of America."

" 'A consummation,' " quoted Stephen, " 'devoutly to be wished.' " He basked in the beaming approval of his wife and children.

"Is it?" Joab grunted, drank deeply, took coffee as a chaser. "Is it for Kittering and Son? We're suppliers of steamboat fittings. Purveyors of foodstuffs and dry goods. Cotton agents with a warehouse and two small steamboats for short-haul freight. When I'm gone, Stephen, and you head the firm, how are you going to like having a custom house at Cairo, Illinois? Or maybe somewhere closer. It ain't proved that Albert Sidney Johnston can swallow his chaw of Kentucky!"

"Now, Pa, once the embargo is lifted and we can ship cotton, without the tariff imposed by the North—"

"Stephen, Stephen! You sat at a desk from time to time, and checked invoices. Didn't you even look at the letterheads? Most of our firm's cotton deals—the most profitable ones—were with New England mills. If all the planters around here ship to Europe through New Orleans, we're cut in two or deeper!"

Stephen frowned, drummed slender fingers on the table. He was annoyed that his father put sordid commercialism above the glorious cause of Southern independence. His sons looked bewildered; his wife poured more coffee. Only Alex turned to hear his answer.

"We'll make out, Pa."

"Sure!" agreed Clifton. "The main thing is to win the war!"

"Sure!" said Joab, with heavy mimicry. "If we do win it the North will start another in a couple or three years. God Almighty! They *need* the river! They *need* New Orleans! They wouldn't let the Spaniards keep it, or the French. The United States cannot allow another country to decide duties and freight rates for shipping on the Mississippi!"

"It's our river," Clifton said, "not theirs!"

"Tell them that in St. Louis when it overflows the levee!"

"Pa," said Stephen, bracing himself to confront his father, "you mustn't say these things outside the house. Everybody in Vicksburg's fond of you and knows your opinions. But that sort of talk makes for bad blood with the war going on!"

"Ah, hell," Joab said, in disgust, "I've been speaking my mind all my life, and I'm too old to change now. The truth makes a bitter pill, but it should be swallowed." He finished his drink, pushed aside the untouched mush, shoved back his chair. "Andrew."

"Yes, sir." Andrew deftly lifted the crutches from the chair, held them in readiness.

Twisted hands flat on the table Joab lurched to his feet. He seemed even larger standing, in rumpled black broadcloth coat, with silk stock askew under the high, old-fashioned collar. Swaying slightly he adjusted the crutches under his armpits, spoke in a carefully casual tone.

"Are you coming to the office today, Major Kittering?"

"Well, Pa—I—I sort of promised Captain Miller of the Vicksburg Southrons that—"

The old man's smile was a brief, bitter twitch. He swung around on the crutches, not waiting for his son to finish the excuse. Alex Kittering

[23]

saw the smile and felt a sudden pang of pity. It was a new feeling. The Ancient, her grandfather, had always seemed indomitable, crippled and hunched by pain, yes, but undefeated. Why, she thought with surprise, he looks his age, and lonely.

She hastily gulped the last of her coffee, rose. "May I come with you, Grandpa?"

"What for?"

The girl had her reason ready. "Well, there'll be a crowd on the riverfront to meet the *Natchez*. That French lieutenant, Henri Duchesneau, is bringing a horse up from New Orleans. He plans to race it against Bryce Furlong's Saladin."

"That's right," said Clifton. "Henri's betting real money, too."

Clay Kittering chortled. "He must be crazy!"

"Why call him crazy, Clay?" asked Epie with mild curiosity.

"I've seen Saladin run."

"That black Saladin," said Stephen, "is Bingaman stock. That's the best breed out of Natchez. Blood lines from Hardheart and Brittania both."

When Joab Kittering nodded, Alex realized that the tension in the room had eased. This horse talk made a congenial topic, a shared interest, that united the male members of the family. She was interested in the coming race herself, but the masculine sporting attitude amused her. Even the war became of secondary importance when the true Mississippian, especially in the river ports, discussed local horseflesh.

"No New Orleans horse," said Joab, "is going to beat Saladin. He's never lost a race."

"Bryce thinks," said Clifton, "that Saladin is in the best shape of his life. At even weights Henri's nag, this Flambeau, won't have a chance."

"Flam what?"

"Flambeau, Clay. It's a French name."

Alex and her grandfather, listening to Clifton, had the same thought. Clifton was Bryce Furlong's closest friend, a little too apt to parrot the other's opinions. The old man believed it smacked of toadyism; the girl attributed it to hero-worship. Alex didn't quite share Joab's disapproval, but she had an uneasy feeling that her brother should not be a copy cat.

"How do we know," asked Joab, "that the *Natchez* will make Vicksburg this morning?"

"Henri Duchesneau had a telegram, Grandpa."

"Well, then, Alex, come along." Joab sounded gruff, but was pleased to have his granddaughter's company. He watched admiringly as she donned a mulberry cloak that matched her dress, and a perky bonnet with a gay, gold feather. The butler helped him into his greatcoat, presented his low-crowned beaver with a flourish.

[24]

"The carriage is ready, sir, and waiting." Andrew never failed to deliver this unnecessary information. The day the Kittering carriage was not waiting at the front door when Joab left the house Andrew would cause a commotion in the slave quarters.

While small Esau held the span of matched gray horses Martin, the coachman, helped the butler make Joab comfortable in the open vehicle. It was a smart turnout, with a shining black body and bright, yellow-spoked wheels. In spite of Epie Mae's objections Joab refused to put his slaves in livery. The coachman wore plain dark suiting, a felt hat. Esau, bareheaded and starched with dignity, sat beside the driver in clean denim.

They were on the crest of one of the many hills when the steamboat blew for a landing. Joab told the coachman to halt the team, and they sat there gazing down at the wide river, the resplendent vessel challenging the current. The slaves were as interested as the old man and the girl. The Kittering firm's two steamboats, the *Tonica* and the *Chickasaw*, were small. This was the *Natchez*, a crack passenger packet, the toast of riverfront taverns from St. Louis to New Orleans.

There was no mistaking her smart lines, the spotless white texas aglitter with gold trim. The ship was doubly famous for palatial accommodations and record speeds. With the critical admiration of connoisseurs the watching quartet noted the skilled handling of the helm, the precise slackening of speed as the low prow swung in toward Vicksburg.

"Tom Leathers made good time," said Joab. "Go on, Martin, we want to be there when she berths."

"Cap'n Leathers always makes good time," Martin said before he chirped at the team.

Alex Kittering smiled at the flat, unqualified statement. The giant captain of the *Natchez* was a legendary hero to his loyal followers.

Martin turned the team down a winding street that led to the levee. Both passengers sat straighter as riverfront Vicksburg came into view.

Along the water's edge the twin smokestacks of the ranked steamboats gave the appearance of an idle, many-chimneyed factory. Cotton in bales seemed to clutter every cranny not needed for traffic. The bales formed shaggy ramparts on the stringpieces of wharves, were piled in clumsy pyramids under the jutting roofs of warehouse loading-platforms. Some were neatly wrapped, some tattered, but they all managed to look forlorn and neglected.

Joab Kittering grunted, made his usual comment. "Jeff Davis must be daft!"

Alex, wisely, kept silent. The Confederate government's embargo on cotton was not popular in Vicksburg. Tempers flared when it was mentioned, and many, like her grandfather, blamed Jefferson Davis, the local politico-planter, who now presided over their new nation. After all he was a neighbor, practically a fellow townsman, who should know that the South depended upon cotton!

The coachman slowed the horses to a walk as they joined the throng moving toward the coils of thick woodsmoke that twisted from the *Natchez'* two forward funnels. Drays and wagons came bumping from every sidestreet and alley; townsfolk, drawn by the whistle, were gathering to watch or welcome arriving passengers. The gangplanks rattled down and black stevedores swarmed around them, waiting the orders to unload.

At the foot of the wharf a group of horsemen, young officers, made a mounted clump of Confederate gray above the patchwork of slaves and civilians. One tall captain backed his bay mare from the group, swung her toward the approaching Kittering carriage.

"There's Bryce," said Alex, as Martin, finding the way blocked by the crowd, halted the team. "Bryce Furlong, Grandpa."

Joab frowned at her tone. He watched the rider skilfully edge his mare through the jostling pedestrians. Young Furlong could ride. He sat in the saddle with easy, careless mastery, an aristocrat from stirrup to hat-brim. Bryce was very fair, ruddy, with a thin brush of blond mustache and long horseman's legs. He smiled politely as he guided the horse past people, but the smile held a hint of arrogance. Bryce was displaying his horsemanship, not worrying about those in his path.

"He's cavalry, isn't he?"

"Yes, Grandpa. A captain."

"Thought so."

The old man knew the whole Furlong family, wealthy planters with pretensions. Bryce's grandfather, long dead, had been Joab's friend; they had arrived in Mississippi in the same year, Furlong from Virginia, Joab from New Jersey. Frank Furlong, this boy's father, was a good businessman who knew cotton and handling slaves, but he had more manners than brains. Joab couldn't understand a gentleman who quoted Latin tags while he raised on a four-card flush.

Bryce was still another generation, the type that rode hell-for-leather to avoid work. He would talk heatedly of Southern chivalry, and risk his life in its defense. Bryce Furlong, decided Joab, would think war a chance to win the fair maiden by riding roughshod over the Northern armies.

As Bryce reined in beside the carriage and lifted his hat, Joab realized that Alex was the fair maiden involved. The old man sighed, uneasily aware that bright young eyes saw love far differently than the aged.

"Mister Kittering, sir," Bryce said, with a courtly bow. "Alex."

"Hello, Bryce."

[26]

"Bryce."

"Come down to see the New Orleans horse?"

"Not only," said Joab. "The *Natchez* should have some cargo of mine. Paxton has my *Tonica's* insides in his machine shop, and needs some parts to move them out. You see Runcey Carr anywhere around, Bryce?"

"Yes, sir. A moment ago." Bryce raised himself in his stirrups to survey the crowd. "There he is yonder. No, sir. To the left. Beside that tall soldier with the beanpole rifle."

Alex stood up to see. Runcey Carr was the firm's apprentice, a gangling, red-haired lad of fourteen, bound to the family more by ties of affection than papers. An orphan who hankered to be a river pilot, Runcey acted as Joab's legs. The girl considered him an unscrupulous urchin and an old friend.

She saw the soldier first. He was staring at her, and that, for a moment, seemed to magnetize her own gaze. He looked young, with wide shoulders and narrow hips, his lanky-legged height accentuated by the tight, ill-fitting, gray uniform jacket. All the soldiers Alex knew, officers like Bryce or even privates in Vicksburg's three select companies, wore trim, tailored Confederate gray. This stranger's shirt and trousers were homespun butternut. His face seemed long and sensitive, too thin, but saved from delicate handsomeness by a square chin and broad mouth. She watched the tanned cheeks darken with flush under her regard; it made him seem older.

Then, as he turned his head to avert his stare, Alex noticed the hat. It was small, flat-crowned with a narrow brim, a bright, new straw made more garish because it perched on crow-black hair. Alex had worn a similar bonnet when she was ten.

"What a ridiculous hat," she said, and giggled.

Bryce Furlong grinned as he dismounted. He tossed the mare's reins to the Kittering's Esau, offered his hand to help Alex descend. He said, "Perhaps you'd like a closer look at this Flambeau as he disembarks?"

"Grandpa?"

"Go ahead." Joab snapped his fingers, beckoned to Runcey Carr.

On Bryce Furlong's arm, Alex sauntered to join the other officers. Joab watched riders swing down from their mounts to surround the couple. He spotted the blue coat that made the Creole, Henri Duchesneau, conspicuous among the young men. They all crowded toward the *Natchez* with holiday carelessness.

"You want me, Mister Joab?" Runcey Carr, beside the carriage, gazed up at the old man.

Joab thought the boy's freckles too big for his face as his head was too big for his body. "Tom Leathers fetch us those engine parts, Runcey?"

"Ain't had a chance to ask."

"Ask."

"Yes, sir." Runcey started to turn, checked the movement as he heard Joab's question.

"Who's your friend?"

"The soldier? Name of Dixon. Tempe—Templeton Dixon, Ninth Mississippi. Detached." Runcey used the military term as if he had always known it. "They sent him down here to wagon supplies. Enafield rifles and such. From our warehouse to the railroad depot."

"He tote that gun everywhere?" Joab hadn't missed the long-barrelled rifle in the crook of Tempe Dixon's arm. It reminded him of the backwoods sharpshooters at New Orleans.

Runcey Carr grinned. "Pretty near. Says he brought it from home. His pappy used it in the Mexican War. Tempe's taking no chances on losing it. Seems they ain't enough guns to go 'round in our army."

"I'm not surprised," Joab said.

"Ahhh!" Martin's exhalation expressed satisfaction; it was echoed by Esau. "Here comes that New Orleans horse, Mister Joab."

The others turned as the crowd murmur buzzed a trifle higher. A big, blanket-clad horse was being urged down a gangplank from the *Natchez*. His neck gleamed sorrel-brown in the sunlight. He had a hogged mane, a long blaze on his nose, two white stockings. A diminutive Negro groom, jockey size, was dragging him by the bridle.

Through a long life Joab Kittering had bought, sold, traded, ridden and driven many horses. He knew a thoroughbred when he saw one. This Flambeau certainly qualified. The horse was also, Joab judged in a glance, high strung, and unhappy. That showed in the flaring nostrils, the rolling eyes, the restless pawing.

He doesn't like the wooden ramp underhoof, the old man decided, nor the chattering crowd. He had probably hated the whole steamboat journey.

"Big feller, ain't he?" said Runcey.

"Sixteen hands," Esau announced with pompous assurance.

Flambeau came gingerly down the gangplank. Joab, leaning forward to watch, relaxed when the horse was safely on the landing. The crowd parted to let the sorrel through. Henri Duchesneau, followed by his friends, pushed forward to claim his property. Ten yards away, the tiny groom, arm extended over his head as he clutched the bridle, grinned, raised his other hand in greeting.

It happened without warning. A big roustabout, concentrated on his labor, not watching, lost his grip on a packing case. The crate tottered atop a pile, slid down at gathering speed. Aghast, the stevedore shrieked a warning.

"Out below!"

[28]

The scream was drowned in the splintering crash as the crate hit. It fell close behind Flambeau, too close. The big sorrel whinnied shrilly in fear, and reared. The little Negro, flipped loose, turned a somersault through the air. Flambeau, hoofs flashing, slammed down, and bolted.

Men scattered, tumbling, out of the way. Henri Duchesneau stood frozen. Bryce Furlong tried to spring forward, bumped into swerving friends, was pinned. Alex Kittering, skirts raised, scampered for the family carriage. Shouts rose; the shouters, unthinkingly, spurred the runaway.

"Look out!"

"Get back!"

"Make room!"

"Jesus God," prayed Joab aloud, watching his granddaughter. Runcey swore, jumped to help Martin control the span of grays in the carriage shaft. Esau had his own troubles; heels scrabbling in the dust he fought to hold the mare steady.

For the old man the whole scene, blurred with exploding motion, was suddenly narrowed in focus. He had never felt so helpless, so chained by crippled limbs. The girl and the sorrel were converging on the carriage, and Joab could do nothing. Alex was running directly into Flambeau's path. The big horse, wild with panic, head tossing, raced toward her with incredible, hammering speed.

Into Joab's vision leaped the young soldier, Tempe Dixon. Half a dozen quick strides brought him to Alex's side. He grabbed the girl's wrist, whirled, flung her away, spinning, with all his strength. The old man caught a glimpse of the outrage on her face, swirling cloak, askew bonnet. His gaze followed her rescuer.

Dixon turned in a swift half-crouch, tensing for his jump. The onrushing animal seemed to loom above him, all teeth and muscle. Joab knew there would be no second chance if the leap missed that bridle.

Tempe Dixon jumped, arms outstretched, diving sideways to escape the full impact. His fingers caught in, and clung to, the sorrel's chinstrap; his other hand clamped on Flambeau's muzzle.

Braced, waiting, Joab Kittering felt the vibration of the hoofs, kept his gaze steady on the linked man and horse. The big sorrel reared, shook the dangling figure through empty space. Those dangerous, slashing horseshoes came very close to the carriage. Joab calculated the distance with detached clarity.

A long moment later the soldier's weight told; the blazed nose came down. Dixon's feet touched ground, scrambled for a purchase. Before he found it there were others around him, helping, and the crisis was over.

"I've got him, soldier."

[29]

"You can let go now."

Tempe Dixon stepped back, flexing his fingers. He was trembling as hard as Flambeau, breathing as fast. The babble of excited congratulations seemed to confuse the soldier. He suffered Henri Duchesneau's violent handshake with a diffident smile.

Did what he had to, thought Joab, and dislikes fuss about it. The old man approved; for all his scarecrow clothing this Dixon showed signs of brains and breeding. Kittering & Son had been built on snap judgments, and its founder decided he liked Templeton Dixon.

Glancing away from the group around the quivering Flambeau, Joab saw his granddaughter. Bryce Furlong was helping Alex to her feet from a sitting position. The girl's skirt hung awry over twisted hoops; her bonnet was over one ear, and her face was very pink.

The Creole lieutenant stooped, plucked an object from the dust. He held it out, a small straw hat crushed into shapeless hay.

"Is this yours, *mon ami?*"

"It was," said Tempe Dixon.

"*N'importe!* Do not look so woeful. I will replace it. We all owe you thanks."

Alex Kittering, joining them in time to hear the remark, did not feel thankful. She had not been frightened, was sure she could have avoided the horse. Instead this soldier had subjected her to an embarrassing, jarring fall. Alex knew her tumble had revealed her legs and bruised more than her dignity. Her voice was coldly polite.

"Thank you, young man. You moved very quickly."

"You're welcome, I'm sure, ma'am."

"You're very strong," said Alex. She pushed back a sleeve to examine a darkening mark on her right wrist.

Joab Kittering swallowed a chuckle. He knew the blaze in Alex's eyes showed temper. But the Dixon boy deserved better than chill thanks. The old man raised his voice in a rasping irony that dominated the noisy crowd.

"Don't gush, Alex. That was a damn fine piece of work. It's a relief to see somebody in a *gray* coat trying to save life and property, instead of hell-bent on smashing it to flinders!"

His glance raked the gathering, noted the reactions to his speech. Alex showed consternation; Bryce Furlong was stiff with disapproval. The Creole officer and Tempe Dixon, side-by-side, both looked astonished. None of the others mattered.

"You, there, Runcey Carr," said Joab, taking advantage of the hush. "Go find Captain Leathers. Some of us still have work to do!"

Far north of Vicksburg where the rolling hills of Kentucky shouldered into Tennessee an invisible war-front stretched eastward from the Mississippi River for some three hundred miles. Behind that wavering line armies assembled; the two men in command watched each other, gazed at maps, and made plans.

Both these men were professional soldiers, West Point graduates, generals. But there the resemblance ended.

The Southern general, Albert Sidney Johnston, was older, handsome, a fine mustached figure of a warrior. Kentucky born, he had served the Republic of Texas and in the United States Army with distinction and success. His military reputation, based on that long career, was very high. Many of his fellow citizens in the Confederacy spoke of Albert Sidney Johnston as the beau ideal of the Southern cause.

Henry W. Halleck, the Northern general, was pop-eyed and balding. He was a bookish-type officer, a translator of French tactics, a writer of military texts, known to West Point classmates as "Old Brains." As a theorist, among a select few, Halleck's reputation was excellent; as a fighter he was untried and practically unknown.

Both generals recognized the importance of rivers as the main arteries of troop transport far more reliable than rural railroads. They knew they would fight for control of those rivers.

Johnston had fortified the banks of the Mississippi, at Vicksburg and elsewhere. Now, early in 1862, he hastily erected forts on the Cumberland and the Tennessee. Watching Halleck's build-up at Cairo, Illinois, he constructed Fort Henry and Fort Donelson to block an expected advance south.

Halleck had more men than his opponent, more supplies. He also had a stocky, bearded, cigar-smoking brigadier general named Grant. The latter's military reputation was almost unsavory, stained with charges of drunkenness; his civilian life had been a succession of failures. But he had captured Paducah, without orders, he knew how to handle troops, and he wasn't afraid of anything.

Grant wasn't even afraid of Albert Sidney Johnston.

THE CROWD that thronged the Vicksburg racecourse gave little thought to the War Between The States. It was not a question of bread and circuses; any race that pitted local horseflesh against an imported steed was more important than either. In spite of the chill, damp weather most of the town turned out to watch the match between Saladin and Flambeau.

The oval track with its whitewashed rail was on a bluff directly above the river. Mist rose from the sluggishly moving water to blend with a sky the color of stale cigar ash. A raw breeze from the Mississippi sifted an intermittent, fine drizzle across the land. It managed to dampen everything without clouding vision. The fence rail was beaded with moisture; the infield grass, lushly high, had a dark, wet gleam; the turf of the track itself was as shining black as lacquer.

The prospect of a mudder's day brought smiles to the faces of Vicksburg bettors, black or white. They knew Furlong's Saladin; many had seen him run. Saladin could move through glue if necessary, and maybe the New Orleans horse needed a fast track.

Alex Kittering shared this local opinion. She was driving the Kittering chaise, only half-listening to the chatter of the two friends whose hoop-skirts bulged the little vehicle. The damp weather had forced her grandfather to stay indoors; Clara Furlong and Emilie Verrier were her guests.

"Henri and Bryce," said Emilie, "should have waited for a nicer day." Her nose was pinched, red with cold, and she sounded miserable.

"They couldn't," Clara said. "Both being officers. My brother is sure to be ordered north any day, and Henri can't leave the telegraph whenever he chooses. There's a war going on, you know."

"Yes," Emilie said, tartly, "I've read about it in the Vicksburg *Daily Citizen.*"

Alex, concentrating on her driving, acknowledged the remark with a smile. Lately, even the printed columns in the newspapers, the familiar editorial denunciation of the enemy, had made the war seem remote, a far-away crisis that concerned other people.

There had been skimpy accounts of sporadic engagements in Virginia, Missouri, and Kentucky. The biggest, closest battle in this new year was reported as two days of fighting near Mill Springs, Kentucky. The 15th Mississippi had been in that, and a Southern general named Zollicoffer had been killed. Alex almost agreed with her grandfather's opinion that claims of a Confederate victory were exaggerated.

"I'm cold," Emilie said.

Clara's snort was impatient. "Land's sake, girl, don't start fretting before we even arrive! Nobody made you come!"

"We've a wrapped stone jug with hot coffee," Alex said. "But I want to get close to the paddock before we stop."

The race-eager crowd didn't bother Dancer, the sturdy cob who always drew the Kittering chaise at his own pace, steady as a Tennessee walking-horse, but Alex found the congestion trying. She'd been promised a place near the paddock, with a good view of the finish, but getting there was a problem.

Occasional rain, and the many raised umbrellas, didn't discourage the spectators from noisy festivity. Carriages and horses already formed a hedge around the outer rim of the elongated oval; their owners craned and waved, or descended to gather in gossiping groups. Negroes, all ages from patriarchs to scampering youngsters, thronged the infield enclosure. If the slaves babbled and bet in constant cadence, their masters were not exactly silent.

Except for the gray uniforms, Alex decided, this might be any peacetime horse race. It was Sunday, and, to judge by the number of soldiers present, only skeleton crews were manning the river batteries.

"There's Runcey Carr, now," said Clara, pointing.

"I see him," Alex said, turning the cob toward the beckoning boy. Runcey had kept a place in the front row of parked vehicles, but the space was barely wide enough for the chaise. Alex maneuvered carefully between jutting wheel-hubs; with feminine obstinacy she ignored Runcey's directions.

"Easy, Miss Alex. Left a little. Just a mite."

"Whoa," cried Alex, reining in. She grinned down at the red-haired apprentice. "You stick to piloting river boats, Runcey. Let me drive the horses."

"I reckon," Runcey said, stroking Dancer's nose.

"Thanks for keeping the place."

"Said I would, Miss Alex. Tempe, here, helped."

Until then, Alex hadn't noticed the tall, young soldier. He was standing a yard behind Runcey, on the fringe of a crowd of wagering men. The girl's first thought was that at least today he wore a new hat, a respectable sand-brown felt, not that ridiculous child's straw that flew off when he leaped for the runaway. She nodded, made her voice gracious.

"Thank you, too, then, Mister Dixon."

"You're welcome, ma'am," said Tempe Dixon, raising his hat.

His gravity amused her but she was careful not to show it. Alex wished to appease her conscience. Her grandfather, who never minced words, had thought her thanks for the rescue on the landing quite inadequate. She didn't want even an uncouth stranger to think her rude.

"Two to one on Saladin," cried a man's voice close by. "I'm giving two to one."

"And no takers," Runcey Carr said.

Alex saw Tempe Dixon quickly glance at Runcey, return to her. She knew that, in spite of the dampness, she looked well in mantua-cut coat

[33]

and full skirt of hunter-green broadcloth. Her hat matched her costume as closely as the shining black buttons that adorned it matched her kid gloves. Winding the reins around the dashboard bar, she pretended friendly interest.

"Aren't you a betting man, Mister Dixon?"

"I already bet."

Beside her Clara struggled to raise an umbrella while Emilie sat in huddled misery. Alex ignored them both as she imagined the probable size of Tempe Dixon's wager. This tacky young man was surely from branch-water folk. She could picture the ramshackle cabin set in piny woods with a blue dog snuffling at the rickety doorstep. Those people always had at least one blue hound.

"I hope you didn't plunge."

"I got good odds, ma'am."

"Oh, then you bet on Flambeau."

"He sure did," said Runcey Carr with disapproval.

"That's right."

"You *are* a gambler, Mister Dixon."

She saw his gray eyes darken at her amusement, gazed over his head at the crowd. My, thought Alex, but he's quick to take offense. Not wanting to show her irritation she surveyed the scene around her with deliberation.

Most of the ladies in the carriages had opened umbrellas; the taut, black, bell-shaped silk, glistening with wet, made a strange wavering canopy over the parked vehicles, like many moving hillocks in a row. The men folk, more hardy, ignored the drizzle, warmed themselves with argument.

By standing on tiptoe Alex could see the open space where the contestants were being readied. Both horses, saddled, were standing quietly.

Henri Duchesneau was talking to his jockey, the small slave who had led Flambeau from the steamboat. The little man, resplendent now in green-and-gold silk blouse, nodded his peaked cap as he listened. The other jockey, in the Furlong scarlet-slashed-with-blue, was also getting instructions from his master. Bryce, thought Alex, seemed very assured and confident.

The slaves looked about the same weight for a fair race, and Alex turned her attention to the animals. Strangely, Flambeau wasn't bothered by the noise around him. The sorrel stood at ease, in his element. However skittish he acted in other places, a racing crowd was evidently an accepted part of his life.

Gazing at Saladin, the girl felt almost sorry for Tempe Dixon. The big, black stallion was a picture horse, lithograph-perfect with his rain-polished coat casting highlights when he moved. There wasn't a gray hair or an ounce of superfluous flesh on Saladin. Alex had never seen him look better.

"Runcey should have warned you, Mister Dixon," she said.

"I tried, Miss Alex."

Tempe Dixon shrugged, said, "A man backs his choice, ma'am, and the horses settle things."

There was a deeper hum of excitement from the group surrounding the paddock, and then it began to dissolve. Both jockeys were up, colorful little figures above the bobbing hats. Men hurried toward the trackside to find viewing points. Runcey Carr nodded a farewell and darted away into the crowd.

Tempe Dixon stared after him, but, before he could move, Alex was introducing her companions. He bowed to each girl, raised his eyebrows as he heard Clara Furlong's name.

"Mister Dixon is wagering against your brother, Clara," said Alex.

"I heard," Clara said. "He's just throwing money away. Saladin never loses. Bryce has a side wager of a thousand dollars with Henri Duchesneau. Even Papa thinks that's a bit steep."

"It's sure sizable," Alex said. She judged from the sudden blankness of Tempe Dixon's face that he was not unimpressed.

"I wish they'd get it over," Emilie Verrier said. "I'm cold."

"It won't take long, Emilie," said Alex. "They agreed to run only one heat because of the weather. Please put your new hat back on, Mister Dixon. It's starting to rain again."

Scowling, he complied, yanking the hat-brim down over his brow. The girl realized that her reference to his new headgear had reminded him of the old one, the silly straw. The poor oaf probably wanted to disappear, but didn't know how to make a polite adieu. She enjoyed feeling superior, was determined to be kindly. Her voice sounded so friendly that Clara Furlong stared.

"You could see the race better from the chaise, Mister Dixon."

"You all are a mite crowded now," Tempe Dixon said, grinning. "But I'd be obliged for a boost on the wheel-hub if I need it."

He has a nice grin, Alex thought with mild surprise. It was no effort to smile back at him. She supposed that his friends found him pleasant company. A sudden hush over the surrounding crowd made further speculation needless and small talk unnecessary.

"They're at the start," said Clara.

"High time," Emilie said. "I'm cold."

Tempe Dixon swung around to watch. He spoke over his shoulder, suddenly assured, a young man who knew a plug from a pacer.

"At a mile and a half I still like the sorrel."

"Saladin," said Alex. "Going away."

"We'll see."

"We will indeed. You haven't a chance."

"There's always a chance."

"Not this time."

"Put up or—"

"Shut up!" Alex finished the phrase with a laugh. She was delighted at the exchange, at his shocked look as he bit off the challenge in mid-speech. She had never teased Bryce Furlong into a wager so easily. The girl hoped her success wouldn't hobble this Dixon man's tongue. Anything was better than him calling her 'Ma'am' every other sentence. "All right. I will."

"You mean—"

"It's a shame to take your money, Mister Dixon, but—"

The horses at the starting line decided to close the betting. They exploded into motion and the crowd roared. The ancient, traditional cry, bellowed from a thousand throats, interrupted Alex, almost drowned Clara's excited squeal.

"They're off!"

Flambeau, on the inside, got away faster, but not by much. Saladin's nose was right beside the brown horse's saddle. They went down the straightaway like that, running hard, practically in step, with a speed that had the crowd in an uproar.

"Come on, Saladin! Come on!"

Alex Kittering, yelling, leaned from the chaise to pound a gloved fist on Tempe Dixon's shoulder. She was no more aware of her action than the man was; he paid no attention to the pummeling. They were both delirious with race fever. The soldier cheered his choice with a wild, wordless shout. Alex didn't even hear him; she had never seen such speed on a wet track.

The horses swept into the far turn, throwing clods of mud. In the infield the slaves seemed to be holding a mad tribal dance. They leaped and screamed, waved their arms, pushed and shoved as they ran around trying to follow the progress of the race.

Tempe Dixon swore when that jostling mob blocked his view. He stepped upon the wheel-hub. The sudden movement disturbed Alex's balance. She teetered, caught his arm to save herself. Intent, craning to follow Flambeau's position, the man shook himself loose.

"Well, really," said Clara Furlong.

Alex glared, speechless with outrage. The near-mishap had caused her to lose sight of the horses. Only the fellow's rapt expression saved him from a tongue-lashing. To Alex the race along the far side of the track was a distant blur, but the soldier seemed able to check it. *He has good eyes,* she thought as she shrieked the all-important question.

"Who's ahead now?"

"Flambeau!" he cried. "Flambeau!"

The girl wasn't sure if it was an answer or just a cheer. But the horses came pounding into the near curve now and she could tell them apart. That blazed brown nose nearest the rail did seem to be still in front.

"Come on, Saladin!"

"Saladin! Come on!"

"*Saladin!*"

Most of the crowd was chanting Alex's cry; they pleaded with their favorite.

At the head of the stretch Zack, the Furlong jockey, went to his whip. His arm rose and fell; the big black horse surged forward. Saladin moved alongside Flambeau. They were racing neck and neck.

"Oh, you, Saladin," yelled Alex.

"Flambeau, boy," Tempe Dixon begged. "Flambeau."

As they charged closer Saladin, bigger, seemed to loom over his rival. But Duchesneau's jockey was whipping furiously too, and Flambeau had something left. With one last sprint the brown horse edged ahead. Flambeau's nose was in front by inches when they swept across the finish line.

The crowd's noise became a turmoil of rage, enthusiasm, exasperation, sheer release. Only a few were certain which horse had won; everybody was willing to voice an opinion.

Tempe Dixon leaped from the wheel-hub, kicking his heels in the air. "What a race," he cried. "Good old Flambeau!"

"Saladin won," Alex said.

"He did not!"

"He did too!"

"It was Flambeau by a nose!"

"I don't see," said Clara, "how anybody could be sure." That won her glares from both arguers.

"*I'm* sure," Alex said.

"Sure and wrong."

Alex bit her lip; the blue eyes flashed. Her anger wasn't diminished by the growing certainty that she *was* wrong. Down the track she could see Duchesneau's jockey grinning as he held up his whip; Zack was slumped in his saddle. The Furlong slave cringed suddenly, and Alex glimpsed Bryce Furlong pale with rage shaking his fist. That decided it. She trembled with an impulse to slap Tempe Dixon's face. Her voice was tight with fury.

"You're just afraid you've lost your paltry bet!"

"And you, ma'am," said Tempe Dixon, "are a sorehead loser." He raised his hat with extravagant courtliness, turned, and walked away.

"Let's go home," Emilie Verrier said. "I'm cold."

"Oh, shut up," said Alex.

· 4 ·

VICKSBURG'S WATERFRONT section, along the levee, never claimed the river-length notoriety of Natchez-Under-The-Hill. But it had its own hectic night life, complete with taverns, light ladies, and professional gamblers. The quarter enjoyed its evil reputation, bragged of its lurid history.

Templeton Dixon, a stranger in town, found the details fascinating as told by Runcey Carr. The Kittering's boy-apprentice used language more colorful than his red hair. He was an ambling encyclopedia of Mississippi River lore and he liked to show his knowledge. Runcey could recite the name, time, captain and pilot of every steamboat that had attempted a record passage upstream or down. He collected such data as a numismatist did coins, treasured it like a miser. As a local boy, he was delighted to impress his new friend with the details of Vicksburg's most sensational hours.

"The riverfront," said Runcey, "was wilder than a pestered alligator in the old days, Tempe. Knifings and shootings, murders and robberies, the whole blasted shebang! I reckon the Devil hisself wouldn't strut Levee Street in the dark thirty years ago!"

"Thirty years ago," Tempe said. He smiled at his fourteen-year-old instructor.

"Pretty near," said Runcey, ignoring the smile. "The gamblers got their come-uppance in the summer of 1835. July, it was. Before that they had the town hooked and bleeding like a landed catfish. It was high, wide, and dump the corpses in the river!"

"But it ended."

"Sure did, though it took doing. Ain't there a marker about it up to the corner of Main and Farmer? Didn't you read it your own self? Doctor Hugh Bodley, it says. To his memory. Murdered by gamblers, it says."

"That's right." Tempe knew the boy could scrawl his name and decipher a printed page, but scorned both accomplishments. Runcey's heroes were river pilots whose reading was mainly devoted to shifting channels.

"Damn right, it's right. That there is where the fight took place. Where

[38]

Doctor Bodley was killed. The gamblers holed up in the courthouse, and the doctor led the attack to root them out."

"The courthouse?" Involuntarily, Tempe glanced upward at the structure on its high hill, shining with newness in the evening's drizzle.

"Not that one!" Runcey spoke with offended civic pride. "That's brand new. Not a mark on her! This was another, older courthouse. I guess it got riddled good with all the shooting. Every man in town that owned a gun was in that fracas! One side or t'other. Doc Bodley, he captained the respectables, but even my Mister Joab went along." Runcey's sigh expressed regret, not criticism. "'Course he don't hold none with shooting."

"Mister Kittering?" asked Tempe, with interest. In his few days hauling supplies from the Kittering warehouse he had learned that its crutch-hobbled owner could display irascibility and friendliness with the same breath.

"Nobody else. I reckon he just grabbed a holt on one of the ropes." Runcey didn't want Tempe thinking his employer was faint hearted. The boy adored Mister Joab, cherished his promise that the apprentice, in a few years, could learn the piloting trade aboard the *Tonica*. Runcey would not have swapped that chance to command the archangels.

"What ropes, Runcey?"

"Why, they hung them crooked gamblers higher than buzzards fly. High as those trees grow on Farmer Street anyways. Seven or eleven of them aswinging in the breeze. Cleaned them out!"

Tempe, amused by the evident relish in Runcey's recital, doubted that Joab Kittering had joined a lynching without great provocation. The old man was violently outspoken in his opposition to secession and the war; he seemed to be a furious believer in existing law and order.

"But you're taking me to a gambling house, Runcey."

"Jump MacGregor's? That ain't the same at all. Jump's games is *honest*. That's why I placed your bet with him." Runcey's freckles seemed to dim as his face darkened. Like most of Vicksburg's horse-racing enthusiasts, male and female, slave or free, he considered Saladin's loss a mournful calamity.

These folks, thought Tempe as he recognized the expression, sure took a whipping badly. The girl, Alex Kittering, had flared into ill temper; Runcey looked as if he'd swallowed sulphur-and-molasses.

"You hear any more," he said, changing the subject, "about those new ironclad gunboats?"

"Just what I told you," Runcey said, brightening instantly at the chance to discuss steamboats. "All the pilots was talking about them in Jump's the other night. Cap'n Abram Auter, his son, Sid, and the rest. The Confederate Navy is building them now up to Memphis. Two real

[39]

whoppers, armored all over, like nothing the old Mississippi ever saw before!"

"Big as the *Natchez?*" Tempe used a newly learned standard of comparison. Before he left home to go to war he had never seen a steamboat, nor really understood the width of the Mississippi River.

"Bigger maybe. And built different. One's going to be called the *Tennessee,* and t'other the *Arkansas.*" Runcey clapped his hands in glee. "Ziggety-damn, Tempe! Once they join the River Defense Flotilla no Yankee steamers will dare come poking down our river!"

"I hope you're right."

"Sure, I'm right," said Runcey with conviction. The boy idolized Southern captains and pilots; he couldn't imagine Yankee ships or sailors besting his heroes.

They had reached the foot of a street leading down to the levee, and they paused to gaze at the river. Even in the murky light cast by the distant, rain-blurred, setting sun beyond the low Louisiana bank the Father of Waters was an impressive sight. Empty of traffic, shadow-black, the Mississippi was a wide, dark, lonely stream. The wavelets that slapped against the levee, gurgled around piles and moorings, seemed muted by the majesty of the silent flood behind them. As always in dreary weather the river's odor was a dank mixture that quivered the nostrils, a scent both chill and menacing.

Runcey Carr, head turning, scanned the wide stretch of water like a farmer estimating his crops. Templeton Dixon stared; once more he was awed by the river's size, sensed its power.

It's even bigger, thought Tempe, than Pa said. If you came from over east in Noxubee County you just didn't get used to the Mississippi in a fortnight. It sure made the Noxubee River in spring flood seem as piddling as a rain-spill off the eaves.

Thinking about his pa gave Tempe a sudden pang of loneliness. He recalled an earlier conversation with the ever-curious Runcey.

"What's your pappy do, Tempe?" the boy had asked.

"Pa? Why, he's a poet."

Tempe smiled remembering Runcey's quickly masked astonishment. The answer, spoken without thought, had been true enough. Lucius Dixon *was* a poet, and his many other trades were merely incidental to his true vocation. He had once explained that fact to his only son.

"Poetry, my boy," Lucius had said, "is not a paying craft. Homer begged his bread, and Horace had a thrifty father."

"What about Shakespeare, Pa?"

"Ah, well, the giants are always exceptions, not like the rest of men. But even Shakespeare made his money by stagecraft, not peddling verses. The age was with him, an age when that raddled old queen herself respected poetry. However, it was play-acting in theaters made him rich."

"But the sonnets—"

"You needn't argue their worth with me, Tempe. The sonnets would have made him famous in any case. Suppose though he had neither trade nor patron? He might have starved before anybody read them!"

Lucius Dixon had been an itinerant printer in his youth, roaming the breadth of the land, as far north as Cincinnati and Pittsburgh, as far south as New Orleans and Texas. He still set the type for the weekly news-sheet that summarized world events for Noxubee County. Lucius had paused there to court and wed Tempe's mother, had left wife, small son and infant daughter to volunteer for the Mexican War. The ankle smashed at the battle of Buena Vista had hobbled him to a lurching gait and ended his wanderings.

Now, at twenty-one, Tempe had a mental picture, real or imagined, of the lithe, graceful man who had gone trotting off to that earlier war. He was sure he remembered his father's return on crutches, and he had never forgotten the look on his mother's face.

The neighbors around Dixon's Place respected Lucius Dixon. He was the rural schoolteacher as well as part-time printer. He was also a carpenter, boot-maker, harness-mender, an occasional blacksmith-cum-veterinary, a perennial farmer. But none of the visitors who listened while Lucius recited in the book-lined corner of his living room ever doubted that he was a poet. Tempe had heard their comments.

"That verse was as good as a hymn."

"Lucius could talk a possum into frisking."

"I reckon, Tempe, your pa's got more books than acres."

That last estimate, Tempe thought ruefully, was only too true. Pa owned sixty acres, but over twice that many books. In the seven years since his mother had died in child-birth, Tempe had grown very close to his father. That was why he had stayed put at home, did his traveling vicariously in the library or by prompting Lucius to reminisce about his gypsy days.

"Don't you ever get restless, Pa?" Tempe had asked.

"With you and three daughters to raise?" Lucius, twinkling, had flashed the bright grin that made his grizzled beard seem tangled. "Not to mention crops, chickens, pigs, two cows and a tired, old horse."

"But you never even bother to print your verses in the paper any more."

"No space. Ever since the secession talk started that little sheet's been crammed to the masthead. Speeches and more speeches. Seems like every fire-eating orator in the South is stumping the country."

"Well, you know best."

"Don't you worry, son." Lucius had laughed at Tempe's frowning disapproval. "The one thing I am not is a mute, inglorious Milton."

Recognizing the quotation Tempe had exploded into laughter. The words culled from Gray's *Elegy* hardly fitted his voluble father. Lucius Dixon would join a cross-road argument before his horse felt the bit, control the conversation before a hat hit the ground. The circuit riders, judges and lawyers, the politicians, peddlers, passers-by or neighbors who spent the night at Dixon's Place found three things: good food, clean beds, an entertaining monologue from the host. Lucius Dixon was probably the only man in Mississippi who delighted an audience by reading from *Uncle Tom's Cabin*. For a man who didn't believe in slavery he made a hilarious parody of Mrs. Stowe's version of that peculiar institution.

Tempe Dixon didn't realize that his own quiet gravity was a reaction from his father's loquacious wit. The family lived well, and snugly, without much money; Lucius was usually paid in kind. But Tempe, who adored his father, thought odd jobs dissipated talents, and knew that drudgery however lightened by cheerfulness still made muscles ache.

Nobody in Noxubee County considered Lucius Dixon's family poor whites, but Tempe had seen that feeling in Alex Kittering's glance. The girl, of course, had been amused by that childish straw hat.

He flushed at the memory of her ill-concealed laughter. The hat, Tempe admitted, had been a mistake, but it had been a going-away present from his youngest sister. She'd spent a whole Confederate dollar for that head-piece; its bright newness was meant to supplement the handmade boots Lucius had stitched for his departing son.

"Whatever Napoleon said," Lucius had insisted, "an army travels mostly on its feet. A rifleman does a sight more walking than riding. It was that way in Mexico, and this war will be the same."

Tempe had waited until the fall harvest was in the cribs before marching off to war. He found that his father had been right in most of his predictions. The delay had not mattered; the South, with more enthusiasm than equipment, had not yet managed to obtain the decisive victories that would establish independence. Tempe found his rifle welcomed, his boots admired. Many recruits who arrived in camp unarmed stayed that way; few privates could afford such elegant footwear.

The recruiting sergeant, impressed, had issued Tempe Dixon a worn, gray uniform jacket. It was too tight, but at least it was soldierly. In Tempe's company the tiny straw hat provoked neither comment nor laughter. Some of his comrades wore even more outlandish headgear, cut-down plugs, tattered coonskins.

Gazing at the Mississippi now, Tempe sighed. He couldn't expect a girl like Alex Kittering to realize that the completely uniformed Confederate troops were either outfitted by private means, or had stripped the

[42]

quartermasters early. The more recent crop of volunteers, like himself, had enlisted at a time when demand outran supply.

"You got a bellyache?" asked Runcey Carr.

The abrupt question jerked Tempe back to the present. "No," he said. "No, Runcey. I was just thinking." He couldn't tell the boy that he was wishing he'd made a better impression on Joab Kittering's granddaughter. "Sort of wondering what I was doing down here in Vicksburg."

"Again?" Runcey sounded impatient. "You're doing what you was told to do!"

"But it's a long way from the war. I'm supposed to be an infantryman and—"

"And they got you hauling supplies. I know. Well, I reckon when they want you doing different they'll tell you that, too. Come on along and collect your winnings."

Tempe let himself be led away from the river. He had risked twenty dollars, hard money, on the horse race, at three to one. Sixty dollars was certainly a lot more important than mooning about a girl who disliked him.

The pair heard the din from Jump MacGregor's tavern at a distance of several hundred yards, before Tempe could distinguish the building from those around it. Closer inspection revealed it to be a long, two-storied structure, unporched, as barren of architectural adornment as the nearby warehouses. But the tavern's closed shutters showed yellow streaks of light that seemed to vibrate from the noise within; the double-door entrance, stepless, had pale panels of curtained glass.

"What kind of place is this?" asked Tempe cautiously. He peered into an alley where hitched horses were clotted into a mass by the deepening shadows. Behind the clapboards he could hear loud voices, raucous laughter, clinking glassware, a strummed banjo, but the blended sounds made an unintelligible uproar.

"Drinks, eats and gambling."

"I know, Runcey, but—" Tempe recalled his father's tales about plush New Orleans gambling halls with elegant furnishings, deep-piled carpets, brilliant chandeliers. He had no wish to play the country bumpkin among dandies. "I'm only a private, and—"

"Jump's is open house," said Runcey. "Anybody can pay, can stay. Besides, he's a friend of mine." The boy swaggered toward the doorway. "He used to work the steamboats, but he retired after the *Bayou Belle* exploded under him. Jump says he was holding four jacks when the boiler blew up!"

Tempe blinked as the boy thrust the door open. A thick cloud of tobacco smoke swirled into their faces, bearing light and heat in its folds.

Tempe fought an impulse to cough, smelled odors of sweat, food and liquor sharp enough to penetrate the pervading cigars.

The big, barn-sized room, lit by a dozen hanging lamps, seemed packed with men, all talking. They stood two deep at the bar that spanned the far wall; their glistening faces, reflected in the ranked mirrors, hung like so many breeze-stirred toy balloons. Others, crowded around a score of tables, were more quiet, intent on games of chance, though the noisiest group was crouched in a corner, playing dice. The sawdust-strewn floor held dozens of polished brass spittoons, obviously receptacles not decorations.

Tempe Dixon noticed that the waiters weaving among the tables were Negroes, the bartenders white. He recognized a railed, sanded circle as a cock-pit, empty now save for two black men, seated tailor-fashion, who sang as they strummed banjos. Their song was gay and brisk enough to be audible when one listened.

> When you go to de boatman's ball,
> Dance wid my wife, or don't dance at all;
> Sky-blue jacket and tarpaulin hat,
> Look out boys for de nine-tail cat.
>
> De boatman is a thrifty man,
> Dar's none can do as de boatman can;
> I neber see a putty gal in my life
> But dat she was a boatman's wife.

A thick-set man in a rumpled white-linen coat lounged by the entrance, removed his cheroot to nod to Runcey. He had a broad, battered face, with a broken nose beneath a perpetual frown of scar-tissue, but his voice was hoarsely affable.

"Evening, Runcey. Still raining?"

"Evening, Smasher," said Runcey. "Some. Where's Jump?"

"At the big table in the big game." Smasher waved the cigar in a vague point. He gazed at Tempe in open, friendly inspection, nodded. "You'd strip down too fine for rough and tumble, soldier. Never fight with no holds barred."

"Why, no, sir," Tempe said, startled. "I won't." He guessed that the jargon referred to prize-ring tactics, judged the advice was well intended.

"The Smasher," explained Runcey as he pushed through the crowd, "used to fight in matches for money. Up and down the river."

He looks it, Tempe thought, but made no comment. He followed the boy past several tables, was not surprised when they stopped at the one surrounded by spectators. The proprietor, of course, would be where the highest stakes drew a crowd. But he was surprised at Jump MacGregor's appearance.

The gambler, easily distinguished as the only civilian in the game, did not match Tempe's notions about professional card players. He looked neither shrewd, nor elegant, nor dangerous. Jump was short and fat, with a red, bald head made pear shaped by plump jowls that jiggled when he moved. He had several chins, a luxuriant white mustache, and wore square-rimmed spectacles. Jump MacGregor's clothes, rusty brown, were without distinction; his linen was soiled, his stock frayed. He smiled and chuckled as he played, seeming as harmlessly happy as old King Cole.

Tempe knew the game was poker, recognized three of the four officers at the table. One was Bryce Furlong, flushed and sullen. Beside him, tossing cards away in disgust, was the young man Runcey had pointed out as Alex Kittering's brother, Clifton. More pleasantly, Henri Duchesneau discarded his hand. The Creole's voice was amused.

"*Non*, I think not. I am out."

Bryce Furlong glared across the table. "Does every bet I make scare you off, Henri?"

"*Mais, oui*," said Henri, with a shrug, unoffended. "I have been too lucky against you already today, my friend."

Tempe saw Furlong's flush deepen at the remark. The sting of defeat had evidently not lessened. Clifton Kittering made that even plainer with a growled oath.

"Lucky is right," he said. "That damned muddy track."

"Fortunes of racing, *mon ami*."

"Play cards," said the other officer.

Jump MacGregor chuckled, pushed chips forward. "I'll just jump you twenty dollars, Captain Furlong."

"Your twenty," Furlong said, "and fifty more."

The spectators stirred. The unknown officer raised his eyebrows, clicked his tongue in mild rebuke. Tempe, feeling Runcey stiffen beside him, realized that Furlong had been discourteous, had committed a breach of poker etiquette. By the rules of play, and his position at the table, the other officer, a lieutenant by his braid, should have had the first chance to speak after MacGregor. Furlong, with reckless impatience, hadn't waited.

"My apologies, Lieutenant Case." Furlong sounded formal and surly.

"You've probably," said the lieutenant easily, "saved me money."

"Well, Jump?"

"I'll just see what you have, Captain Furlong."

"Three queens."

"Too bad," Jump MacGregor said. He laid down his cards one by one, chuckling as each face was displayed. "A full house here, Captain. As you see. Tens over fours."

Tempe didn't know the values of the different colored chips, but he saw there were a lot of them. He figured the pot held several hundred dollars, and the murmurs from impressed spectators made him raise that estimate. Judging by the stacks in front of each player, MacGregor and the Creole seemed to be doing most of the winning.

"Jump," said Runcey, who had only waited for the hand to be played, "you owe my friend here sixty dollars. From the horse race."

The speech quelled talk within earshot, and attracted stares. Tempe Dixon, looming beside the boy, felt suddenly conspicuous, a stranger in a hostile town. But MacGregor merely glanced up from his winnings, and nodded.

"Evening, Runcey," he said, and raised his voice in summons. "Floyd!"

A saffron-colored mulatto, very thin, appeared at the gambler's shoulder. Floyd's thinness was accentuated by his gaily striped waistcoat, and by the broad leather sack that dangled from his neck. He spoke with a weary drawl.

"Yes, sir, Mister Jump?"

"Gentleman on the winning horse, Floyd. Wishes to collect." MacGregor glanced at Runcey. "Name of?"

"Dixon. Templeton Dixon."

Henri Duchesneau uttered a crow of delight, waved smoke from before his face as he leaned forward for a clearer view. He said: "My good friend Tempe Dixon! But of course! *You* would bet on Flambeau! You saved him from bodily harm, perhaps felt his power, eh? Come, *mon ami*. We must have a toast to our victory. Waiter! Glass and drink for *M'sieu* Dixon."

"Private Dixon," muttered Clifton Kittering.

Furlong said nothing, but Tempe felt his hostility. The captain was pale now with suppressed rage, his tight lips thinner than his mustache. He looked, thought Tempe, as tense as a crouched wildcat.

Actually, Bryce Furlong was seething. He took defeat as a personal affront, a reflection on his breeding. It had been bad enough to lose the race and over a thousand dollars. It was worse that the code demanded he endure Henri Duchesneau's celebration of victory while continuing to lose at poker. But, at least, the Creole was an officer and a gentleman. This upstart, Dixon, was a nobody.

He checked his scores against Tempe Dixon. The butternut-clad private had dared manhandle Alex Kittering, rescuing her from real danger while her true escort stood helpless. He had also bet against Saladin, and won. Now, he was demanding his winnings in Bryce Furlong's presence. That was intolerable!

You will pay for this, Bryce promised silently, glaring at Tempe Dixon. As truly as Zack, the jockey, was whipped for losing the race.

[46]

A gentleman punished his slaves for faults, and did not accept insolence from inferiors.

"Mister Jump, sir," said Floyd, scanning a slip of paper. "The gentleman is correct. He wins sixty dollars."

"Pay him."

The mulatto fumbled in his sack, drew out a sheaf of currency. Nimble saffron fingers began to deal out bills.

Tempe winced when he saw the bright color, the crisp newness, of the money. These were Confederate dollars, and patriotic enthusiasm for their tender was waning as rapidly as their value decreased. He had wagered a gold coin brought from home, a treasure obtained by much trading and careful saving. He had risked it blithely, as a gambler should, on a fair chance at good odds. But sixty Confederate certificates was not really three to one for twenty dollars in gold. He swallowed, hesitating to object, aware he was the alien, a winner among many losers. There would be little sympathy from those who had bet on Saladin.

Runcey Carr had no such qualms. The boy's voice was shrill, but assured. "It was a hard-money bet, Jump. That was understood."

"I'm paying off," said Jump MacGregor.

"I made the bet with you myself," insisted Runcey. "You know I gave you a double eagle!" He was distressed by the gambler's genial blandness. "I told my friend you'd pay in coin."

"Now, Runcey," said MacGregor, "you shouldn't have done that. I can't remember the circumstances of every wager placed in my establishment." His spectacles gleamed as he surveyed the listening crowd, noted Bryce Furlong's attitude, Tempe's discomfort. Jump MacGregor believed in taking every possible advantage. "But suppose we let the young man speak for himself."

"Well," said Tempe, "I'd like my coin back, sir, but—"

"You have some objections to paper money?"

"No, Mister MacGregor, if you want to pay the rest that way, why—"

"Private Dixon!"

Bryce Furlong, seizing the chance for vengeance, rose to his feet as he spoke. His tone was more startling than a shout. Henri Duchesneau, negotiating for a fresh drink, whirled; his brown eyes darted toward the speaker. Clifton Kittering leaned forward, wet his lips. When his friend addressed someone like that it meant trouble.

In the sudden quiet Jump MacGregor chuckled.

"Captain," said Tempe, rigid at attention.

"Are you trying to disgrace your uniform?"

"No, sir."

"What's wrong with Confederate money, Private?"

"Nothing, sir."

[47]

"Perhaps you don't believe we'll win this war?"

"We'll win, sir." Tempe had learned early not to argue with officers. He knew Furlong was baiting him, but kept his face blank and his answers respectful. The damned aristocrat had him in a trap, before a crowd, and could tease him at will.

"Those bills, Private, are your government's promise to pay on victory." The scornful voice showed Bryce Furlong's contempt, but not his relish. "The word of gentlemen, accepted by gentlemen. Do you understand that, Private Dixon?"

"Yes, sir."

"I doubt it," Bryce said. "I doubt if you know the meaning of the term."

"Oh, come, Bryce," said Henri Duchesneau. The Creole was annoyed. He recognized bullying when he saw it, realized that Tempe Dixon, outranked, was defenseless. "Enough of this. *Sacré nom!* Why a tempest over nothing? What is it that Tempe Dixon did?"

"He didn't want to take Confederate currency," said Clifton, as always supporting his friend Bryce.

"Pooh!" Henri snorted, shrewdly struck at the source of the trouble. "Or is it, *peut-être*, that my friend won this currency on my horse?"

"Are you," asked Bryce Furlong, stung, "inferring that I am a poor loser?"

Jump MacGregor was suddenly anxious. He sensed tension around the table, felt the whole room was too quiet. The gambler wanted no trouble in his place. These planter gamecocks were always too ready to fight. He said quickly: "In this case I'm the one who's the loser. Pay the wager, Floyd."

Knowing his master the mulatto offered the sheaf of bills. Tempe took the paper money without comment. Runcey, beside him, started to splutter, was stilled by Tempe's quick clutch. All the private wanted was to get away from these wrangling officers. He would be the sure loser no matter who won.

Bryce Furlong saw the movement. His eyes narrowed. He had made this Dixon back down, berated him publicly, cost him his precious gold coin. Any quarrel with the Creole, for whatever reason, might cause critical comment about sportsmanship. But there was a chance to strip Tempe Dixon of his winnings. Furlong's voice was gently mocking.

"If the private is such a gambler perhaps he'd care to try his luck at cards?" Bryce picked up his chips, let them click through his fingers as he counted. "There's about eighty dollars here, Private. You seem to like odds."

Tempe was silent, thinking. He had been goaded enough, was tired of acting mouse to Furlong's cat. The watching men, gamblers all, eagerly awaited his decision.

"You do play cards, Private?"

"Old Sledge, Captain."

"Old Sledge?"

"Seven-up," said Jump MacGregor. "Fours."

"Then you know the value of the cards?"

"Yes, sir," said Tempe.

"Well? Will you wager? On the turn of a card?"

"Yes, Captain Furlong. High card wins." Tempe placed his money on the table.

"*Bien!*" cried Henri Duchesneau.

"Jump, if you please?"

"Sure, Captain." MacGregor shuffled the cards, set the deck in the center of the table. The spectators pressed closer.

Bryce Furlong, coolly smiling, gestured toward the pack of cards. He misread Tempe's impassive countenance as frozen fear. The soldier probably thought the sum involved was a fortune; Bryce had paid more for cuff-links. His politeness was elaborately indifferent.

"You may cut first, Private Dixon."

"Thank you, sir."

Tempe, ignoring Runcey's audible indrawn breath, reached with a steady hand. He wanted fiercely to win, but not because of the money. This man, pulling rank, had challenged his courage.

He cut the pack about half-deep, turned his palm half to view. Tempe's voice sounded calmly indifferent.

"Ace of clubs."

The captain's eyes bulged. Incredulity, stupefaction, outraged fury showed on his face in successive waves of flush and pallor. He felt betrayed, duped; his plan had gone awry through some trick.

With an oath Furlong swept up the rest of the pack. He made no cut, showed no card. He flung the playing cards, full force, into Tempe Dixon's face. As they spattered around the other's head, Bryce Furlong turned on his heel, shoved an onlooker from his path, and stamped from the room.

Clifton Kittering scrambled after his friend. No one spoke until the door slammed behind them.

"*Mon ami,*" said Henri Duchesneau, brushing a card from Tempe's shoulder, "you have won more than money. *Mais, oui.* You have won yourself an enemy."

5

The strategy was Major General Halleck's, but he picked Grant to lead a speedy invasion. With seventeen thousand men, plus a flotilla of transports and gunboats, the Union army swept down the Tennessee River to engulf Fort Henry like the flood waters of a sudden February thaw.

Albert Sidney Johnston, the Confederate leader, had tried to defend too much with too little. Most of his available force was still far to the east, at Bowling Green, Kentucky, when the Federal warships opened fire on Fort Henry.

These craft were strange, makeshift vessels, new to the inland waterways of the continent. In a hundred days, at a hastily created shipyard called Mound City, near Cairo, Illinois, an ingenious, hard-driving contractor, James B. Eads, had converted seven river steamboats into ironclad gunboats. The idea wasn't new; every naval designer, North or South, was experimenting with armor plate. But Eads had his ships ready first, and the little fleet, under Flag Officer Foote, reduced the enemy fort after a short, spirited battle. Grant arrived in time to accept the surrender.

Without dawdling, he went after Fort Donelson. While the gunboats darted back to the Ohio River to steam down the Cumberland, Grant marched his soldiers overland. That second week in February, 1862, was sleet cold, and the military textbooks said no attackers could take a fortification bravely defended by almost equal numbers. In spite of weather, rules, and resistance, Grant's army took Donelson.

It was the first really decisive victory of the war. Grant captured thirteen thousand Confederates, and made his name a rallying cry.

Replying to a request for terms, Grant used the phrase, "Unconditional surrender." Since his initials were, officially though incorrectly, U. S. Grant, the stocky general was widely hailed as Unconditional Surrender Grant!

The double victory thrilled the North, sent a shock of fear through the South. Even the rival governments, at Washington and Richmond, with their splendid armies massed in Virginia, turned to gaze West.

This new sensation, Grant, was a man to watch.

VICKSBURG, slumbering through the winter, with business at a stand-still and cotton choking the warehouses, was startled by Albert Sidney Johnston's swift withdrawal through Tennessee. His new base, at Corinth, Mississippi, was a sight closer to home than Bowling Green, Kentucky.

The local planters grumbled into their toddies. But the same telegraph keys that clattered warnings, like a mechanical Cassandra, rapped out reassurances from Richmond. Take heart; gird your loins; rally 'round the flags: the Bonnie Blue Flag, the red-and-white State flag, the popular new battle flags with the blue St. Andrew's Cross on a scarlet field. Fort Pillow stood firm. Island No. 10 alone could keep the Yankee gunboats from descending the Mississippi.

There was concrete evidence that the Confederate Government intended to regain the lost ground. Reinforcements were being sent to Johnston, and the cream of the South's generals were hurrying to his support. Some of their names were familiar in Vicksburg—the romantic P. G. T. Beauregard, Braxton Bragg, Leonidas Polk. Hadn't that same Bishop Polk, in his peaceful role, laid the cornerstone of the town's Anglican church?

Vicksburg, slave and free, no longer talked about the Yankees quitting. Now, the arguments concerned inevitable battle, and the triple-damned enemy blockade at the mouth of the Mississippi. Even when cotton was allowed to move again, somebody was going to have to run it out of New Orleans through the Federal fleet.

Of course, a way *would* be found. Cotton, after all, was king. Europe, especially those English mills, couldn't do without it. But it seemed silly to have more cotton bales stacked on the waterfront than cannon on the bluffs.

Not that Vicksburg was likely to need more batteries. She was sending her young men away in gray uniforms to make certain of that. Only a small garrison stayed behind to guard the town; so many were leaving by rail or steamboat, afoot or riding their own horses, that the hundred hills seemed somewhat desolate.

Mimosa, the Kittering's slave-maid, gazed out at the emptiness of Cherry Street with cold, tearless eyes. The girl was sullenly angry.

"They didn't have to take Benjie," she muttered.

Only a few minutes before, the now-deserted street had been filled with bustle. Major Stephen Kittering and his son, Lieutenant Clifton, were riding off to war on Corngold and Shuffleshoe. The ladies of the family, young master Clay, even most of the slaves, were accompanying the officers as far as the steamboat landing. But, far more important to Mimosa, her husband, Benjie, the Major's body-servant, was going with his master. Now, for the first time, she felt rebellious, irked by the difference between slave and free.

"Sitting on that horse," said Mimosa. "Waving and grinning like he wanted to go!" After three years of marriage Mimosa had no illusions about her husband's brains. Benjie was coal black, but he was the butler's son and the marriage assured them and their children of a permanent place.

"Leaving a wife and two poor children," she said, squinting into the thin morning sunshine filtering through the window curtains. Mimosa ignored the fact that her mother-in-law, big Sarah, took charge of the children.

She saw the young soldier turn in the front gate, hesitate, come on toward the house. He was tall, with a blanket-roll over his shoulder and a long rifle in the crook of his arm. Mimosa frowned; she was well trained but she couldn't place this face among the family's friends.

The slave girl let the knocker sound twice before she opened the door. Mimosa's manner betrayed none of the hostility she felt today for all who wore the gray uniform. She'd been taught to greet every caller politely, and instinct told her that this one, for all his butternut shirt and trousers, carried himself like a gentleman.

"Yes, sir?"

"I would like to see Mister Joab Kittering. My name is Templeton Dixon."

"This way, sir."

Tempe followed the maid into the living room where Joab, hunched under his shawl, sat close to the fire, reading. The big head did not raise until Mimosa spoke.

"Gentleman to see you, Mister Joab."

"Oh, it's you, son," Joab said. "Come to take leave?"

"Yes, sir. I've been ordered to join my regiment at Corinth."

"You, too, eh. Corinth will be crowded. Mimosa, fetch us a couple of drinks."

"I'm not sure I've time, sir," Tempe protested.

"Nonsense." Joab flipped the fob from his waistcoat pocket, glanced at his watch. "Always time for a drink. The *Tonica* won't cast off for another hour."

Mimosa slipped away, with silent ease.

"I wanted to thank you, sir," said Tempe.

"For what?"

"Everything. Letting me sleep at the warehouse with Runcey. Arranging for me to ride as far as Memphis on the *Tonica*." Tempe's sudden grin was boyish. "I've never ridden on a steamboat, sir."

"Enjoy it while you can," Joab said, gruffly. He liked this young man, his independent spirit, the interest he'd shown down at the warehouse. The South was crazy, Joab thought, to waste youth like this as cannon fodder.

"I—I wonder if I could ask another favor, sir." Tempe was hesitant. He didn't want to abuse the old man's kindness.

"Speak up."

"Yes, sir. You see, I'm carrying quite a bit of money, sir, and—"

The shaggy eyebrows rose in surprise. Joab said, "Where'd you get this windfall?"

"Won it. On the horse race." Tempe tried not to grin at Joab's grunt. Mister Kittering, he judged, might not agree with his fellow townsfolk on most matters, but he shared the local loyalty to Saladin. "And elsewhere. I'd rather not take it to camp, sir, or—or battle."

"Sensible."

"I'd sort of like my father at Dixon's Place, over in Noxubee County to get it." Tempe took out the sheaf of bills. "But no matter how I wrap it to mail you can tell what it is by the feel."

"And the postal service," said Joab, grinning, "was a mite more trustworthy under the United States, eh?"

"I wouldn't say that, sir."

"I would. But hand it over, son. Nobody tampers with goods sent by Kittering and Son. I'll make sure it reaches your pa."

"Thank you, sir."

"Want a receipt?" Joab was pleased by Tempe's quick headshake. He was stuffing the money in his wallet when the Vicksburg bells began to ring, first one, then another, then the whole clangorous chorus. Joab's gnarled fingers were still as he listened. "What in thunder—?"

Outside in the street a man's voice rose in a shrill, elated yell. A horse clattered past at full gallop.

"Must be a fire or—"

"No, sir," said Tempe. "I reckon they just heard the news. About the ship."

"The ship? What ship?"

"Why, the ironclad. The *Merrimac*, over in Virginia. It got out into Hampton Roads yesterday, and—well, I guess it just about broke the blockade."

"Broke the blockade?" Joab, for once, was gaping. "I don't believe it!"

"It's true, sir." Tempe nodded with enthusiasm. "I was telling good-by to Lieutenant Duchesneau—he's the telegraph officer—when the news came over the wire. The *Merrimac* sank two or three big Yankee warships, and they couldn't even dent her. You know what *that* means, sir!"

"Yes, son," said Joab heavily. "I do. It means a longer, bloodier war."

"But, if the blockade's broken—"

"Even if it is, son, the Yankees will mend it. One ironclad, no matter how mighty, isn't going to win this war. If the South can build them, so can the North." The big head jerked toward the sound of the bells. "They'll be celebrating like that through the whole Confederacy, Tempe. But to me it sounds more like a death knell."

Why, thought Tempe with a sudden chill, the old man really means it. He can't imagine the South winning the final victory. Tempe tried to keep pity from his gaze. He had no wish to hurt Joab Kittering.

You just couldn't argue with the aged. They didn't understand.

Alex Kittering, seated at the Pleyel piano in the Cherry Street parlor, pecked at the ivory keys nervously. She played passably, but not really well, and she knew it. Besides, the delicate air of Gottschalk's *La Savane* might be proper mood music for this evening, yet it certainly didn't soothe her flutters. She felt sorrowful, anxious, drained by the emotions of her father's, and brother's, departure. She was, also, terribly aware of the importance of Bryce Furlong's expected visit.

He, too, is leaving to do battle for the Confederacy, she thought with tragic bathos, like a knight of old. Alex was determined to behave in a heroic fashion. She wondered why something seemed off-key, why she felt a jarring uneasiness.

The girl glanced over her shoulder at her mother. Epie Mae, placidly doing embroidery by the fireplace, neither heard the discord, nor sensed tension. Her fingers were deft; her face was untroubled. Nothing disturbed Epie when she was absorbed in handiwork.

Alex usually admired such composure, but this time she resented it. She brought both hands down on the keyboard with a crash. The resulting jangle shook through the room, drew her mother's unstartled attention.

"Yes, dear?" asked Epie.

"I—I don't feel like playing."

"Very well." With a gentle sigh Epie put her embroidery on the inlaid table beside her chair. She considered herself very artistic, regretted the hours stolen from this natural talent, but realized her duties as mother of a family. After all, she thought, the boys and Alex are my creations, too.

"If he's coming," Alex said, "I wish he'd get here!"

"He isn't late." Epie studied the ormulu French clock on the mantelpiece as if inspecting it for dust. Then, with the same expression, she surveyed the room. Everything in it was imported—the Belter furniture from Philadelphia, the chandelier, piano, and ornate gilt-framed mirror over the mantel from France, the heavy damask drapes from Italy. Epie, who had arranged all this, gazed at it complacently.

Alex said, "Bryce isn't usually so formal."

"Formality," said Epie, "is required on occasion." Having decided the setting was eminently suitable, she regarded her daughter with critical detachment. Alex did look lovely this evening; the blue brocade gown was very becoming. The stylish width of crinoline emphasized Alex's slender waist, made tightly laced stays unnecessary.

The girl herself felt constricted but not by stiff, heavy clothing or the over-cluttered room. Those were normal, every-day parts of living. She only knew she was flushed and uncomfortable. "It's warm in here, Ma."

"Do you want a fan, dear?"

"N-No."

"We could ask Andrew to send Mimosa to fetch one."

"No, it's all right."

Epie Mae smiled at the flames in the fireplace grate. She knew they had nothing to do with her daughter's heightened color. That was due to nerves, a condition Epie recognized from pure observation. She couldn't recall suffering such qualms when her husband, Stephen, came to propose, but it was a common ailment among young ladies. Fortunately, Alex's cheeks were enhanced by a blush.

"The house seems empty," Epie said, making conversation, "without Clifton and your father." She was trying to put her daughter at ease, succeeded.

"I know," said Alex. "The Ancient isn't very good company these days."

"I wish you wouldn't call your grandfather by that ridiculous name. Some day he'll overhear."

"He wouldn't care. It sounds like something from his beloved Dickens."

Epie Mae pursed her lips, without comment. She disapproved of Mr. Dickens as well as her father-in-law. Both were too crude, too outspoken, for her taste. But she made it a practice never to criticize Joab to his grandchildren. Opposition made unseemly behavior more attractive to youthful minds.

Drawing a leg up under her, Alex sat, side-saddle fashion, on the piano bench. Frowning, she said: "Ma, what about the Ancient? He's still pretty sharp, you know, and he doesn't say these things just to hear himself talk."

"What things, dear?"

"Oh, the war. Secession. All that rigmarole."

"Your grandfather is an old man. Behind the times."

"He thinks we're going to—to lose." Alex's tone was hushed.

"We shall not lose," said Epie, without raising her voice. Her political beliefs were simple, fixed not fervent. God had ordained that she was born a Clifton, into a family of slave-holding cotton planters. She had married a charming widower, a Southern gentleman by choice in spite of his father. "God will defend the righteous cause."

"The Yankees most likely say that, too."

"Yankees will say anything, Alex." Epie Mae's logic was above attack. She could not have defined a syllogism, true or false, but she lived by a rigid self-made one. Only gentlemen were fit to govern. No Yankees were gentlemen. Therefore: no Yankees were fit to govern. "They said they wouldn't fight, then turned right around and made war on us!"

"We've just got to win!"

"We will, dear," Epie said, with quiet conviction. "Don't bother your head about it." She uttered a soft chirrup of laughter that dismissed the subject. "Why should a woman of sense care to talk about anything but dress or servants?"

Alex stared, a trifle appalled, slightly rebellious. She didn't agree with *that* for a moment. She realized the question was rhetorical, knew better than to attempt an answer. While still in pinafores the girl had learned it was futile to try to change her mother's opinions.

She's like a rock in the river, Alex thought, that you can't move so you just steer around. She smiled affectionately at Epie, recalling the many times in the past when she and her brothers had steered around in thought or deed. Ma was never troubled by anything, but she wasn't informed about *everything*.

"You letting Clay go upriver, Ma?"

"Yes, dear. A visit to Cuddin Bess in Memphis will do him good." Epie was pleased by the turn of the conversation. Clay, her youngest, was her favorite though she never openly admitted it. He was the best looking, the wittiest, the most mischievous. Of course, she loved all three, but Clay, her baby, deserved a special place in her heart.

"What about his schooling?"

"He's ahead of the others already, Alex." A shrug helped make the words sound unimportant. Epie had secret plans for her younger son's future. "He's real pert. There isn't much more poor Mister Fenable can teach him."

"No," said Alex, "I guess there isn't at that." She knew how often Clay avoided his lessons to go traipsing around with Runcey Carr and Esau.

"No. Not Clay." The mother believed that all her children did her credit. Clifton was the image of his father, even to his gentlemanly disregard for learning. Alex, while not beautiful, had turned out well, would take her fit place as Mrs. Bryce Furlong. But Clay, with that easy manner that brought a lump to his mother's throat, was pure handsome!

In a few years, Epie thought, he'll have all the girls swooning. Not just here in Mississippi, either, or even throughout the Confederate

States. But in England while he attended Oxford, and on the Continent when he made his Grand Tour. He was destined, by Epie, for all those things as soon as the war ended.

Alex stiffened, listening. "Ma, didn't you hear a horse?"

Epie, wrapped in dreams, hadn't, but the noise was repeated. She heard the shod hoof paw gravel, the greeting from Martin, the stableman, a reply. Bryce Furlong had arrived.

"Alex, dear. Play something."

"But, Ma! It's so—so—"

"Appropriate, Alex. Play that hymn—the 'Volunteer Song.' You know, the one we came across in that copy of the New Orleans *Picayune*."

Feeling foolish, Alex struck the opening chords. At least it gave her something to do while Bryce made his entrance. She concentrated on the melody, recalled the words as solemn, not sentimental. Softly, impressed by the lyric's meaning at this particular moment, she began to sing.

> *Go soldiers, arm you for the fight,*
> *God shield the cause of Justice Right;*
> *May all return with victory crowned.*
> *May every heart with joy abound,*
> *May each deserve the laurel crown,*
> *Nor one to meet his lady's frown.*

The girl was moved, near tears as she finished the verse. She swung around, held out a hand toward the officer standing beside her mother in the hall doorway. Bryce looked very handsome and tall in full regimentals. He stood at attention, erect, unsmiling.

"Go on, Alex," said Bryce, gently. "Finish it."

She bowed, played, began the second verse. Her voice was tremulous, but that only accented the simple sincerity of her song.

> *Your cause is good, 'tis honor bright,*
> *'Tis virtue, country, home and right;*
> *Then should you die for love of these,*
> *We'll waft your names upon the breeze:*
> *The waves will sing your lullaby,*
> *Your country mourn your latest sigh.*

As the song ended, Alex sat motionless, gazing at the keys through a blurred mist. She heard her mother murmur something, and leave the room. Head bent, waiting, she sensed Bryce Furlong's approach, was not surprised when his fingers touched her shoulder.

"Alex?"

"Yes, Bryce."

"Alex, look at me."

She turned then, drawn but piqued by the pompous gravity of his tone. Could this be Bryce, a childhood playmate, Clara's brother? She had teased, twitted, even wrestled roughly in games with him as a boy; she had flirted with and kissed this young man. Now, towering above her, Bryce's face had such a look of solemn, rapt devotion that Alex fought an insane impulse to giggle.

"You know why I'm here, Alex?"

"Yes, Bryce."

"I spoke to your father before he left. He and your mother give their full consent."

"Yes." Alex lowered her eyelids demurely. This was part design, part necessity. Bryce's square chin was too resolute; the quivering blond mustache and troubled hazel eyes stressed the emotion in his voice. She couldn't gaze at him so closely too long without laughter. And this was no moment for laughter.

"What I have to say will hardly come as a surprise."

"No, Bryce."

If only, she thought, he'd get on with it, say it! These formal expressions were proper, according to the code, but they certainly became tedious. Alex fastened her gaze on the brass buckle of Bryce's sword belt, on the laurel-entwined letters: C.S.A. That helped her recall the cause, the war, her lover's imminent departure.

"Alex, will you—will you—do me—"

The husky faltering as Bryce choked and stammered touched Alex. She felt a rush of tenderness, a rekindled patriotism, a sudden excitement. Whatever bookish phrases he used, Bryce's emotions were genuine. She could not laugh at them.

Trying to help she reached, took his hand. His grip surprised and pleased her. There was blood and strength in the Southern chivalry beyond the fine rules of conduct.

"Go on, Bryce," she said, raising her glance. She gave him her full attention now, lips parted, the blue eyes dark with repentance.

Bryce cleared his throat, tried again. "Alex, will you—do me the honor to—become my wife?"

She saw the pulse beat in his neck, that his florid complexion had turned brick red. His clasp was hurting her fingers, and that, too, thrilled her. Here stood a perfect example of a Confederate officer, no playmate but a budding hero, asking her to be his bride. To accept would be like marrying the South itself.

"Yes, Bryce," she said. She spoke without tremor. No other answer seemed possible; a negative would have shocked them both.

Bryce bent and she rose to his embrace. The song, the occasion,

Bryce's request, her acceptance, all combined to stir Alex to ardor. She was ready and willing; her mouth eagerly awaited his kiss.

He kissed her with firmness and despatch, a capable demonstration of how a gentleman should kiss his betrothed.

But, thought Alex with dismay, he's kissed me like this a dozen times! Tonight should be special, different. She was half-panting with passion, and Bryce made no attempt to caress her. It was a jolt as physical as missing a step coming down a staircase.

"Oh, Bryce," she whispered, trying to move him, "you do love me, don't you?"

"Why, of course."

The declaration, too, was disappointing. Was this all there was to becoming engaged? Wildly she told herself that true love didn't need display, or wanton tricks. But she felt vaguely unconvinced.

Epie Mae's discreet cough from the hallway parted them. They were holding hands, flushed and smiling, when the mother entered. At a glance she knew that the expected had happened; she raised the tray of drinks like an offering.

"Am I in time to toast an engagement?"

"Yes, Ma."

"I reckon so, Miz Kittering."

Well, thought Epie Mae, handing sherry to Alex and bourbon to Bryce, that is that. She said, "I only wish Alex's father were here to do the honors."

"He'll do them at the wedding," Bryce said. He fumbled inside his uniform tunic, drew out a box. "We'll all be back—victors to claim the spoils. Alex, dear, your ring."

It was a heavy gold ring with a square-cut diamond. Alex recognized the stone. She had seen it sparkle from Bryce's ruffled shirt front several times before war changed his civilian dress. As he slipped it on the proper finger Alex said, "You must have been sure to have it made."

Bryce laughed, a smug, masculine laugh. "I always play my hunches, Alex."

Somehow, Alex heard again an inaudible jarring note. Bryce wasn't pompous now, nor uncertain. He seemed to reflect her mother's calm assurance. The decision had been made; they only waited to be happy ever after.

You're engaged to be married, she said silently. But the ring felt strange and heavy on her hand.

6

THE BRIGHTENING DAWN tinted the tree-tops to rosy red, but shadows still clustered in the underbrush of the wood where Templeton Dixon stalked. Dew-wet grass swished against his legs as he went forward into battle.

There was no doubt there would be a battle. Ahead, only a few miles now according to the cavalry reports, was a big Union army, encamped at a place called Pittsburg Landing, near Shiloh Church. That was newly promoted Major General Grant's Army of the Tennessee, and it had pitched its tents between spring-swollen streams with its back to a curve of the Tennessee River. Behind Tempe, coming on in his tracks, was an army of 40,000 Confederates, foot, horse, and guns, that had been gathered together for this day by Albert Sidney Johnston.

That much Tempe knew, as he knew his mouth was dry, his heart pounding. He had even heard of the handsome general's boast that they would water their horses in the Tennessee by nightfall. It wasn't hard to figure they'd have to whip the Yankees to do so.

Tempe wished he was sure how he'd act when the fighting began. He shared his comrades' confidence in the coming victory, but that was an army feeling, not personal. Of course the boys would win, just as the general claimed. But Tempe wasn't so all-fired stuck on himself as to think he might not be scared.

"Scared green," he said, softly, "and funking."

So far it had been easy, more like an early-morning hunt than anything else. The trees around him were sporting a bright April green and the spring air was soft here in southern Tennessee. Even the position of his long rifle, cocked, held across his chest ready to shoot if anyone kicked up birds, reminded Tempe of hunting. But his blue hound, Junior, was far away, and the careful, quiet men to right and left were soldiers, not hunters. The gleaming steel bayonet they'd given him branded the gun a man-killer. He was aiming to flush Yankees, not game.

Skirmisher was the proper term. They had trained him for that down to Corinth. Mostly, he guessed, because he could shoot, had a rifle, and wore a uniform jacket. Whole companies in the Ninth Mississippi were clad in everyday clothes; many of the boys were carrying shotguns.

He remembered the commands. "Skirmishers fire and fall back." Or the other one. "Skirmishers fire and join the charge." Whichever it was they were the fellows out in front, the first to meet up with the enemy.

Ahead, thinned by tree screen and distance, bugles blared the wake-up call.

Sergeant Tazewell, a yard from Tempe's right elbow, raised his voice in a hoarse whisper. "Soft now, boys. We're getting close."

Tempe glanced toward the speaker, seeking encouragement. He liked the big sergeant, a balding, barrel-chested veteran, ex-U.S. Army regular, who had fought at and escaped from Donelson. Tazewell's nod seemed to dismiss the enemy bugles as unimportant.

Well, the sergeant should know, Tempe thought. He himself still couldn't imagine why anybody expected to surprise the Yankees. Not after that noisy march up from Corinth with half the army acting like tomfool rowdies at a county fair. Firing their guns to check the priming in Thursday's rain; whooping and hollering at every deer they saw. It had taken them over four days to come eighteen miles. Unless all the bluecoats were deaf they must be awaiting visitors.

Anyway, the boys were quiet this morning. He could sense the tread of the numbers behind him, but there was very little noise. Barring the sergeant no one in his own squad had spoken since the start at half-past five.

He looked to his left, at Lack Norris, who shared his bed-roll. Lack kept wetting his lips, but he managed a wink. Tall Stackpoole loomed beyond Lack; Tempe couldn't see Enright, the flanker. Strung out, on the sergeant's far side, would be the Ganzell brothers, and the funny little Englishman, Jollibee. He didn't bother to spot them. He didn't want Sergeant Tazewell to catch him gawking like a Sunday-go-meeting hillbilly.

Today is Sunday, thought Tempe, and gulped. He was out to kill men on a Sunday, and the old folk saying blazed in his brain: Nobody ever won a battle they started on Sunday.

Maybe the Yankees would start it by firing first. There was comfort in the quibble.

Tempe saw more light ahead where the woods thinned to clearing. It seemed very quiet under the trees, but he could hear bustle and talk at no great distance. Somewhere, closer, clearer a stream gurgled as it tumbled toward the Tennessee.

A rifle cracked. He never knew which side loosed the first shot.

"Pickets!" yelled Tazewell. He threw up his gun, and fired.

Tempe heard a quick crackle like a suddenly caught brush fire. Smoke and flashes speckled the fringe of bushes in front of him. He saw a lone Yankee shoot; the bullet ripped through nearby leaves. The blue-belly leaped away, behind a tree, before Tempe could move.

"At 'em!" the sergeant's voice boomed. "On the run!" He bit into a cartridge as he bounded forward.

"Bull Run!" shouted Stackpoole.

Lack Norris began to scream the shrill yell the Southern troops had used at Donelson. The wordless cry gathered volume as others echoed it.

Then, they were all running, shrieking. The whole, long wavering line of skirmishers charged for the edge of the woods.

They plunged into the clearing, a sloping strip of cockleburr meadow, bordered by the tall, wigwamlike Sibley tents of the enemy camp. Tempe saw Yankee soldiers standing frozen, in attitudes of shocked amazement. Others were running about in frenzy, upsetting cookpots.

He felt a sudden surge of wild elation. This, then, had been something like a surprise; Tempe realized he hadn't yet fired his rifle. He recalled the adage to go slow and aim low, but he wanted to pick a target.

There was a tall Yankee officer, red beard bright against rumpled blue tunic, sitting his horse within range attended by a younger horseman. The officer was holding binoculars. That made him at least a colonel.

He dropped to one knee, drew breath as he sighted, squeezed off the shot. Only when the younger man pitched from the saddle did Tempe remember he hadn't corrected for windage. To add to his shame the red-bearded officer seemed to be still watching him through his glasses.

"Oh, damn," cried Tempe. He fumbled for cartridge, cap, ramrod, all thumbs in his haste to reload. He almost dropped everything when Sergeant Tazewell grabbed his shoulder.

"Get back out of this! Back to the Ninth!"

"But, Sarge," shouted Enright, "they're running." He raised his rifle, fired harmlessly into the air as a bullet knocked him spinning.

"They ain't all running," Tazewell said. "And they won't. These blue bastards can fight!" He gazed over his shoulder, grunted in relief. "I thought we'd lost the main attack!"

Tempe, reloading, paused to stare as the Southern column, in tight, close-order battle line rushed from the woods. The long, uneven rows of glittering bayonets were very impressive; so was the steady rattle of musket fire. Yelling soldiers swept around him as they rushed for the tents. He saw some men in gray fall, realized that Tazewell was right. The Yankees weren't running, that drone was passing bullets, and a battle-field was no place to stand gaping.

He ducked, pushed in among the charging throng. During the confusion he went along with the rest, lost contact with Tazewell and his own unit. He ran, aimed low when he fired, reloaded, ran some more.

They darted into the enemy camp, drove the Union defenders out. Once broken by the tall tents the Confederate formation lost impetus. Men stopped to cheer, to forage, to rummage in abandoned haversacks.

Some of them, careless of rations, hadn't eaten in hours. They were hungry. It was all over anyway.

Tempe cheered with the others, gulped a hot cup of coffee from a captured cookfire. He gazed at dead Yankees huddled on the camp ground with pitying condescension, feeling sick but triumphant. The poor fellows shouldn't have started it.

A shell, bursting close overhead, shocked him back to reality. The Federals had only retreated a short distance, were rallying, still yielding ground but slowly, defending every yard with deadly, steady fire. Somebody had brought up a battery that was shelling the camp.

He clutched at a Confederate soldier staggering rearward with a dangling arm. "What outfit?" asked Tempe, shouting above the din. "Whose troops?"

The private looked at him with agonized eyes, mumbled a few words in French.

It was enough. Tempe knew that accent from Henri Duchesneau. Louisiana men. That was Beauregard, or should be. He didn't belong that far toward the left flank. The Ninth was under General Chalmers, in Bragg's command, much nearer the center unless Johnston had changed plans. Tempe wasn't sure about the generals, but he felt he had to find his own company.

He couldn't bind the Frenchman's wound, but he helped him back to the woods, left him with other wounded. Then, he went coursing along the battle line, heading always for the bright pimento flags that the color bearers carried with the attacking Southern troops.

The sun was ten o'clock high before Tempe found his comrades. The hours passed like a dreadful nightmare in which the gray and blue lines smashed at each other, charge and counter charge. In an ever-increasing crescendo the earth shook around him as cannon pounded; volleys of musketry swept across fields; bullets ripped grass, leaves, tree bark to shreds. Twice, he was involved in bitter, swirling pockets of fighting that almost became hand to hand. Men fired at each other as close as thirty feet.

He stumbled over Stackpoole first. Tall Stackey was lying dead with a ramrod in his stomach. Some Union recruit had forgotten to remove it after reloading, but it had proved a killing iron arrow.

Tempe had no time for tears, no time to be sick. He heard Tazewell's voice shrieking his name. Only a momentary lull made it possible.

"Dixon! *Dixon!* Over here, Dixon!"

He ran toward the waving figure, barely recognizing the big sergeant. Tazewell was hatless, in a blood-stained uniform, his face streaked with black powder.

"Where the hell have you been?" he rasped.

In hell, Tempe thought. He said, "I got lost."

"Well, come on! The Ninth is going in!"

They went in at a charge, into a withering fire that seared and blinded. Dead and living went down before it, but the living fought forward, shooting as they crawled. They re-formed and charged again. A nest of enemy, penned in a blind ravine, were slaughtered from its rim. Tempe fired down into that mass of struggling bluecoats only once.

During a respite, while he searched dead and wounded for more ammunition, Tempe learned the enemy he faced was an Illinois brigade under General Prentiss. Tazewell, on the same mission, always managed to know such details.

"He's pulled them back and anchored them in a sunken road. It's a sure-enough hornet's nest in there."

"Who's Prentiss?" asked Tempe.

"Who the hell knows?" The sergeant's grin was made more sardonic by his blackened face. "They got more damn brigadiers that come out of nowhere. *We* got all the reputations. For all the good that does."

Tempe stared around, trying to get some idea of the general situation. It seemed as mixed as the battered dead strewn nearby, blue coats merely darker clumps among the gray. The cries of the wounded were piteous as they pleaded for water, attention, death's relief. Trying to ignore them, Tempe concentrated on watching Confederate light artillery wheel to a fresh position and open fire.

That, he thought with weary disinterest, would be friend Duchesneau's bunch. He couldn't recall the name. Aloud, he said: "Bragg's hitting them with everything he has."

"He'll need everything," Tazewell said, "including us. Let's go, boy."

They rejoined the ragamuffin, un-uniformed Ninth Mississippi, fighting like veterans for all their scarecrow appearance. Again and again the ragged lines charged the Hornet's Nest, and men were tumbled in windrows like hay beneath a scythe.

For Tempe, the next hours made the morning an almost pleasant memory. He was fighting with hate now, hate for these Yankees who wouldn't quit, hate for the carnage that never stopped. Rage made him ignore fatigue, forced his weary muscles to answer, turned everything to a white blur.

Once he fought, in single combat, bayonet to bayonet, with a bluecoat soldier about his own age. They slashed and stabbed, forgetting all training, in a furious clumsy duel; they might have been alone on the field. Neither realized how well they symbolized both these maiden armies, novices at war learning their trade the hard way. When Tazewell finally shot the Federal down, Tempe felt cheated.

At last, after six hours, surrounded and outnumbered, Prentiss surrendered his remnant of two thousand men. That segment of the battle was over, and Tempe could think again.

He was drained of emotion, physically exhausted, but he gazed on the Union prisoners with sheer astonishment. Why, he thought, they're no older than myself, as dirty, as bone weary. Just farm boys from up North.

"Well," said Tazewell, "it's over for today anyway."

"Over?"

"Finished. The word just came down. Bragg blew his boiler, but Beauregard gave the order."

"Beauregard?"

"Johnston's been killed."

Afterwards, Tempe Dixon recalled that he never saw the Peach Orchard, where the bullets ripped the pink blossoms from the boughs to flutter down in horrible carnival mockery on redder ground below. After many futile attempts Albert Sidney Johnston himself had led the last attack on the Peach Orchard. Flushed with success he had sat his horse laughing while his life drained away into a blood-filled boot.

Tempe never drank from the Bloody Pool either, where wounded from both sides turned the water's color. That was behind the Peach Orchard where the Federals held with massed artillery at their backs.

"I was at the Hornet's Nest," Tempe would say as if that made further explanation unnecessary.

At the end of that first day after the shooting died and twilight gathered Sergeant Tazewell refused to let his men rest until they found captured stores of food and ammunition. Soldiers were wandering everywhere to search for friends, to gape at prisoners, aimlessly seeking shelter, but the sergeant kept his group together.

"Tomorrow's another day," Tazewell said. "There'll be more of the same in the morning."

"We drove them, didn't we, Sarge?" asked Lack Norris.

"We drove them one, maybe two miles. We took three camps, a lot of guns, and plenty prisoners. But they've got another whole army coming up—the Army of the Ohio. And all we got's right here now."

Tempe was too tired to worry about the morrow. He ached in every muscle, twitched with fatigue, but couldn't sleep. All around them in the deepening shadows wounded begged for help. He heard the steady pom-pom from the enemy gunboats in the river that sent shells whining overhead to burst with a clatter among the trees.

The squad was sadly diminished. Stackpoole was gone, and Enright; one of the Ganzell boys was missing. His brother sat in stupefied silence. Only the scrawny, bandy-legged Englishman, Jollibee, was talkative.

"I been soldiering all my life," he said, in his high-pitched voice. "I was in the Crimea, and I saw the cavalry charge at Balaklava. But I ain't never spent a day like this."

"What brought you over here anyway, English?"

"Why, Sarge, fighting's my profession, ain't it?"

It rained during the night, a drenching downpour complete with lightning. That and the gunboats made sleep impossible. Tempe had never spent a night under shellfire, found himself quivering as he listened for the next burst. In a way it was worse than battle. The damned things seemed to be searching for victims. You never knew where they might hit.

The second day, Monday, brought gray morning and the red flash of cannon. From the opening gun it seemed to Tempe like an aftermath, a needless repetition with a foreordained conclusion. The fighting was bitter and endless, but he remembered it only in flashes.

This time it was the bluecoat lines that came charging. The Southern infantry fought to hold the ground; every bush became a fortress, every tussock a redoubt. Tempe aimed low now without thought, reloaded with automatic motions. Always there seemed to be more and more Union soldiers in front of him, coming on; it was a nightmare in which two enemies leaped up for every one that fell.

Toward noon, while his shattered company rested in the high grass of a hollow clearing, Tempe Dixon saw Bryce Furlong. The captain led a small troop of cavalry into the clearing, evidently gave orders for a charge. His troopers drew sabers, jostled their mounts into a ragged line. Tempe recognized Clifton Kittering at Furlong's side while the captain shouted, pointing his sword.

"What the hell is that idiot doing?" asked Sergeant Tazewell.

"Looks like he's aiming to charge that Yankee battery yonder," Lack Norris said, nodding toward the enemy cannon gleaming in the distant underbrush.

Jollibee spat. "Blooming Light Brigade!"

Tempe opened his mouth to shout a warning. There was a whole Union brigade massed behind that battery. Furlong's men didn't have a hope. Only a feeble croak came out of Tempe's mouth; his tongue was too dry for speech.

The sergeant stood up, waved, but the cavalry paid no attention. They started at a trot, broke into full gallop. Furlong's bay mare carried him well in front, his saber flashing. Young Kittering, crouched low, rode a length behind the captain. The rest, farther back, did not seem to be spurring quite so vigorously.

Furlong was halfway across the clearing when one of the enemy howitzers fired. It was only an opening, range-finding shot, but the shell hit Clifton Kittering!

[66]

The horse turned a complete somersault; the rider was dead before he reached the ground. The cavalry troop veered away at once, racing for shelter, but Furlong went on alone until he was within musket range. A volley slammed from the bluecoats before he swerved his mare, cantered away, shooting back with his revolver.

"More guts," said Tazewell, "than sense. Can't hit them with a handgun at that distance."

Aiming carefully, Tempe shot the screaming, kicking animal beside Clifton Kittering. Then, he stared at the gray-uniformed figure crumpled in the grass. Somebody, thought Tempe, will have to tell that girl. He was glad it wasn't his job, hoped it was Furlong's. That boy's life had been thrown away in a reckless, stupid dash!

There was no time for reflection or recrimination. Tempe, and the others, charged with the Ninth Mississippi when General Chalmers snatched battle-flag from color bearer to lead them back to the Hornet's Nest. They retook the position, held it until told to retire. Chalmers was the only general Tempe saw close hand on either day.

They fought for eight hours, were, at last, driven from the field in mid-afternoon. Even the fresher Federal reinforcements were too exhausted to pursue with much vigor.

The road back to Corinth was a tortured pathway. It rained again that evening, a cold, stinging rain that changed from sleet to hail. Tempe, trodding through the mire, thought it unfair that they should be pelted by Nature after two days of gunfire.

"Armageddon," he said, aloud.

"What?" asked Tazewell, floundering beside him.

"The battle. Armageddon. Like it says in the Book."

"The name of this place," said Tazewell, "was Shiloh. And don't you forget it." He sounded bitter from defeat.

Sometimes, decided Tempe, the sergeant liked to repeat the obvious. It wasn't probable that anybody who had been there would ever forget it.

· 7 ·

Shiloh stunned both the North and the South. Never before had a battle of such magnitude, such bloodshed, taken place on this continent; the number of casualties, on both sides, was staggering.

The South mourned the loss of Albert Sidney Johnston, and used his death as an excuse for the second day's defeat. But on that same

[67]

day Island Number 10, the Confederate bastion that blocked the upper Mississippi, fell to Union forces under General John Pope. A chill wind of foreboding swept down the great river valley; now its defense would not be easy. There was also a sudden revision of the estimate that one Southern soldier could whip ten Yankees.

In the North premature prophecies that the war was won mingled with sharp criticism of the losses at Shiloh. The bereaved said that Grant's army had been surprised on the first day, almost routed. Only crazy Sherman's stubborn resistance, and rescue by the Army of the Ohio had saved the Army of Tennessee from annihilation. Grant's budding fame lost its bloom; people recalled that the man drank.

Back east in Virginia McClellan, moving at last, had begun his Peninsula Campaign to test his huge army against the defenders of Richmond commanded by Joe E. Johnston. At the mouth of the Mississippi a U.S. fleet under Farragut threatened the forts guarding New Orleans.

Major General Halleck took personal charge of a ponderous advance on Corinth. Shunted aside, Grant found himself second in command with rank but no power. Only fast talk from his new friend, Sherman, prevented him from leaving the army. The clinching argument was the importance of the Mississippi valley as a future combat theater.

Chewing his cigar, Grant nodded agreement. He would wait for another chance. In a war, there was usually for the living another chance to fight.

Fighting was one business Grant was sure he knew.

TONICA HILL, the Kittering summer house, was about a dozen miles southeast of Vicksburg, on its own eminence near a branch of the Big Black River. It was far from any railroad stop, could only be reached by driving or riding out from town on the Baldwin Ferry Road until the turn-off onto the even more winding, narrower dirt track that Joab Kittering had made when he bought the land. This curved upward through an avenue of shade trees until it looped in front of the steps before the tall, white columns at the entrance. The house was sheltered by a clump of walnut trees, and there were terraced gardens on both sides.

Now, in mid-April, the trees were a dark, cool green, the gardens in full bloom. Alex Kittering, from the front gallery, could see roses, yellow and red, clusters of violets, beds of verbena and mignonette, white magnolias and pink crape myrtles. Along the terraces ran borders of passion vine, not yet at full fragrance, the petals barely tinted with pale lavender, the tiny plum-like berries far from ripe. Black birds and blue birds darted, singing, among the boughs; a hidden mocking bird joyously imitated them both.

Truly mocking, thought Alex sadly as she listened to the repeated trilling. So were the bright gay hues of the flowers. They should be wearing black bombazine as she was. Tonica Hill had been a house of mourning ever since it received word that Clifton Kittering had been killed at Shiloh.

"Poor Clifton," murmured Alex. "Twenty. In his first battle." There was no doubt about it. Stephen Kittering had gazed on his son's body. The father, wounded himself, had fainted, been carried from the field. Clifton, like so many others in blue or gray, had been buried in the blood-drenched ground where he fell.

"Miss Alex."

"Yes, Mimosa?" Alex turned, aware of the subdued tone used by the maid. There had been wailing in the slave quarters for the young master, genuine grief, until Joab put a stop to it.

"No sense," said Mimosa, "to stand here watching down the road. It sure ain't going to get them here no faster." Mimosa felt sorry for the family, hid her own elation that Benjie, unscathed, was fetching Mister Stephen home.

"Where's my mother?"

"Missus Epie's lying down."

Alex accepted the answer with a nod. Epie Mae had reacted to her eldest child's death in characteristic fashion. She had wept copious, ladylike tears, but there had been no hysterics, no rent garments, no disheveled hair. Her mother, Alex thought, merely retreated deeper behind the defenses built by years of proper behavior. She wore mourning with careful propriety; her infrequent smiles were wan, but her voice showed no emotion.

"And Grandpa?"

"He's upstairs waiting. Sitting in his chair." Mimosa hesitated, blurted the rest. "He's holding a book, but he ain't reading in it."

"I know." Alex had expected recriminations from Joab. Instead the old man had frozen into impassive stoniness. It was almost as if the stiffness in his joints had afflicted the muscles of his face. Joab spoke little these days, and that gruffly, but made no mention of war, rebellion, North or South. It was, the girl realized, because the dreaded tragedy had occurred.

"Mister Joab, he's taking it mighty hard."

"Aren't we all, Mimosa?"

"Yes, Miss Alex."

"Did you put flowers about the house?"

"Yes, Miss Alex."

There would be, Alex knew, no flowers on her brother's grave. The girl felt a spasm of pain that brought eye sting without tears. She had done her crying privately, was finished with it. But Clifton, she remembered, had liked flowers, had enjoyed their formal presentation on every occasion.

"That's all then, I think, Mimosa."

"All but the waiting."

Alex gave the maid a smile of understanding. She was grateful for Mimosa's company; the slave's presence helped her self-control. Left alone, Alex was troubled by the guilty knowledge that she and Clifton could have been closer. After a few childhood squabbles when, as older brother, he tried to dominate, they had settled for mutual respect and affection. But Clifton, a hero-worshipper, showed more devotion for his friend, Bryce Furlong.

"Mimosa?"

"Yes, Miss Alex?"

"We did send word to the Furlongs and the Verriers?"

"Soon as we heard."

How much, Alex wondered, would Clara take on over Clifton's death? He had been a popular escort, attentive to many girls, but recently Bryce's sister had seemed to be front runner. The couple had been a recognizable, pale imitation of herself and Bryce.

She shuddered, as she did whenever she thought that it might have been Bryce.

"You all right, Miss Alex?"

"Yes, Mimosa. Quite all right."

The girl was sure, uncomfortably sure, that she would have mourned her fiancé with stronger passion. Of course any death for the South from General Johnston down to the least private like that Dixon, merited a tearful prayer. For all she knew that obnoxious young man, too, might have been killed at Shiloh.

"There's they dust, Miss Alex!" This time Mimosa forgot to hide the excitement in her voice. In a few minutes she would see Benjie. He was her man, returned at last safe and sound.

"I see it," said Alex, watching horses and carriage take shape in the dust cloud far down the driveway. "Would you please tell my mother and Grandpa?"

She wasn't surprised that Mimosa scurried. Alex shared the slave's excitement. Father and master was coming home, wounded but alive! She felt her throat clog with tenderness for her hero father. From childhood she had given Stephen unquestioning devotion. Even after she was old enough to recognize his weaknesses, she instinctively dismissed them as minor flaws, not faults. She knew that Epie Mae was stronger, Joab was wiser; that only made her more protective toward her father. Her love needed no rationalization. It showed that complete loyalty given by some women to stupid, gentle men.

Where the dirt roadbed changed to gravel the matched grays, nearing home, visibly increased their pace. Alex judged at once, from their freshness, that Martin had not pressed the team. The girl swallowed, clenched her fists. If the coachman had driven so far that carefully it meant that her father's wound was serious, perhaps unhealed, unable to take the jolting of a speeding carriage.

"I mustn't show worry," she murmured. Stepping to the edge of the steps, she forced a smile, raised a hand in greeting.

The horses pranced to a smooth halt. As Martin reined in, other slaves, attracted by the rattling wheels, appeared at the corners of the house. One moment there was no one, the next field hands, kitchen help, women and children were grouped in clusters, watching.

Stephen Kittering, hat over his face, was slumped on the seat of the open carriage. Benjie, his body servant, was holding him, carefully cradled, in his arms. The slave, plump face shining with sweat, rolled his eyes at Alex as she hurried forward.

"He's all right, Miss Alex," said Benjie, grinning. "Just worn to a frazzle by the journey." Benjie shook his cannonball-shaped head as if to belie grin and cheerful tone.

"Pa," said Alex hiding her emotion. Her heart was pounding; her smiling lips were dry.

Slowly, using his left hand, Stephen removed his hat. He blinked at the sunshine, nodded to his daughter. His voice sounded very tired. "Hello, Alex."

"You're home, Pa. It's all right now. You're home."

"Home," repeated Stephen.

"Miss Alex," said Andrew, edging past the girl, "let me give Benjie a hand now." The butler leaned into the carriage, solicitude in his very posture. "Welcome home, Mistuh Stephen. Welcome, sir."

"Thank you, Andrew."

"Easy now, Benjie. Easy now."

"I'm not made of glass, Andrew," said Stephen and sat up as if he were.

The two slaves helped Stephen from the carriage. Alex tried to gaze without staring. Her heart seemed to twist when she saw the bulge at her father's right shoulder, the dangling coat sleeve, the swollen fingers peeping from his unbuttoned tunic. His uniform had been washed and mended, but she knew the faded stain, an ugly blotch, for what it was. The white thread made a puckered scar on the gray cloth.

"Lean on me, sir," Andrew said.

Benjie said, scowling, "I brung him this far, I can go the rest."

"Oh, get him inside," Alex said. She had never seen her father look so fragile, move so woodenly. Benjie had shaved him, but all health and color seemed to have been planed away by the razor. Even his mustache, she thought, now looks too big, false as an actor's.

"Patience, Alex. Patience."

"Yes, Pa." She bit her lip, furious at herself for showing anxiety. "How—how bad is it?"

"Bad enough. But better than it was." Stephen concentrated on climbing the steps. He straightened at the top. He gazed around, saluted the assembled slaves, sounded stronger. "Nothing at the moment that a good stiff drink won't cure."

"Andrew."

"Yes, Miss Alex. In two shakes!"

Epie Mae was waiting inside the threshold. Stephen let go of Benjie and walked toward his wife. He didn't totter, held himself stiffly erect. Alex saw her mother's eyes widen, then close, open again.

"Epie."

"Oh, my dear."

"Clifton—I—"

"Yes, Stephen, we know."

"There was nothing I could do," said Stephen heavily. "Nothing. I didn't even know he'd been hit until—until long afterward. By that time I—I had this." His left hand made a half gesture toward his right shoulder.

He mustn't apologize, thought Alex, for Clifton's death! He mustn't! He's wounded, hurt, sick, and he sounds so hangdog! It wasn't his fault. Ma should run to him, kiss him, show something besides calm pity.

"It's past and done, Stephen," said Epie with mild finality. "Now, my dear, we must get you well." She regarded her husband speculatively, judged that he looked worse than during his periodic seizures of malaria. Her voice changed to quiet competence. "Perhaps a nice, warm bath after the dust of—"

"Stephen!"

Joab's rasping interruption drew every face, black or white, toward him. The old man, buttressed by his crutches, was standing at the top of the long stairway that rose from the central hall. Shoulders hunched, big head thrust forward, Joab loomed above them like a massive gargoyle.

"Hello, Pa," called Stephen.

"How are you, son?"

"Middling, Pa. Middling."

At that moment Andrew arrived with a tumbler of whisky. Stephen took it, raised it to his father, drained it with one toss. He blew out his breath, said, "Another, please, Andrew."

"Yes, sir!"

Epie glanced at her daughter. Alex was watching her grandfather, waiting for his next speech. Joab would never interrupt a man's drinking, but he would hardly confine himself to the amenities. The girl feared his attack might be vitriolic. After all, son and grandson had gone to war against the Ancient's wishes.

"Son," Joab said in a curiously softened rasp, "you mosey up here to your room and get comfortable. Nobody's going to pester you until you're ready."

"Thanks, Pa." Stephen waited for his second drink, drained it with the same quick motion of head and hand.

Alex's raised eyebrows were mirrored on Epie. Fashionably, according to Southern custom, Stephen had always consumed his share of liquor, but he'd never been a hurried drinker. The whisky visibly helped him now; he approached the long stairway more confidently than he had managed the broad, shallow steps outside.

They ascended in procession. Epie led the way, wide skirt lifted to shoetops. Stephen, good hand clutching the bannister, followed. Andrew and Benjie hovered, ready to assist. Alex, last in line, noted that three men could climb abreast on the narrow staircase where modishly dressed women could only pass by turning sideways.

Mimosa was already in the master bedroom, removing the spread, fluffing up pillows. The mosquito netting, drawn back, masked the bed's four posts like filmy draperies. The slave girl darted a single glance at her husband, turned back to her work. Benjie's solemn countenance went as blank as an erased blackboard. He helped Stephen out of his coat, eased him onto a chair, while Andrew, at Joab's signal, went for more liquid refreshments.

Stephen mopped his forehead, waved away his body servant. "That's all now, Benjie."

"Your boots."

"Later. Later." Stephen smiled at his servant. "Get along now. You, too, Mimosa. You must have plenty to talk about."

"Yes, sir, Mister Stephen." Mimosa needed no urging. She reached the doorway in three gliding strides. Standing there, beside Benjie, her fingers trembled from the effort of not touching him before the white folks.

"Take along Mister Stephen's coat and hat for brushing," said Epie.

"Yes, Missus Epie." Benjie gathered the garments. If he knew the look in Mimosa's eyes the brushing would wait a while, but that was their business. His master had been his charge and he'd delivered him safe home; Benjie intended, after Mimosa was thoroughly impressed, to regale the whole slave quarters with his adventures.

[73]

"And Benjie."

"Mister Stephen, sir?"

"Thanks. Thanks for everything."

Benjie bowed, grinning, and let his wife drag him away. Stephen settled back, gazed around the room. His ruffled linen shirt, too, had an empty sleeve, neatly pinned across the chest. The assembled family waited for him to speak, awkwardly aware that he needed these moments of orientation. He seemed to rouse when Andrew returned with a tray holding decanters and glasses.

"Benjie behaved splendidly, Andrew," said Stephen. "You can be proud of your son."

The butler beamed, jerked his woolly head in a series of delighted bows. "Thank you, Mistuh Stephen."

"He found me among the wounded," Stephen explained. "Nursed me like a baby. Hardly slept those first few days."

"As it should be, Mistuh Stephen. As it should be."

"We won't forget it, Andrew," said Joab, trying to hide his impatience. He was still standing, leaning on his crutches. "That'll be all, I think." He waited until the butler left, nodded to his granddaughter. "Alex, will you do the honors?"

Pouring drinks, Alex was aware that her father had again lapsed into silence. There was no sound in the room but the tinkle of glass on glass. From outside came the soft hum of the spring evening as the insects came to life. The delirious mocking bird was even more intoxicated by its own repetitive performance. She passed the glasses, bourbon for the men, springhouse-cooled wine for her mother and herself.

As he took his tumbler Stephen said, abruptly, "I gave Corngold away, Pa."

"All right, son."

"To an Alabama captain. He'd lost his own horse."

"All right."

"Shuffleshoe was lying beside Clifton." Stephen looked at his wife, winced. "The shell got them both. He—he never felt anything, Epie."

"Don't talk about it, dear," said Epie.

Joab glared at his daughter-in-law. He realized the necessity for Stephen to talk, to drink, to relive and release the whole terrible experience in a babble of words. Can she really, he wondered, believe it's healthier to keep it corked in tight? Joab's question was gratingly blunt.

"How bad is your wound?"

Holding her breath, Alex waited for her father's answer. The telegram had given no details. Even Epie stiffened, raising her head as if scenting danger.

"I'll never use the arm again," said Stephen slowly, gazing into his whisky. His glance flicked up at Alex's gasp, Joab's muttered curse. "The ball tore through my bicep, shattered the bones." With careful fingertips he touched the bulge of his shirt. "There's a splint on, and it should mend, but stiff."

"Oh, Pa!"

"Hush, Alex," said Joab. "Who says, son? We'll get Doc Randall to take a look at it."

"He'll have to anyway," Stephen said, "because it isn't fully healed. But he can't put bone splinters back that aren't there. Luckily the ball went clean through."

"You have laudable pus?" Joab knew doctors thought suppuration necessary and beneficial.

"I guess so, Pa. I didn't know too much for a while there. What with pain, and thinking about Clifton, and maybe fever. Yes, and fighting the surgeons."

"Fighting the surgeons?"

"Yes, Alex. Tooth and nail." Stephen gazed at his drink as if surprised he still held it, gulped it down. This time he coughed, and a pink flush tinted his cheeks. "You see, they wanted to cut it off."

The quiet statement, spoken with slow deliberation, turned Alex's stomach. She fought nausea. It was her father talking! Her father! She watched his face as if hypnotized. Stephen, eyes wide, was staring into space; a note of hysteria came into his voice.

"That first day, the day we thought we had them beat, we drove the Yankees back several miles. I reckon you all know that. It was bloody, fierce fighting, and a lot of poor devils on both sides went to meet their Maker.

"Maybe you think a staff officer doesn't get up in the thick of battle, but there weren't any lucky officers like that at Shiloh. Not on Johnston's staff, or Bragg's, or Beauregard's, or the Bishop's. Some of Breckenridge's family had a respite in the beginning—he had the reserve—but they all were under fire before it was over.

"True for us, true for them. The bluecoat generals were right up there with their men, too."

"All right, son," Joab said. "We realize that." He had wanted Stephen to talk, but this spate of words disturbed him. Something, liquor or memory, was driving him close to raving. Alex looked white as milk, and even Epie, for once, silently implored Joab to calm her husband.

Stephen paid no attention, went on as if he hadn't even heard his father. "Not that I'm any great warrior. I never fired my revolver the whole two days. Nor drew my sword. But I was always within call—as much as one can be in a mixed-up hurley-burley like that scrap. I was only twelve yards behind Johnston when he went into that damned Peach Orchard to his death.

"No matter. It was around then that we over-ran one of the Yankee hospital tents. God! There were piles of limbs outside that place. Arms and legs stacked up like—like cordwood! Fingers still clutching scraps of paper, bones sticking through boots. And inside it was worse, with the stench of blood and men shrieking in agony.

"The Union doctors never even looked at us. They were busy. Covered with blood, haggard with strain, one of them even amputating with his hat on! It was a—a charnel house!

"Jesus, God and Saviour!"

Stephen buried his face in the crook of his elbow. His shoulders shook; he still held his empty glass.

"Stephen, dear—"

"Pa. Oh, Pa—"

"Son, maybe you'd better—"

"No!" Stephen shouted the word, glaring. "No, no, no! I want you to hear! Everybody should know!"

"Yes," Joab said, "they should." He nodded at Alex, pointed to the whisky decanter. The girl hesitated; Joab stabbed his finger toward the tray, toward Stephen. He said, mildly, "Wait a second, son. My drink's empty. Talking is dry work." He knew that Stephen had to finish his tale, but the liquor might deaden the pain of recital.

Stephen nodded, held out his glass for Alex to refill, continued. The interruption seemed to have steadied him. His tone became flat, almost unemotional.

"That was worse than the battle itself. The battle was hell on earth, but that was a special corner of it, filled with poor damned souls. God help me, it was a relief to get back and face the cannon!

"Nobody slept much that night what with thunder and lightning and shelling. But that wasn't why I couldn't sleep. I was afraid to close my eyes lest I'd see that tent in nightmare."

He paused to gulp some of the whisky. The others drank, too, as if aping his action. Epie, surprisingly, drained her glass.

"It was practically all over," Stephen said, "on the second day when I was hit. Beauregard sent me to Chalmers with a message to retire. The Yankees were smashing us back. I was alone, cantering Corngold.

"Something from nowhere, more blow than pain, knocked me out of the saddle. I hit my head, lost consciousness. I don't know how long I lay there. When I came to, Benjie was bending over me. Corngold had run back to headquarters where he'd had his last meal, and Benjie had ridden in search of me.

"He bandaged me, best he could, got me back on Corngold. Riding

[76]

double we started from the field. I had quite a bit of pain. On the way we saw Clifton. Dead."

Stephen finished his drink, dropped the glass on the carpet. He watched it roll idly, shook his head. Alex wanted to comfort him, knew it wasn't the time.

"What with that shock, pain, and loss of blood, I fainted. Benjie kept me from falling off Corngold. And the next time I woke up—the next time I woke up—oh, Jesus!—I was *in* a charnel house!

"Men were screaming, moaning all around. I couldn't breathe for the blood smell. And a surgeon was standing, saw in hand, ready to cut off my arm!"

He wiped his wrist across his brow. The sleeve turned dark with perspiration.

"They tell me I fought like a madman. That I said terrible things. I guess I did all right because I know I went out of my head with fright. I remember I drew my gun, left-handed, cocked it, and threatened to blow that surgeon's brains out. He gave up at last, patched me as best he could.

"I rode all the way to Corinth, Benjie behind me, with revolver cocked. Another surgeon, a Georgian, told me when I reached a bed I gave Benjie the gun, told him to kill anybody tried to come near me. I don't believe that—me giving a slave, even Benjie, a weapon. But the next four, five days aren't very clear. There was fever and pain and Benjie pouring whisky—wet fire!—on the wound.

"Then, the fever left, my head cleared, though I was limp as wet moss. The Georgian surgeon came around, sniffed at my wound, rigged up a splint, and told me I was lucky."

Stephen cackled with laughter. He smacked the arm of his chair with his palm. "Lucky!" he cried. "Lucky! I should say! I kept my arm! You hear that, Epie? Hear, Alex? I kept my arm! God damn them, they didn't cut it off!" He laughed again, a peal of wild, triumphant glee.

Alex wanted to clap her hands over her ears, stood as if frozen. Epie Mae, bewildered, stared at her husband. She had never known Stephen to display such uncontrolled emotion, not even during their honeymoon. It was Joab, clumping forward, who took command of the situation.

"Good boy, son," he said. "You beat them in the end. Fine. Fine. I'm proud of you."

"Are you, Pa?"

" 'Course I am. You're going to be all right, now. We'll send Martin for Doc Randall first thing in the morning. Now, you'd better get some sleep. Epie, can you undress him?"

Epie, wetting her lips, looked faintly shocked. She wasn't; she was frightened. For the first time in their married life Stephen seemed a stranger. She had nursed him in sickness before, but now she thought him dangerous.

"I—I don't know, Father," she said. "I think perhaps Benjie—"

"Not Benjie," said Joab. "Andrew. Benjie's had enough." The old man gazed at his son. Stephen, chin on chest, was beginning to breathe heavily. "He'll sleep the sleep now it's off his mind. I'll send Andrew up."

"I'll go, Grandpa," said Alex.

Outside in the upstairs hall the girl and her grandfather stood for a moment in silence, and looked at each other. Through the mistiness of her own tears Alex saw her grandfather's grim sadness. She was, she thought, learning to tell the many different faces of sorrow. The town's elation over the *Merrimac's* initial victories that supposedly shattered the blockade had lasted a single day; it had been replaced abruptly by distress on hearing how the Yankee *Monitor* had fought the bigger ironclad to a standstill. But the news of Shiloh, with the long casualty lists, brought a deeper, stronger emotion. Alex had never known a Vicksburg so stunned by universal grief. People walked the hundred hills in a daze, with pale, set faces; the merchants spoke in hushed tones. Even the slaves were subdued.

She knew that Joab felt no satisfaction that he had been right in his predictions. Her own doubts about eventual Confederate success were growing; now they had to be rejected, could not be easily stifled. If the Ancient had been correct so far—

Alex refused to complete the thought. The important thing, right now, was the immediate present, her father's condition.

She said, chokingly: "Oh, Grandpa. Poor Pa. Poor, poor Pa."

"I tried to tell you," Joab said. "I tried to tell you all. Clifton. And your pa. That's what war really is."

· 8 ·

As SPRING BLAZED into summer Alex Kittering found each week spent at Tonica Hill harder to bear. Always before she had enjoyed the family's hot-weather stay in the tall, spacious, white-brick house that her grandfather had built for his bride. Now, daily, she longed to return to Vicksburg, even though the town was sweltering under rising temperatures.

The girl never mentioned her feeling to anyone, especially not to old Joab. He was proud of Tonica Hill. It was designed in the great tradition, the Grecian style that had swept the South in the halcyon, successful days of Joab's young manhood. For years he had boasted that it was bigger than Jefferson Davis's Brierfield, and had smiled when anyone mentioned that The Hurricane, Joseph Davis's manor, was far larger. All Vicksburg chuckled at Joab's standard reply to such criticism.

"So's Joe's income. I reckon he's the richest man in these parts, but you can't buy taste."

Since the war the town had stopped quoting the further remark that brother Joe made money and brother Jeff made trouble.

Alex envied her grandfather his bi-weekly trips to town. The firm did little business now, but at least he learned the latest news when it was fresh. She was forced to wait until he returned, or for the unscheduled occasions when Runcey Carr brought mail and messages from Vicksburg. The waiting made her feel very isolated; Tonica Hill seemed a stagnant backwater unruffled by the wind of great events.

Her confinement was a necessary duty. She was needed to help her mother, and Mimosa, nurse Stephen through his long convalescence. He shuttled between the netting-shrouded four-poster and an easy chair in the garden. In both places he stayed motionless for hours, staring into space.

"He is doing as well as can be expected," said Doctor Randall on every visit. Poll's father had a surprisingly deep voice, softened by bedside assurance, and he made the trite statement sound like a profound medical discovery.

"And how well is that, Doctor?" asked Alex after her fourth hearing of the pronouncement.

George Randall was a short man, with a small head atop a rotund, demijohn torso. He smoothed the waxed points of mustache and Vandyke as he reflected. The whiskers were, like his collar-long hair, spotless, almost as white as his linen duster and leghorn hat. "The wound is healing nicely, Alex. No putrefaction. No hospital gangrene or traumatic erysipelas."

"But, George!" Epie Mae's complaint barely hinted at impatience. "He doesn't show interest in anything, not even his own health."

"Well, he needs building up, Epie. Building up, strength and tissues. I prescribe silk weed root in a glass of whisky at regular intervals."

Alex recognized this as a familiar remedy, but was sure she'd heard younger, more modern, physicians flout such old-fashioned concoctions.

"A tonic, my dears," the doctor had said, and chuckled. "A tonic at Tonica Hill. Did you know the two have a relationship? The Tonica Indians, who once infested these parts, gave their name to some tribal libation. Now, it is applied to any medicinal, and obnoxious, beverage."

Stephen swallowed the medication without protest, not even smiling when Joab protested that the mixture ruined good bourbon. Sometimes, watching the two together, Alex thought that her father personalized the Ancient's low opinion of the Confederate government. Stephen was wounded, weak, suffered from recurring attacks of pain, awaited the next onslaught with dull apathy. She had heard Joab's summation of the situation as translated from the more optimistic pages of the Vicksburg *Daily Citizen*.

"McClellan is advancing on Richmond. The Union fleet under Farragut is attacking New Orleans. And our western army, at Corinth with Beauregard, waits for a Yankee invasion. Everywhere the South is outnumbered, on the defensive. Jeff Davis and Company had better stop talking and start acting."

"They're doing all they can, Grandpa."

"Your wish fathers that thought, Alex."

The girl refused to admit that defeat, anywhere, was inevitable. She listened avidly to every word-of-mouth report that reached Tonica Hill, scanned each written or printed line. Runcey, the doctor, newspaper editors, letters from girl friends and fiancé, were all more optimistic than her grandfather. The Confederacy was assailed, but uncowed. Let the Yankees come, on land or water; they would be thrown back by a united South, fighting valiantly for hearth and home.

Alex's young brother, Clay, made his ardent patriotism vocal. Summoned hastily from Memphis where he had been visiting, young Clay arrived at Tonica Hill two days after his father. Stephen's condition hardened the boy's resolve to avenge his brother's death. Clay spoke of the war as a personal, family feud.

"Those damned nigra-loving Yankees," said Clay, dark scowl making his tow-hair seem albino, "killed Clifton and crippled Pa. They're going to have to pay for it! The South needs every man. I'm going to volunteer!"

For once, for the only time in Alex's memory, Joab and Epie Mae joined forces. Both opposed the youth's expressed intention. The arguments raged for weeks. Joab roared; Epie wheedled; Clay, made boyishly uncertain by the voices of authority, tried to win approval by fiery, but illogical oratory.

"We'd have won at Shiloh if we'd had more men! There was soldiers up to Memphis younger than me. The cabin boy on the new ram, the *Arkansas*, wasn't half my size. I saw him when they towed her out to take her up the Yazoo River for finishing. No Yankee gunboat on the Mississippi will be able to whip the *Arkansas* when she gets in action!"

"She won't see much action," Joab said, "in the Yazoo City shipyards."

Epie calmly repeated her favorable objection. "You're only a boy, Clay."

"I can ride and shoot as well as anybody." Long discussion would bring

Clay close to tears. "As good as Clifton, almost as good as Bryce Furlong. Tell them, Alex. Tell them what Bryce wrote you. That only Southern chivalry stood between Tonica Hill and the abolitionist barbarians!"

"Yes," Alex said, "Bryce did write that." She flushed under Joab's stare. The girl was trying to stay neutral. She understood Clay's feelings, but sympathized with her mother and grandfather. Sixteen was awfully young for the hazards of war. They had lost Clifton; they didn't want to risk Clay.

Besides, she was disappointed in Bryce's infrequent letters. They were short, scrawled in wretched handwriting, full of flowery sentiments that seemed boastful. Even his most affectionate sentences had a mannered air that caused Alex uneasiness. About love or war, Bryce seemed incapable of expressing plain, honest emotions.

With mutual, unspoken agreement the family carefully kept the debate away from Stephen's hearing. Clay, in spite of growing impatience, realized that his wounded father must not be bothered by any problem but mending health. Epie Mae, unruffled by her son's vehemence, saw no reason to involve her husband in constant, ridiculous scenes.

"Poor Clay," she told Alex, "is all unstrung by our recent misfortunes. Family and country. But he's only a boy, and, of course, he will listen to me in the end."

Alex hoped her mother was right, but bad news continued to stoke Clay's patriotic fervor like tallow tossed in a steamboat's firebox. The Yankee fleet, under Farragut, smashed its way past the forts defending the Mississippi River's mouth, routed the Confederate navy in a short, furious battle. New Orleans, the fabulous city, the magnetic market place, the gay Mecca of most Vicksburg citizens, fell to the enemy, was occupied by Federal troops.

The girl, reading aloud the account of this defeat, saw her shaking voice reflected in her brother's quivering lips. As more detailed reports filtered in Tonica Hill seemed as gloomy as a tomb. The two giant, new ironclads built at great expense to make the Confederacy invincible at sea had not even contributed to the city's defense. One, the *Louisiana,* had proved too heavy for her engines, was towed into action as a floating battery; the other, the *Mississippi,* named for her own state, had not been finished in time. Both had been destroyed to prevent capture.

"What damn bad luck!" exploded Clay when he heard about the fate of the ironclads. He ignored his mother's frown at his language.

Joab was more succinct. He said, "Blunderers!"

The Ancient, thought Alex, whatever his Unionist feelings, was still a steamboat-man, outraged by the incompetent tardiness of the ship builders. Joab, too, seemed downcast that Yankees patrolled New Orleans. Everybody in Vicksburg, even the slaves, the girl decided, regarded the Mississippi River as a personal possession. It had been bad enough that geography placed its source in enemy territory; the loss of the great port at its mouth was a blow to pride and ownership!

There was worse to come. On a bright mid-May morning Poll Randall, home again from college, and Emilie Verrier accompanied the doctor to Tonica Hill. Both girls were aglow with excitement, could hardly wait for Poll's father to go attend his patient. Though Emilie had not seen Alex in more than a month, and Poll for a whole season, neither wasted time in small talk.

"Alex," cried Poll, "what do you think? The Yankee fleet has reached Vicksburg!"

"Just below," Emilie said. "They're anchored in the river."

"We saw them from Sky Parlor Hill."

"Dozens of ships. Frigates. Gunboats. Mortar vessels."

"I'm not surprised," Alex said slowly. She was telling the truth. There was nothing down river that could prevent an enemy fleet's passage to Vicksburg. She had expected this arrival, but now it came as a distinct shock. Her stomach muscles tensed, then fluttered. It was like hearing, at last, of the anticipated death of a loved one after a long, incurable illness.

"Nobody was really surprised," Poll Randall said. "Henri received warning from Port Hudson by telegraph. The Yankee steamship *Oneida* was the first to appear."

"Her captain," said Emilie, "had the impudence to send a note ashore. It was politely worded, of course, and addressed to the authorities at Vicksburg, but it was a request that we surrender the town."

"Oh?"

"Yes! Imagine!"

Poll's blonde ringlets bobbed in an indignant toss. "Colonel Autry, the commander at Vicksburg, put him in his place! His reply was a sure-enough gem."

Emilie rose, struck a dramatic pose. With a Gallic love of rhetoric she quoted, with feeling, from Autry's answer. "Mississippians don't know and refuse to learn how to surrender to an enemy. If Commodore Farragut or Brigadier General Butler can teach them, come and try."

"Do you think they will?" asked Alex.

"Attack? Who knows? But they can't take Vicksburg!"

"*Zut, alors,*" Emilie said. "They haven't a chance! Troops are pouring in from General Smith by every train. Captain Harris, the engineering officer sent by General Beauregard, has them digging emplacements for new, big cannon sent from the Tredegar Works in Richmond. The most modern weapons. Parrotts. Brookes. Wentworths."

"Henri says," said Poll, "that all Vicksburg, along the bluffs, from below the racecourse to the mouth of the Yazoo River, is a natural fortress. He claims that the Fifth Washington Light Artillery alone, *his* company you know, could prevent the Yankee soldiers from landing."

Alex hid her amusement at this glib recital of military knowledge. Henri Duchesneau, she gathered, had been busily instructing both girls in the art of war. Knowing the handsome Creole's tendencies, Alex was fairly certain that his two pupils had been flustered and flattered during their studies. But if Vicksburg was threatened she could not rely on girlish prattle, hearsay evidence. She would have to see for herself.

"I'm going in to town," Alex said, "as soon as Martin can harness the grays." She knew her mother, and Joab, would make no objection. Lately both had insisted that she relax from her nursing. Stephen was much better and she needed a change. "Would you-all ride with me?"

"Of course," said Emilie.

"We knew you'd say that." Poll, having heard about Alex's engagement, no longer considered her a rival. She felt very friendly to anyone not competing for Henri's favor. "Papa has some other patients to call on, and we'd waste the whole day with him."

Driving toward town on the Baldwin Ferry Road, Alex was surprised to find several other vehicles moving in the same direction. The summer dust raised by hoofs and wheels seemed much more than normal, and the girl realized that the countryside shared her curiosity about the enemy fleet. Whole families were in transit, attended by their slaves. The Yankee ships were a great attraction.

"It's been like that every day," Poll said. "Folks stand around for hours just staring down at those gunboats."

"I declare," said Emilie, "there's not a slave in all Vicksburg who's done a lick of work since the Yankees dropped anchor."

"Don't they realize those sailors are bent on *our* destruction?" Alex, feeling guilty, was righteously indignant. She kept the gray team at a steady pace, not hurrying, as if undue haste would betray her motive to be as capricious as the crowd's.

"Shucks, Alex," said Poll. "It's just been a side-show so far. Those Yankees are careful to stay out of range of our batteries."

"You know," Emilie said, "it gave me a real turn to see that old, candy-striped flag again after all this time."

Alex nodded in understanding. She, too, had been taught to revere that banner. It was hard to remember it was an alien, enemy ensign now, a hated gaudy rag whose appearance on the river was an insult. Her loyalty was to the newer flag atop the Vicksburg courthouse. She could see it ahead in the distance, a scarlet swatch hanging limply on its pole.

They passed through the outskirts of the town, climbing the first ridge of the hundred hills. Alex noted the heat-haze shimmering over the river, but caught no glimpse of shipping. The grays needed little guidance; they were on familiar ground, headed for their stable behind the Cherry Street house.

"Henri has a spyglass," Poll said, "and you can see every button on—"

At that moment the air shook with a shuddering blast. That first salvo seemed to erupt with a crash like some giant tree falling through thick forest.

"What's that?" cried Emilie.

"Cannon!"

"The Yankees are shelling the town!"

Alex fought to quiet the frightened team. For an instant everything within sight seemed frozen. A pedestrian stopped in mid-stride; his wife gulped in mid-sentence. Two slaves lounging on a picket fence stiffened as if stung.

Glancing upwards Alex saw black smoke draw a streak across the sky. Instinctively, she knew what it meant. Rising, she braced herself, twining the reins taut around her wrists. Her voice was sharp, but controlled.

"Hang on, girls. And duck!"

Crump!

Emilie's scream was lost in the explosion as the shell burst overhead. Alex never heard the deadly patter as the fragments showered down. She was too busy, trying to hold the grays. The horses tossed their heads as they fought the bits, reared in a panic urge to bolt. Alex swayed, arms rigid, using all her skill to prevent a runaway.

"Let them run," Poll said. She was more thrilled than scared.

Emilie said, "Gracious sakes!" in a very subdued voice.

Another ragged cannonade, like rumbling thunder, sounded from the river. The Yankee sailors were evidently well drilled in rapid-fire gunnery.

Vicksburg is under siege, thought Alex. She eased the writhing leather lines, gave the team a chance to gallop. As long as the grays knew she was master they would be less frightened. She had no desire to stay on an open road under shellfire.

As the carriage rattled, full speed, toward Cherry Street and safety, Alex glanced up at Vicksburg's shining, new, white courthouse.

It made a really splendid target.

The Union fleet commanded by David Farragut shelled Vicksburg nearly every day through the month of June. The town soon learned to live with the noise, even boasted of the small amount of damage. Only the Yankee mortar vessels could lob shells over the rooftops; the big steam warships couldn't elevate their cannon high enough to bother

Vicksburg atop the bluff. Sometimes the Confederate batteries answered, but the enemy stayed well beyond effective range. The courthouse, amazingly, was unscathed.

The townspeople, slave and free, behaved with a nonchalance that was close to bravado. They were the front line now, attacked but impregnable. They were amused by the way General Beauregard had outtricked the Yankees in evacuating Corinth, undismayed by the loss of the place. Sure, it was close, but in Vicksburg a man could look down the cannon muzzles of the U.S. Navy. Not even Richmond was so besieged.

Vicksburg's importance was stressed by the arrival of a new general. Earl Van Dorn was practically a local boy, born in Port Gibson, only a few miles down river. Everybody was delighted that he had been given the command. Anecdotes about the general's career were as plentiful as Confederate banknotes, and more willingly exchanged. He was a Mississippi's judge's son, a West Pointer, a distinguished cavalry officer who had fought in Mexico and been wounded by Comanches.

"He's handsome, too," Alex Kittering said.

Poll Randall told everyone that General Van Dorn was the image of Napoleon III. He wore the imperial beard and mustache. They helped people remember his bold capture of the U.S. Steamer *Star of the West*, the same vessel that had vainly tried to supply Fort Sumter. The town was more than ready to make excuses for Van Dorn's defeat at Pea Ridge, Arkansas, the previous March. Since Missouri's General Price was also involved, why put the blame on a native son?

Young Clay Kittering was wildly enthusiastic about the new commander. With boyish stubbornness he still clung to the popular theory that Southern horsemen, on splendid thoroughbreds, could scatter any Northern army of ribbon clerks and farmers.

"Now we'll see the fur fly around here," said Clay. "Van Dorn's a cavalry officer. He'll soon be riding rings around the Yankees, the way Jeb Stuart is doing in Virginia!"

Joab Kittering couldn't agree. He said, "My boy, this war will not be decided by cavalry charges."

"We've got the best riders!"

"Clay's right, Grandpa," said Alex, trying to keep the argument peaceable. "Certainly Stuart's men have proven that."

The old man's smile was grim. "Well, Alex," he said, "I've a great admiration for a fine horse, and a good rider. But this war won't end in any hurry, and horseflesh can stand just so much. Armies need transportation, and already our railroads are falling apart because the mechanics were all Yankees who went home when the trouble started."

"Good riddance!"

"Was it, Clay? You can fix a busted machine, but a worn-out horse is finished. The North knows that. If you doubt me go down to the river and look at Farragut's fleet sitting there unchallenged. All the cavalry Earl Van Dorn can raise won't give Farragut one sleepless moment!"

"We still have the *Arkansas*, Grandpa."

"Yes, Alex, for what she's worth. Bottled up in the Yazoo River and forced to fight a fleet single-handed if and when she steams out." Joab raised a hand to check the young people's objections. He had heard enough hopeful boasting about the new, giant Confederate ironclad. "Oh, I know what the *Merrimac* did in Hampton Roads against wooden ships like Farragut's, but you're asking a lot from one lone gunboat!"

"The Yankees haven't any *Monitors* on the Mississippi."

"They'll get them if they need them, Clay."

"We'll see," said Clay, unconvinced. At times he disliked his grandfather intensely, blamed him for a carping logic that belittled the Southern cause. Truth, to Clay's boyish mind, was a thing of unquestioning belief.

He found a fellow believer when Bryce Furlong returned to Vicksburg as aide to General Van Dorn. The captain had sought the assignment through family influence, obtained it for his local knowledge. Bryce wasn't searching for a sinecure; he wanted to help defend Vicksburg. Besides, he was glad to get away from Forrest's cavalry. Nathan Bedford Forrest fought his horse soldiers as mounted infantry, with savage success, but he was no gentleman.

"A half-literate slave trader," Bryce said, with a sniff. "He's a demon in battle, and valuable, but I'd much rather take orders from someone like General Van Dorn."

Alex was slightly irked by this viewpoint. It was all right to prefer a fellow Mississippian to a wild man from Tennessee, but Bryce seemed to carry secessionist feelings to absurd conclusions. He was a fiery advocate of Southern freedom, states' rights, and slavery, but sometimes he sounded as if these principles were the exclusive property of planter society in a small segment of Mississippi, his own family and a few, select friends.

War, the girl noted, had honed Bryce to a keener, more hardened fighting man. He was thinner, burned russet, with crow's-feet evident around the hazel eyes. He spoke and moved with quicker nervous energy, impatient of opposition, ready for action.

"Alex," he said, as soon as they were alone, "when are we going to get married?"

"Why," said Alex, startled and stalling, "you said—after our victory—when the war ends—"

"Did I?"

"Yes, Bryce."

"I've seen more war since then. We'll win, of course, but it will not be easy or soon. Those blue-bellies fight, and any stray shot or chance bullet—" He stared at her, leaving the sentence unfinished. Bryce didn't believe that the Yankee lived who could kill him on purpose, but he had learned that anything could happen in battle.

Alex swallowed, then met his stare. She said, "I—I'm still in mourning for Clifton, Bryce."

Bryce winced at her mention of his friend's name, but it was grief not guilt. He believed that Clifton had died as a Southern gentleman should, charging the hated Yankees. His condolence notes to the Kitterings had said as much; he felt no need to elaborate. Anyway, poor Clifton had gone down at Shiloh, and that was many months, miles and skirmishes ago.

"I've paid them back for Clifton, Alex."

The flat statement amazed her. How childishly like Clay, she thought. As if revenge was the answer; as if a dozen girls weeping for Yankee brothers filled the empty bed in Cherry Street. She tried to make excuses for Bryce, told herself that war and hardship brutalized men. But doubt persisted. This gallant captain facing her, fiancé, beau, husband-to-be, sounded like a total stranger.

"You—you'll have to give me time to think, Bryce."

"About our wedding?"

"Yes."

"How much time?"

The abrupt question annoyed Alex, but she kept her voice calm. "Well, I don't know. Vicksburg is all sixes-and-sevens from Yankee shells. And there's Pa's health. He still needs—"

"He's getting better." Bryce's smile dismissed Stephen's weakness as unimportant; it showed the healthy soldier's patronizing pity for less hardy comrades. "You women fuss over him too much."

"Fuss?" Alex spoke sharply, angered by his smile. Bryce Furlong, however brave, had no right to criticize her father. The girl flushed; her blue eyes turned very bright. "How dare you use such a term to—"

"Alex, let's not argue." Bryce, stirred to sudden desire by her flaring, became a man of action. Even as he interrupted, he reached, swept Alex into his arms.

It was the wrong tactic, at the wrong moment. Alex stiffened at his touch. Her body didn't recoil from the fierce embrace, but it was rigid against the man's muscular pressure. She didn't struggle; her lips flattened under his kiss, yielding without response. Alex was coldly unmoved. Once she had wanted Bryce to show more fervor, more passion,

[87]

to sweep her off her feet. Now that he was, quite recognizably, doing just that, she felt nothing but faint dismay.

Bryce, no novice at love-making, let his hands rove. One stroked Alex's back, drew her even closer; the other fumbled at her bosom. He murmured against her throat.

"Alex, Alex, I want you so."

"Not here, Bryce. Not now."

"I love you, Alex."

"Please, Bryce. Stop!"

"We're engaged, dear."

"Please! You mustn't!"

Her whispered, shaken pleas calmed Bryce. He was a gentleman, and he had gone far enough. He drew back, smiled down at the girl's flustered face. Bryce mistook bright cheeks and wet eyes for indications of aroused passion instead of helpless outrage. Alex, a lady, had allowed him to touch her intimately, to kiss her thoroughly. That was enough to convince Bryce that she loved him. An inflated masculine ego made him speak with smug confidence.

"It's all right, my dear. You mustn't feel ashamed."

"No," said Alex, chokingly. "No." It wasn't shame she felt, but desperation. Bryce was a hero who deserved her love, but she had held back. She had suffered his caresses without enjoyment. Surely, there was something lacking in her, something that would be disastrous in a marriage.

"I am sorry if I was—importunate."

The formal apology, baldly impenitent, changed Alex's mood. She giggled, amused by her lover's obtuseness. When Bryce laughed in return, her giggle exploded into honest mirth. If the poor lamb, she thought, was pleased at her wooden reaction, she could certainly make him happier.

"Dear Bryce," she said, tenderly. She kissed him gently on the cheek, slipped from his arms. "Come, we must join the family."

After that, with a complacent swagger, Bryce Furlong resumed his official duties as fiancé. He did not notice that he was never alone with Alex for more than a few minutes. His day-time duties increased when Farragut ran his fleet upriver past the Vicksburg batteries, and Alex took care to see that his free evenings were crowded. Their status as an engaged couple gave them local prominence. When they danced together beholders beamed on an ideal picture of true Southern romance—the handsome Confederate officer and his vivacious belle.

Alex, aware of the picture, enjoyed her position as a central attraction. The town's undaunted spirit stimulated her own gaiety. Memphis was occupied by Yankee troops; their ships had dropped shells on several of Vicksburg's hundred hills too. These things hardly disturbed Alex's social whirl. When the enemy cannonade played a rumbling counterpoint to the fiddles, the gay, young dancers never missed a step.

The girl realized that Bryce displayed her like a proud possession. She was more than willing to gratify his feeling, honestly tried to please him. For that reason she discarded the black bombazine of mourning for brighter colors and furbelows. At the party the Furlongs gave to celebrate Lee's victory in Virginia, the seven furious days that saved Richmond, she was radiant in the Confederate colors, red and white. On Bryce's arm Alex seemed to typify the cotton chivalry's dream. She was the lovely South waiting to deck her returning knights with laurel.

"Don't they make a stunning pair?" Poll Randall asked Henri Duchesneau.

"Stunning," agreed Henri. "That is to say, capable of addling the brain." His irony was intentional. Both Clara Furlong and Emilie Verrier, separately, had poised the same question. Henri, an old hand at flirtation, recognized an arch hint when he heard one. All women, he decided gloomily, considered engagement fever a beneficent plague.

Poll tapped him with her fan in playful rebuke. She said, smiling, "And the fox said the grapes were sour."

"*Mais, non!*" said the Creole, shrugging. He conceded that Alex Kittering was attractive, but there were others, including Poll. The fabled fox, like himself, probably forgot the grapes when the next pullet crossed his path. "She has made her choice. I wish her well."

"You don't like Bryce, do you?"

Another shrug served as answer. Henri would not criticize a man in his own home. This Bryce Furlong had shown his true colors with Tempe Dixon in the gambling house. The captain was a poor loser, an ugly bully when thwarted. And, unless Henri was a poor judge of females, an unthinkable conclusion, Alex had a strong will and a temper. There would be a fine clash some day when the bloom was off this story-book romance.

"Henri," said Poll, almost gushing, "you mustn't resent Bryce because he's seen action. Your work here is important, too!"

He smiled, very aware of her blondeness, heightened color, the shadowy cleft in the white bosom revealed by her low-cut ball gown. "Vicksburg," said Henri, "has its attractions. Even the war has come to its watery doorstep. May I have this dance?"

Alex Kittering hailed him as they moved toward the dance floor. "Henri," she called, "isn't it wonderful about the *Arkansas*?"

"Isn't what wonderful?" asked Poll.

"Why, she's all finished, and coming here."

"Here? To Vicksburg?"

"That's right, Poll. She's moving down the Yazoo River tomorrow."

[89]

The Creole lieutenant was startled. He had thought such detailed information a military secret. Sometimes his telegraph dispatches seemed much slower than Vicksburg gossip. Scowling at Bryce Furlong, he said, "And where did you hear that?"

"Oh, come," Bryce said, haughtily. "It's common knowledge, Henri. A couple of dozen Vicksburg mechanics went up to Yazoo City to work on the *Arkansas*. Some of them are back."

"But the day and the hour," Henri said, shaking his head. He was a volunteer, a citizen-soldier with a dislike for martinets, but surely such carelessness endangered victory. His voice was tart. "*Mon Dieu!* One might as well signal the news to Farragut."

Bryce Furlong stiffened. "There are no traitors here!"

"Why worry?" said Poll Randall. "The Yankees haven't any ships to stop the *Arkansas* even if they do learn she's coming!"

Alex, watching Henri's face, understood his obvious discomfort. The Yazoo River's mouth, where that sluggish stream entered the Mississippi from the delta country, was only a dozen miles north of town, but between it and Vicksburg lay the entire Yankee fleet. The girl hoped the Confederate ironclad was as invincible as touted. If the Federal sailors, forewarned, were ready and waiting, the *Arkansas* might need luck as well as armor.

Bryce dismissed these fears as groundless as soon as Henri moved out of earshot. "For a flibberty-gibbet," he said, "Duchesneau is a great worrier. The *Arkansas* was built to fight against odds, wasn't she?"

His tone exasperated Alex. He had, she realized, little interest in naval warfare, less knowledge, and a cavalryman's contempt for lumbering steamships. Bryce accepted the big ram as a Confederate achievement, praiseworthy but relatively unimportant to the war.

Next morning, when he escorted her to a vantage point on Sky Parlor Hill, his attitude was unchanged. Bryce seemed politely willing to be amused like an adult at a child's puppet show. As they left the carriage to climb the steep wooden stairway on the landward side of the hill, Alex discovered that her fellow townsmen, and women, were much more enthusiastically curious.

She was shocked at the size of the crowds assembled on the Vicksburg bluffs. It was one thing for her friends to discuss the ship's planned arrival at a private party; it was decidedly indiscreet to give the news such widespread circulation that the young slaves told it to their cronies. She recalled her grandfather's scornful refusal to attend. Joab had made remarks about gladiators in the arena and the blood-thirsty rabble in the seats!

There was, she admitted, a carnival air vibrating from the bustling, chattering assemblage. This throng, though scattered along a mile of waterfront, was as gay, as varied, and as numerous as holiday spectators at the race-course! Every hillcrest had its knot of people; parked carriages blocked the sloping streets. Slaves climbed to roof-tops, hung in the branches of the taller trees. There was a group in the courthouse cupola; others leaned from its windows.

Surely, she thought in dismay, the stupidest Yankee tar could guess the reason for such a turn-out!

"Quite a gathering," said Bryce, gazing around. He unslung his binoculars, focussed them. "There's General Van Dorn's party over there. Yes, and Father with the family yonder."

Alex felt a sudden anger that he turned first to the crowd, not the more important, distant black shapes of the enemy fleet on the river. She vaguely remembered reports that hundreds of spectators cheered the bombardment of Sumter, flocked to the battle at Bull Run, watched the *Merrimac's* duel with the *Monitor*. The unthinking, on both sides, seemed to find the war an entertaining spectacle!

Runcey Carr, ruthlessly pumping his elbows, pushed through those around them. The boy, as usual, was bursting with information. "Miss Alex," he cried, "there's been a wig-wag signal come from Fort Snyder!" Runcey named the redoubt at the Yazoo River's mouth without further identification; everyone in Vicksburg knew its position, the very names of the gray-uniformed gunners. "There's been a fight! The *Arkansas* met three Yankee gunboats in the Yazoo, and scattered them like—like hen feathers in a hurricane!"

"Three, Runcey?"

"Are you sure?" asked Bryce.

Runcey's eyes darkened with scorn. He did not like Bryce, but politeness kept his voice pleasant. "Three. The *Tyler*, the *Carondelet*, and the *Queen of the West*." He grinned, slapped fist into palm. "That ole *Arkansas* drove them running, helter-skelter, right out into the Mississippi!"

"Oh, my," said Alex. "Then Farragut will surely know she's coming!"

Bryce nodded, turned his glasses on the fleet. "They must have warned him."

"I reckon not," Runcey said. "There ain't no signal flags flying from the *Hartford*, nor no smoke from their stacks. Looks like the damn-Yanks have been caught napping with cold boilers."

"One has steam up," said Bryce, handing the glasses to Alex.

"Yes, but that's just the *General Bragg*. No converted steamboat will bother the *Arkansas*."

"The *General Bragg?*"

"That's right, Captain. She's Yankee now. They captured her in the fight at Plum Point."

Alex, using the binoculars, surveyed the enemy's naval power. She had gazed at the fleet before, but never so carefully or on so important an occasion. Here, magnified in the glasses, were warships of every description—huge twenty-four gun sloops, armed schooners, big gunboats and small broad-beamed mortar vessels, even skiffs and dinghies. There were wooden hulls and ironclads, steam-and-sail, screw propelled, side-wheelers and sternwheelers. They were anchored in parallel lines on both sides of the river, leaving a broad channel in mid-stream.

"It will be like running the gauntlet," she murmured, thinking of the *Arkansas*. Cold boilers would have no effect on Yankee gunnery.

"Don't you worry," said Runcey. "She'll do it."

She could not help worrying as they waited under the hot glare of the mid-July sun. It was a long wait, interminable seconds that became tedious minutes. The crowd around them was quiet now, restless, suffering from the heat. Alex shared in the general unhappiness; the air was stifling, breezeless. Under the hoop-spread lawn petticoats and linen skirt her body fairly steamed. She could feel the perspiration trickle down her thighs.

Bryce became bored, lit one cheroot from a consumed butt. Runcey, borrowing the binoculars, chanted the names of the enemy ships in a soft, baleful litany. "The *Winona*. The *Itasca* alongside the *Essex*. The *Brooklyn*. The *Signal*. The *Benton*."

Alex sighed, fanned herself with her handkerchief. She said, "Any sign of bustle aboard them, Runcey?"

"No, ma'am. Nothing yet."

Then, he tensed, knuckles whitening as he tightened his grip on the glasses. Alex caught the boy's excitement, swung around to stare. Even across that long stretch of shimmering river she saw the tiny pennants fluttering up on Farragut's flagship, the *Hartford*. An instant later a distant cannon thundered.

"It's her!" yelled Runcey. A roar from the crowd echoed his shout. Men pushed and pointed; women and children clapped their hands. The noise seemed to bounce from hill to hill. Runcey was nodding madly to emphasize his words. "It's the *Arkansas*, Miss Alex! Here she comes!"

Bryce Furlong reached for his binoculars, but Alex snatched them first from the boy. The captain frowned, shrugged, blew a smoke ring. These civilians, he thought, sure made a great fuss over nothing.

Alex, staring through the glasses, saw the cannon smoke before she heard the reports. Both columns of anchored Yankee vessels seemed to explode at their upriver ends. She could not see the target, the *Arkansas*, guessed at its position. The smashing bursts of smoke and flame visibly spread down the ranks of the enemy ships. Every Union gunboat in the fleet was opening fire.

There, at last, framed in the circular lenses, was the *Arkansas*! The

Confederate ironclad, in mid-stream, guns blazing, was fighting her way down the river!

Alex noted the strange, new design first, thought irrelevantly of a metal hen-coop on a low platform. Wood-cut reproductions of the *Merrimac* had looked much more nautical than this reality. Only the white water churned by the ram-nosed prow, the pitch-blackened plumes streaming from the two forward funnels gave any indications of speed. The big, ugly vessel looked adrift, assailed on both sides.

The girl saw shot and shell strike the *Arkansas,* saw cannonballs ricochet. The ironclad shuddered, rocked, but plowed on her course. She *was* making progress! Battered, scarred and staggered, she was half-way through the gauntlet. Alex could make out the figures on the conning platform in front of the smokestacks.

Runcey called their names in senseless encouragement. "Come on, Cap'n Brown! Lieutenant Stevens! *Come on!*"

The noise of the enemy cannonade was a continuous series of blasts that quieted the watching crowd. There were few cheers now; Vicksburg waited in anxious silence. When an *Arkansas* broadside smashed back at her tormenters the concussion seemed to riffle through the spectators.

"Oh, my God!" moaned Alex as a Yankee shell burst on the conning platform. Splinters flew; the uniformed figures tumbled. She trembled with relief as the men scrambled back to their stations.

Under a canopy of smudged, drifting gunsmoke the *Arkansas* charged downstream. It was as if she carried her own shadowy pall overhead. The ram's smoke, cannon and furnace, trailed astern as she moved, but the enemy fire surrounded her like fog.

Alex's heart leaped as the ship moved out of it! There was open water behind her, and the hairpin turn above Vicksburg dead ahead. Alex watched that beautiful, brown, empty, sunlit stretch of Mississippi lengthen as the *Arkansas* put distance between her stern and her anchored adversaries.

"She made it! She made it!"

"She got through!"

"Oh, Runcey! How brave!"

Runcey was hugging Alex now. All around them people were shouting, dancing, throwing hats into the air! There was no question of pursuit. The *Arkansas* would be safe under Vicksburg's guns before the Yankees could raise a head of steam!

Even Bryce was infected by the feat. He threw back his head and screamed the shrill rebel yell made famous by Southern soldiers.

Alex beamed at him. For an emotion-blurred moment he was again the ideal officer!

When a single vessel could fight off the whole Yankee fleet, who could doubt in eventual Confederate victory?

· *9* ·

For both North and South 1862 had provided a summer of discontent. Confederate sympathizers bemoaned their losses in the west; loyal Unionists mourned over blue-coat armies beaten in Virginia.

The whole Confederacy toasted the defenders of Richmond, when Robert E. Lee, replacing the wounded Joe Johnston, drove McClellan back to his transports. Marse Robert, and his able lieutenant, Stonewall Jackson, were the new heroes, legendary leaders of an invincible gray host. Sentimentally, while the bands played "Dixie," the safety of the Old Dominion outweighed control of the Mississippi valley where low water forced Farragut's fleet to withdraw downriver.

Lincoln, the Northern President, beset and harried, turned to the west, his native section, for proven leaders. He brought Halleck to Washington as general-in-chief, put Pope in command of the Army of the Potomac. In the great northeastern cities, too, a Virginia campaign seemed more important than policing distant rivers.

August's history repeated the familiar pattern. On the lower Mississippi the North's troops repulsed a Confederate attempt to recapture Baton Rouge. But Lee and Jackson won the South's adoration when they defeated Pope's army in the second battle near Bull Run.

Vicksburg, snug and unassailed, began calling itself "The Gibraltar of the Confederacy." Major General Grant, U.S.A., stuck in Corinth, Mississippi, apparently was impressed. Halleck's garrison policy had dispersed the Federal strength, but Grant was blamed for the western stalemate.

Now, in September, the South seized the initiative in both theaters. The Army of Tennessee, revitalized by General Bragg, made a bold thrust north for Kentucky. Lee's Army of Northern Virginia, fifty thousand confident men, crossed the Potomac into Maryland.

Northern newspapers had panic headlines. McClellan was hastily restored to his command; Halleck telegraphed instructions to all the western generals. The invaders must be stopped.

Grant, unflustered, gazed south toward Vicksburg.

Cheer, boys, cheer! no more of idle sorrow;
Courage, true hearts shall bear us on our way;
Hope points before and shows a bright tomorrow,
Let us forget the darkness of today.

CORPORAL TEMPLETON DIXON smiled as he listened to the lusty masculine chorus. He had just replaced the sentry mounting guard at the Monroe Street gate before the McNutt house, command headquarters in Vicksburg. Tempe knew the song. People said that Breckenridge's Kentuckians had sung it before they went in at Shiloh. It was a popular ditty. The Ninth Mississippi used it around campfires and on the march.

Then cheer, boys, cheer! for Dixie, Mother Dixie.
Cheer, boys, cheer, for the willing strong right hand;
Cheer, boys, cheer! there's wealth in honest labor;
Cheer, boys, cheer, for the new and happy land.

Applause in polite, staccato handclaps saluted the end of the chorus. Tempe shifted his bayoneted Enfield, and nodded in agreement. It sure sounded fine on a warm, moonlit night. Made a listener feel good, no matter what he thought about soldiers who found time to sing during battles. He was willing to believe that some men, companies, regiments, did rouse their fighting spirit with bellowed lyrics. Tempe knew it took all kinds to make a war. But he just hadn't happened to hear any singing around when the guns started, and the bullets flew past.

"Not at Shiloh," murmured Tempe. "Nor anywhere else."

The remark held a veteran's cynicism. Tempe realized that, and compared the untried recruit who had left Vicksburg with the tested corporal who had returned. He had two faded chevrons on his uniform sleeve now, and a new rifle. For a while after Shiloh there'd been Enfields to spare and Sergeant Tazewell had helped him pick out the best. Lucius Dixon's elongated Mexican-War relic was now safely back in Noxubee County.

Yes, Tempe told himself, you've done a heap of marching and shooting since you sent that rifle home. In a way getting back to Vicksburg had been a sort of homecoming. He had civilian friends here, knew the town well. He'd paid a call on old Mister Kittering, spent an evening in Jump MacGregor's with Runcey Carr. On both occasions Tempe had carefully avoided Alex Kittering or Bryce Furlong. The news of their engagement had dampened his return.

Still, he reflected, there was a lot less pleasant duty than standing sentry in a flower-scented garden. He'd been assigned to Vicksburg because somebody in the army hierarchy had sent out a call for sharpshooters. The marksmen were supposed to make river traffic hazardous by knocking Yankee helmsmen right out of their pilot-houses.

"Might work at that," Sergeant Tazewell had said. "A good pilot's sure necessary on these here rivers."

"But, Sarge, I don't cotton to picking a feller off when he doesn't even know you're stalking him."

"You're in a war, Tempe. You goes where you're sent, and you does what you're told."

Jollibee had been even more succinct. "A soldier's job is to shoot enemy soldiers."

Well, thought Tempe contentedly, it had worked out fine for the crack shots drawn from the Ninth Mississippi. He and Taze, Jollibee and Lack Norris, among others, had been sent to Vicksburg. It wasn't their fault that the Yankee steamboats had made themselves scarce since they'd arrived. Sooner or later some idle staff officer would discover that no enemy pilot in his right mind would steer within rifle range of the Vicksburg bluffs.

Cocking his head as the banjos and fiddles inside the house shifted to a livelier melody, Tempe identified "Jim Crow." In Vicksburg even the sudden visit of a distant cousin was cause for celebration, but tonight the whole town had good reason to feel festive. Henri Duchesneau himself had brought the message to headquarters, racing from the telegraph office. Before the hour was out the hills had rocked with cheers. Tempe tapped his foot in time to the music as he recalled the news.

Lee's army was deep in Maryland, probably threatening Washington. And two days ago, on September 15th, Jackson, the fabulous Stonewall, had led his fast-stepping troops on a brilliant dash over the mountains to capture Harper's Ferry. Because of John Brown every white adult in the South knew about Harper's Ferry, its location and its arsenal. Tons of stores and ammunition had been seized by Jackson's men; they had taken more than twelve thousand Yankee prisoners.

"Stonewall sure paid them back for Donelson," Tempe said softly. He knew the South had needed a victory, shared the general elation. Now the North was feeling the pinch of invasion. Tempe wondered what it would be like to serve under those two Virginians who seemed to go from success to success without tasting defeat.

But now voices, crisp with anger, sounded in the quiet garden behind him. Tempe stiffened to attention as befitted a headquarters guard. He wanted no criticism from any officer. Light duty in Vicksburg was better than camp drill or forced marches; any dull task far behind the lines was safer than battle.

Then, he recognized both voices, and froze. Suddenly, he seemed as cold as the moonlight gleam on his bayonet.

"You had no right to do it, Bryce!" cried Alex Kittering. "You knew how we all felt!"

"Alex, the boy wanted to go!" Bryce Furlong said.

This, Tempe recognized, was no lovers' spat but a real row. The girl's voice wasn't loud, but she was furious. Captain Furlong was biting off his words with cold clarity. Tempe had a sinking feeling in his stomach, aware that as witness to the quarrel, he, disliked by both participants, was the one liable to get hurt.

"You call him a boy, but you sent him to war!"

"I didn't send him, Alex. I merely—"

"Made it easy for him! Went straight to General Van Dorn. Against my parents' wishes, my grandfather's!"

"Your grandfather is not exactly loyal to the cause!"

The couple was close now, and Tempe risked a sideways glance. They were not noticing him. Even by moonlight Alex's eyes were blazing, her face flushed. She looked, he thought, very lovely in corn-colored silk trimmed with black lace. The captain wore dress uniform, complete with sash and gloves. Tempe had seen Furlong coldly angered once before.

"My grandfather's right about this! Clay is too young to realize what war is!"

"He'll learn!"

"From you, Bryce?"

"Well, yes. I'm due to rejoin my company, and Clay was posted there at his own request. I'll teach him myself, Alex, and in no time—"

"How much did you teach Clifton?"

Tempe winced, recalling Clifton's death. She was, he decided, in fine, feminine fettle, reaching for any remark that cut deep. For an instant he felt sorry for Furlong. But that feeling vanished at Bryce's cold reply.

"To die like a hero."

He can believe *that,* wondered Tempe, after throwing his friend's life away in a senseless charge! If the girl knew the truth she'd toss his engagement ring in his face. But Alex sounded contrite, less angry.

"I'm sorry, Bryce. I shouldn't have said that."

"No, you shouldn't."

"I said I was sorry. But that doesn't change my feelings about Clay. You went behind my back and helped him volunteer."

"Alex," said Bryce Furlong stiffly, "even your wishes must bow to the South's needs, and she needs every soldier she can raise."

"Not boys of sixteen, Bryce."

"Those like Clay, yes. Right now, especially. Bragg took most of our troops north, but General Van Dorn has a plan to recapture Corinth."

Oh, fine, said Tempe in silent disgust, tell it to the women, shout it from the house-tops! You dumb, blabbing horse officer, tell it to everybody but the men who'll do the fighting. He had the infantryman's distaste for cavalry, and he didn't like Bryce Furlong.

"And Clay, of course, will make all the difference."

"Alex, be reasonable."

"I don't feel what you'd call reasonable. I'd like to go home. Would you call your carriage, please?"

"You can't leave now, Alex! The general—"

"I spoke to General Van Dorn. That's how I learned about Clay. He congratulated me!" Her laugh was sharp and brittle. "I thanked him politely!"

"Now, Alex—"

"Will you call your carriage, Bryce?"

"Now, listen—"

Alex spoke without looking, a polite request that took prompt service for granted.

"Sentry, would you please fetch me a carriage?"

Here it comes, thought Tempe. In a moment now the lightning strikes. Neither of these proud peacocks will relish the idea that Tempe Dixon heard their fight.

Bryce Furlong didn't glance at the soldier by the gate. He treated sentries, all lesser ranks, as he did his slaves, with serene indifference. They were to be seen and not heard; there to command, not to listen. His voice was childishly pleased. "The sentry can't leave his post."

"Is that right?" Alex, unbelieving, swung around to consult the soldier. Her eyes widened in surprise; it showed in her changed tone. "Oh! You!"

"Who?" Bryce's head came up. For a moment he squinted, then recognition brought a glare. His whisper was shaken with hostility. "By God, it's Dixon!"

Tempe, not moving, wished that the earth would swallow him. This, through Bryce's enmity, could cost him his stripes. He saw the girl's quick look at her escort, noted her lips twitch in a suppressed smile. She would be delighted to make matters worse.

"Corporal Dixon," said Alex coolly, "is a friend of the family, Bryce. As you know he once saved me from serious injury. I am sure that under the circumstances, he finds our presence here quite embarrassing."

Very neat, thought Tempe in admiration. With one speech she treed the coon, peppered his hide, and got her own way. She had made Tempe an ally, forced Furlong to choose between a scene or retreat. The officer looked ugly.

"Corporal."

"Captain?" said Tempe.

"When did you return to Vicksburg?"

"Ten days ago, sir."

"I see."

"Bryce," said Alex, "I really must get home. If Grandpa's found out about Clay the fur will be flying." She placed a hand on Bryce's arm. "Shall we go?"

"Yes, of course." Bryce tried to sound polite. He would not argue with her in front of Dixon. The damned fellow was always around where he wasn't wanted.

As they passed through the gate toward the parked carriages Tempe slapped the Enfield to present arms. Alex's wide skirt swayed close, and away. She called back over her shoulder, smiling.

"Good evening, Corporal Dixon."

"Evening, ma'am," he said. Tempe didn't dare show amusement at her impudence. Whatever the price he was glad she'd made Bryce Furlong dance to her tune. She was right about her young brother, too. War was no place for youngsters.

Tempe Dixon sighed. From the look on Furlong's face, he had a hunch that one sharpshooter from the Ninth Mississippi wouldn't have a soft berth in Vicksburg much longer.

The minute Alex Kittering entered the house on Cherry Street she knew that the family had heard about Clay. That was evident from Andrew's impassive countenance, from Mimosa's tight clutch on a crumpled newspaper. It was emphasized by the rumble of Joab's voice from upstairs. The Ancient was obviously on a rampage.

"Clay?" asked Alex.

Andrew nodded. Mimosa offered the paper, said, "He done found it in this here *Daily Citizen*. 'Bout near an hour ago, Miss Alex."

Alex smoothed the sheet, read the item. "Clay Kittering, of this city, has left the family domicile to join the First Mississippi cavalry. Thus does our chivalrous Southern youth pluck our own magnolia flower, safety, out of this Yankee nettle, danger. We wish Clay every success, crowned with laurels, running over." Such effusive sentiments must have driven her grandfather to frenzy.

"Master Clay's been gone all day," said Andrew.

"Bed wasn't slept in," Mimosa said. Her eyes narrowed as she added, "He took Esau with him." Mimosa still didn't approve of white folks dragging slaves to the war.

"Didn't he leave a note?"

"Yes, Miss Alex. But it was only just delivered. He told that Runcey Carr to give it to Missus Epie after supper."

"Did you know he was going, Mimosa?"

"I suspicioned, but I didn't rightly know."

"You might have warned us," said Alex, without rancor. She realized that the slaves would not tattle on Clay no matter what they knew. You couldn't blame them. He might some day be master, and masters had long memories.

Mimosa didn't bother to reply. The butler, too, ignored the remark. He said, gently, "They're all in your pa's room, Miss Alex."

"Thank you, Andrew."

Raising her skirts, Alex ran up the stairs. The higher she climbed the more audible Joab became. On the landing through the closed door she could hear him plainly.

"Children! Clay and Esau! Children in a holocaust! God help us! The sins of the fathers—" He paused as Alex opened the door.

The girl found the trio in varied positions. Her grandfather was propped against the wall. Stephen was pacing; Epie Mae sat on the edge of the bed, rigid as its posts. She wasted no time on greetings.

"You've heard about Clay, Alex?"

"General Van Dorn told me."

"Van Dorn," said Joab, and made a rude noise.

"That fool boy," Stephen said. "That fool boy."

"Stephen," said Epie, "that's just the point. He *is* only a boy. Even the conscription laws puts the proper age at eighteen." Her tone was calm but not placid. For once, a tense pallor betrayed Epie's emotion.

"Clay wasn't conscripted, Ma."

"He enlisted."

"Then, you must take action, Stephen."

"The time for that," Joab said, "was before he left. You had reams of warning from the way Clay talked. Now, you want to lock the barn too blasted late!"

Alex silently agreed. She blamed herself for not noticing that Clay and Bryce Furlong had their heads together a lot recently. She was still furious at Bryce, but she wouldn't betray him as Clay's accomplice.

"How can you say such a thing, Father? We had no idea Clay would run off like this!"

"That's right, Pa."

"No," Joab admitted, "I don't suppose you did." Everybody in the room was equally guilty. He himself had neglected to heed his grandson's hints. Stephen, morosely nursing his crippled arm, had no time for anything else. Epie, in the midst of war, lived in her own protective shell. Alex was in love.

"Nobody took him seriously, Grandpa."

"No, Alex, but Clay took that secesh buncombe straight, in hundred-proof gulps."

"His brother died for the Confederacy, Pa!"

"Yes, son, I know." Joab accepted the reproach. He could not tell his son that Clifton's death did not make the war holy. "But your problem is Clay. It's a sight easier to join an army than to get somebody discharged. You'll have to petition the right people, speak to generals, write letters, ask favors. That all takes time."

"How long, Father?"

"There's no telling, Epie. I only know that the Yankees won't wait for you."

"Will you help us, Pa? You know everybody and—"

"Everybody knows *me*, son. I'm sorry, real sorry." Joab sounded sad, but grimly harsh. "I've spoken my mind too often. If I made the rounds trying to get a Confederate soldier—any soldier, much less my grandson —out of uniform, they'd clap me in the hoosegow and throw the key in the Mississippi."

Alex realized he spoke the truth. Bryce considered her grandfather little less than a traitor. She touched the big diamond ring on her left hand.

Epie Mae stared at her father-in-law, slowly nodded. All along she'd believed that his rude, bitter opinions would alienate decent people. Now, when he was needed, Joab was useless. Her agreement was coldly definite, a dismissal.

"Yes, of course, Father, you'd do more harm than good."

"You—you think so, Epie?"

"Yes, Stephen."

Joab saw his son's glance shift toward him, and away. Stephen, as usual, would follow his wife's leadership. The old man suspected that Epie would find Clay harder to persuade. Feeling helpless, Joab teetered in a turn, jerked his head at Alex.

"Come, Alex."

"Yes, Grandpa." The girl recognized that her mother was in charge again, wanted to talk to her father in privacy.

On the threshold Joab made one last effort to advise his son. He did not stress the pronoun.

"Do what you consider best, son."

The latch clicked as Alex closed the door behind them. Stephen blinked; the wide oak panel seemed to shut the problem in the room. He was not sure what course of action to take. The code of a Southern gentleman called for pride in Clay's behavior.

"Stephen."

His wife's voice sounded remote, farther away than across the room. Stephen looked at her, stirred by a memory. Through the fever-distorted dreams as he lay wounded, Epie had called to him like that.

"Yes, Epie?"

"We must do something. Unless you ride after Clay—"

"Please don't start that again," said Stephen abstractedly. The suggestion had upset him when previously made, now it merely seemed absurd. He was home, safe in Vicksburg. He had no intention of leaving it until he had been passed as fit by Doctor Randall.

"Unless you ride after Clay immediately," repeated Epie, with firmness, "it may be weeks, months before we have him back." She was sure her husband realized that Clay would be in more danger with each passing day.

"You don't know what it's like, Epie. Out there with the army."

"Well, it's certainly not for Clay."

"Nor for me." Stephen moved closer to the bed, gazed down at his wife. "Nor for me. Do you think I want the boy to suffer as I suffered? Battle and death, screaming men, the stink of blood!" He dropped to his knees, put his head in her lap. "Oh, Epie, Epie, I was so scared."

Surprised by his action, by the emotion-shaken voice, Epie stroked her husband's hair. He hadn't mentioned the war since that first day at Tonica Hill; she thought his worry was for their son. For a moment her feelings were moved by Stephen's emotional outburst.

"Poor Clay mustn't go through that," she murmured.

Stephen didn't hear. His whisper was muffled against her silken skirt, but he spoke with fierce intensity. "You were the one I thought about. Not the children, not even Clifton. You, Epie! I was sure I'd never see you again, never touch you, never hold you! And I wanted you so, needed you. All that torturous ride back to Corinth. In my dreams and nightmares!"

Epie listened to this long speech with growing wonder. Somehow her husband seemed to have lost the thread of their conversation; they had been talking about Clay.

"Stephen, dear, you've forgotten—"

"No," said Stephen, raising his head. His gaze was blurred by tears. "No, Epie. I remembered every detail. Your hair, your eyes, your breasts and body!"

"But—"

"I longed for you then, and it's been worse since I came back. But I had to wait. I wasn't strong enough. Pain and weakness unmanned me. That's passed now."

He reached with his good arm, placed his hand behind her head, drew it down.

"Oh, Epie!"

The kiss startled Epie Mae. She had no time to stiffen in resistance; Stephen's urgent lips bruised her mouth. She gasped, and his darting tongue took instant advantage. Its touch shocked her. Her stomach quivered as she flinched.

"Stephen, wait—"

"No, Epie, the waiting's over."

Twisting her head, Epie tried to recapture her calm attitude. She couldn't believe this was happening; it couldn't be Stephen kissing her ear, her cheek, her throat. Epie had thought conjugal love a thing of the past, a dim, fairly pleasant memory. They had not practiced it since Clay was a baby.

Clay! The name rang inside Epie's head. This childish nonsense wasn't as important as her son's future.

"Now, Stephen. No. Stop!"

"Epie, Epie!"

"We must think of Clay!"

"To hell with Clay," said Stephen thickly, and pressed her back across the fourposter's candlewick spread. His mouth found Epie's again, clung.

She squirmed under his weight, senses reeling. Even on their honeymoon they had not been ardent. She had been a curious innocent submitting to the advances of a gentleman husband. They had found pleasure in a polite, genteel relationship. Stephen had never been demanding, importunate. Epie knew her wifely duties, but this—this was savage!

Her protest was a panted, trembling whisper, but it came from the depths of Epie's fears. She had even slept apart, on a trundle bed, while nursing Stephen, and now she beseeched him in behalf of prim dignity. "Not here. It's—it's broad daylight!"

"Here. Now, Epie. Now!"

Not knowing how to fight, Epie pleaded. She had never imagined that people made love with all their clothes on, and her pleas were based on insipid, conventional terms. "My hoops!"

"Darling, darling!"

"Stephen!"

"Let me."

"You're tearing my petticoat!"

Stephen was doing more with one hand, she thought wildly, than he ever had with two. His caresses were brutal; her flesh tingled. She made a last, feeble attempt to restore sanity.

"Stephen—your arm!"

" 'S all right."

Epie surrendered, accepting defeat. She shut her eyes tight, waited for the final horrible degradation. This she supposed was rape, a word whispered behind hands, a crime that happened to slave girls and fallen women.

Then, her eyes popped open as her body began to respond to the act in a totally new manner.

Her cry was a wordless tribute to passion.

[103]

BOOK TWO

———◆———

The Bayous

10

FROM VICKSBURG's hundred hills citizens, soldiers and slaves watched the autumnal haze thicken over the Mississippi River. There was little else to see. The great stream, flowing sluggishly past the bluffs, seemed to darken muddily as winter weather approached, but, for long hours, the wind alone disturbed its waves.

There was some sporadic traffic. An occasional ferry pushed across to DeSoto on the western bank, returned. Fishermen rowed back and forth; supply ships at times blew for a landing. But the busy days of the mighty steamboats were only a memory, less vivid than the shellfire of the Yankee fleet. Both were remembered with much talk, the former nostalgically, the latter with bitterness. Nobody, gazing down at the eternally restless currents, could find evidence that these things had ever happened.

The town showed a few scars. Mostly these were windows boarded against the coming wintry blasts. Other damage had been swept away or repaired but there was no window glass in Vicksburg. The South was finding, to its dismay, that a slave trained as a glazier could not replace a shattered pane without glass. Every month of war showed more eyesore patches plugging window frames throughout the Confederacy. It was a small matter, but irritating; another sign that their newly formed nation, fighting for independence, was dependent on outside aid.

Through the autumn there had been no Yankee activity against Vicksburg. The batteries along the bluffs, now reinforced to a formidable array of heavy guns, kept a silent vigil. Few enemy gunboats poked their noses as far south as the Yazoo River, and these scouting ships kept well out of cannon range. Still, the war was ever present, and the literate in town smudged their fingers grabbing ink-damp daily papers.

In the Vicksburg press, as in all contemporary newssheets, North and South, published results of distant battles were always late. Initial telegraph reports were tardy as well as brief; more complete stories, with casualty lists, came days later by mail. However by careful, constant perusal a reader could learn certain facts, and pass them along to those unable to read.

Both Confederate invasions had failed. At Sharpsburg, Maryland, the

Army of Northern Virginia had fought with valor, inflicted equal heavy losses, left a much-larger Yankee army listlessly licking its wounds. But, though Southern pride, in editorials, called it a drawn battle, that unbeatable gray-clad army was back in Virginia. A glance at a map showed that Robert E. Lee had retired a long way from Antietam Creek.

Braxton Bragg's invaders, too, had met with disappointment. On the promises of politicians, Bragg had carted fifteen hundred rifles into Kentucky to arm an oppressed, rebellious people. The weapons were never used; even slave-holding Kentuckians showed no great desire to rally to the Stars-and-Bars. Trying to escape battle against superior forces, Bragg's retreating army was forced to fight free at Perryville, with heavy losses.

Vicksburg needed no newspapers to learn of the three days of furious fighting around Corinth, Mississippi. The wounded brought into town told the tale.

Earl Van Dorn and Sterling Price, unlucky partners in Arkansas, had joined forces once again in an abortive attempt to recapture Corinth. Their army fought its way into the town's outskirts, occupied outlying houses, but the Federals were too strong, too well entrenched. Those two bloody days at Corinth, and a rear-guard action at the Hatchie River bridge on the third, cost the South 4800 men.

Stunned by this defeat the people of Vicksburg hardly questioned the appointment of Lieutenant General John C. Pemberton as the new Confederate commander in the district. Not even the rumor that the man was a Pennsylvanian caused much stir.

Old Joab Kittering glowered in silence until the family learned that Clay had survived Corinth unharmed. Epie Mae seemed less placid, sometimes gazed at her husband with a puzzled frown. As Stephen's health improved, Mimosa watched him like a wary animal. The slave-maid had no intention of letting Benjie go off to the white folks' war again.

With the other ladies of the town Alex Kittering helped nurse the wounded in the hospital run by the Catholic sisters. Poll Randall proved a good nurse; Clara Furlong was clumsy. Emilie Verrier fainted at the sight of blood, but rolled innumerable bandages.

Vicksburg spent November trying to do business as usual. House slaves performed their regular tasks; field hands who worked on the ramparts admired the cannon and the gunners' uniforms. Food and whisky were plentiful, though the blockade had stopped imported luxuries.

Henri Duchesneau supervised a work-party stringing telegraph wire from DeSoto to a point ten miles below Lake Providence. Runcey Carr fretted, fished, and got into mischief. Doctor Randall was the busiest physician in town. Jump MacGregor figured the odds on leaving or staying. He told Smasher the damned Yankees were sure to return, but the gambling hall was thriving.

December brought cold rain, blustery gales. It was gray weather, depressing and ominous.

Tempe Dixon didn't like to bivouac anywhere in the delta country at any time, but he thought the bluffs on the bank of the Yazoo River even more miserable in December's squally weather. Every gust of rain that drove a spatter-curtain across a bayou reminded Tempe of the Texas Brigade's charge on the second day at Corinth.

This was not a pleasant memory. He had watched that gray line, screaming the yell, sweep over open ground in a mad dash for the Yankee breastworks beyond the railroad tracks. Colonel Rogers, on horseback, led his Texans on that last, desperate lunge to break the Union line. For a few minutes it had looked as though they were going to make it. They'd reached the tracks when that searing blast of Yankee fire smashed in their faces. Those poor Texans were lying like tumbled cornricks, Rogers among them, when the smoke from that terrible volley lifted.

"Corinth," murmured Tempe, remembering, "was Shiloh all over again."

He knew that many more men, on both sides, had been engaged at Shiloh, yet Corinth, for a rifleman, had repeated the same pattern of hellish combat. Once more an initial Confederate success had turned to bitter defeat. On the first day Tempe's unit had gotten close enough to read the sign on the Tishomingo Hotel, but the Yankees were stronger on the second. There always seemed to be fresh bluecoats coming from nowhere!

The size of a battle didn't matter much to the men in it. It was the volleys, the cannonade that counted. Any soldier who fell at the Hatchie River bridge was just as dead as Albert Sidney Johnston.

Shivering now, Tempe turned back toward his comrades. At least they had all come through unscratched. He shared their opinion that Van Dorn, a cavalry officer, was a mite too fond of charging enemy batteries, but he did not repeat the common jeer, "Who ever saw a dead cavalryman?" Tempe had seen Clifton Kittering, and dreamed of his sister.

Trudging through the mud, Tempe noticed that the rain had stopped. Not that it mattered much. Bayou duty was a melancholy, irksome task at best. The nights featured a raw, damp chill that made a campfire a pallid, guttering smudge-pot without cheer or much warmth.

Give me open woods, Tempe decided as he neared the fire, that a man can hunt over without constant fear of snakes. He hated the tainted breezes from the bayous, the way the lush undergrowth retained the smells, steaming hot in summer, a dank mire in winter. The high bluffs above the Yazoo made a natural fortress, especially here on the south bank, a dozen miles or so, crow-flight, north of Vicksburg's outskirts. It seemed a good place to defend the town, but Tempe couldn't figure any Yankee general foolhardy enough to try landing troops on such wretched terrain.

Big Tazewell, squatting on his heels, held his hands closer to the flickering flames. At Tempe's approach he glanced over his shoulder, but his question wasn't addressed to anyone in particular.

"You reckon those contraptions will work?"

"If they don't," said Lack Norris, wearily, "we all got mighty wet for nothing."

Tempe nodded in grim agreement. The squad had spent a long, tiresome day acting as boatmen, as handymen, while the experts from Vicksburg strewed the Yazoo's channels with sunken explosives. Fussing around in that ice-cold water soon made the whole procedure a hardship, an unreasonable test of endurance.

"Torpedoes," Jollibee said, with professional sureness. "That's what they calls them, Sarge. Torpedoes. They ain't as new-fangled as you'd think. But I never heard of them sinking anything."

"They look," said the sergeant, "like iron whisky jugs. A demijohn, maybe, of Tuscaloosa rye."

"And don't we wish they was," Lack Norris said. He chuckled, poked at the fire. "They might be more use at that if they was chock full of rye or bourbon."

"Easy," Tempe said. "They'll hear you." He glanced over his shoulder at another fire where the experts huddled.

"Let 'em."

"Now, Lack, it wasn't their fault the water was freezing."

"Do tell. We worked like slaves out there, but that Mike Tansey feller explained they was ascairt to use nigras around explosives. Might lose a valuable field hand if something blew up!"

"He never said that, Lack."

"He as good as, Sarge."

"No, no." Tazewell shook his head. "What he meant makes sense. Slaves is careless when they're miserable. And it was sure miserable on that river. You get a careless black with his teeth a-chattering and those powder kegs might have blasted us to smithereens."

"Accidental like, sure," Jollibee said. "But it's anybody's guess whether they can be exploded on purpose when wanted."

"Mr. Weldon," said Tempe, "and Mike Tansey, and that Lieutenant Cowan seem to know what they're doing." He was surprised at his support of the experts. For a while, before cold dulled his interest, Tempe had been fascinated with the work, the intricate rigging, the elaborate precautions. He knew that Mr. Weldon had designed the mine, that the Paxton works had made them. Certainly the mechanic, Mike Tansey, and Cowan considered them lethal weapons.

A floating log kept the metal bomb at the proper depth; an attached weight anchored it in place. The trigger wires stretched to the bank, were supposed to explode the powder by electricity. Tempe didn't know much about electricity, but he was sure it could make sparks. You didn't have to be a scholar to realize that one spark was all that was needed for a blast.

"You think they'll work, then, Tempe?"

"*They* sure think so." He jerked his thumb backwards in a point. "Let's wait and see."

"Seems to me," Jollibee said, "that making torpedoes is a lot different from designing courthouses. Maybe Mister Weldon should stick to his last."

"He the one built the Vicksburg courthouse?"

"That's what I hear, Lack."

"Well," said Lack Norris, "I don't know about you-all, but that sure makes me feel heaps better. That's a mighty pretty building. This Weldon man ain't likely to be frittering his good time away on mere foolishness."

"Here's a change of tune," Sergeant Tazewell said.

"Aye," said Jollibee with a sniff. "Lack, you're not very strong on logic."

"That's a schoolbook word. I ain't unreasonable, English. An honest man admits when he's wrong, and I keep an open mind."

Tempe sensed that Lack Norris was laying the groundwork for a joke. The lad liked to bait Jollibee, to trap the Englishman into displaying ignorance of Southern customs. Lack's wink made Tempe certain.

"Your mind is open all right," Jollibee said. "So open the wind blows right through."

"Oh, I don't know," Lack said, casually. His tone brought a quick glance, followed by poker-faced impassiveness, from the sergeant. "Seeing is believing, Jollibee. Now, it don't seem logical that a toad would eat a live coal, but I've seen it."

"Toad?" Jollibee sounded bewildered. "Who was talking about toads?"

"I am," said Lack. "I caught me a couple this afternoon. Poor little critters was too cold to jump away. Fetched them back here in an old cigar box. They makes nice pets."

"Loathsome things!"

"Nonsense, Jollibee. It ain't true that they cause warts. But it is true that they'll tongue swaller a glowing ember."

"Are you pulling my leg, Lack?"

"Am I which?"

"Funning him," translated Tempe.

"Me? What would I go and do that for? I'm just aiming to demonstrate a simple fact. Matter of science. Toads eat live coals—coals of fire. They flicks their tongues out, catches them, and gulps 'em into their lil ole tummies."

"You're daft! You're straight out of Bedlam!"

"Well, then, Jollibee, you just put your wager where your mouth is. Let's see that English sporting blood. Place your bet or hold your peace."

Tempe, watching doubt and wariness cloud Jollibee's face, wondered if the Englishman deliberately stepped into Lack's snares. It was this sort of game that made Lack Norris almost invaluable to the squad. They might be down, dog-tired, bored stupid by the endless repetition of military routine, but Lack always managed to supply a fresh bit of foolery.

"Have you seen this, Sarge?"

"Uh-uh." Tazewell shook his head. "I've heard tell a toad will do it, but I've never seen it."

"Tempe?"

"This is between you and Lack. Even a toad should know better than to go burning his mouth."

"Well, Jollibee?" Lack took a cigar box from his jacket, carefully reached inside. He held a toad cupped in his palms, the tiny eyes shining in the firelight. "This one I calls Sherman. He thawed out better than his friend."

"You're willing to try him?"

"Sure enough. But I don't want to cheat you, Jollibee. This here toad will think the ember is a lightning bug."

"In this weather!"

"Well, he's *seen* fireflies. I reckon he ain't never had a calendar anywhere handy."

"For how much?" asked Jollibee.

The sergeant stroked his mustache to cover a smile. Tempe, eyes twinkling, gazed fondly at both bettors. He still suspected that the little Briton knew he was being duped, played along for entertainment's sake. Jollibee seldom won from Lack, but he generally retrieved his losses before long.

"For how much, Lack?"

"Who has money, even Confed?" asked Lack, pondering. "For my Bowie against your jack-knife with the corkscrew gadget. I'm giving odds because you're a poor ignorant foreigner who don't know beans about toads."

"In my country," Jollibee said, "we do not make pets of vermin. You have a wager. Tempe, Sarge, you're both witnesses."

"Fair enough."

"Sure."

"Of course they're witnesses," Lack said. He edged a trifle closer to the fire. "Somebody lend me a spoon."

"Use your own," said Jollibee. "I have no intention of supping from anything licked by a toad!"

"Fussy, ain't you?" Lack took a battered tin spoon from his belt. Leaning forward he scooped a live coal from the fire, blew on it.

The others watched with breathless attention worthy of a grander spectacle. Tempe judged that the ember, glowing red, was about the size of a black-eyed pea. The toad blinked, but gave no other sign of life.

"Hold it closer," suggested the sergeant.

"So it can see," Tempe said.

"Maybe it isn't hungry," Jollibee sounded confident. "Maybe the whole thing is a fairy tale."

"Now, wait. Wait." Lack rubbed his thumb on the toad's spine. "Give him time. He's had a cold, hard day." He blew on the coal again, dangled the spoon in front of the toad. "Come on, Sherman. Here's a tasty firefly!"

The toad stirred. Almost too fast to be seen the long tongue darted, flicked against the spoon. The bright ember vanished.

"By God," cried Tazewell, "he did it!"

"I'll be damned," Jollibee said, in disbelief.

"It didn't even bother him," said Tempe. "He—he just downed it like it was cane syrup."

"Told you," Lack said, smugly. "Told you, didn't I?"

"You sure he swallowed it? He didn't just knock it on the ground or something?"

"Jollibee, you're a suspicious man. But you ain't blind."

The sergeant nodded. "For my money he swallowed it all right."

"Try it again. Try the other one."

"Nothing doing," Lack said. "I always quit when I'm ahead. Besides it's time to hit the blankets." He put the toad back in the box, accepted Jollibee's knife without comment.

When no one argued Tempe realized they were all tired. Each man made his bed in his own fashion. Tazewell stood to wrap his blanket around him; Lack rolled up in his. The Englishman fussily made an envelope on the ground, crawled into it. They had served together long enough to know personal habits and preferences. It was understood that Tempe, by choice, took the first watch.

He made a shawl of his own blanket, broke a cheroot in half, sat smoking one end. In this camp his only duty was to keep the fire bright; the sentries on the parapets, in the battery emplacements, along the river bank, stood guard. Tempe didn't bother to remove the protective rag-wrappings from his rifle.

Storm clouds scudded past overhead; somewhere nearby a bullfrog croaked. Tempe could distinguish individual snorers, and the hiss from the damp wood in the fire. These were familiar sounds, common to most army camps. They did not disturb his reflections.

Mostly, because of the day's work, Tempe thought about the war. There were many rumors of a coming Yankee advance; the torpedoes were evidence that somebody took the rumors seriously. Another general besides Pemberton had arrived from the east, an artillery brigadier named S. D. Lee. He'd made his reputation with Robert E. Lee's army, but didn't seem to be related to the famous commander. The new brigadier was a South Carolinian, not a Virginian. Tempe only hoped the man knew his business. He was busily collecting Negroes to build more fortifications. Tempe heartily approved. While General Pemberton kept the bulk of his army in the north, watching the Yankee concentration at Oxford, the more redoubts and cannon on the Vicksburg bluffs, the safer the garrison.

After two hours Tempe rose, stretched, woke Jollibee. As the Englishman rubbed his eyes, his predecessor curled close to the fire. Tempe had learned the soldier's trick of falling asleep anywhere, at any time. Tonight, for no reason, his slumber was restless, troubled again by dreams of Alex Kittering.

He awoke with a start, roused to another gray dawn by a distant rumble. Thunder, Tempe thought, then knew better as he kicked his covering aside. That was cannon, a big gun with a loud bark, probably a rifled Parrott.

"Ain't no sunrise salute," Sergeant Tazewell said, sniffing the air like a bemused beagle.

Lack Norris grinned, said, "No sun."

"Sounds like the Fort Snyder battery," said Jollibee. He was already reloading his gun. The Englishman didn't like to trust even a percussion cap after a night's dampness.

Tempe and the others followed his example. They were sharpshooters, marksmen who made fetishes of their rifles. The guns were the tools used in their trade, handled with a skill that had made them a select group. No member of the group listened when the bugles blared around them, summoning other units, infantry and artillery, to their stations. The riflemen knew where to go and what to do; they would be ready in plenty of time.

[114]

They even paused to prepare breakfast and break camp. Veterans did not go hungry into a fight if it could be avoided; they wanted to find their belongings later.

Lack Norris fried thick slices of bacon. Jollibee cut slabs from a wedge of cold cornpone. Tempe brought last night's coffee to a boil. Sergeant Tazewell rolled the blankets, cached them under a sheltering bush, made sure the canteens were filled.

"All right," said the sergeant, accepting the passed coffee can. "Let's move. Eat the rest on the way." He took a swig of the steaming liquid, made a face.

"Sorry, Sarge," said Tempe, "we're out of coffee."

"That brew's three days old," Lack Norris said, cheerfully. "Here, Jollibee, have a hush-kitten."

"A what?"

"A hush-kitten." Lack brandished the bacon-and-pone sandwich. "It sure ain't morsel enough to be a hush-puppy!"

"If you're through playing end-man at a minstrel show," said the sergeant, "kick that fire apart, and shake a leg out of here."

They went off at a dog-trot, trailing their rifles. Tempe swallowed the last of his food, licked his fingers. He and Lack shared a shallow rifle-pit on the face of the bluff above the river. Behind them, higher, a two-gun battery poked its cannon snouts over a log rampart. Below, closer to the water's edge, the three explosives experts, hidden in a natural gully, huddled over their terminals.

Tazewell stopped at Tempe's pit on the way to his own position. The big sergeant's voice was quick, but calm.

"Wigwags say enemy gunboats are coming upriver."

"How many?"

"Four. Two little ones, a big one and a ram."

"That's no attack."

"Uh-uh. Reconnaissance. Poking and prying."

"Sounds like," said Lack Norris, "they've heard about the melons we've been planting in the water yonder."

"Could be. Aim careful now. We can't sink gunboats, but we can sure discourage their people." Tazewell tapped each man on the back in turn, trotted away.

Tempe snuggled into the pit, making himself comfortable. He stuffed a rag as cushion in a prepared hollow, slid his rifle into position. Gazing down the barrel, foresight centered in rear notch, he aimed at a previously selected mark on the far bank. Beneath them this stretch of the Yazoo ran wide and straight, a muddy highway, made slightly turbulent by recent rains. Midstream was a good shot, farther a long one; the morning haze would make a target tricky at any range.

"Them fellers down there," said Lack, nodding at the trio clustered below, "remind me of three moonshiners fussing over a mash of mule."

"Let's hope the still blows up." Tempe could see the wet strands of wire as they emerged from the river.

"You really think them torpedoes will do more damage than us or cannon?"

"Maybe. If they work as they're supposed to." Still amused by Lack's metaphor, Tempe peered down the slope. The three men certainly appeared busy. Lieutenant Cowan's gray uniform made him seem twice as active in contrast to the darker civilian dress—Mike Tansey's homespun, Mr. Weldon's broadcloth.

"*If*," said Lack, hitching up on an elbow to stare at the Yazoo. "You know, Tempe, I ain't even sure now where we put those things."

"They know." Tempe studied the river's surface. He was pretty sure he recalled three places near the far bank, less certain about the torpedoes in midstream. That funny ripple there might mark one, he thought, though it shouldn't.

"Well, it ain't my worry. I aim to get me a Yankee pilot."

As they waited, listening to the sporadic gunfire downstream, trying to separate the batteries from the answering enemy ships, Tempe pondered his companion's last remark. Lack was right; their job was to shoot Yankees. This wasn't the same as sniping at an unsuspecting helmsman. That had worried Tempe, but this morning was different. The Union sailors were coming up the Yazoo deliberately, trying to draw fire, to discover strength. This was fair fight, part of war.

"Hey, Tempe, you hear a chug chug?"

"No, but our gunfire sounds closer."

Lack squinted in concentration, straining to hear the noise of engines, of paddle-wheels. No steamboat, especially under forced draught, approached in silence. Tempe saw that Lieutenant Cowan was standing, gazing through binoculars.

"They're a-coming," said Lack, nodding to Tempe. He cocked his rifle and the hammer click seemed to signal that the fight had reached them.

Tempe heard riflefire crackle close, guessed that the nearest infantry had started shooting. Then, around a bend, the first enemy vessel edged into view.

He was surprised at her small size and slow speed. This was a little sternwheeler, double-stacked up front, pilot-house just aft. She looked no bigger than the *Tonica*. He counted four gun ports on her lightly plated lower deck, noted the structure above was wood. The steamer, moving forward at half-speed, was hugging the far bank.

"What the Yanks call a tinclad," said Lack. He tensed, loosed a test shot.

"Let her get in range," Tempe said.

A second ship, a twin to the other, was chugging along about four lengths behind, farther into the river, near midstream. Between the two sternwheelers, well back, was a bigger gunboat, a real ironclad. Her cannon were slamming at the Confederates on the bluff.

The battery above the riflemen opened fire. Tempe cringed at the sudden double-blast. He braced, sighting on a cluster of Yankee sailors in the bow of the front ship. They seemed to be fishing in the river. The cannonballs, falling short, showered them with spray.

He fired, thought a man dropped behind the gunwale. The range was long, but possible. He could see chips fly as gunfire peppered the wooden superstructure.

Strangely, Tempe thought, the ship in midstream seemed to be drawing less fire, though it had cannon and muskets working. The infantry must all be blazing away at the lead vessel.

Beside him, Lack's rifle cracked again. Tempe felt a nudge, heard a delighted chortle.

"I put that smack in their pilot-house window!"

"Hit anything?"

As they reloaded Mike Tansey scuttled from the shelter below. The big Irishman scrambled up the bank at a half run, half crawl. He tumbled, panting, into the rifle-pit.

"That—that *Marmora*—she's digging out our torpedoes!"

"The *Marmora*?"

"That's the first sternwheeler. The other's the *Signal*. The big ironclad is the *Cairo*. There's a ram down the stream a bit, but I can't put a name to her yet."

"Do you know them all?" asked Lack in amazement.

"I know these, lads! But for God's sake stop them filching them torpedoes!"

"Can they do that?"

"All it takes is to snip the wires!"

Both riflemen nodded, settled gun butts against shoulders. Tempe drew a breath, held it. For an instant his frontsight was against a dripping iron jug being drawn across the *Marmora's* bulwark. He shifted his aim to the man holding it, squeezed off his shot. Lack fired at the same second.

Two of the Yankees grouped in the ship's bow visibly reeled back, spinning as they fell. The others scattered, diving for shelter. But the black torpedo, too, toppled inside the rail. Stern wheel churning, bullet raked and shuddering, the *Marmora* began to back water.

"She's had enough," mumbled Lack Norris, biting open a paper cartridge.

"So's the *Signal*," Mike Tansey said. The remark was half lost in the thunder from the battery above them as both cannon roared in unison.

Tempe didn't look; he was too busy reloading. He had taught himself never to be distracted from that important task. Dropping his ramrod, he fitted a fresh percussion cap with deft fingers. Not until he thumbed back the hammer to cock the rifle did he look up.

At that moment a steam whistle shrieked. Tempe saw that the white jet came from the ironclad, saw, too, that the *Cairo* had increased her speed. That was evident from the thicker smoke pouring from her funnels, the wider waves at her prow. The *Cairo* was charging upriver, gun ports blazing, to rescue her smaller, lighter-armored, sisters.

"Damn," said Lack, aiming, "she's big as a house, but there's not a head showing."

"Wait'll she's broadside," Tempe said. He was ready, watching the *Cairo* slide into his sights, waiting for a clear shot at the pilot-house.

"Glory be to God!" said Mike Tansey.

The awe in his tone drew the riflemen's attention. Mike was rigid, staring down at the *Cairo*. He looks, thought Tempe, like a man beholding a vision.

"What is it, Mike?"

"The *Cairo*! If she keeps on that course she'll run smack over one of our torpedoes." The Irishman pointed a quivering finger. "It's right there! Dead ahead of her!"

"Who cares?" Lack said, returning to his own task. He stiffened, fired, swore softly. "The men on her are nothing but shadows, Tempe."

"Mmmm." Tempe grunted agreement. The drifting cannon smoke was a hindrance. He saw a blur of movement as a wisp cleared away from the pilot-house, squeezed the trigger. The rifle bucked in his grasp. There was no telling if he'd hit anyone.

"Come on." Mike Tansey sounded as if he were praying. "Come along there! Just a wee bit more! *Come on!*"

"They can't hear you," said Lack, working his ramrod. "And if the cannon can't even dent—"

"Now!" shouted Mike Tansey. "Lieutenant Cowan! Mister Weldon! *Now!*"

The yell, so close to his ear, made Tempe jump. He stopped reloading to glare at Mike; the mechanic's rapt expression quelled his annoyance. Tempe glanced at the pair crouched over their wires, straightened to peer at the *Cairo*.

A blinding, blue-white flash suddenly ripped out of the river with a tremendous explosion that seemed to tilt the sky. Tempe blinked, felt the earth beneath him shake from the concussion. The *Cairo's* foredeck was completely hidden by a smoke-twined waterspout. Scattered specks of debris erupted from that thrusting geyser. Gaping, Tempe followed the flight of one object, recognizable as the ship's anchor.

With feather-like ease the anchor rose to tree-top height, lazily turned at the end of its arc, then plunged into the Yazoo. By the time it struck the river the ironclad, mortally wounded, was sinking.

"Holy Mother and all the Saints," said Mike Tansey. "Holy Mother and all the Saints." He kept repeating the phrase in a stunned litany.

Lack Norris sounded equally dazed. He spoke in a toneless whisper. "They sure enough work, don't they?"

In the sudden silence that followed the blast Tempe could hear the yells from the Yankees on the *Cairo*. Men were leaping, diving, over the side into the river. For a full minute or more there was no gunfire from cannon or rifle. Below him Tempe saw Lieutenant Cowan pounding Mr. Weldon on the back, but every other Confederate soldier was probably standing motionless like himself, stupefied by success.

The two sternwheelers were in full flight; the Federal ram, a long, squat vessel, tried to pick up survivors. Her advance ended the self-imposed truce. Once more the battery and the riflemen sprayed the river with fire.

Lack Norris cursed, shook himself, finished loading. He fired, shrilled a triumphant rebel yell. There was no doubt that Lack took some personal credit for the torpedo's success.

"I reckon," he cried, "we showed you something that time, you blue-bellied varmints! That'll learn you to stay out of our rivers!"

The *Cairo* sank fast. When the ram pulled away ten minutes later only the ironclad's chimney showed above the river's surface. The current bubbled around the jutting funnel, tossing flotsam in a widening circle.

Tempe only fired at the ram twice, carefully aiming high. He could not bring himself to shoot at the dark heads bobbing in the water, or the dripping rescued clambering over the ship's side. The poor devils had barely escaped a death terrible even for Yankees. He had no idea how many of the *Cairo's* crew survived, but surely the majority had been blown apart or drowned.

"We must have killed a couple or three hundred," estimated Lack Norris.

"Aye," Mike Tansey said, "at least. It's a horrible thing to think about. Three hundred souls dashed into eternity without a moment's warning."

"Well, hell," Lack said, "wasn't that why we planted the torpedoes?"

"That it was, lad. Sure, it's a glorious achievement. I'm not denying that. But it's horrible at the same time."

Tempe Dixon watched the Yazoo flow past and said nothing.

11

CHRISTMAS EVE was a blustery day in Vicksburg, and after nightfall
the wind howled with increased fervor. But nobody with an invitation
stayed away from the Grand Ball at General Martin L. Smith's headquarters.

No true Mississippian, rich or poor, let stormy weather interfere with
a festive occasion. Vicksburg intended to celebrate the Yuletide season
in *ante-bellum* fashion, with all the old pomp and merriment. There
would be crowded taverns and packed churches, suitably decorated. In
spite of war and blockade there was still plenty—turkeys, yams, cornmeal and grits to eat, bourbon whisky to wash them down. Since gunpowder was now needed for sterner uses, the children might miss the
holiday fireworks, but even the slaves would receive their usual gifts.
Why blame them for Yankee villainy? The town had seen enemy gunboats on its river, heard the whine from enemy shells. Let the wind
buffet its way from hilltop to hilltop. Neither hurricane tempest nor
Federal might could daunt the South's spirit.

This was shown by a formal expression of sentiment in various places.

"Gentlemen," said the general as his officers rose from that evening's
mess, "I give you the President of the Confederate States of America!"

The same toast was repeated over damask-covered dining tables and
flask-littered bars. Vicksburg's citizens clinked glasses to the office and
the man. It was a pleasure to salute Jefferson Davis, friend and neighbor, practically a fellow townsman.

In flowery rhetoric they forgave past mistakes. Jeff was a credit to the
valley; he'd won his spurs—to quote the Mississippi state motto—"By
Valor and Arms."

Partly this was due to Christmas spirit. Partly it came from a feeling
that the Confederate States had already suffered the worst that war could
bring. They believed they'd seen the high-water mark of Northern invasion, that the South had fought it to a standstill. Now it was a question of endurance, and surely the money-loving Yankees, as the costs of
the conflict mounted, would weaken first.

Alex Kittering, changing to her dancing slippers in an upstairs chamber of the general's temporary home, didn't bother her head with such
thoughts. She was happy, gay, among friends, anticipating a delightful
party.

The room was crowded with chattering girls, the younger bevy of Vicksburg belles. Their mothers, and the other married women, discarded wraps elsewhere. Here, there was laughter and giggles when wide skirts collided as their wearers contested for places before mirrors. These young ladies gossiped with the intimacy of long acquaintance, but one topic was taboo. There were no feline remarks about last year's ball gown, made over and freshly beribboned. New styles and fabrics were blockaded out of existence.

Clara Furlong, smoothing ringlets rumpled by wind in the short scurry from carriage to doorway, was atwitter with excitement. Her voice bubbled from topic to topic without pause for breath.

"Isn't this like old times? Did you-all know there was fighting on the Yazoo today? Yankee gunboats again. I do wish that gallant General Van Dorn was still here. Cavalrymen make the best dancers. And Bryce. Don't you miss Bryce, Alex?"

"Of course."

"That's a downright chittery question," said Emilie Verrier, nudging Clara aside to adjust her neckribbon in the mirror. "When you're engaged to someone you just naturally miss him."

The remark gave Alex a twinge of guilt. She hadn't been thinking of Bryce Furlong, or feeling very engaged. In fact his absence was a distinct relief. But she didn't intend to reveal her qualms about Bryce to anyone. That was their own affair.

"Well, I sure don't miss that General Pemberton any," Clara said. "Isn't he a stick? You know, he's a Yankee."

"From Pennsylvania," Poll Randall said.

Emilie giggled. "Imagine ole Vicksburg having a Yankee for a general."

"Girls," said Alex, frowning at them, "he's a Confederate officer. Jefferson Davis thinks very highly of him."

"And besides," Poll said, "he's keeping the Yankees away with his army."

"Listen at our Miss Napoleon. You sound like a sure-enough military genius."

"Why, Clara, she should," Emilie said. "She's been studying from a French text. Name of Henri."

"Pot to kettle," Poll said, blushing. "I'm not the only one."

Alex said, smiling, "A beau like Henri is hard to find these days. And does he know it!"

"Oh, you," said Emilie. "You've got Bryce."

"Yes," Alex said dryly, "I've got Bryce." She gave her hair a final readjusting pat. "We'd better go along down."

Her friends, Alex judged, would be the prettiest damsels at the ball.

They made the other girls in the room look faded, though none were wallflowers. Poll, her fair complexion heightened by the wind, glowed in mulberry satin. Emilie wore white, Clara blue; by pre-arrangement they had adorned their gowns with contrasting ribbons. All the dresses, including Alex's own gold brocade, were cut modishly low.

They descended the stairs in a group, automatically tripping to the strains of "The Bonnie Blue Flag," played by the headquarters band. The hall was bright with many candles, decorated with green garlands and Confederate flags, the popular Beauregard banner with its scarlet field and blue, star-studded St. Andrew's Cross. There were some worn uniforms among the waiting officers, but gloves and sashes were spotless, every button sparkled.

Alex stopped to chat with her parents, but the other girls were whirled away at once. She noticed, with amusement, that Poll had managed to capture Henri Duchesneau. They made a striking couple—the tall, dark Creole officer and his statuesque blonde partner.

"Good evening, daughter," said Franklin Furlong at Alex's elbow. Bryce's father was a balding, heavy-set man. He offered his arm, while Katie Sue, his wife, smiled approval. "May I have the honor of the first dance?"

Stephen Kittering looked surprised, but Epie Mae nodded at her daughter. The Furlongs, Alex decided, shared her mother's sense of propriety. An engaged girl was not expected to be too strait-laced in her fiancé's absence, but to open the dance with her future father-in-law reminded everyone of her status.

Franklin Furlong danced gracefully, but with a slightly hesitant tempo as if he recalled the steps from dim memory. Unfortunately for Alex there was no hesitation in his speech.

"Alex, my dear, have you heard from Bryce?"

"Not recently, Mister Furlong."

"Is there anything wrong between you two?"

The question startled Alex, made her wonder if Bryce had written his father. She said, "Why, whatever makes you think that?"

"My son can be difficult. It's the Furlong pride."

Alex realized that the man made the statement as an indisputable fact. The Furlongs were evidently proud of their pride. She tried to keep her own voice casual.

"I can be difficult, too."

"Of course. 'Tis a lady's prerogative."

That, Alex judged, dismissed it as unimportant. The girl had always known Bryce's parents as a remote, polite couple hovering in the background. Even now they seemed to belong to the "big people" of her childhood, the grown-ups, who lived in another world. She was slightly shocked by Franklin Furlong's assumption of his position as her prospective father-in-law.

"Bryce writes so infrequently, Mister Furlong."

"Ah, yes. Well, he's a man of action, not letters."

"I know."

"Have you made any plans, my dear?"

"Plans?"

"About the wedding."

"No," Alex said slowly. "Not really." She felt a flash of rebellion. This was neither the time nor the place for such a discussion. Was the man trying to spoil the music, the dance, her gay mood? "The—the war comes first."

"But it shouldn't."

"It shouldn't?" Alex gaped at him in amazement. Franklin Furlong gave her a bland smile and a paternal pat on the shoulder.

"No, Alex." A touch of oratory came into Furlong's soft drawl. "This cruel war must not disturb our habits of living, our code, our manners. That is why we are fighting. The Yankees wished to change our society. We want things to be as they were before."

"But—that's impossible!" Alex was too astonished to be vehement. Everything *had* changed! There was a new flag, a new government. Boys like her brother, Clifton, were dead on remote battlefields. The South had changed the course of history, and Bryce's father had vocally supported the move.

"I am speaking of essentials," said Franklin Furlong. The ruffles of his snowy shirtfront fluttered as he moved in the dance. His face was shining from the exercise but no more than the satin lapels on his black broadcloth coat. "We have had tragedy, and hardship. And will endure more, no doubt. Tonight, for example, I broached my last pipe of Madeira wine. But these things are unimportant, will pass. We must not allow the enemy to thwart us in spiritual matters."

The Ancient, thought Alex irrelevantly, should hear this! How old Joab would bellow at such garbled thinking. But a well-bred young lady did not contradict her elders on a dance floor. She said, politely, "I don't think they can do that."

"Fine. Then you and Bryce should arrange to be married in the near future."

It was such a smooth transition that Alex was caught by surprise. She didn't think wedlock all that spiritual, or that important. Personal, yes, but not a public concern. Anyway, Bryce should do his own arguing, not send his father to persuade her.

"I will think about it, Mister Furlong."

"Do that, Alex. Both Mrs. Furlong and myself have been highly pleased that Bryce showed such good taste. We would hate to lose you, my dear."

"Thank you," said Alex. She was very annoyed. Why must they keep pressing her for an immediate decision? She wanted to be let alone for at least this one evening, Christmas Eve, to enjoy the ball with no thought of the morrow, or war, Bryce Furlong or matrimony. Nothing was going to stop her!

Franklin Furlong relinquished Alex to their host, the general. The girl found Vicksburg's garrison commander a ruddy-faced, pleasant gentleman, who executed ballroom turns with a military snap.

The next hours passed in a kaleidoscope of melodies and partners, swirling skirts and flashing candleflames. Alex was happily confused; moments, faces, tunes seemed jumbled together. What officer led her through most of "Old Folks At Home"? Who held her close while they played "Lorena"?

She was exhilarated by exercise, entranced by music, flattered by compliments. Alex swung, dipped, stamped and waltzed, in the arms of friends and strangers. It amused her to keep tally of the latter by rank instead of names or faces. Her score was two privates, a sergeant, ten lieutenants, six captains and a colonel, not counting repeaters. The occasional civilian partner was a familiar Vicksburg older citizen like Doctor Randall.

In the intervals when the band stopped there was no relief from the heat in the over-crowded rooms. Men and women fanned themselves, sought refreshment at the punch bowls, perched for rest on chairs, stairs, sofas. Some of the older ladies paused to trade scandals; most of the older men eased aching feet with whisky. But everybody stayed indoors. On such a raw, blustery night there was no strolling out into the garden.

Alex, eyes closed, was waltzing with Henri Duchesneau late in the evening. She knew that Clara, Poll and Emilie were probably glaring, but didn't care. The Creole was a light, skilful dancer; his low baritone harmonized softly with his partner's singing.

> Soft fall the dews of evening
> Around our valley bowers;
> And they glisten on the grass plots
> And tremble on the flowers,
> And tremble on the flowers
> Like jewels rich to see
> But the tears of one I left there
> Are richer gems to me.

"You can't go in there!"
"Let us pass!"

"Oh, no, you don't!"

"Hold on!"

The loud voices jangled harshly over the music. They jarred Alex back to reality. She bumped against Henri as he stopped abruptly, stood staring at the commotion in the doorway. The girl felt bewildered, slightly frightened. Around them other dancers halted and turned toward the noisy altercation.

Two sodden figures, a man and a boy, were trying to force their way past the sentries at the entrance. The man was expostulating, spraying water drops as he gestured. Struggling in one guard's grip, the drenched urchin ripped out a lurid oath.

Ladies gasped; the band's playing grated to a shuddering death.

"You hush!" cried a sentry.

"Who are they anyway?" somebody asked, too loudly.

"Why," said Alex, in startled recognition, "that boy—that's Runcey Carr!"

Runcey heard his name, swung toward the speaker. His red hair was dark, plastered with wet, but a few freckles showed on his smudged face. His voice was shrill with excitement.

"Miss Alex! Miss Alex! We just got to see the general!"

General Smith stamped forward, ignored the lad, addressed the man. His tone was brusque, peremptory; he pointed an accusing finger. "Well, sir, what do you want? What's the meaning of this?"

The man straightened, saluted. His movement revealed the bedraggled uniform under his cloak. It was soaked colorless but had military buttons.

Henri Duchesneau grunted, dropped Alex's hand, and pushed forward. He said, "It's Colonel Fall, General."

"Colonel Fall?"

"Yes, sir. Philip Fall, telegraph officer at DeSoto across the river."

"That's right, sir," said the colonel.

" 'Course it is," Runcey Carr said. "He has a message and nobody over there except me would risk the river to row him across. The old Mississippi is raging! Waves as high as houses!" The boy was enjoying his recital. "And we rowed, and bailed, and tried to keep that blasted red lantern lit so's the batteries wouldn't fire on us and—"

"That's enough, Runcey," said Fall.

"Well, we damned near drowned!"

"What is it, Phil?"

"Trouble, Henri." The colonel turned to General Smith. "Sir. Eighty-one enemy gunboats and transports have passed Lake Providence, bearing south!"

This time the gasp was like a chill gust sweeping through the crowd.

Alex saw the general's ruddiness slowly pale. Eighty-one ships, she repeated mentally, and knew it was a full-scale attack.

"You're sure?" asked Henri.

"Lee Daniel counted them from Tibbot's plantation. He rode inland and sent the message himself. He signed it, Henri, and it was his fist!"

"His fist?"

"Telegrapher's term, General," said Henri. "His way of sending by key. Major Daniels is the telegraph officer at our outpost station ten miles below the lake."

General Smith nodded, raised his voice to parade-ground volume. "This ball is at an end. The enemy are coming down the river. All noncombatants must leave the city." He saluted Philip Fall. "Our thanks for your service, Colonel. My apologies for not recognizing you, and my impolite manner."

"Oh, that's all right, General," said Runcey, with cheerful impudence. "It's just lucky I was over there to watch a cock-fight."

"Excuse me," muttered Henri, brushing past Alex without seeing her, "there is much to do."

The girl stood motionless in the midst of hubbub and bustle. Officers were hurriedly taking their leave of dancing partners. The musicians were packing their instruments. Chaperones beckoned to their charges; wives searched frantically for husbands; girls wrung their hands, paled or flushed, clustered in groups or darted about as if lost. Servants, eyes and teeth very white in black faces, were huddled behind the bandstand as if already seeking shelter.

She saw Emilie and Clara tearfully clinging together in a dramatic tableau. Poll Randall, very pale, was shredding a dance card with nervous fingers.

Alex refused to panic, was plagued by a dimly recalled literary parallel. Wasn't there a similar scene—an interrupted, scurry-beset ball—in some book she'd read? She smiled suddenly, immensely relieved that she'd placed it. The eve of Waterloo in Thackeray's *Vanity Fair!*

That should, she thought, be a good omen. Waterloo had been a victory for the summoned dancers. She couldn't remember how Becky Sharp had acted, not that she'd ever emulate that scheming minx!

"Alex! Alex, over here, dear!"

She heard her father's hail, waved in answer, shoved and twisted her way through a dozen distraught females. Her parents were waiting at the foot of the main stairway; Epie Mae had already donned her wrap, Stephen was buttoning his overcoat. He was nervously flushed, but wasted no words.

"Frank Furlong's gone for both carriages, Alex. Go home with your mother. Leave for Tonica Hill at once. Don't even let Martin unhitch the team."

"You're not coming, Pa?"

"I'm reporting to the general for duty!"

"Stephen—"

"Don't argue, Epie. By God, I'm fit enough for this! An eagle with a limp wing still defends his own nest! Vicksburg is my town!"

The grandiose speech impressed Alex. For once her father sounded certain, fervently patriotic. The girl glanced at her mother, nodded in agreement.

"As you wish, Stephen," said Epie calmly.

"The Ancient will never go, Pa," Alex said.

"Oh." Stephen scowled, considered. He couldn't imagine Joab obeying his wishes. "Well, then," he said, desperately, "then, you must leave without him!"

"I'll get my cape," said Alex. She didn't intend to desert her grandfather, but that could be decided later. "Wait right here, Ma."

She dashed up the stairs sideways, hugging the wall to avoid those clattering down. Nobody paid her much attention. These men and women, her friends, were too busy with their own concerns.

It was the same in the crowded cloakroom. The giggling leisure of a few hours previous was replaced by frantic haste. The same girls now shoved and snapped as they searched for their belongings. Even the candlelight no longer cast a flattering glow, but revealed tense, haggard faces. Alex snatched up her red-velvet cape, but couldn't find her street shoes. She gave them up for lost, and left.

Downstairs, Epie Mae competently took charge of their exodus. She led the way to the Kittering carriage with unswerving decision, gave crisp, definite orders to the coachman.

As they rattled through the dark streets, Alex leaned in the vehicle's window to let the still forceful wind cool her face. She was grateful that her mother sat in immobile silence, while the team toiled slowly uphill, or trotted in rapid descent. The girl stared out at the familiar terrain.

Usually, at such a late hour, Vicksburg was bleakly empty, the huddled houses black blocks on the many hills. Tonight was different. There was noise and movement. Figures darted along the roadside, grouped at corners, at gateways. Voices shouted, called, mumbled in talk; hoofbeats drummed and turning wheels made a whirring racket. The Kittering carriage trailed another; both halted at an intersection to let vehicles cross. Once, a soldier horseman overtook them, passed at a gallop. Every building was marked with yellow squares of lamplight.

The town was awake and restless, spreading the news that the Yankees were coming. Alex shared the excitement, the anxiety. She had been away at Tonica Hill when the enemy fleet arrived, had missed this pulse-quickening anticipation.

She wondered for a moment if General Smith meant to include slaves in his order for non-combatants to leave town. If every Negro in Vicksburg left with his or her master the place would resemble a graveyard. Nothing would function. But it was hardly fair to leave your slaves to face danger and flee to safety yourself.

I'll not go, Alex resolved, unless Mimosa, Andrew, big Sarah and the rest, can go, too. The girl didn't really want to desert Vicksburg.

"Do you think we'll be shelled again, Ma?"

"Speculation," said Epie Mae, "is useless. I'm sure we'll be safe at Tonica Hill."

"I meant the town. Vicksburg."

"That, dear, depends on our soldiers."

Alex chewed her lip, annoyed by her mother's phlegmatic attitude. Of course, she thought, the town's fate depended on the soldiers! Didn't Epie realize that some boys her daughter had danced with tonight might die defending Vicksburg?

The team swung into Cherry Street, but the news had sped before them. Lights streamed from windows to speckle the roadbed. Upstairs and down, the front of the Kittering house was all ablaze as if a party were in progress. As the coachman reined in the team Alex was surprised to see three armed soldiers at the driveway's edge.

She recognized Tempe Dixon immediately. He stepped forward, shifting his bayonet-topped rifle, offered a hand to help her from the carriage.

"What is it?" asked Alex. "What are you doing here?"

"Orders," Tempe said. "General Lee—Stephen Lee, that is—has requisitioned every able-bodied slave in Vicksburg to help dig fortifications. We're out rounding them up."

Epie Mae spurned his assistance, climbed down unaided. Her voice was a cool, unhurried drawl. "You can't mean our servants, young man."

"I'm afraid so, ma'am. Only men, of course."

"Nonsense," Epie said. "These are household slaves, not field hands."

"So the old gentleman, Mister Joab, told us." Tempe's smile was brief, but genuine. "Among other things. Mostly cuss words. It didn't help at all that we've been friendly."

"Oh, my!" said Alex, imagining her grandfather's wrath.

One of the waiting soldiers, about Tempe's age, chuckled at her distressed exclamation. The other, older, coughed and spoke with a strange accent.

"I say, Tempe, we haven't all night, you know."

"Yes, Jollibee, I know." Tempe looked at Alex, lowered his voice.

"We've been waiting around quite a spell. Not wanting trouble. Mister Joab threatened to use a shotgun on us. We could have just taken the three we picked, but—well, knowing the family—"

"Which ones?" asked Alex, thankful that Tempe had come instead of a stranger.

"The groom. The gardener. One named Benjie."

Above on the box Martin, the coachman, wheezed a gusty sigh of relief. Epie Mae glanced upward, expressionless, back to Tempe.

"Benjie is my husband's personal body-servant, Corporal."

"He's still husky and fit, ma'am."

"Of course he is," Alex said. "A little hard work won't hurt him. Ma, you go inside and try to pacify Grandpa. I'll take care of this."

"Make sure you receive proper papers, Alex," said Epie. "And you, Corporal, see that they are returned in good condition." She gave Tempe a regal bow, walked up the steps, and entered the house.

Tempe removed his hat, took a bundle of papers from inside it, shuffled them. He said, "I have the requisition right here, all filled out and—"

Raising one finger Alex interrupted. "Martin," she said, "show these other gentlemen to the slave quarters 'round back, while I settle things with the corporal. Tell Ned, and Calico, and Benjie, they're to go along and do as they're told."

The coachman clucked to his team, and giggled. "That Mimosa," said Martin, "sure ain't going to be pleased." He let his horses walk at their own pace.

"Come on, Lack," said Jollibee, following the slowly moving carriage. Lack Norris gave Alex an amiable wink and ambled after the Englishman.

From inside the house came an unintelligible rumble as Joab Kittering roared at his daughter-in-law in protest. Tempe shrugged sheepishly, offered the requisition slip with an apologetic gesture.

"I'm afraid we've caused a sight of trouble."

"That's just Grandpa."

"I know."

"Wait'll he learns he's supposed to leave Vicksburg." Alex took the paper chit, began to fold it into tiny pleats. She was aware that they both watched her fingers with intense concentration. "Will the slaves be gone long?"

"I don't know, but I shouldn't think so."

Alex thought she understood his reasoning. The slaves would only be needed until the Yankee force arrived. After that it would be too late to complete fortifications. Her throat seemed to tighten, making speech difficult.

"Tempe."

"Yes?" Her use of his first name seemed natural.

"Will there be a battle?"

"Seems as if. They sure ain't—aren't—bringing all them bluecoats down this way to visit."

"Can—can they take Vicksburg?"

"No." He said the word flatly, repeated it when she raised her gaze to his. "No! I mean that. Honest. Don't you worry about them."

She was thrilled by his vehemence. This was the way a Southern soldier should talk, without hedging, without doubts. Alex felt that Tempe realized the Yankees had greater numbers, that he gave her a studied opinion.

Suddenly, Vicksburg's bells started to ring. The first peal came from St. Paul's Cathedral; the Episcopal church, the firehouse, and the others followed immediately. For a moment, listening to the wind-tossed clangor, Alex thought it was an alarm. Then, she saw Tempe's lips moving as he counted the strokes, and knew they were sounding the hour.

"Twelve," he said. "Midnight."

"Yes." Alex remembered what day it was. So much had happened in the last few hours—the ball, its sudden end, the hurried ride home—that she had forgotten the date in the imminence of deadly battle. "Tempe."

"Yes?"

"Merry Christmas."

Yielding to impulse Alex leaned forward, kissed him gently on the lips. She was stepping back, smiling, before he recovered from his surprise.

But then Tempe moved fast. Without warning his arm swept her close, tightened. This kiss was a fierce meeting, a moment of desperate clinging. They both knew it might be the only one, the first and the last. When they drew apart with dazed reluctance, Tempe's voice was shaking.

"Merry—merry Christmas—Alex."

The girl, blue eyes wide, touched her lips. Her whisper fluttered the paper still in her fingers. "Go now. God keep you safe from harm."

Turning, Alex ran for the house.

· *12* ·

The government known as the Confederate States of America still believed its destiny was independence. Most Southern citizens supported

[130]

that belief. In spite of the blockade and some staggering defeats, the vast central core of seceded territory was untouched. The South had lost Tennessee, part of Arkansas, the great port of New Orleans, but these were not mortal wounds. Two hundred miles of Mississippi River, from Port Hudson to Vicksburg, remained in Confederate hands, and the gray armies everywhere were intact, undaunted.

Besides, the man the South had rejected, the Northern President, Abraham Lincoln, was obviously fumbling as he tried to find generals who could win. McClellan was again in disgrace, removed for his failure to pursue the enemy after Antietam. A popular officer named Burnside, more noted for his luxuriant whiskers than his military skill, now commanded the huge Army of the Potomac.

In the western theater of war the Federal armies were scattered as occupation troops. Buell had lost his command in Tennessee because he let Braxton Bragg escape, but no Union general showed much initiative. They fought when attacked, busied themselves with governing hostile populations. Even U. S. Grant, of whom so much had been expected, seemed shackled by red tape.

When Grant moved, it was suddenly, an action precipitated by the knowledge that Lincoln wished to appoint a friend, McClernand, to head an expedition against Vicksburg. That fortified town had become Grant's pet objective; he wanted no politician-general getting in his way. Not while he had the red-bearded Sherman for a field commander, and Admiral Porter to take the gunboat flotilla any place it could float.

The plan was simple. As Sherman and Porter sailed down the Mississippi from Memphis with forty thousand men, Grant would move south from Holly Springs, fighting his way along the railroads. His advance would batter Pemberton's army before it, prevent the Southern General from sending aid to the besieged town. Surely, Sherman's force could overwhelm Vicksburg's tiny garrison of six thousand.

Grant got only as far as Oxford, Mississippi.

THE WIND and the rain lashed the land with a daily flogging. Stormy gusts howled through the trees at different volumes, but the downpour seemed steady, ceaseless.

After four days the delta landscape was flooded. The gale-swept waters in the bayous overflowed to hide the twisted cypress knees on their banks; swampy ground became quagmires; cottonwood hillocks were soaked into swamps. Tumbling and noisy, the Yazoo River swelled into a torrent, racing through its many-curved course like a millstream, at record levels, with a new, even muddier width. That fast current, channel drowned and boiling, made a formidable moat for the high bluffs along the Yazoo's south bank.

Both armies suffered, but the disembarked blueclad attackers endured the greater hardships. They had to move to get anywhere, and movement meant wading or slogging through gluey mud. The Southern troops, the defenders, were entrenched in clay or behind log ramparts, looking down on their enemy. Although they were soaked and miserable they were determined not to move.

Tempe Dixon, prone in the shallow advance rifle-pits hastily scooped beside the bayou's edge by a Louisiana company, knew that he'd do some moving. For the ragged skirmish line in its exposed position, the rule, once more, was fire and fall back.

He was not thinking of Alex Kittering's farewell kiss. That sort of nonsense was for quieter moments in more comfortable surroundings. Not that Tempe placed much importance on what had happened. It was a nice girl's gesture, hail and farewell to a soldier bound for battle, a Christmas greeting without mistletoe. She was engaged anyway; he had only acted as kissing-boy for Bryce Furlong.

Blowing on his fingers, Tempe hoped something would take place soon. Drenched to cold stiffness he had spent the early morning shooting through murky half-light at vague shadows. Out there, beyond his sights, protected by their own pickets, Yankee engineers were building an approach. The perpetual gray dusk made every shot haphazard, but marksmen on both sides kept up a random, desultory fire.

A withdrawal, Tempe thought, a fight, any action that stirred congealed blood would sure be welcome.

"Tempe," said Lack Norris, "this here Louisiana boy wants to know just where he's at."

"Hell of a time to ask," Tempe said, not turning.

A soft, Creole voice spoke somewhere behind him, near Lack's stand. "Well, now, I beg your pardon, sir, but we all have been too busy promenading down to this parish to make proper inquiries."

"Vicksburg!" Another Louisiana soldier made the name a plaintive complaint. "High-tail your britches on down to Vicksburg. If this Godforsaken place is any kind of town at all, I am the good St. Louis himself!"

"The Gibraltar of the West. A pea-patch mud hole scooped out of the top of a bluff. There ain't no hundred hills around here, Johnny."

"The town," Lack said, "is about a dozen miles behind us. Give or take a hoot and a holler."

"And this, where we are?" The Creole spoke with gentle insistence. "A gentleman prefers to know precisely in which accursed pool of stagnation his corpse may pickle."

"It's a bayou," Lack said.

"We have eyes, *mon ami*—my friend—but which?"

"Tempe?"

"Chickasaw or McNutt's. Take your pick." Tempe considered question and answer equally unimportant. He was fairly sure the high ridge some two hundred yards back, to the left, was called Chickasaw Bluffs, but that didn't matter much either. He was too grateful to wish to sound abrupt, so he mollified his tone. "We're right glad to see you-all here anyway, Louisiana."

"Do tell."

"It ain't no lie," Lack said.

Tempe watched a distant reflection quiver on a bayou eddy, squinted at the shadow-clogged brush above it. The Louisiana troops, he thought as he cocked his hammer, were a belated Christmas present from General Pemberton. Reinforcements had poured in almost as steadily as the rain, were in fact still coming. At least Vicksburg's garrison of six thousand wouldn't face the Yankee assault alone.

Across the eddy an enemy rifle cracked; the darting flame was mirrored on the water.

Aiming at the flash, Tempe fired. He curled on his side to reload. The exchange sparked other sharpshooters. Guns spat and crackled from both picket lines.

Two days ago, Tempe recalled, with the battery on Drumgould's Bluff, our riflefire was like a continuous volley. The light was as bad, if not worse, but at least there the targets were bigger. Yankee gunboats, mindful of the *Cairo's* end, made daily sorties to clear the torpedoes from the Yazoo. They, or the raging floodwater, had been successful; the enemy transports had come upriver to land troops without an explosion. But, day before yesterday, opposite Drumgould's, four ships and a tug were caught in a withering, tornado-spin blast of gunfire from artillery and infantry.

Even that onslaught, thought Tempe gloomily, failed to sink a single vessel. The tiny tug skittered away like a frightened water-bug; the four warships—the *Benton,* the *DeKalb,* the now familiar ram, *Queen of the West,* and the *Signal*—were raked and battered, but escaped.

He, with Taze, Jollibee, and Lack, had poured deliberate, carefully aimed volleys into every crevice on the *Benton*. She was the biggest, a long, dirty-faced ironclad, homely as a privy, with an armor-encased hump over her sternwheels. Firing at the sergeant's word, the quartet was sure they'd made a shambles inside the gunboat's pilot-house.

"In de mornin' an' all day. In de mornin' an' all day."

The snatch of song drew Tempe back to the present. He realized the sporadic riflefire had reached another lull, turned toward the singer. Sergeant Tazewell, hunched over his gun to fit a fresh cap, was crooning in an absent-minded way as he worked.

Tempe smiled in recognition. Those words, that tune, were stuck in his head, too. It was a slave spiritual, improvised by the Negroes while they toiled on the fortifications. The soldiers on the bluffs first heard it chanted above the wind-scream of a slashing rainbeat. In rhythmic cadence, singing with pure, natural harmony, the many voices ignored the tempest's noises, imprinted their song indelibly in a listener's memory.

> Oh, dat ole nigger pick-ax
>   Is swingin' down from high.
> Oh, dat ole nigger shovel,
>   She make de dirt to fly.
>   In de mornin' an' all day
>   In de mornin' an' all day
>   In de mornin' an' all day!
>   Till de Lord do call us home.

That had been Tempe's first witnessing of the birth of a spiritual. He knew, of course, that slaves sang to lighten labor, in the cotton fields, at plow or picking. But his pa, Lucius Dixon, back in Noxubee, kept no slaves; Tempe had never before heard black workers improvise a song as they labored.

Big Jules from the Furlong plantation had bellowed the opening two lines as he swung his mattock. Little Jules, his partner, chimed in immediately with the next two. Kittering's Benjie supplied the refrain, taken up by a dozen voices with each repetition. In full, deep-throated chorus, without hesitation, the whole group sang the last line as if they had rehearsed it.

"Like they was ready," muttered Tempe, still surprised at his thrill on hearing it. They called such efforts spirituals with reason. This one, Tempe felt, appealed to the spirit while it stimulated bodily action. An ancient, mournful plea ran through it in undertone to the work tempo.

"Till de Lord do call us home," sang Tazewell. He tilted his head back to gaze into the storm-marbled overcast, and said: "De Lord better get around to it. It's nearing ten."

"That, Sergeant, is a guess."

The Louisiana rifleman's remark made Tempe chuckle. The sharpshooters had long since learned that Taze's ability to tell sky time in any weather was uncanny. If the big sergeant did guess at the hidden sun's position, he was surprisingly accurate.

Lack Norris spoke in the mild tone that meant he sensed a favorable wager. He said, "If one of you boys should happen to have a watch on—"

Yankee artillery interrupted the sentence. All along the dark hedge of trees that bordered the bayou the enemy field guns opened fire. The howitzers slammed; the heavier pieces thundered. Smoke and flame burst from the dense cover in successive eruptions as battery after battery joined the cannonade. The noise blended into a single tremendous roaring that seemed to shake air, earth and water.

From their fortified emplacements on the bluffs the Southern cannon blazed in reply before the Yankee barrage reached its peak. The gunners handling the Napoleons and rifled Parrotts jumped to reload faster than drill had taught. This was the hour that justified the long wait, the endured misery.

Beneath this fresh gale created by passing projectiles from both sides the infantry waited, crouched, burrowing into the sodden ground. The foot soldiers, in gray, blue or butternut, knew that they, in the end, would decide who owned the Yazoo, whether that river defense-line could be held or taken.

In Tempe's sector, where he huddled in the advance rifle-pits with the 26th Louisiana, and some companies of the 17th, the artillery exchange was intense. Yankee shells whined overhead, burst or plowed yellow clay from the steep banks. The South's answering missiles, on a higher trajectory, crashed among the trees beyond the bayou.

Even the rawest Creole drummer boy realized that this was the prelude to attack. The infantry's orders were to show resistance and withdraw to prepare positions before the enemy charged.

Tempe shot without aiming now, tried to judge the weight of the Yankee rifle fire. The bluecoats were evidently shooting at will, every man for himself, but the musketry rattle seemed a mosquito buzz compared to the thundering cannon.

Bullets zipped past Tempe's ears, spattered mud close to his face. The fight wasn't as fierce as Shiloh, but he knew it would get worse.

"All right!" Tazewell punched Tempe's shoulder as he shouted. "The captain says get out of here!"

"Sweet talk," said Tempe. "You sure won't need to tell me twice."

"We stick with Louisiana, Sarge?"

"Till we're told different, Lack."

Jollibee popped from a hole like an intrigued groundhog. He rubbed his powder-smeared mouth, and spat. His complaint sounded more annoyed than bitter. "This here blooming haze is wetter than a ruddy London fog."

"Write a letter to Pemberton," suggested Lack.

They withdrew on the double, cringing under the shellfire, grateful that the morning's murkiness, thickened now by black gunsmoke, helped hide the movement. The Louisiana companies broke formation as they climbed the slope to the new position, but the four marksmen kept together.

The entrenchments stretched across the crest of a tall bank extending from the higher bluffs called Chickasaw. They were fortified by a solid, clay-chinked, log breastwork, crooked as a rail snake-fence, but tolerably bullet-proof. From above on the bluff the nearest battery could enfilade attacking troops, while fire from the embankment itself would sweep the level approach.

"Snug as a suckling pig a-feeding," Lack said as he patted a smooth rest for his rifle.

"Just don't get a Yankee musket apple stuck in your mouth!" Jollibee inspected the firing step, swapped an approving nod with Tazewell. "This ought to be a nappy shooting gallery."

"If we hold it," said the sergeant.

Tempe watched the last files of the Louisiana infantry scramble down into the trench. He, too, considered the place a good one. To get at them the Yankees would have to come across open ground made treacherous by the swollen bayou, through the abandoned advance rifle-pits, and up the slope. It was hazardous terrain; they'd be under fire all the way.

"You reckon they'll attack this whole stretch of river, Tempe?" asked Lack.

"Where they can. Only a couple of spots a body can land troops. Like here. I reckon there's enough of them out there in that swamp to make this a mighty interesting slice of pie."

"Peach," Lack said. "Hot baked and oozing juice through the crust."

Jollibee groaned. "Lack, would you please stop talking about food!"

"Hush your clabber, Lack," said the sergeant. "This won't be no picnic. I counted them Yank transports, and this feller, Sherman, must have twenty, thirty thousand blue-belly soldiers to throw at us."

"Hell!" Lack was unimpressed. "We've scotched that many snakes around here in a single day!"

Suddenly, the Federal cannonade stopped. Tempe, having turned his back to the enemy, was watching a shell streak through its flight. The projectile burst above the snout of a Confederate howitzer. That gun muzzle belched fire, and its report sounded sharp and loud. Too loud. The silence seemed to box his ears.

He whirled to stare over the breastwork, unable for an instant to hear even raindrip or wind. Then, the Yankees began to shout in their familiar bellow that was so much deeper, at any distance, than the shrill Southern yell.

"They's a-coming," Lack said.

Tempe grunted in shocked surprise as the Yankee battle line, a solid mass in the day's gloom, emerged from the woods. He'd not watched an enemy charge since Corinth, had half forgotten it was a sight different than shooting at gunboats. His first glance at the distant foreshortened figures made him suck a gasp through his teeth.

Their array, he thought, looked as wide as the horizon, as dense as the thick delta forest. A moving black wall, the soaked uniforms without color, the tricky light jelling the intervals together. Only the polished bayonets glittered, a garland of cold steel points strung across the advancing line.

As always, Tempe's stomach fluttered a salute to the bayonets. They had their own sheen, and it seemed more deadly in haze than in sunshine.

The cannon began again; the blast from the nearby bluff battery steadied Tempe's nerves. He cocked his gun, took aim.

These blue-bellies would not be easy to stop, but then they never were. The Yanks, too, had learned a lot since Shiloh.

"Hold your fire. Hold your fire."

Tempe heard the familiar command repeated along the line by officers and non-coms. The refrain wasn't really needed for veterans, but it might calm a few trigger-happy recruits. This was no place for fancy marksmanship; only short-range volleys could shatter a charge.

"Hold your fire," said Sergeant Tazewell, automatically. "Let 'em come closer."

"They will," Lack Norris said.

The Yankees were getting closer with every step. They splashed out of the bayou's puddles onto the muddy ground, and came on. Tempe could distinguish the white blurs that were faces now, the candy-striped battle flags. He drew bead on a tall officer brandishing a revolver. But the man disappeared as the enfilading Confederate cannonade ripped a swath through the blue ranks.

They're good, Tempe thought, watching the files close, the column reform under that murderous barrage. These black-hats were very damned good indeed! He felt a soldier's admiration for the enemy troops that kept coming through that hell of crossfire.

Then, the charging blue line reached the abandoned rifle-pits, stumbled and leaped across them, started up the slope. There was no more time for admiration. Now they were suddenly close, too close! Tempe could see the contorted expressions, the dark, gaping mouths.

"Fire!"

As Tempe shot into a knot of bluecoats he felt the breastworks rock from the volley's slam. It was as evident as the gun butt bucking against his shoulder, as the thick billow of powder-smoke that erupted to hide the Yankees.

Snarling in haste, he bit open a paper cartridge, rammed it into place. This, the act of reloading, was the rifleman's vulnerable moment, but he didn't dare glance up to peer for the telltale gleam of advancing enemy bayonets.

When the gun was ready, Tempe saw that the Yankees were stopped, but shooting. Their first line was a shambles of fallen, and reeling wounded, but the second, bent like men facing a gale, was trying to fight back. The enemy muskets crackled, the spurting flames lurid in the haze. A bullet struck the barricade; another tugged at Tempe's hat.

"Get them out of there," he said.

"On the double," said the sergeant.

Again, the Confederate rifles blazed in a volley. Tempe heard no command, fired with the rest. The Louisiana boys seemed to know their business.

The Yankees tried to cling, couldn't. A color-bearer bravely planted his standard in the ground, then buckled over and snapped the staff as he fell. The bluecoat who snatched the flag from the mud was staggering back with a limply hanging arm. The whole column was wavering. Only a few were fleeing, but the rest were beaten.

A third volley crashed from the breastwork, sent the Federal troops into full retreat. They scurried back down the slope, and the Confederate cannon drove them, plowing gobs of mud and men from the field.

"By God!" Lack Norris said, mopping his face. "By God, it's good to see them whipped for a change!"

The sergeant grunted assent. He said, "Now they know how it felt charging their works at Corinth!"

"You think they'll try again, Sarge?" asked Tempe.

"Not unless that Sherman's as crazy as they claim. He's been three days trying to gain a foothold and that there—" Tazewell gestured toward the huddled Yankee bodies on the slope—"that's as far as they got."

"They made a damn good try," Tempe said in tribute. He didn't think Sherman would waste more men attempting the impossible. You didn't have to be a general out of West Point to realize the Yazoo's bluffs couldn't be carried by a frontal assault. Not while the defenders had plentiful ammunition for cannon and rifles.

He gazed out across the battlefield, trying to ignore any crawling wounded. Most of the enemy force was retiring across the bayou, but several companies were digging in at the rifle-pits.

"What," asked Lack, "do those damn fools down there think they're doing?"

"I dunno," Sergeant Tazewell said, staring. "There must be three, four hundred of them. I count four flags. Tempe?"

"I make it four, too," Tempe said.

"That ain't no place to stay," said Jollibee. "Our cannon is dropping shells behind them."

A low Louisiana voice drawled a question. "What do you say, boys? Shall we go catch us a passel of Yankees?"

Tempe saw that the idea was infectious, watched it spread through the gray ranks. He sighed and made sure his bayonet was fastened tightly. There wasn't much doubt that a swift charge would capture the bluecoats in the rifle-pits, but he wished they'd had sense enough to pull out with the others. They sure made a tempting prize.

"I hope it's worth it," he muttered.

Tazewell grinned, nodded. "I know what you mean, Tempe. It's a good move, but a feller could get killed making it."

"It's decided," Lack said. "There goes the yell."

The shrill yelling started at the end of the line, but everybody joined in. Tempe saw the Louisiana boys scrambling over the breastwork. Then, he vaulted to the top, screamed with the rest, plunged forward into the charge.

As they raced down the slope he tried to avoid trampling the Yankee dead. Lack Norris, slightly ahead, leaped high over a crumpled body. Tempe caught a glimpse of a wounded Yank, white face mutely pleading. There was no thought of pausing. In a charge a man ran all out because those who hesitated never made it.

The Yankees foolishly rose to meet them, as if disdaining the shallow protection of the rifle-pits. The bluecoats, thought Tempe, must be stunned stupid by the cannonade. They wasted powder by scattered, ragged shooting. He heard a bullet whine, realized the Confederate gunners were holding their fire while the gray infantry charged.

Then, the sharpshooters reached the pits. A hatless, blueclad stripling made a bayonet lunge at Lack, and missed. Tempe felled the boy with a sweep of rifle butt. Jollibee went in low, tackled a color-bearer. A Yankee captain, cursing, clicked his empty revolver in Tazewell's face. Reaching a big hand, Taze took the pistol, and the officer burst into tears.

It was over in one minute. As the Louisiana troops hustled their prisoners up the slope, Tempe heard the cannonade begin again, covering them. He thought the captives looked older than they had at Shiloh. But then, so did everybody in the Confederate army.

They tallied the bag after nightfall. That one quick charge had taken twenty-one Yankee officers, three hundred and eleven lower ranks, as well as capturing four stands of colors, and five hundred stands of arms. It made a fitting climax to the day's victory.

Next morning Sherman put his army back on its transports, and started them out of the Yazoo River.

· *13* ·

VICKSBURG celebrated the arrival of another year, and the victory at Chickasaw Bluffs simultaneously, with gay confidence. The battle's result made the coming months look brighter; surely, 1863 would bring success and independence to the Confederate States.

Those non-combatants who had left town under orders streamed back, taxing the already limping railroad. Everyone felt that a residence on the hundred hills was a reasonably safe sanctuary. Hadn't their brave soldiers proved that Vicksburg could not be taken? They had repulsed a vastly superior Yankee army with heavy losses, and their own casualties were negligible. Scholarly citizens, like Franklin Furlong, mentioned Thermopylae with a patronizing smile. Even the slaves who had worked on the fortifications boasted of their labors. By Twelfth Night most of the townspeople were intoxicated with the idea that their city was invincible.

Alex Kittering shared this general enthusiasm, refused to be deflated by her grandfather's gloomy comments. She and old Joab, with Mimosa and Andrew, had stayed behind on Cherry Street when Epie Mae led the rest of the household slaves to Tonica Hill, and had not suffered. The windows had rattled from the storm, but not from enemy bombardment. Runcey Carr, who went everywhere with a boy's disregard for regulations, had sloshed through the garden with the first news of the Yankees' defeat.

"We sent them skedaddling, Miss Alex! They took off like a buckshot-riddled chicken thief! And they was riddled, too, good and proper. That ole Sherman must be having fits!" Runcey had paused to guffaw, oblivious of the puddle forming around his feet on the Kittering's best carpet. "Them Yanks just flounder about lost in bayou country. They spent most of a night building a road across one in the wrong direction. Had to take it all up when they found it wasn't going anywhere!"

"Did—did we lose many men?" asked Alex, thinking of Tempe Dixon.

"None that I saw. Somebody said about three-score."

"You ought to stay out of the lines, boy," Joab scowled his disapproval.

"Shucks, Mister Joab, I don't bother nobody, and nobody bothers me."

The three conscripted slaves also returned with loud tales of Southern glory. They had watched the battle from a safe distance, and loafed home. Alex didn't notice how Mimosa glowered at Benjie's sniffles. The slave-girl resented the task of nursing her husband through a feverish cold. Mimosa tallied another black mark against the war and folks that sent a houseboy out to dig in weather unfit for field hands. Benjie's proud account of the work, as told to young mistress and old master, didn't mollify his wife.

"You just ain't got sense enough," Mimosa had stated, in the slave-quarters, "to get in out of the rain!"

Joab grouchily kept to his room to avoid his granddaughter's evident happiness. The old man began to doubt his own logic, was half-convinced that his neighbors had been right all along. There was no sense in thinking any place invulnerable, but this whole war was conducted in a senseless fashion. He found no cheer in the reports that the Yankee army had steamed north to capture Arkansas Post, a Confederate fort on the Arkansas River.

When it took thirty thousand Union soldiers, Joab decided, to subdue five thousand Rebels in a rag-tag fortress, Vicksburg could hold out for years. The longer the war lasted the worse would be the carnage and the killing.

Alex tried without success to jolly her grandfather from this mood. She was distressed by his refusal to congratulate Stephen on his appointment to General Smith's staff, hurt when the old man gave no homecoming welcome to Epie Mae. Her parents, from long experience, shrugged away these slights, but the girl, for the first time, resented Joab's attitude.

"He acts like a kill-joy," Alex said. "I know he's against the war, but he ought to be glad Vicksburg at least is safe."

Her mother nodded, glanced at Stephen. "The Kitterings," she said, "all get crotchety notions with advancing age." She spoke tonelessly.

"He is getting on," agreed Stephen, smiling fondly at his wife. She must be pleased that his new duties as staff officer would keep him in town, available as husband and buffer against Joab.

"How do you mean?" asked Alex, puzzled.

"Oh, Alex, dear," Epie said, "he's notional. Touched. It's been coming on for years."

Alex, scowling, shook her head, nettled by the bland remark. She simply did not believe that Joab's brains had deteriorated overnight, and she knew his thinking had been keen until recently. Neither Epie Mae nor Stephen, in their daughter's opinion, had ever seen the day they could out-smart the Ancient. Whatever her parents thought it wasn't wise to underestimate Joab.

"I doubt that, Ma," she said, "but this time I'm not going to let him spoil our victory with croaking predictions." Alex sounded defiant, as if bold statement would bolster her confidence.

That confidence was still unshaken in late January when Bryce Furlong and Clay Kittering came home on leave. Mimosa saw them first as they rode up, recognized them in spite of the heavy, blue Yankee greatcoats they wore. She was at the door to greet them, as gushingly effusive as ever.

"Well, well, Master Clay! Ain't you a sight for eyes? Regular soldier. Welcome home, Master Clay. Welcome, welcome, Cap'n Bryce."

"Thanks, Mimosa."

"Where is everybody?"

"Around, Master Clay. Your ma's upstairs—just wait'll she hears your voice! Miss Alex's nursing at hospital, but she'll be here directly." Then, as she helped Clay out of his coat, Mimosa casually asked her important question. "Where you leave that Esau, Master Clay?"

"Esau?"

"Him. He went off with you, but he ain't come."

"Oh, Esau's back at camp. He cooks for our whole mess. He's having a fine time, Mimosa."

Mimosa, slipping away as she heard Epie Mae on the stairs, scowled. Just like I figured, she thought. Take that poor little boy to war and leave him behind. Poor little Esau! Mimosa ignored the fact she'd always disliked Esau. Now he was a symbol, another slave endangered by an inconsiderate master.

Alex, coming home, found the returned warriors entertaining Epie Mae. The girl stared at her brother. Clay was smoking, strutting before his mother, while Bryce, lounging in a chair, watched indulgently over his whisky glass. The lad had changed to a slight, trim trooper in spurred boots. He wore a short, gray tunic, and blue trousers with a broad yellow stripe, newer than the jacket. Clay had a dark forage-cap on the back of his tow head; a sheathed saber and holstered pistol hung, dragging, from his wide leather belt.

The weapons, thought Alex, seem too big for him. She knew Clay was wearing everything to impress their mother, a gamecock displaying his plumage. Aloud, she said, "Well, I declare, the prodigal returns."

"Hi, you, Alex," said Clay, grinning. His scabbard clanked as he waved his cheroot in greeting, stuck it back between his teeth.

"Don't smoke too much, Clay, dear."

"Everybody smokes in the army, Ma."

"Doesn't he look well, Alex?"

"Yes, Ma. Just fine." She was pleased to admit that Clay was tanned and healthy, but the thin cigar made his face appear very boyish.

"Oh, I thrive!" Clay struck an attitude, sang a snatch of song. "If you want to have a good time, jine the cavalry." He laughed his own applause.

Alex felt Bryce's gaze, turned toward it. He had unbuckled his side-arms, was sitting cross-legged, smiling at her with smug condescension. The expression was almost a cold sneer. Bryce might as well have said the words. "I told you so, Alex. Your worries were female foolishness. Clay's made out in high style."

She felt the hot flush rise, bit her lip to prevent angry speech. Bryce's smirk dared her, but Alex wouldn't spoil her mother's pleasure in Clay's return. The girl hadn't doubted her brother would make a soldier, but deplored his runaway as reckless and unfeeling. Putting a youngster in uniform, she thought, didn't change his age.

"Tell them where you got the outfit, Clay," said Bryce, tutor prompting his protégé.

"Gifts from Uncle Sam!" Clay chortled, slapped his thigh. "Courtesy of Abe Lincoln. Trousers, cap, saber and Colt's revolver." He hefted the polished-leather holster. "And a nice, warm greatcoat besides. All spoils from the raid that saved Vicksburg."

"The *what* that saved Vicksburg?" Alex was genuinely astonished.

"The raid that saved Vicksburg," repeated Bryce.

"Bryce and Clay," said Epie, "just told me, Alex. It seems that General Van Dorn—"

"Now, Miz Kittering, it's Clay's story."

"That's right, Ma."

"Of course, dear."

Alex's stare shifted from mother to brother to Bryce. She guessed that her grandfather had deliberately avoided this narration. Whatever the exploit was, Bryce wished her to be impressed.

"Go on, Clay," said Bryce. "Spin your tale."

The youngster nodded eagerly, plumped himself into a chair. Clay found his saber annoying, unhooked it, laid the curved scabbard across his lap. "We don't use swords much any more," he explained. "At least we didn't on this raid. Six-shooters are much handier, eh, Bryce?"

"As the Yanks found out," said Bryce, "but start at the beginning."

"Oh. All right." Clay took a deep breath. "Of course, I'm just a plain trooper as yet, a private, Company G, Bryce's company, in the 1st Mississippi Cavalry under Colonel Pinson. None of us knew General Van Dorn's strategy until it was all over."

"Never mind the strategy," Bryce said. "Just tell how it happened."

Alex caught the faint note of annoyance, said sweetly, "Give him a chance, Bryce." She smiled as he scowled at her.

"Anyway," Clay said, "we all figured something was going to happen. We were camped on the north bank of the Yalobusha River, near Grenada. The Texas Brigade joined us, and the Tennessee Brigade, and the 2nd Missouri. All cavalry. Even I knew the general wasn't collecting that many horse soldiers together without a plan."

"About twenty-five hundred men," Bryce said.

Clay nodded, wet his lips, and chuckled. "And almost as many accents. The poker games in Ante-up Church sounded like the Tower of Babylon."

"Babel," corrected Alex.

"Did you say Ante-up Church?" asked Epie Mae.

"The fellers quartered there just called it that, Ma. Antioch Church. Ante-up, see, for the poker."

"Clay, you didn't play poker in a *church?*"

"It was empty, Ma," said Clay, flustered, "and I wasn't quartered there myself. I was outside with the rest of the Deupree mess. There's six Deuprees in my squad, all kin, and we eat together so naturally it's the Deupree mess." He laughed, beginning to enjoy his narration. "During the night of December sixteenth we started a ruckus by accident. You see we built a fire at one end of a fallen log, and we hung our tack—saddles, overcoats, and guns—on the limbs of a tree smack against the other end."

Alex noticed that Bryce was frowning, but he didn't interrupt. She said, "What happened?"

"Damndest thing," said Clay happily. "While we were all asleep the flames licked along that there log, and smack up into the tree. The whole shebang caught, and blazed. Our clothes got burned to pieces, and the guns—the guns went off!"

"My," said Epie Mae.

"The whole camp turned out, Ma. Thinking it was the Yanks come a-shooting. Bryce, you recall how Colonel Bob McCullough from Missouri plunged out his tent roaring? 'What in hell is all that shooting for?' "

"I remember," said Bryce.

And you wish you didn't, thought Alex, because it sounds like a pretty childish stunt. She realized that Clay considered it a lark, a schoolboy prank that disturbed his elders.

Clay sensed his captain's disapproval, hurried on with his story. "Well, next morning we were all issued three days' rations. Everybody, except maybe Bryce and a few other officers in General Van Dorn's family, thought we were going out to hit Yankee cavalry under Dickey who were raiding in the neighborhood. At nightfall we saddled up and rode off.

"We started east, not fast, and we didn't halt to feed the horses until just before sun-up. Before noon we passed through Pontococ, and, you know something? All the ladies in that town was out in the road with baskets of food. Fried chicken, baked yams, corn bread. Scrumptious, wasn't it, Bryce?"

"Very patriotic," said Bryce.

"A regular picnic," Alex said.

"I hope you thanked them," Epie said.

"Sure, we did, Ma. But just about then I was riding in the van, right behind Bryce, and near General Van Dorn. One of the scouts came galloping in to report. I could hear every word. The scout, a Texan, was all het up.

" 'General, sir,' he says, 'there's a large Yankee force moving out from Tupelo.'

" 'Cavalry?' asks the general.

" 'Cavalry,' says the Texan.

" 'Well, now,' says Van Dorn, pulling at his whiskers, 'we'll just swing this column around, and head away from them.'

" 'But, sir,' says the Texan, 'the enemy is firing in our rear.'

" 'Are they still in your rear?' asks the general.

" 'Yes, sir!' says the scout.

" 'Very good,' says General Van Dorn. 'That's where I want them, son. In your rear.' "

Clay paused to view the effect of this dramatic exchange. Bryce's nod was an accolade; Epie Mae beamed, suitably impressed. Alex thought the lad had imitated the separate voices very well, even managing the flat Texas accent. She winked at her brother.

"After that," said Clay, encouraged, "we all knew we wasn't out to meet Dickey's Yanks. We swung northwest, and some of the boys wondered if we weren't heading for Ripley or Bolivar in Tennessee. There were Federals in both places, Jay Gee Deupree claimed. We camped that night on the banks of the Tallahatchie, at New Albany. The horses needed a rest, and I was as stiff as Grandpa and near as lame. I reckon we'd been in the saddle for over thirty hours.

"Long about midnight it rained. Sheets and torrents, cats and bullfrogs! A real downpour that flooded the camp! We had to go wading after stuff that floated away—blankets, saddle-cloths, hats. I reckon we splashed around for an hour before we got everything up on higher ground.

"But the next day was beautiful, blue-bright and shining. It was a cold morning and it didn't get warmer. Around noon we turned toward Holly Springs, and right away the whole column knew where we were heading. Holly Springs, in which Grant's bluecoat army, down to Oxford, had its supply base, chock full and overflowing with pretty near everything!

"General Van Dorn put the Texans out in front to arrest anybody moving on the roads. We wanted a complete surprise! By late afternoon, when we halted to feed the horses, we were placing guards at every house we passed so's nobody could sneak out to warn the Yanks we were around."

"Warn the enemy?" asked Epie Mae. "Our own people?"

Bryce Furlong shrugged. "Sometimes it's wiser not to take any chances. Some families have their Union sympathizers."

Including ours, thought Alex, and dared Bryce to mention Joab's name. She said nothing, aware that Clay wanted to continue.

"At ten that night, December nineteenth, the general split us into two columns and we went forward on parallel roads. We stopped and dismounted about five miles outside Holly Springs. It was bitter cold without fires. I'd lost my heavy coat when that silly tree went up in flame, but I was wearing five shirts. Five shirts and I was still cold! By the time it started getting gray, just before dawn, my teeth were chattering.

"Company G drew the van and was in front under Lieutenant Day. We mounted and formed fours at Bryce's command. He led the advance guard himself, twenty of us. I was in the very first four along with Jay Gee Deupree, Bob White and Groves Dantzler. Wasn't nobody but Bryce in front of us."

Bryce, thought Alex, was trying vainly to look modest. Clay, eyes dancing, sounded gleeful.

"We were to go in fast from the northeast, pass through the bluecoat infantry, and smash their cavalry which was camped on the Holly Springs Fair Grounds. The others had different jobs."

"The plan was the general's, of course," said Bryce, implying his approval. "The 2nd Missouri, dismounted, was to follow on foot. Half the Texans were to charge in from the east by the railroad depot, the rest were to attack from the south. The Tennessee detachment was to enter the town from the north, and had the duty of watching the roads from the east and west."

Alex nodded, visualizing the gray column moving darkly through grayer morning. The horses, sensing the excitement, would blow smoke-vapor in the cold air; their hoofs would thud on the frost-hard road.

Clay, carried away by recitation, swayed in his chair as if riding. His voice quickened. "We spurred to a hard gallop as we hit the town. I was on Sadeye, the same horse I fetched from home. We swept through Holly Springs like a dust cloud." Clay's laugh rang with triumph. "You should have seen their infantry tumble out of their tents half dressed. Some only in shirts, and some without. They opened fire in spite of being surprised. Sadeye was grazed. I guess every mount in the advance guard was hit, but we paid them no mind and raced straight for the Fair Grounds.

"The Yank cavalry—we learned later it was the 2nd Illinois—was swinging into the saddle when we rammed into them. It was a nice fight, short and sweet. They tried using their sabers, but we did better work with revolvers, like we'd been taught. I had a Leech and Rigdon Confederate Colt that Bryce had given me, and I emptied it in less than a minute."

Clay shook his head, but his voice stayed happy. "Sadeye took another ball and went down under me. But it was all over by then. Some of our boys got cut up a little, here and there. Little Jerry Beasley was slashed in the face. Major Wheeler had his thumb nearly sliced off. A few others. Nothing that couldn't be patched."

Alex swallowed, aghast at her young brother's carefree indifference. Her mother didn't seem to notice.

"Then, from seven in the morning till about four in the afternoon we had a high old time. There was a trainload packed with clothes and rations drawn up by the station. The courthouse was piled high with supplies. What we couldn't carry, we burned. There was plenty to eat and enough whisky to float the *Tonica!*"

"We destroyed," Bryce said, "over a million dollars worth of Federal stores. We completely ruined Grant's base of supplies."

"And, then, after paying our respects to Mrs. Grant, who was staying in the Walker house, we went away from there. I hope the lady tells her husband how politely she was treated.

"We came back by way of Davis Mill, Coldwater, and Middleburg, pestering any Yankee garrisons we came across, but not wasting time over them. We returned to Grenada thirteen days after we set out."

"Wasn't it wonderful, Alex?"

"Yes, Ma," said Alex, "but I'm not sure how it saved Vicksburg."

"Without a base," said Bryce coldly, "Grant was forced to withdraw his army. You can't fight battles without a base of supply. His withdrawal allowed Pemberton to send reinforcements down here. That's what saved the town."

The girl gazed at him, unimpressed. She remembered the sodden wounded she'd tended after Chickasaw Bluffs. The men on those drenched bayous saved Vicksburg, Alex thought indignantly. Tempe Dixon and the others who faced Sherman's bayonets and threw them back.

"I never," said Clay, "had so much fun in my life!"

Epie Mae said, "That's nice, dear."

Alex made no comment. She could hear old Joab's rasping insistence that war was not fun. In that at least he spoke the truth. Admittedly, Van Dorn's raid had damaged the enemy severely, perhaps helped the defenders of Vicksburg. But she refused to believe the horsemen had played a more important role than the gunners and riflemen who fought the battle.

No wonder, she thought, that infantrymen were less than enamored with the cavalry.

A few days later her estimate of the raid was supported when Runcey Carr burst in with the news that the Yankee army was back. The blue-coats could be seen by telescope from the courthouse cupola. They were disembarking from their transports at Young's Point, on the western bank of the Mississippi, opposite the mouth of the Yazoo.

This time, Grant was with them. Somebody had recognized the stocky general in spite of his rumpled uniform. Grant, who had taken Fort Henry and Donelson, who had won at Shiloh, had his army digging in within sight of Vicksburg.

It was, Alex figured, exactly one month since the cavalry raid had pillaged Holly Springs. Now, Grant was just across the river.

That kind of persistence seemed coldly ominous.

· *14* ·

Loyal citizens of the United States faced a bleak winter in deep mourning. Sherman's repulse in the bayous of the Yazoo River, with 1700 casualties, seemed a smaller repetition of the terrible tragedy enacted, earlier that same month, in the east.

There, in Virginia, the latest Union general, Burnside, had lost his reputation and over 12,600 bluecoat soldiers. Moving the Army of the Potomac in an inept and bungling advance that wasted its vast numbers, Burnside had crossed the Rappahannock into Fredericksburg, and assaulted Marye's Heights. Robert E. Lee, with a firmly entrenched, competent army, needed little genius to shatter the Federal attack.

Both battles greatly encouraged the South. The gray armies had held, against odds, Marye's Heights and Chickasaw Bluffs, two elevations. There were mountains and ridges studded throughout the Confederacy, east and west, that could be equally fatal obstacles for Yankee invaders. Vicksburg, alone, was sprawled across a hundred hills.

From Richmond and Washington, the two Presidents anxiously watched the opposing generals commanding in the Mississippi valley. The officers were as unlike as their executives.

Lieutenant General John C. Pemberton, C.S.A., was an austere professional soldier, impeccably dressed, severe in manner. On the great river's western bank, at Young's Point, the cigar-smoking, taciturn Grant looked as if he slept in his uniform. The men had met once, been friendly enough, in Mexico. War had brought them to this second meeting to contend for Vicksburg.

Pemberton's orders were to hold the town. He scattered his forces from the Memphis-Charleston Railroad in the north to the batteries on Vicksburg's bluffs. They could be moved like chessmen to counter any enemy thrust. The delta country, bayous and swollen rivers, swampy terrain, helped this defense.

Grant intended to capture Vicksburg. He didn't yet know how; he would try any half-feasible plan. But he had come down the river to take this town, and he would not go back until it was done.

Grant had a phobia about retracing his steps.

TEMPE DIXON tossed a dampened cotton-wad into the flames of the campfire. The thick smoke from the smudge made a man cough, but it didn't seem to discourage the swarms of mosquitoes.

"That should help some," said Sergeant Tazewell, squatting on his hunkers alongside.

"Help us get lung fever," Jollibee said, coughing.

Lack Norris chuckled; he had been born on the fringe of this half-drowned terrain, felt its hardships less than the others. He said: "It's worse for them Yankee sailors. They dassn't light a blaze, and they ain't used to our salubrious climate."

Tempe stared balefully at his friend. His own dislike of the delta country had hardened to a numb, dogged hatred. At night a man slapped at unseen, buzzing insects; by day the gnats were visible cloud clusters, billowing from among the leaves like the tattered, hanging tendrils of Spanish moss.

For two months the gray riflemen had lived in mildew, marching and counter-marching from swamp to swamp. Their rations were green with mold an hour after supplies reached them; their lice-infested clothing was coming apart from constant dampness. There seemed no end to the dark, glossy jungles interlaced by mud-brown or clay-yellow rivers. Even the occasional, abandoned cotton plantations, soggy clearings, were a relief from the lush, steaming undergrowth.

"Salubrious for snakes," Tempe said, trying to quell a fear by mentioning it.

He had always been afraid of snakes, with an intensity that prevented him from telling harmless black from deadly cottonmouth. To see one coiled asleep made him queasy; to watch a reptile slither from a comrade's blanket gave him the trembling horrors. He was sure the mere touch of a slimy form would make him scream, disgracing himself before his fellow veterans. The size and number of snakes in this benighted landscape were as variable as the streams.

I have seen enough swollen creeks, Tempe decided, and stinking bayous to last a lifetime.

"At least this time," Lack said, "we were Johnny-on-the-spot. Not like at Fort Pemberton."

The others nodded in unison. They all knew their movements were dictated by the enemy's plans. Whenever anybody reported that the Yankee gunboats had steam up, gray soldiers throughout the delta country rolled their blankets into carryalls, and prepared to march. Through February the bluecoat army had kept probing along the Mississippi's eastern bank, well north of Vicksburg, trying to find a waterway that would carry troops around the defenses on the bluffs of the Yazoo River.

Tempe recalled their forced march the previous month. Grant had sent the ubiquitous Sherman, with Admiral Porter, to cut the levee at Yazoo Pass opposite Helena, Arkansas in an attempt to push his transports into the Coldwater and Tallahatchie Rivers. By the time Tempe's company of sharpshooters had splashed their way north to Fort Pemberton, its guns had driven Porter's ships back on the stalled transports.

"That Porter," said Jollibee, critically, "must be a real addle-pate. Why, back home, the First Lord would cashier an Admiral who tried such a fool stunt. He'd probably be court-martialled and shot."

"It's my fixed intention to do just that tomorrow."

"Do what, Lack?"

"Shoot Porter, English. Without benefit of court-martial." Lack grinned, patted his rifle stock. "Sure was a regular turkey shoot out there today. Fixed distance, bobbing targets and all."

"More like sitting ducks," the sergeant said. He threw up a hand, cocked his head, as a rifle cracked nearby.

The others stiffened, listening. Another sharp report, more distant, slapped across the insect hum. A third sounded like an echo. Then, the night was quiet again, except for the fire's green wood hissing.

"Some of the boys," Tempe said, "keeping the Yanks honest. You know, we're likely to be the first foot soldiers that ever captured a fleet."

"Don't count your chickens," Tazewell said.

"Hell, Sarge," said Lack, "they ain't going anywhere."

Jollibee grunted, said, "I just hope we don't have to chop down any more trees to make sure."

Tempe examined a blistered palm and agreed. In regiment strength the riflemen had pushed through to a branch of the Big Sunflower River to find the Yankee gunboat flotilla halted by a tangled barricade of felled trees. They had wasted no time grabbing axes to send more twisted cypress trunks and cottonwoods into the stream behind the enemy vessels.

Now Porter's ships were landlocked, blocked fore and aft. The Yankee crews were unable to clear a passage because it was worth a sailor's life to show his head. For two days, from snug, brush-concealed rests on the bank, the Confederate sharpshooters had riddled the gunboats.

"How in the world," asked Tempe, "did they ever get up here anyway?"

"Through Steel's Bayou, I reckon," Lack said, "to Deer Creek. But who cares? Be thankful for favors, Tempe. Here they are, stuck firm like flies in a saucer of molasses."

Jollibee said, "Tomorrow should do it. They must be running short of victuals, and a couple of those ships are beginning to look like colanders."

Tazewell shrugged. "Unless they got word out somehow."

"Word to who, Sarge?"

"Stands to reason, Lack, they didn't try this on their own. Even Porter ain't that harum-scarum. There must be a Yankee army back aways."

"Nobody got away with any message, Sarge."

"Maybe. Maybe not."

"If the Yank soldiers haven't arrived so far," said Tempe, reasoning, "they must be too far back to hear our rifles. And if they're that far back, getting them here won't be easy." He knew the difficulties of marching a sizable force through the terrain.

"Listen," Lack said, "I know this here river. Places the trees hang over it so low you can spit into the branches from a canoe. I'm surprised Porter got here with a single smokestack standing. But those big, clumsy transports ain't never going to make it."

"I hope you're right."

"I'm dead certain sure. We caught us a whole school of Yanks and tomorrow we start to haul in. Porter's got to give up, Sarge, or starve." Lack snickered, exploded into laughter. "Can you picture Grant's face when he hears he's lost his gunboats?"

"He'll be through," Jollibee said. "Finished. The Yanks can't mount an attack against Vicksburg without that flotilla."

Tempe saw that the magnitude of the prize within their grasp had them all awed. The North's river fleet, ironclads and tinclads, had been a scourge from the beginning; the Yankee warships had driven deep into Southern territory, demolished every Confederate naval vessel that opposed them, made a dozen ports untenable, and protected the water passages of the blue armies. The Lord, he thought, has delivered the Philistines into our hands. War still inspired apt reminders from his Bible-reading boyhood.

"Even if Porter scuttles them all," Sergeant Tazewell said, "they'll lose their strangle hold on the Mississippi. It'll be up for grabs again."

Big Taze, Tempe noticed, had trouble keeping elation out of his voice. Excitement was shining in every eye, like the reflected firelight. Lack's grin might have been painted in place; Jollibee kept toying with a loose button. Nobody wanted to sleep. The pickets guarding the stranded gunboats were probably more drowsy. Tomorrow's dawn promised a great victory, and waiting made them all restless.

Somewhere in the darkness a chuck-will's-widow, the Southern whippoorwill, wailed its piercing trill. The quartet listened in silence until Tempe mentioned the old superstition.

"That's bad luck, some say."

"Means a death," Tazewell agreed.

"For the Yanks," said Lack. "For the Yanks, that's all. Anyways, I've heard them a million-trillion times without no bad luck pestering me."

Jollibee spat into the fire. "You Rebels are a bunch of old wives," he said. The plump Englishman's smile softened the insult. He was the only one ever used that Yankee term of reproach. "But I'll admit that bird ain't no blooming nightingale."

Shivering, Tempe rubbed sleeve across forehead, smearing a feasting mosquito. He felt very strange, decided it was due to anticipation. Close to the fire he was sweating hot; away from the flames he seemed uncomfortably chill. He licked his dry lips, wished the night would end. This nervous, almost giddy, realization that the enemy was neatly trapped was a new experience.

The mid-March dawn was a bleary dilution of night in which the blackness above the treetops faded to desolate gray. An early breeze riffled through leaves and thickets, seemed discouraged by the heavy growth. Before the riflemen trudged to their positions the wind had died. In flat calm, while the sun mounted slowly through haze, the sharpshooters checked their weapons and snuggled into yesterday's pits.

Gazing down from the bank, Tempe found the scene almost unreal. The enemy ships were crowded into the backwater like logs in a lumber jam. Smoke curled from the funnels, leaked from the bulletholes that punctured them. The water under the hulls seemed the same color as the dirty armor plate. Only the vessels nearest the bank attempted to answer the Confederate fire; the others lay huddled and helpless, showing no more life than the limp flags at their sterns.

Crack. Crack. Crack-crack-crack.

All along the thicket-crested bank the rifles began to shoot with quickening tempo, rising to drumbeat roll as more marksmen joined the day's sport. The rattling drowned out the few Yankee muskets that spat back at their tormentors. At intervals a naval cannon, roaring defiance, sent a shell crashing among the trees, but even the gunners knew it was ineffectual.

Tempe glimpsed movement in the nearest pilot-house, fired at it. He saw his ball rip splinters from an already scarred window frame.

He grunted disgust at the miss, reloaded clumsily. His eyes were smarting, and he rubbed them, aware of intolerable heat burning through his body. It was funny, he thought, that the day had turned scorching this early. The shimmering waves that blurred the gunboats made him squint as he aimed.

"Tempe!" Sergeant Tazewell pounded his shoulder. "Look yonder."

"Where?" asked Tempe, with a suddenly thick tongue.

"No. Downstream. By those old Indian mounds. Near where we cut the trees behind Porter."

The sergeant's pointing finger didn't help. Tempe was unable to distinguish anything at that distance, could see only dark foliage wavering. His voice was strained. "What is it?"

"Yanks. See? There go their muskets."

"It's only a couple of companies," Lack Norris said. "They must be trying to keep us from cutting down more trees."

"Let's go help roust them out of there," said Tazewell. "Come on, lads."

Tempe stumbled along with the others, trying to keep up. His Enfield seemed very heavy now; his legs were surprisingly weak. He heard gunfire ahead, getting closer, recognized it as an infantry exchange.

Then, as he shook with chill his vision cleared. He saw the glinting line of bayonets, watched the bluecoat battle array charge, close-packed, from the woods.

"Couple of companies, hell," said Tazewell. "That's at least a brigade!"

"I know those boys on the left," Lack said. "They're Missouri. That's Sherman!"

The sergeant cursed in doleful agreement. "That red-bearded son of a bitch," he said, "got here after all. A lone regiment can't keep a corps from reaching Porter."

Tempe Dixon, overcome by weakness, stricken with disappointment, began to weep. They had lost the grand prize, the trapped flotilla! Sherman had arrived in time to rescue Porter, and they were helpless to prevent it.

Helpless, Tempe thought, in dazed despair. He made no noise, but the tears trickled down his flushed cheeks.

The ladies of Vicksburg, like others throughout the world, had thrilled to the tale of Florence Nightingale's work in the Crimea. Their own war gave them a chance to emulate the lady with the lamp, and what at first they lacked in efficiency they compensated by willingness. Some of the most sheltered learned nursing by trial-and-error; others, less adaptable, visited the bed-ridden soldiers daily, bearing fruit, dainties and calves-foot jelly.

Doctor George Randall made his own rules for tending the patients under his care at the hospital. The Catholic sisters, trained by rules, assisted at surgery, and nursed the more severely wounded. Matrons who had reared large families were chosen to attend the helplessly ill. Single girls, in Doctor Randall's wards, were only allowed to feed or dose the sick. The female slaves who accompanied their mistresses to the hospital willingly did the heavy work, the scrubbing and cleaning.

The fussy little physician made two exceptions to these rules. He knew that his daughter, Poll, was a capable, dependable nurse; he discovered that Alex Kittering was another. Both were given wider latitude, and more work, than the other unmarried volunteers.

"Pay the gossips no mind," Doctor Randall told the nuns. "Poll's been helping me since she could toddle. And Alex's a Kittering, a tough chip off old Joab. She pitched right in and nothing bothers her."

He was wrong about Alex. The girl nursed from a sense of duty, but hated every minute of it. A screaming patient made her nauseated; a death gave her nightmares. She hid her distress behind a smiling mask that reminded onlookers of her mother. The men on the pallets were Southern soldiers, stricken while fighting for the cause. Every afternoon, except Sunday, found Alex trying to ease pain or cheer spirits.

She nearly dropped the medication tray when she suddenly encountered Tempe Dixon. There was no warning. Alex turned from one bed to the next, and met his gaze.

"Tempe," she said, feeling her hospital smile tremble.

"Hello, Alex."

He looked, she thought, pitifully gaunt, burned haggard by fever. Tempe's eyes were sunken, and a stubble of beard made his pallor almost livid. Alex had not been working in this room for several days; her first reaction was the choking realization that he could have died, and she'd never have known.

"How—how long have you been here?"

"About three days," Tempe said, smiling. "The worst was over before they dragged me in."

His smile made her heart turn over. She put a hand on his brow, felt it was cool and moist. He sounded very weak but cheerful. Her own voice seemed a trifle loud.

"What was it, Tempe?"

"A touch of malaria."

Doctor Randall, making his rounds, paused as he heard the medical term. The rotund figure slumped wearily; the plump face seemed flabby. There were circles under the doctor's eyes, blood specks in his white

Vandyke, smudges on his hands. He wore a burlap apron to protect his broadcloth suit.

"You know this lad, Alex?"

"Yes, Doctor."

"Another case due to the miasms in the bayou country. But this one's out of danger. No complications but a touch of dysentery. No erysipelas or pneumonia."

"Thanks to you, Doctor," said Tempe.

"Nonsense. Nonsense." The doctor glared at his patient. "Might just as well thank your comrades. The damn fools doused him with turpentine, Alex."

"Turpentine?"

"That was Jollibee's idea," said Tempe with a feeble grin. "He'd heard about it somewheres."

"God deliver us," said Doctor Randall, "from all amateur physicians! Lay meddlers." He snorted, tugged his beard. "But I'll admit it didn't harm you. The fever was breaking when they brought you in."

Alex nodded her relief, knowing there were always more sick soldiers than wounded. She had learned that malaria and dysentery, the "camp fevers," were only too often assisted toward fatality by measles and scurvy. As every gunshot wound flirted with hospital gangrene, every disease seemed to invite pneumonia.

"Whisky and quinine, Doctor?" she asked, naming the standard remedies for malaria.

"Just whisky now, Alex. It's more plentiful than drugs. Not that this one used any great amount. A little opium for the dysentery. He never reached the butterfly root and sanquinara stage."

"Silk weed root in the whisky, Doctor?"

"I'll take it straight, Alex," said Tempe.

"Let him. Let him." The doctor smiled at Alex. "You remembered, eh? What I prescribed for your father. But it didn't help until I added phytolacca to the mixture. That pinch of poke's what set Stephen on his feet."

"Doctor," said Alex, "if Tempe's nearly well, could I—we—take him home?" She knew that Joab kept a store of quinine in the house, a staple for recurring bouts of fever. It was customary now in Vicksburg for families to take in walking wounded and convalescents. The practice relieved the overcrowded hospitals. "We have plenty of room with Clay away."

"I wouldn't want to be any bother," Tempe said. He was torn between the desire to escape the depressing hospital odors and the fear that Alex's proximity would make life difficult.

"You won't be," said Alex.

[155]

"What about old Joab?" asked Randall.

"Grandpa likes Tempe, Doctor. He'd be the first to agree."

"Well." The doctor fumbled with Tempe's wrist, found the pulse. He took out a hunting-case watch, flipped up the lid, and stared into space, lips moving as he counted. "All right," he said, at last. "Speak to Mother Dolorosa. Tell her I give permission to move him. Keep him on low diet for a couple more days."

"Yes, Doctor."

"Low diet," said Tempe. "That's milk and rice. I'd as soon lie down and let the moon shine in my mouth."

"You'll do as you're told," Doctor Randall said. "Now, excuse me, Alex. I've a gangrene waiting for musket balls to be melted to make sulphide of lead." He hurried away, coat tails aflutter, heels clacking.

Alex supervised Tempe's removal to Cherry Street. She brought Benjie to the hospital to shave the patient; Martin, the coachman, helped chair-carry Tempe to and from the Kittering barouche. Far from objecting Joab approved the transfer, showed an interest that was alertly pleased. Even Epie Mae and Stephen, humoring the old man's good mood, were politely cordial to their daughter's charge.

For Tempe, the next ten days were a luxurious change. He had a wide, four-poster bed, with down mattress and linen sheets. Three slaves waited on him. Big Sarah and Mimosa took turns nursing him; Benjie acted as barber and valet. He only wished his father could see him living planter-style.

His health improved rapidly. He progressed from the low diet through the half diet of soup and toast to the full diet of beef, corn bread and greens. After that he had real meals, cooked to a turn, too rich and satisfying to be insulted by the word "diet." There were even delicacies—ripe strawberries in cream, hot biscuits, figs in molasses syrup, fresh eggs.

"If Lack Norris ever finds out," Tempe told Alex, "he'll make himself sick just thinking about such food."

"You need filling out," Alex said.

The girl still spent her afternoons at the hospital, but the other day-time hours belonged to Tempe. She took pleasure in watching his strength and color return, felt a maternal joy when he began to sit up in an armchair. Alex would have denied any emotion stronger than friendship, but she rushed home to talk to him.

Joab Kittering took his granddaughter's place when she was away. He sat with Tempe for long periods of amiable discussion, smoking and drinking whisky. The old man spoke of many things—books, business deals, the great steamboats, his past. He also managed, without prying, to learn a goodly amount of Tempe's background. Lucius Dixon, Joab thought, sounded like a man he would understand.

Once, Joab had an argument with Alex over the merits of Scuppernong wine. Tempe listened with delight as the two Kitterings bridged the intervening generations with crisp debate. It was obviously an old game which both enjoyed. The anger was pretended; the insults were friendly.

"Scuppernong bilge," said Joab, disparagingly. "I'd as soon drink Lubin's Extract Perfume."

"Listen at the connoisseur."

"Georgia grapes that ain't fit to eat."

"They make a nice, aromatic wine."

"Stuff tastes like plums."

"It'll be good for Tempe."

"What's the matter with bourbon?"

"There are other drinks, you old reprobate."

"Doctors give whisky for malaria, not Scuppernong wine!"

"Tempe's over his malaria!"

"Then, why cause a relapse?"

To settle matters Tempe drank the wine, thought it palatable, but not in a class with bourbon. Both debaters claimed victory.

Not until Tempe was able to come downstairs to bask, bundled, in the sunshine, did Joab mention the war. In the early Southern spring the garden was redolent with honeysuckle and roses. The old man didn't rant or criticize; the gruff voice was friendly.

"You'll be going back to the war in a couple days, Tempe. But you should be thinking beyond it. There'll be a sight of picking-up to do after this thing's over—whoever wins or loses. I probably won't live to see it, but you're young. You should have plans."

"It's hardly the time, Mister Kittering."

"I don't agree, son. *I* have plans. There's the warehouse full of cotton and sundries down to the riverfront. There's my two steamboats, the *Tonica* and the *Chickasaw* chafing at their moorings, but Runcey makes sure the engines don't rust too bad. Those things are assets, and they'll still be assets when peace comes. Specially the steamboats."

"Yes, sir," said Tempe, thinking, in the quiet, flower-scented air, that peace belonged to the nebulous distant future.

"But somebody has to run things, Tempe. I won't last forever. My son isn't interested in business. Neither was Clifton. I had high hopes for young Clay; he's quick, but I'm afraid war has spoiled him. He's joined the cavalry—the good-time cavalry—for life. That leaves me and Runcey Carr. A youngster and a gaffer."

"You've years yet, sir."

"Maybe, Tempe. Maybe. But some days I sure wish Alex had been a boy. I don't suppose you'd go along with that?"

"No, sir," said Tempe slowly, "I can't rightly say that I do." Whether gratitude or illness undermined his defenses, the simple speech betrayed his love.

He glanced, met Joab's level gaze, realized the old man knew how he felt. Tempe drew a deep breath, and waited, bracing himself against sympathy or advice. He wondered how to escape the discussion without rudeness. Alex was engaged to Bryce Furlong.

Joab merely sighed, and shook his head. He could not interfere; there were some areas in a girl's life where even a meddling grandfather had no place. Alex's choice was her own. There was no sense in making sorrowful noises because Tempe might get hurt.

"Anyway," he said, changing the subject, "slavery as an institution is finished. I know we scoffed at Lincoln's Emancipation Proclamation as a scrap of paper only enforceable by bayonets. But it did its work, Tempe. Now, the South stands alone. No government in Europe will support us on that issue."

"We don't need them, sir."

"Not yet, son, but it'll get lonelier with every passing week. Oh, our slaves are loyal; they'll stick to the end, barring a few malcontents. Most folks in the North can't understand that, any more than my neighbors around here understand that the nigras are bound to be free eventually. Bond or free, the poor blacks have no say in making war, or waging it."

"My family never owned slaves, sir," Tempe said. "I'm fighting for Mississippi's right to leave a Union she freely joined."

"A lawyer's argument," Joab said, "pleaded on the battlefield instead of in a courtroom." The wide shoulders lifted in a weary shrug. "But that's all beside the point. I grow garrulous with the years. Plan ahead, Tempe. Plan for the days of victory—or defeat."

Tempe's nod was polite, but unconvinced. The old man meant well, he thought, but he was a civilian. No soldier planned beyond the next meal, the next skirmish. If a man considered defeat inevitable, the logical move was desertion. You could only forget logic and fight to win.

He saw no future for himself that contained Alex Kittering. No other kind seemed worth bothering his head about.

That evening Tempe sat at the dinner table for the first time. He wore a clean uniform, dead Clifton's extra one, that Alex had wheedled from her mother, and Andrew's skilled needle had stitched to a decent fit. The polished buttons, the neat, unpatched gray cloth made Tempe feel self-conscious. Even with the braid removed, the new butter-yellow chevrons showed that the tunic didn't rightly belong on a veteran rifleman.

The family, following a code of hospitality that treated all guests with courtesy, ignored the soldier's initial awkwardness. Alex, thinking he

[158]

looked very smart, was pleased by his table manners, annoyed at herself for noticing. Joab drew him into the conversation, and Stephen, conscious of his rank, contributed patriotic platitudes. If Epie Mae, gazing at the uniform, was reminded of Clifton, she displayed no emotion.

Still, Tempe was glad when the meal ended. The food, the linen, the silverware, candlelight and servants, were a world away from corn pone wolfed around a campfire. He was fit again, belonged in the field with Lack, Taze and Jollibee.

After supper Joab clumped upstairs to bed. Stephen, on night duty, departed for headquarters. Epie May stayed in the parlor with the young people for a while, chatting aimlessly, until the butler summoned her away with a whispered question about some housekeeping problem. She had no qualms about leaving her daughter alone with the young soldier. It never entered Epie's mind that a girl engaged to a Furlong would look at another man.

She left an uncomfortable silence behind. Tempe stared at the rosewood piano as if admiring its polish. Alex twisted a handkerchief, suddenly tongue-tied.

They had enjoyed many talks, sharing laughter and knowledge, while he recuperated. Now, without warning, they seemed to have run out of topics. Neither realized they had reached saturation point in discovering each other's likes, dislikes, feelings and opinions. They were standing on a threshold that led to a more intimate subject than friendly discourse.

Then, both spoke at once, and the questions collided.

"Do you play, Alex?"

"Would you care for a drink?"

Alex laughed, and relaxed. This, she thought, was safe ground, requiring no emotional involvement. She said, "You first."

"I'm not thirsty, and you've never mentioned that you played the piano."

"I'm not very good, Tempe. I haven't touched the keys in months." Alex spoke frankly, without coyness. Somehow, with all her skill at parlor palaver, she never felt it necessary to pretend with Tempe. "You may find my playing a trial."

"I'll take that chance."

"Gambler," said Alex.

She moved to the Pleyel's bench, sat down, automatically massaging her fingers. For an instant she recalled, with dismay, the last time she had played for a Confederate soldier in this room. The dreadful war had seemed a gallant tournament then, and Bryce Furlong a knight-errant. It was only a year ago, but she had been so young, starry-eyed with romance, plighting her troth to Bryce and the South.

Trying to reject that memory, Alex plunged into the rollicking melody of "Camptown Races." The tune gave her a chance to cover mistakes with noise, to work the stiffness from her hands. But its joyous tempo sounded false.

Too gay, she thought as she finished. Too brisk for us this evening. Anxious to please, she shifted, without pause, to hymns that Tempe would recognize, the familiar strains of "Old Hundredth" and "Lead, Kindly Light." A glance at his face showed him listening with a smile that made her blood race.

Tempe was stirred, strangely touched. Alex was playing for him alone, and the hymns seemed to solemnize the occasion. He paid no attention to the swiftly moving fingers, gazed at the bent, flushed face, the magnolia-white bosom revealed by the low-cut blue brocade gown. That shadow-clefted expanse, made tremulous by the girl's exertions as she leaned over the keyboard, roused no lust in Tempe. He was enthralled by music and beauty.

God, he thought, how splendid!

Alex felt his mood, shared it. She tried one of Chopin's easier pieces, aware that she had never played better. That led her into Gottschalk, the native composer, the pride of the Southland. She guessed this music would be new to Tempe, was curious to see how he would react.

Tempe met her gaze with a slow, appreciative nod. The unfamiliar airs seemed even more fitting than the hymns. They took him to a strange, unexplored land where only Alex belonged. Surely, these moments would remain indelible in his memory.

Then, he held his breath as the girl began to sing.

> The years creep slowly by, Lorena,
> The snow is on the grass again;
> The sun's low down the sky, Lorena,
> The frost gleams where the flowers have been;
> But the heart throbs on as warmly now
> As when the summer days were nigh;
> Oh, the sun can never dip so low,
> Adown affection's cloudless sky.

The popular ballad and its soft accompaniment closed the concert. Alex sat with bowed head, not seeing the black-and-white lattice of the ivory keys. The hush in the room held her like an enchanted spell. She was grateful for Tempe's silence; any sound might destroy the magic.

"Alex," said Tempe, at last. "Alex." His voice was very low, unnaturally strained. He could find no other words, spoke his love by repeating her name. "Alex."

The girl drew a breath, turned. She knew what he meant, welcomed

[*160*]

it. Her mind whirled, spun by her quickened heartbeat. She had kissed this man once, for Christmas, on impulse, to erase earlier quarrels before he risked death. She had tended him, helped him back to health. Now, happily, her only thought was that he loved her.

"Yes, Tempe," she said, and held out her hand.

It was her left hand and the diamond caught candlelight. The sudden flash struck Tempe like a blow. He blinked, swallowed, stepped back. The engagement ring, Bryce Furlong's ring, shocked him sober.

Alex read his face, clapped a palm over her ring. It was a futile gesture, too late. Her whisper was almost a moan.

"Oh, Tempe."

"Good—good night, Alex," said Tempe. "Thank you for the music." He had to flee; if he stayed he would blurt out his love. She was, he guessed, not unwilling to listen, intoxicated, like himself, by melody. But she was also Bryce Furlong's fiancée.

"Please, Tempe."

Tempe ignored the plea. Stay-at-homes, safe behind the lines, had stolen girls from fighting men since the days of David and Uriah, but it was a sneaky, dirty trick. Tempe Dixon couldn't do it, wouldn't try. He was a soldier with a hard learned code. Kill or be killed was fair; filching was a necessity. Only a coward stole from a comrade, behind his back, in the face of danger.

I almost did, thought Tempe, and looked at Alex with longing. He didn't like Bryce Furlong, right now he hated him, but the man was out there somewhere tonight, maybe riding against the enemy. While Tempe Dixon, well fed in fine linen, betrayed him.

"Good night, Alex," he said, again, and left the room with swift, abrupt strides.

Alex stared after him, frustrated but understanding. She, too, had been trained by contemporary standards. A word was not given lightly, nor easily broken. The conventions surrounding a formal engagement were almost as strict as those about marriage. Nobody cared if a belle was engaged a dozen times before the match was announced and approved, but once acknowledged there were rules. Bryce had his faults but he didn't deserve to be jilted while he was off fighting.

She clutched the ring so fiercely that the prongs of the setting dug into her palm. Tears stung her eyes, but she tried to weep soundlessly.

"We are all," Alex said, sniffling, "so damn noble!"

· 15 ·

VICKSBURG'S INHABITANTS, black and white, considered the Yankee army across the river at Young's Point the daftest besiegers in history. The Federal cannon were too far away to harm the town; the blueclad troops were too helplessly mired to make any sudden, threatening moves.

The Union encampment had few secrets from the watchers on the opposite bluffs. Everyone knew at once when the Yank engineers tried to build a canal across the hairpin bend that jutted into the mighty stream. It was obvious that Grant wanted to use this means of floating his transports past the Vicksburg batteries beyond cannon range. The slaves chortled with glee to see so many white soldiers digging in muck with pick and shovel. The Confederate gunners, grinning, shifted and sighted their big guns to enfilade the canal, confident they would blast the clumsy transports out of the water.

Before the ditch was half-finished, the Mississippi, as if annoyed by such liberties, rose in a roaring freshet that destroyed the labor of weeks, drowned equipment, and sent men scampering for safety. In taverns and parlors, behind sheds in slave-quarters, the town's drinkers toasted that tumbling yellow flood, wagered it would wash away the enemy tents it now surrounded. What did those Northern boys from prairie states know about building proper levees anyhow? That old Mississippi River sure slapped them back in place!

Spies brought information that rumor inflated to grotesque proportions. The blue-bellies were suffering from a dozen virulent "camp fevers." Smallpox was rampant; Yankee regiments were dying by companies, and the remnants were too sick to fight. There was dissension among the generals, despair in the rank-and-file. Grant was drinking heavily again.

Northern newspapers, still available by telegraphed digests from the east, confirmed some of these rumors. The congressmen of the old government were blaming the Union commander with outraged cries. But Vicksburg learned, and cherished, one tidbit not printed in the press. Grant had lost his false teeth when a careless servant emptied a washbowl!

The resulting laughter diminished the man's stature, lessened his menace. Runcey Carr expressed the town's opinion to Tempe Dixon in a single sentence.

"Poor ole Grant bit off more than he could chaw, and now he can't chaw at all!"

"Maybe," Tempe said. "Maybe, Runcey. But don't skin that coon just 'cause he's treed. Whenever we figure we've got that feller whipped to a frazzle, he perks up and starts a-coming. And he keeps a-coming and a-coming!"

"Boy," said Runcey, shifting his tobacco-cud to one cheek while he drank, "what's biting you? You sure are mister gloom hisself these days."

Tempe admitted it with a frown, swishing the whisky in his glass. They were sitting in Jump MacGregor's place, and he wished he was somewhere else. Neither the liquor nor the gambling helped him forget; the banjos sounded tinny and the raucous laughter grated.

He had left the Kittering house to report for duty, expecting to return to the sharpshooters. But a pimply-faced callow lieutenant-doctor fresh from the board of medical examiners at Tupelo decreed otherwise. The stripling had some fool notion that a man just over malaria should stay away from the bayou vapors for a while.

"My squad's on the Yazoo," Tempe had said in protest.

"Worst place for you, Corporal."

"But I'm a rifleman, a sharpshooter."

"Fine! We can use you guarding the river batteries."

"But—"

"Report to Colonel Higgins' aide at the Cowan house."

"I want to go back to my outfit!"

"Corporal, haven't you been in the army long enough to learn to obey orders?"

"Yes, sir," Tempe had said.

He had, Tempe thought morosely, been in the army a damn sight longer than that pipsqueak doctor. This fact, of course, impressed no one in authority. His repeated requests to be sent back where he belonged collected dust on an adjutant's desk through the first warming weeks of April while he paced a post as sentry. At the racecourse battery, too, the southernmost Vicksburg gun emplacement, where not even field glasses could spot hide or hair of a single bluecoat.

Tempe had fretted through the days, anxious to leave town before he encountered Alex Kittering. He couldn't enjoy easy duty in a place where she might turn the next corner. Runcey told him the family had not left for Tonica Hill.

Their parting had been polite and painful, an interview that included the girl's parents and grandfather. Tempe had not been alone with Alex since the night she played the piano, had seen her once, in the distance, after leaving Cherry Street. He was sure this careful avoidance was correct behavior, and even surer that it made him miserable.

"You ought to be cakewalking for joy," Runcey said. "You got the orders you wanted, didn't you?"

"Finally," Tempe said. He measured the depth of his drink, drained it with a toss. Quiet persistence had prodded officialdom into action; tomorrow he left to join Taze and the others at Haines Bluff. "It took them long enough."

"Well, for God's sake," Runcey said, "act a little happy about it." He snapped his fingers at a waiter, gestured to order another round, spat a brown jet neatly into the nearest spittoon. "This ain't no place to be crying in your liquor."

"Who's crying?" Tempe asked, harshly. He had no intention of confiding his troubles to Runcey. The boy was precocious, but he'd never understand that Alex Kittering was different. Now that he had attained his wish to leave, Tempe was convinced he would never see Alex again.

"You ain't laughing," said Runcey.

"What's funny?"

"Look a-here, Tempe. Drinking bourbon is as tricky as playing in Jump's poker game. When you're up, winning, it lifts you. When you're down, losing, it kicks you."

And at your age, thought Tempe, you shouldn't be downing it. Runcey's presence and capacity raised no eyebrows among Jump Mac-Gregor's customers. Tonight, like himself, they were mostly off-duty soldiers seeking diversion with liquor and cards.

Tempe glanced around at the crowded tables, noted, with satisfaction, that every pot held heaps of crumpled Confederate bills. Jump's own game was no exception; the portly gambler raked in chips and paper money with equal aplomb. There was not much coin in evidence, and, with the South's dollar now worth less than fifty cents, the bets seemed tremendous.

"You ain't thinking of playing, Tempe?"

"No, Runcey. Once bitten."

The boy nodded, with relief. Runcey had revised his opinion of Jump's honesty. The proprietor wouldn't deal from the bottom, if watched, nor welch on a wager before witnesses. Tempe would be a lamb among wolves bucking any game in the house.

A commotion at the doorway drew their attention. Smasher, the doorman, was arguing with a tall, bearded captain. Massed behind the officer were gray uniforms and bayonet-topped rifles. The loud voices penetrated the smoky room, quelled other noises, brought irritated glances from the most preoccupied gamblers.

Tempe rose to his feet when he saw the bayonets. Runcey's question was a quick whisper.

"What is it?"

"Provost guard."

The captain pushed past Smasher, raised his voice to a shout. "Gentlemen! Your attention, please!" He waited, thumbs hooked in gun belt, until the room was quiet, ignoring Jump MacGregor's falsely cordial invitation.

"Step right in, Captain. No trouble here."

"All officers and men," the captain roared, "of the Confederate army are to report to their posts immediately! On the double! Invalids on passes are to return to their quarters. By order of the general."

Hubbub and bustle made the cigar smoke swirl as soldiers grabbed money, and cashed chips. The mulatto cashier, Floyd, appeared at his employer's elbow to count bills into outstretched hands. Jump detached himself from such sordid matters by pushing back his chair, snipping the end from a cigar with a cutter. His bland countenance wore the look of a resigned Buddha.

Tempe and Runcey joined those clustered around the provost captain, asking questions. The man ignored the inquisition with stiff dignity; even his beard seemed to bristle.

"What's up, Captain?"

"Are the Yanks coming?"

"Is it an attack?"

"What's all the fuss about?"

"Just obey orders," said the captain. He nodded to his men, who began a familiar, contrapuntal chorus.

"Come on, boys. Move out. Move out."

"Get cracking there, soldier."

"Don't stand in the doorway."

"Shuffle along, fellers."

A quiet authoritative Georgia voice made itself heard. "Wait a little minute, Mannion. You must have some idea what's going on."

Tempe grinned at the captain's startled apology.

"Oh. Sorry, Colonel. I didn't see you, sir."

"You see me now, son. Elucidate."

"Word's come down from the Yazoo," said the captain. "The Yankees are massing ships up beyond Young's Point. It looks like they might try to run past our batteries."

"Wow!" cried Runcey Carr. "We'll smash them to flinders."

"Let's hope so, boy," the Georgia colonel said as he pushed out the door.

Tempe and Runcey followed. The night air felt cool after the stuffy gambling hall. Their eyes were still adjusting to the moonless dark when they heard the cannonade begin. From the northern outskirts of the town came the slam-slam of the big rifled guns; the distant reports clanged, flat and clear.

"There goes Fort Hill," said Runcey. "The Yanks are really going to try it."

"Seems as if," Tempe said. He wondered what desperation had driven Grant to such a hazardous gamble. Ironclad warships might make it past the batteries, but the transport steamboats were slow, unarmored craft. "They must be fever-raving."

"Farragut did it."

"Not in the face of the guns we have now. Every transport we sink will cost them about a thousand or more men."

"Good riddance," Runcey said, cheerfully. "You aim to report somewheres, Tempe?"

"To Haines Bluff sometime tomorrow after I hoof it out there. I'm not part of Vicksburg's garrison now."

"Then, come on! Let's get a front-row seat!"

"Hell, Runcey, I'm not even armed. I stashed my Enfield under your bed."

"It's safe there. Come on!"

As they raced through the shadows along the uneven waterfront street, aware of other dim, scurrying figures, the cannon-thunder became louder; they could see far-away flashes reflected like heat lightning against the murky sky to the north. Tempe thought he could distinguish the bluff batteries from the enemy gunboats; the Yankee naval cannon, closer to the water, had a different sound.

They reached a stretch of river bank with a clear view in three directions. Skiffs were moored at the water's edge, unmoved by lapping wavelets. Without a moon the quiet, wide Mississippi was the color of dusty pewter, marbled with streaks of currents, smudged by eddies.

Glancing south, Tempe saw calm emptiness, a lake-like expanse as unruffled as a mirror. The low Louisiana bank, directly across from him, was a ragged, dark furrow between stream and sky. But, to the north, was panorama and pandemonium.

"Holy me beads," said Runcey, with awe.

"Amen," Tempe said.

The Yankee ships, toy boats at that distance but black on the dull water-sheen, were hugging the far shore as much as channels permitted. The leading gunboats were fighting, firing broadsides that lit the river with vivid yellow flares. Shells burst above the spark-flecked funnels; water-spouts spurted up like midget fountains. From the northernmost Confederate batteries came an increasing flash-and-slam as if the bluffs themselves were spitting volcanic flames.

"This way," yelled a voice.

Footsteps pounded toward them, and gray uniformed men plunged out of the surrounding darkness. Tempe, surprised, stared at the oars they carried as they swarmed around the tied skiffs. Runcey recovered his speech first.

"Who's that?"

"Volunteers for DeSoto."

"DeSoto?" Tempe glanced across the river, guessed at the position of the town on the opposite bank. No lights showed from DeSoto.

"That's right," drawled the speaker, evidently the officer in command. He wore a sidearm, called a casual order. "Don't take any scow that leaks, boys."

"What's in DeSoto?" asked Runcey.

"Houses. We aim to burn them."

A soldier chuckled as he cast aside a mooring line. He said, "So's our gunners can see the Yankees better."

Runcey clapped his hands, jigged in excitement. "Black Jack!" he cried. "Their ships'll be outlined against the blaze! Let's go along, Tempe!"

"You're sure welcome," said the officer.

"The more the merrier," another voice said gaily.

I'll just bet, thought Tempe, noting that there were more skiffs than volunteers. A quick count numbered the group at a dozen, or less. The river looked a mile wide, and the shooting, from bluffs and gunboats, would get nearer every minute. If there were Yankee troops in DeSoto, as seemed likely, they'd gobble up this foolhardy handful in two shakes.

"Come on, Tempe!" Runcey tugged at his sleeve as the first boat was launched. Another, closer, battery must have opened fire because they felt a slight vibration.

Before he could refuse Tempe found himself scrambling over a gunwale. The skiff rocked; somebody thrust an oar at him. He was seated on a thwart beside Runcey, rowing, before he realized what had happened.

Either recklessness was contagious, Tempe decided, or he'd consumed too much whisky. Here he was, a slipshod oarsman, in a small boat manned by crazy hellions who hadn't learned the veteran's rule about never volunteering. It would serve him right if he got himself killed.

When the shoreline blended back into the shadows he knew they were out on the open river, felt the current against the hull. The man rowing in front of him wore a major's leaf; his partner was a private. Steering in the stern was a scarecrow civilian in a riverman's visored cap.

"A motley crew," muttered Tempe. The oar handle nearly bucked from his grip as he caught a crab.

"Watch it!" Runcey said. "Take the beat from me."

Tempe obeyed, cursing under his breath. He followed the stroke more carefully, moving back and forth, back and forth, until the steady rhythm became automatic. The gray water splashed white when the blades dipped; they seemed to be moving pretty fast.

He couldn't really blame Runcey's eagerness for getting them into this madcap venture. Nothing short of violence would have kept the boy ashore, but he was too river-wise to need a guardian. Tempe grudgingly admitted that his own feeling for Alex Kittering was the true emotional percussion-cap.

Melancholy had tricked him into seeking relief through action. Although he hadn't recognized it until now even the danger had been a lure. Risk had a fascinating attraction to a man with his nose out of joint.

Gritting his teeth, aware that his palms were beginning to smart, Tempe saw that the helmsman was staring upriver. He growled an unspoken wish that the fathead watch their course.

Then, he glanced over his shoulder in the same direction, and gasped.

They were past mid-stream, and the enemy flotilla, bearing down on them, was about a half-mile away. Tempe could see the white prow-plumes of the leading gunboat, blinked as its cannon roared, illuminating hull and water in lurid glare. A shell burst above another ship; the instant of explosion outlined the twin chimneys in stark silhouette.

From the Vicksburg bluffs flame-streaks darted in continuous, thrusting bursts that split the dark mass of the hills asunder, here, there, high, lower, scattered widely, crammed together. The sky, thick with rolling clouds of powder smoke, gleamed from the firelight, and the river reflected the sky. Thunderclap ripped across crashing thunder in the cannonade's loud fury.

"Goddam it, Tempe," cried Runcey. "Row!"

Tempe rowed, feeling guilty. He kept his gaze on the major's collar, irrelevantly noticing that the officer needed a hair trim. Tempe's hands burned, his arms tired and his back ached, but he didn't miss another stroke.

It seemed to take forever before they scraped against pilings, climbed out onto a rickety pier. A sergeant dispensed torches, soaked cotton wads, reeking of turpentine, nailed to wooden handles. Holding one to a matchflame Tempe was pleased by the evidence of planning. It took the spur-of-the-moment foolishness from their sortie.

The men scattered, without orders, to spread arson. Runcey, waving his flaming torch, raced from the pier, whooping like a drunken Indian. Tempe, following, figured they all must resemble raiding Comanches, but he was glad the cannon-thunder drowned out the boy's war cry.

Without the Enfield, the sharpshooter felt almost naked, hoped they wouldn't meet a Yankee patrol.

"The best I could do," Tempe said, aloud, "is throw my hat at them."

DeSoto's waterfront was deserted, abandoned. The burning took very few minutes. Tempe helped Runcey kick in a boarded shop window, found carpenter's shavings that started a roaring blaze. They passed on to a fisherman's shack that caught like tinder.

By that time the little town's whole river bank was a wall of flame from ferry house to slave shanty. The raiders threw their torches into the conflagration, and gathered on the end of the pier to escape the blistering heat.

Tempe gazed on a Mississippi River which was a stage for a procession with fireworks. The Vicksburg waterfront had been put to the torch, too; he could see the flickering orange-yellow hedge beneath the bluffs, a different hue, a steadier glow, than the blazing batteries on the hill-crests. The Yankee fleet, running this fiery gauntlet, was strung out in column as it passed. He counted six gunboats, three transports, a string of barges.

He recognized the *Benton*, leading the way. There was no mistaking the long, black shape of that ugly, humpbacked sternwheeler. She was rocked by her own fire, by the waterspouts, tall as her funnels, that erupted from Confederate fire, but she plowed steadily down the river.

"They're going to make it," Tempe said.

Runcey nodded glumly, then crowed as a Yankee transport was hit. The ship exploded into flame, started to sink as the cotton bales strung along her rails for protection caught. Sailors, stripped to the waist, dived through that flaming rim to the river.

Tempe said, "No soldiers on that, just crew. They sent the transports down empty."

"Dirty sneaks," Runcey said.

The enemy vessels slid past, one after another. A tattered wake was still visible in front of Tempe when the last churned out of range of the southernmost Vicksburg battery. In the sudden quiet the flame-crackle sounded very loud. It had been a good hour, Tempe judged, since the first cannon slammed.

They rowed back to Vicksburg in silence, moving from ruddy glow through cool gray midstream to ruddy glow. The thole-pins creaked a doleful plaint.

The riverman at the steering oar put it into words. He spat tobacco juice over the side, gazed up at the hundred hills, and spoke.

"I reckoned them batteries would stop them, but they swept right on by. Man only proposes. You can't stop the rampaging Mississippi either, no matter how you build the levee."

When the bombardment started Emilie Verrier's party was in full swing. The provost guard had not reached the place, and the first intimation that the enemy ships were trying to pass came from the cannon.

It was neither a large party, nor a special occasion. In convivial Vicksburg, one never needed a reason for a social gathering that included cards and buffet, pleasant conversation and mild flirtations. The Verriers, in particular, were noted for these small, civilized entertainments. Emilie, the hostess, reared on vaguely recalled tales of Madame de Staël, believed she presided over a *salon* when she invited guests to a *soirée*.

This *soirée* ended abruptly with playing cards scattered on tables and carpet, food barely touched, empty glasses everywhere, and the punch bowl half full. Officers hurriedly departed, herding their wide-skirted charges before them. Only the combined efforts of the four girls who had planned to stay the night kept Henri Duchesneau in attendance.

"You can't leave us here alone, Henri," said Poll Randall.

"Even the servants have vanished," Clara Furlong said.

"But, yes!" Emilie said, giggling. "You all saw how Maurice bolted at the first shot. He is major-domo, and when he panics, the whole household has hysterics. By this time every black on the place is huddled under beds in the slave-quarters."

Alex Kittering filled a glass with punch, handed it to the Creole lieutenant. She said, practically, "You are more needed here, Henri, than crowding the telegraph office."

"True," said Henri. "How many men does it take to send messages that the bluecoats are trying to run the batteries?" He raised his glass, contemplated the strawberry floating in the drink, and sipped. His lips moved as he savored the spiced mixture of white wines. Only the Verriers, he thought, still have a few bottles of true French vintages. "But this will be one magnificent artillery duel and—"

"At least stay," Emilie said, "until Mama and Papa have returned. They are off the hill, down in the town visiting."

"And you needn't miss your artillery duel," Alex said. "There's a fine view from Emilie's dining room."

Both remarks bothered Henri. They reminded him that the house was in a very exposed position. He smiled back at the attractive quartet, pleased that for once duty and beauty were combined. For a certainty he could not leave them in a place that might be dangerous.

"Please stay," said Poll Randall.

"I would be charmed," Henri said, truthfully. They were four very pretty girls, probably the handsomest group in town. He had canvassed Vicksburg's belles like a candidate seeking election, and these won the *cordon bleu*.

As he followed the girls into the candlelit dining room, carrying the punch bowl, the lieutenant admired their costumes.

Blonde Poll wore cerise silk trimmed with white point; dark Emilie was dazzling in pearl brocade. Clara's plump curves were tightly stayed beneath emerald velveteen, and Alex's chestnut hair was flattered by her gold-beribboned gown of Confederate gray.

"You are not frightened, eh?" asked Henri, ladling wine into the glasses.

"After Farragut?" Alex said. She shook her head.

"We've been under shellfire before," said Poll.

Clara nodded agreement, and Emilie shrugged. All the girls considered themselves hardened veterans tempered by experience. They had lived through the days when the Federal navy shelled their town, recalled the whine and blast of mortar fire. Surely, this time there was even less cause for fear. The Yankees had fewer ships; Vicksburg had many more cannon.

They crowded around the high French windows that faced the Mississippi, pushed aside lace curtains to peer north through the moonless night. Already they could see gun-flash and shellburst lighting sky and river like a festive firework display.

"It is exciting, *n'est-ce pas?*" said Emilie. She made a fussy ritual of clinking her glass against the others, raised it high. "To the destruction of our enemies!"

"On our river," Clara cried.

"Let them sink or swim," Poll Randall said.

Alex drank without comment. The toast seemed bloodthirsty, though she shared her friends' confidence. Like the majority of Vicksburg's population, Alex believed that the bluff batteries—the heavy cannon imported and emplaced with such arduous labor—made the local stretch of Mississippi impassable.

Refilling the glasses, Henri Duchesneau hid his doubts behind gaiety. A trained artilleryman, he knew the difficulty of placing a mortal hit on a moving mark. The gunners would need luck as well as skill; sheer weight of metal might not overwhelm all the speeding ships.

He wished the girls wouldn't press so close to the window panes. This hill, lower than its neighbors, was within easy range of the Yankee gunboats.

Les Noyers, the Verrier house, was old, dating back to Newlet Vick's early settlement. The builder, Emilie's great-grandfather, wanting an estate, had purchased the whole hill well north of the pioneer community, and raised a New Orleans type structure on its summit. In fifty years the town spread to surround this isolation, but the Verriers sold no property. The family still took its meals in the long rear dining room that overlooked the river, so close to the bluff's edge that stables and slave-quarters were sprawled to one side. Only a narrow terrace, bedecked with fragrant wreaths of passion vine, separated the house's rear from the sheer drop to the waterfront.

"Here they come," Alex said, watching the black bulks on the silvery river take the shape of ships. In the spasmodic lurid flashes of gunfire she could see the smoke pouring from funnels, the cotton bales strung like fenders on a transport's sides.

Emilie, holding her glass in both palms, hiccuped into her wine. If the young Alabama couple invited as chaperones had stayed, she would not have been drinking so fast, but it was excitement that made her nervous.

"Double column," said Henri, "with the ironclads shepherding the transports, and the transports towing barges. There! That broadside! That's a gunboat."

The leading Yankee vessel looked the biggest. It was directly opposite them now, moving downstream at full speed. They could see the white wake churned by its armor-encased stern paddle-wheels.

Kee-rash!

Without warning the Confederate battery on the very next hill opened fire. Its guns loomed above the Verrier roof top, within shouting distance, and the concussion shook the house.

"Get back," cried Henri, as the windows rattled. One pane cracked with a sharp report.

"Goodness," said Poll Randall.

Clara, stumbling back, bumped Emilie. The hooped skirts swayed as the girls clutched each other to prevent a fall.

As she moved away, staring, Alex glimpsed twin waterspouts, like book ends, bracketing the Yankee gunboat fore and aft. Then, she blinked at the sudden flare of the answering broadside. A reddish-yellow curtain, smoke-speckled flame, erupted, hiding the ship's hull.

Henri's shout was lost in the cannon thunder. He neither heard nor saw the shell, but instinctively leaped between the girls and the windows.

The shell hit with a tearing explosion. It ripped across the roof, splintering shingles; ricocheting metal whined through the violent shudder that seemed to twist the house on its foundation.

Debris and bricks from the smashed chimney tumbled down into the fireplace, sent a cloud of dust billowing into the dining room. The cracked window pane jumped from its frame, shattered on the floor. This sound of breaking glass was echoed in miniature by Emilie's dropped drink.

"My God," she said, stunned. "My God."

"Let's get out of here!" Poll grabbed Henri's arm. "Get us away, Henri!"

Clara, whimpering, skirts lifted, was already scurrying through the doorway. The others rushed after her, jamming the portal, but Alex paused to blow out the candles. One, toppled from its holder, was smoldering on the carpet.

The action calmed her; she was more surprised than frightened. She walked, unhurriedly, through the parlor, pinching out candleflames as she passed. There's no sense, she thought, in letting the house burn down through carelessness.

"Alex, hurry!"

"Alex, come on!"

"She must be hurt! Henri, go back and—"

"I'm all right, Poll," called Alex. "I'm coming." She joined the group huddled on the front steps. Poll and Emilie were hanging onto Henri; Clara, fidgeting, was chewing her lips. They winced in unison when the nearby battery fired.

"We'll have to run for it," Henri said. "Stay together."

They scampered down the steps, skirts tucked above shoetops. The Verriers had a long, winding gravel driveway, but Henri hustled them across it. He steered them in a straight line over the front lawn, into the formal flower garden. In the darkness petals and leaves were equally colorless.

A shell whistled above them, coming closer.

"Down!" yelled Henri. He tried vainly to clasp the entire quartet in one embrace, ended by shoving at them indiscriminately.

They fell together in a jumbled welter of skirts, twisted hoops, flaring petticoats. Clara whimpered and Emilie squealed, but the rest panted as they waited.

Alex, face on her arms, tried to make herself small. She was vaguely aware that her clothes were very disordered, that her right knee smarted, that there was a scent of crushed jasmine in the air. Somebody's elbow prodded her ribs; another's weight pressed her shoulder.

The shell burst in a grove of walnut trees. They glimpsed the explosion, heard the charge slashing through the boughs.

"Up!" cried Henri. "*Run, mes amies!*"

Alex rose with a bound. A hand had patted the bare flesh at the back of her thigh, high under her petticoats! She whirled, scarlet with indignation, but the running foursome swept her with them.

As they pushed through bush and bramble, trampling flowers, tripping on vines, Alex's outrage dissolved. That was an accident, she thought. She could no more blame Henri than the thorns that caught and tore her gown. This pell-mell flight put safety above convention, or even modesty.

"Down!" shouted Henri above the screech of another approaching shell.

This time Alex tried to control her skirts as she dropped to the ground. A bush foiled her, twitched the hem loose, helped the bouncing hoops flip the garments to her waist. She twisted, flailed behind her, struck a cringing body.

"Ow!" said Clara.

Emilie giggled. Poll gasped, and said, "Henri!"

"Keep down," Henri said, busily pressing the girls flat. He was enjoying himself immensely. It wasn't every day that even Henri Duchesneau had a bevy of beautiful girls for a soft couch. Under the stress of circumstances he could fondle and pat with impunity, identify round curves by touch, even, at such close proximity, admire long, slim legs, totally exposed.

Vraiment, thought Henri, danger brought its blessings, and comforting the frightened its rewards.

The second shell crumped closer, cast its glare over the prone figures. Alex blushed to think what the bright light revealed.

"Up, girls! Run!" Henri, hands busy, helped his charges rise. He was not surprised when Alex pushed away his wrist. It was only proper for an engaged girl to have scruples, but at night all cats were gray.

They sprawled for cover once more at Henri's command. When this shell burst, high and farther away, Alex felt a deliberate pinch. She snarled, ready to scratch, but Henri's bland voice gave her an irresistible urge to laugh.

"Be calm, *mes amies.* Do not excite yourselves. I think it is over. A few more steps and you all are out of danger!"

They staggered into the nearest house, a bedraggled quintet. Henri's uniform was torn; the girls were smudged and disheveled. Alex, a petticoat trailing, hair a-tangle, thought all the gowns were hopelessly ruined. But her three friends had never looked more flushed, or more innocent.

Henri Duchesneau was the only man in Vicksburg who kept a pink garter-ribbon as a souvenir of the night when the Yankees ran past the batteries. He was never completely sure to whom it belonged.

16

The North, dazzled into pinning its hopes on a commander called "Fighting Joe" Hooker, watched the Army of the Potomac and paid little attention to events in the Mississippi valley.

The Confederate government, less hypnotized, and aware that Lee and Jackson, however skilful, were out-numbered in Virginia, glanced nervously over its shoulder toward Vicksburg. Jefferson Davis sent General Joe E. Johnston to find out what was happening down there.

By the time Johnston arrived a great deal had happened. While marching two corps of his army down the river's west bank, Grant had ordered a cavalry brigade south from LaGrange to create a diversion. These horse soldiers, under Grierson, rode through the state of Mississippi, razing and destroying, to emerge in Federal-occupied Louisiana. It was the most successful cavalry raid of the war.

Pemberton, in Vicksburg, receiving wild reports, almost believed that the elusive Yankee horsemen were the spearhead of a Union advance from the north. His conviction was strengthened when Sherman's bluecoats demonstrated up the Yazoo River on the last day of April. But, as Sherman feinted, Grant, using the transports that had run the batteries, ferried the rest of his army across the Mississippi.

Grant was supposed to wait for General Banks from Louisiana, but the latter wasn't ready. As he thrust northward, driving his troops between Pemberton and Joe Johnston at Jackson, Mississippi, Grant disregarded the sacrosanct military rule that an army was helpless without a supply base.

The Federal administration in Washington, stunned by Lee's brilliant victory at Chancellorsville, was scared stiff by Grant's move. Frantic telegrams advising caution arrived too late to stop the campaign.

Through heavy rains, along muddy roads, the Yankee troops raced north. They foraged the countryside, and ate well. Pemberton's probing vanguard, seeking to cut Grant's non-existent supply line, found nothing. The Confederates were beaten outside Port Gibson, and again near Raymond. Joe Johnston, with only 14,000 effectives, was driven out of Jackson.

Grant, then, swung his army around, marched on Vicksburg.

AFTER TWO DAYS of downpour the morning of May 16th, 1863, was clear and hot. Strung out with the other skirmishers in the tall grass bordering the rutted Raymond Road, Tempe Dixon had no time to think about the weather. The long-range riflefire exchange with the Yankee pickets was the heaviest he'd ever seen. At seven-thirty the blue-belly skirmish line had started shooting through the early mist, and the artillery, on both sides, had joined in before the haze was burned off the damp ground. The cannon and rifles made a continuous din that rose in volume to a steady, rattling crescendo.

Tempe, lying prone, fired at a distant bluecoat, and rolled on his side to reload. He was sandwiched between Lack Norris and Tazewell. The big sergeant mopped his face with a bare forearm, grinned.

"Hot, ain't it?"

"Sarge," said Tempe, "what the hell are we doing anyway?"

Behind him Lack's laugh was as sharp as a bark. "Iffen you got any doubts, Tempe, just stand up."

Tazewell hugged the ground as an enemy fusillade whipped through the grass. He said, "I reckon we're holding them, and they're sure holding us."

"At this range? Without anybody charging?"

"Seems as if," Tazewell said. He propped himself on his elbows, aimed, squeezed off a shot. "The live-long day," he said with resignation.

"The Yanks," said Lack, "ain't anxious to come at us over open ground. And we sure ain't going to do any charging when we're supposed to be pulling out."

"Pulling out?" Tempe twisted to stare at Lack. "Who says?"

"I says. That was the chat around Bowen's tent when Taze sent me back for breakfast rations this morning."

"But we only got here last night. The rain washing out that blasted bridge over Baker's Creek held us up two days."

"I'm just telling what I heard, Tempe. Some cavalry feller got through from Joe Johnston. Rode like blue blazes around the whole Yank army. Foundered his horse but brought a message to Pemberton. A major named Furlong."

"Furlong? You sure?"

"You know him?"

"Yes," said Tempe. "I know him." He kept his voice toneless, in grudging tribute to Bryce Furlong's achievement. The man could ride, and had courage. It was no mean feat for a courier to avoid the Yankee flankers.

"Well, anyway," Lack said, "Johnston wants us to pull back through Edwards Depot and link up with him somewheres north of the railroad." He cocked his rifle, turned on his stomach to shoot.

"Sarge?" asked Tempe.

"Makes sense," Tazewell said. "We've been trying to latch on to Johnston for days." He fired, nodded at the rifle smoke. "But there's a couple of Yank divisions out there that ain't aiming to let us go through or go away."

Lack Norris, reloading, said, "There's more of 'em on the south road, and still more massed around Champion's Hill to the north."

"That means a battle."

"Yeah," Lack said, "I just hope somebody's told Pemberton."

The sergeant's grunt indicated agreement. Tempe scowled, aware that the men's faith in the skill of their commanding general had dwindled to zero. Grant's army had out-witted them at every turn, out-marched them by miles, beaten them in two fights. Pemberton as the highest-ranking officer got the blame.

"Caught with his trousers down," Jollibee had said as they marched out of the trenches on the Yazoo. Admittedly, Sherman had shifted his troops like the operator in a shell game, but a Lieutenant General wasn't supposed to be fooled by trickery. How those Yanks must have laughed as they steamed away!

"He sent too blooming few, too late," Jollibee had said, when they reached the fork in the road between Grand Gulf and Port Gibson. They had staggered in, dog tired, to find the gray soldiers under Bowen fighting for their lives against McClernand's corps. That out-numbered Confederate force had barely escaped by retreating at dusk across Bayou Pierre.

Wounded in a skirmish near Raymond, the Englishman had cursed Pemberton roundly. From a wagon ambulance Jollibee had shouted his opinion. "His Lordship better forget Vicksburg, and come out and fight with all he has! He won't stop Grant with no piddling, piecemeal sorties!"

Well, thought Tempe gloomily, General Pemberton had come out and here they were. There was still a big garrison in Vicksburg, but some twenty thousand Confederate soldiers had marched eastward along the railroad to crowd into the little village called Edwards Depot. There, about twenty-five miles from the Mississippi, the torrential rains that flooded Baker's Creek had delayed the advance.

Most of this army was still confident, sought battle with high hopes for victory. But Tempe's company, the sharpshooters, an elite unit that excelled at patrol duty, felt differently. The riflemen, fighting edge dulled by successive defeats, groaned at orders that shifted them to still another skirmish line. They had marched almost forty miles to cover General Bowen's retreat, been hurried vainly to reach General Gregg's command before McPherson's Yankees slapped it back from Raymond.

We're bone-weary, Tempe thought, too fatigued to recover in four days. In the sodden camp around Edwards even big Tazewell had been listless, sneered at the bragging done by fresher troops. Pessimism gnawed at the sharpshooters like a persistent hunger-ache. They blamed Pemberton for everything, including the washed-out bridge that made the creek impassable.

Tempe had finally seen General Pemberton, close-to, on yesterday afternoon. The Pennsylvanian had a sallow, pallid face, dark brooding eyes. He held himself with ramrod stiffness, never seemed to smile. The kind of officer that privates saluted on sight, but seldom cheered.

"Big casino!" cried Lack Norris. "I done saw that there Yank go down. Told you these minnie balls sure enough carried farther."

"Who's arguing?" Tempe asked, and fired his piece without aiming it. The Minié balls, conical-shaped bullets named for a French officer, were a comparatively recent issue, ammunition captured from the enemy.

"That's right. It was Jollibee wouldn't admit it."

"National pride," Tempe said, glancing at the pointed lead pellet in his fingers. His professional interest in the greater force and range of the Miniés was no longer lively. "The British reckon any French invention is immoral."

"Huh! Was a minnie hit him."

"Well, the Yanks got more than enough to spare."

The casual conversation, under fire, illustrated their veteran judgment that the front had crystallized to an unchanging stalemate. Both sides had been pinned down on the same ground, sniping at long-range, for almost four hours. Neither the gray infantry, nor the blue, was making any belligerent moves to engage at closer quarters.

Content to maintain this position, Tempe was a trifle surprised. The skirmishers were out in front of Cockrell's brigade, Bowen's division, and neither of those brigadiers was noted for avoiding a scrap. Among the ranks John S. Bowen had a fine reputation as a skilful, fighting general.

Well, Tempe decided, Bowen didn't earn it consulting half baked sergeants. He'd been promised field promotion for helping burn De-Soto's houses but it hadn't been officially confirmed. There'd been no time to stitch on a third stripe anyway. Tazewell was a real sergeant, a non-com who could teach officers their trade.

As if sensing Tempe's thoughts, the sergeant rolled over on his back to gaze up at the sun. "Getting on to noon," he said. "And listen!"

The rifle crackle had settled to a steady, fire-at-will sputtering, and the cannon, front and rear, clanged with the deliberate beat of striking clocks. Through these surrounding noises came a distant rumble from the north, the thundering sounds that meant clashing combat, deadly battle.

"Somebody up yonder," Lack Norris said, listening, "is sure getting it."

"Yes," said Tempe, drawling the word, "that's a fight."

Tazewell nodded, said, "Must be Lee's crowd."

"Stephen D. not Robert E."

"Let's hope he's as good as his namesake, Lack."

"Or Reynolds," the sergeant said. "Both of Stephenson's brigades was behind us last night. Loring's bunch was ahead. They camped south of us, and they're on our right now, probably blocking that other road to Raymond, the one we took going in with Gregg."

"But who's facing us, Sarge?" asked Lack.

"My guess is McPherson, but it doesn't feel like his whole corps. Enough to keep us busy."

"Do tell," Tempe said. He glared at the enemy, loosed another shot. How those blue-bellied bastards had marched in the past week! They should be stuck in rain-soaked mud about half-way to Jackson instead of where they were. It spoiled a man's whole day to wake up and find Yankees right under his nose. Who'd ever figure they'd get here so soon, tramping out of the dawn, down a road no better than a cow path?

The skirmishers with Bowen's division couldn't know they were near the cutting-edge center of a battleline shaped like a farmer's sickle. The Yankees massed on the ridge north of Champion's white house formed the wooden handle; the other blue-clad regiments stretched southward, along the hooked blade. Sergeant Tazewell's estimate of the other Confederate positions was roughly correct, but the hilly terrain masked and twisted the alignments of both armies. Soldiers in one sector couldn't see what was happening in the next.

Three roads from the east, converging, led to Baker's Creek, and there was a separate fight on each. It was that kind of battle.

Gunfire was lightest at the clash on the south Raymond Road, heavier in the middle beside the rustic track Tempe Dixon called a cow path. But the main Federal attack poured along the northern route, the Clinton-Bolton Road. Almost as soon as they met opposition these Union veterans, Hovey's division of McClernand's corps, swung wide, skirting Champion's Hill, to flank the Confederate left.

General Pemberton, like an unlucky gambler, guessed wrong again, and again. He made his first mistake at six-thirty in the morning, and by noon the battle was completely out of his hands.

Joe Johnston's despatch told Pemberton to change direction, slip north away from Grant, try to unite both gray armies. Obedience to regulations was Pemberton's creed; he issued the necessary orders at once. Johnston, a famed strategist, was the superior officer.

The Confederate supply train rattled back across Baker's Creek into

Edwards Depot. Turning about, Reynolds' brigade, twenty-five hundred men, marched after it. The rest of the army was to move out as the roads cleared.

Then, the spluttering rifle-fire of engaged pickets signalled the enemy's approach. As the sound increased every listener in gray realized it was too late to withdraw. Within an hour it was impossible. The Yankee army was pressing forward in force.

John C. Pemberton had not picked the hill-cluttered landscape surrounding the Champion property as a battlefield. On the previous midnight his army had encamped strung out in marching order. The Southern general from Pennsylvania was forced to fight against heavy odds to defend ground chosen by circumstances.

A military genius would have had trouble. Pemberton, mistaking the Federal flanking movement for a feint, nearly lost his army.

The Yankees stormed down from the north at nine-thirty. Their repeated charges were meant to crumple the Confederate left flank, drive a wedge between the gray army and Baker's Creek. The attack, if successful, would cut the Confederate line of retreat, sweep down behind the embattled gray troops that faced east. Hovey and Crocker, the Federal generals commanding in this sector, saw the chance for victory. They kept their artillery hammering to support the charging bluecoats.

One thinly stretched gray brigade stood in the way. Seeing the danger that threatened the army, General S. D. Lee had swung his infantry to the north, extended his line far to the left. The jumbled terrain aided the defenders, but they were no more familiar with the countryside than their opponents.

Lee had only the men and guns left in Stephenson's depleted division, halved by Reynolds' withdrawal. These were widely deployed around the Champion holdings in a formation like an elongated number 7.

From mid-morning to early afternoon furious battle raged across this area. The contested ground reached from thick woods far to the west, near the creek, to a crossroad a mile below the hilltop house inside the numeral's angle. It was vicious, hurly-burly fighting, charge and countercharge, volley and bayonet. Men, in blue, gray or butternut, died on slopes, in gullies, beside bullet-scarred trees, in Champion's cornfield. And, in ceaseless, violent requiem, the roaring field guns clouded the bright May sunshine.

By one-thirty Lee's desperate stand seemed a lost cause. Bravery could not overcome the Yankee superiority in men and metal. On the far left the gray soldiers still held in the woods, making every brush a redoubt, but one regiment had been driven back to the bridge that spanned the creek. On the right the bluecoats had smashed through the angle, threatened to crush the entire wing on the southern slope. The 24th Iowa, charging like demons, overwhelmed the Alabama battery defending the crossroad, and captured every gun.

Only the news that help was coming kept the reeling gray line resisting the repeated Yankee onslaughts. The battered Confederates wavered and fell back, yielded this crest, that roadbed, but they refused to quit. Cursing their laggard, long-awaited reinforcements, decimated regiments stubbornly fought on, protecting each square yard with the maniac ferocity of claim-jumped gold miners.

Bowen had finally disengaged troops from the Confederate center. He sent two brigades hurrying to bolster Lee's sagging front.

In this shift of position to their left, north, the sharpshooters, Tempe Dixon's unit, lost touch with their proper command. They received the order to move late, were hustled down a ravine, climbed through trees, and found themselves alone in wilderness.

"What the hell?" asked Lack Norris. "Where's the lieutenant?"

"He got it an hour ago," Tazewell said.

"Where are we heading, Sarge?"

"That way." The sergeant pointed toward the rumble of heavy gun-fire. "They need us up around Champion's."

"Well, let's get there," Tempe said. He felt the nervous stomach-flutter that always preceded action. It made him impatient, aware that he really wanted to stay in the woods where the bird songs were clearer than the cannon.

The riflemen crossed the tree-covered crest at a fast dogtrot. They emerged into the open, on a height with a good view to the northwest. For a few minutes they paused, to stare down at a landscape busy with moving men, splotched with drifting powder smoke.

Tempe gazed at the dusty, brown-gray companies forming in battle array below him. The bayonets glittered, fencing the near edge of a cornfield. Farther away, to his left, he could see the crossroad declivity where Yankee soldiery massed, swarming blue flies as they tried to turn the captured guns. A chocolate road twisted, rising, through the hills to the north; there were solid, dark nests of Federals clustered on both its banks.

"Jesus," said Lack Norris, prayerfully. "I'd no inkling the blue-bellies was nudging our elbows."

"Now, you know," Sergeant Tazewell said.

Tempe said, "I reckon we'd better get down there and help push them back." He tried to sound confident. From where he stood there looked to be a hell of a lot more Yanks than Southern troops. Squinting, he tried to identify the nearest Confederates, shook his head. "That doesn't look like our outfit, but they're getting ready to go in."

"Latch on and ride," Tazewell said.

They scrambled down the slope, joined the gray ranks restlessly bordering the cornfield. Tempe noted the grim, sweaty faces, the stripped-down, packless backs, the muttering uneasiness. He knew the signs; these were men awaiting the order to charge.

That, he thought, had been obvious even from above. There was no alternative. The Yanks were in their laps, and had to be rooted out. This brigade would attack on this side of the road; there was another, yonder, that would sweep up the other side.

"You ain't Cockrell," said Lack, addressing a tall, rangy soldier.

The man shook his head, spat tobacco. He was wearing patched butternut and an unraveled straw hat. Except for his belt, cartridge case, and bayonet-topped rifle he might have been a poor white farmhand. His laconic answer was a slurred twang.

"Green."

"What outfit?"

"1st Arkansas cavalry. Dismounted."

"Gaffed mudcats," Lack said. "We must be right hard up if we got the cavalry down off their high horses to do a mite of fighting!"

"Ha," said the Arkansan. "Ha."

"You got your toothpick with you, Johnny?"

"I got it." The cavalryman touched the hilt of the long bowie knife in his belt. "You itching to taste it?"

"No," said Tempe, soothingly, "he isn't. Save it for the Yanks. We were attached to Cockrell, but it looks like we'll have to string along with you-all."

"You're welcome." A shorter, bow-legged soldier grinned at the sharpshooters. "Don't pay no mind to Hadley here. He gets rampacious when there's a tussle brewing."

The tall Arkansan nodded. "It sure ain't going to be no revival meeting hallelujah. There's more damn-Yanks out there than weevils in a voodoo-cussed cotton patch."

Tempe sighed as he checked his rifle. He slid his bayonet from its scabbard, clicked it in place on the barrel. Around him, the other marksmen, fixing bayonets, made the same noise, like metallic crickets.

A chill, unlucky chirping, Tempe thought. His mouth was dry. Every time a man charged lessened his chances of living. If you didn't think about that, your legs would carry you forward. When the word came.

Down the line a bugle blared. A loud voice roared through the brassy summons.

"All right, boys! Sic 'em!"

Then, they were in among the ripening corn, moving at a walk. Tempe, rifle at the ready, stepped between glossy green leaves, silky tassels, waist-high stalks. He heard the snapping as others crushed through the crop, smelled the sweetish odor of trampled ears. There would be no harvest, nor tasty eating, from this planting.

"Dress to the left," Tazewell said. "Keep close."

Ahead, musketry sounded its familiar ripping clatter. The walk quickened to a shuffling trot.

Tempe could see the enemy ranks, busy waders, dark above the green corn. Riflefire flashes lit the blue coats; smoke wreathed the black hats.

"We go!" Lack Norris shouted.

The Southern yell, the sharp, throat-tearing war cry, shrilled as the gray lines lunged into a headlong run.

Racing, trying not to stumble, Tempe shrieked with the rest. He knew that the harsh bellowing spurred them to the charge, drowned thought and fear in its waves of sound. That was worth the loss of breath. He pounded forward, not pacing himself, sprinting at full speed.

Somehow the Yankees seemed to sweep to meet them. The solid blue mass broke into segments, no longer ranks but individuals. Contorted faces made a mottled, uneven frieze; the thin bayonets glinted and flickered as they were shifted in the sunshine.

Ten paces from the enemy, Tempe leveled his rifle, fired from the hip. He heard no order, but his shot blended with a crashing Southern volley. Ears ringing, he plunged through the smoke barrier.

The volley had shattered the blue wall; the charge flushed the remnants into full retreat. There were only a few moments of hectic, hand-to-hand combat. Tempe, bounding out of the corn, impaled a turning bluecoat with sheer impetus. The man screamed as he fell, nearly twisted the rifle from Tempe's grip. His rush carried him, reeling, into another Yank. In the collision they both went down, but the body under Tempe collapsed in death.

"Sorry," muttered Tempe, as he saw the bleeding bullet-wounds. He scrambled to his feet, reloaded as he stared after the fleeing Union infantry.

They were running away all right, scurrying across an open meadow, but they wouldn't go far. Their second line was formed behind a snake-rail fence on the meadow's opposite side. There were plenty banked along the fence, and more hurrying down the slope behind it.

Judging the distance, Tempe grunted. Two hundred yards of grazing and not even a cornstalk for cover this time. He knew his comrades would keep going; they'd only paused to catch breaths and reload. Lack and Taze raced past him as the order came.

"Arkansas! Missouri! Forward!"

Again, the yell, and the pounding charge. There were blue-clad bodies crumpled on the grass, still as boulders. Tempe, on its right, was dimly aware that the charge was crescent-shaped. He ducked, involuntarily, when the Federal volley blazed in his face, but he kept running. He thought, thankfully, that they'd fired a mite too soon.

The Southern rifle blast scorched the fence-rails, toppled several. The sharpshooters went over the barricade like a cresting wave. Tempe's boot ticked the top rail as he hurdled it.

Along the fence the scrimmaging fight was bitter and violent. The Yankees tried to hold the position, cutting, thrusting, swinging musket-butts. Tempe stabbed, whirled, kicked loose from a tackle. He went down in a wrestling group, fought free. More and more soldiers, outlined for an instant against the sky, poured over the fence. The enemy infantry wavered, and broke.

Blue uniforms mixed with the gray as the struggle swept up the hill, a running fight. Tempe, hatless, panting, raced forward in a white blur of pain, aching lungs, and blood lust. He fired, reloaded, charged, stabbed in endless succession. He was bleeding from a nicked cheekbone and slashed knuckles. Once big Tazewell shouted in his ear.

"The boys across the road took back our battery! Hear it?"

Tempe nodded solemnly, not hearing anything above the tumult raging around them.

Green's brigade carried the hill, re-formed to charge through thick woods. Once more, they drove the Yankees back, and these were fresh troops, recognizable by clean, unsmeared faces. But beyond the woods were stony ridges, and ravines enfiladed by Federal artillery.

"We come a country mile," Lack Norris said.

"Or more," said the sergeant. "It's after four. We've been at it for two hours."

"You got any ammo?" asked Tempe, showing his empty pouch.

They didn't. Neither did the rest of the brigade. They were exhausted, battered troops who had won back lost ground, and a mile beyond, but they could go no farther.

Bowen's charging brigades saved the Confederate army. Nothing could save the day. All that was left was escape.

The road back was long and weary, threatened by cannon rumbling to the east, where the enemy was pressing a fresh attack.

As they splashed across Baker's Creek, fording it below the bridge, the sharpshooters were too dejected to curse General Pemberton.

17

FOR OVER TWO WEEKS, while Grant's army rampaged through the state, refugees from the countryside poured into Vicksburg. The planters came by rail and road, bringing wives, children and their most valued possessions, including slaves and heirlooms.

It was a demonstration of confidence in the town's impregnability; the unexpected guests found hospitable welcome. Houses already crowded opened their doors to kinfolk and friend. Most slave-quarters more than doubled their population. None of the wealthy begrudged food and shelter. The poor were more worried, but as generous. Everybody accepted the Negroes as a responsibility. Vicksburg had known times when flooding Mississippi waters threw similar burdens on her resources. Even penurious tradesmen gave credit to the suddenly homeless. The Yankee invasion, too, would pass away, recede in defeat from the many high hills.

When Pemberton's beaten army returned, hurrying through the outskirts with sullen steps, the civilians felt relief, not alarm. He had left a strong garrison behind when he marched out, but the battered gray veterans crowding down the Baldwin Ferry, Jackson, and Graveyard Roads, wheeling to man the fortifications, increased the town's defenders to an impressive host.

Admittedly, these same regiments had been whipped at Champion's Hill, had failed to hold on the Big Black River. But neither loss mattered as long as the bulk of the army returned intact to Vicksburg.

Amateur tacticians spouted the theory over their bourbon. Battle in the open, where the Yankee superior numbers told, made victory well-nigh impossible. The town's strong fortifications would double the Confederate might.

Everybody knew about those landward defenses; many had lent slaves to help build them. After months of labor they stretched around the town in a wide semi-circle, from Fort Hill in the north to the riverbank west of the Warrenton Road.

Eight miles of rolling land, bluffs, ridges and vales, had been turned into a honey-comb riddled with redans, lunettes, rifle-pits, intertwined trenches. The engineers had embellished every favorable feature the terrain supplied—height, depth, this cliff, that gully. Each hill was a tall fortress and the spurs that jutted from them, front and rear, were earthwork bastions. Now an army was moving into this empty maze, nestling behind these defenses. Cannon, a hundred and two guns, were being jostled into place.

Fort Snyder on the Yazoo was evacuated; the outpost stationed in the suburb village of Warrenton was withdrawn. Vicksburg lay inside a bristling steel stirrup, with the riverfront batteries the horizontal bar.

Alex Kittering only managed to drive a mile out on the Jackson Road before the traffic guards stopped her. The girl had packed hampers in the carriage. Poll Randall and Emilie Verrier were along to help distribute food to hungry soldiers.

"Sorry, ladies," said an unshaven, sun-burned lieutenant, a Georgian by his speech. "You-all will just have to turn back. We need this road clear to move the troops. Grant's whole blasted army is a-treading on our heels."

While Poll smiled and Emilie batted her eyelids, Alex pleaded.

"But we heard the men were hungry."

"You heard true, ma'am. We've done a heap more fighting than eating the last two days."

"We have food, Lieutenant."

"And some whisky," Poll said.

Emilie nodded, fluttered her fingers. "And a whole box of my papa's best cigars!"

The Georgian's grin flashed, broad and greedy. "Well, now," he said, "that's right nice of you, ladies. You just leave those victuals here with us, and my men will see they get proper handling."

"Uh, huh!" a guard said, licking his lips.

Alex frowned in doubt. Standing in the carriage she could see the soldiers filing off the road. Those were the ones she wanted to feed, the tired, dust-stained infantry who had done the fighting. Even at a distance their fatigue was evident from their sagging shoulders and trailing rifles. Neither bank looked steep but the climbers slipped and struggled as they ascended. To left and right the gray-brown files weaved across the green slopes and disappeared among the hills.

"We're all in the same fix, ma'am," the Georgian said.

"Of course." Alex decided it wasn't her place to choose between units or search out individuals like Tempe Dixon. "I'll pull over to the roadside to let you boys unload."

"We'll need the hampers back," Poll said.

"Now, you be sure," Emilie told the men, "you stretch these things as far as they'll go. Pass them around to your comrades."

"We ain't hogs, ma'am," a soldier protested.

Alex said, "There's plenty." As she jockeyed the team to the side of the road, she wondered exactly how large a food supply remained in

Vicksburg. The town hadn't yet felt the pinch of the enemy's foraging, but now the large farms were outside the iron ring of fortifications.

While the hampers were being emptied a group of mounted officers cantered down the road. Alex noted only well-groomed horses and glittering braid before Poll nudged her.

"General Pemberton," the blonde girl whispered.

The tall commander, stiff in the saddle, rode with his eyes fixed straight ahead. His hand lifted in automatic reply to the jerky salutes of the traffic guard, but he didn't glance at them. Alex thought the general seemed very grim and unhappy.

She remembered her grandfather's comment. At the dismaying news from Champion's Hill the old man had been less caustic than usual. Even Stephen had been mildly critical of the defeated general, but Joab had expressed gruff sympathy.

"Poor Pemberton tried to serve two masters. Jeff Davis told him to stay put, and Joe Johnston ordered him to pull foot. So he divided his forces and got whipped. Not even a juggler can milk two cows at once without spilling the pail!"

Alex found little time to feel sorry for the general. The guard returned to the unpacking; the dust wake from the staff officers was still settling when another rider trotted his horse through it. He reined in beside the carriage, voiced a startled exclamation.

"Alex!"

"Bryce Furlong," cried Poll.

"Wherever did you get that horse?" asked Emilie.

Staring, chilled by his sudden appearance, Alex realized she had never seen Bryce so poorly mounted. He was riding a cold-blooded hack, duncolored with black points and a shaggy coat. As Bryce winced at Emilie's question, she spoke quickly.

"What are you doing in Vicksburg?"

"God knows," Bryce said, with cold anger. His gaze glowered at the girls, shifted to the traffic guards. "I sure don't belong here!"

"But—"

"Johnston sent me to Pemberton with a message. I ran a good mare into the ground on a footless errand, and this is the remount they gave me!" He tugged savagely at the reins, yanking the horse's head from its drooping posture.

"The poor beast is tired, Bryce," said Alex.

"And useless! There's a whole Yankee army between me and Johnston now, and this cob's as slow as a mud tortoise!"

"But you weren't with Johnston."

"Poll's right," Emilie said. "You were supposed to be up in Tennessee with that charming General Van Dorn."

"Van Dorn's dead."

"Dead?" The three girls spoke in unison. They had all danced with the gallant cavalry commander, taken pride in his exploits.

"Ten days ago."

Emilie, tongue protruding, counted on her fingers. "Right after Stonewall Jackson succumbed. Another brave sacrifice to the South's noble cause."

"Well, not exactly," Bryce said, uncomfortably. "Van Dorn was killed in a private quarrel." He could not tell these maidens that the general had been assassinated while sitting at his desk in the Spring Hill headquarters. "A personal matter."

"A duel?"

"N-No. Duelling's forbidden in the army."

The trio sensed his embarrassment, exchanged glances. With unerring feminine instinct Poll and Emilie scented scandal. They waited for Alex to speak. If a girl couldn't ask her fiancé for the latest gossip, who could?

Alex frowned, more puzzled than curious. She glanced at the listening lieutenant, thought she understood the reason for Bryce's reticence, lowered her voice.

"We hadn't heard."

"It was—well—complicated." Bryce scowled at his halting explanation. The general's murder had a spicy motive involving honor. Doctor Peters, the civilian who fired the shot, alleged that Van Dorn had betrayed a female relative. Nobody wanted that bandied about in bivouacs or parlors.

"Complicated?"

"Yes, Alex. That's why I took the—er—details down to General Johnston." Bryce changed the subject, ignoring the disappointed looks from Poll and Emilie. "If you know old Stonewall's dead, you've learned of our brilliant victory at Chancellorsville."

"Yes, Bryce."

"The news came," Emilie said, "before the Yankees cut the telegraph wires."

Poll said, "Henri Duchesneau received the message himself. Lee and Jackson smashed the enemy."

"And then poor Jackson was accidentally shot by his own men."

Bryce nodded gloomily. He refrained from saying that the South could ill afford to lose generals who won. The girls might renew their questions about General Van Dorn. His voice rose, sharply impatient.

"Lieutenant!"

The Georgian stiffened, saluted. "Yes, Major?"

"Are you going to fuss over those baskets the live-long day?"

"No, sir. We've finished." He motioned his men to lift the hampers into the carriage, made a courtly bow to the girls. "You have our most grateful thanks, ladies."

"You're welcome," Alex said.

"Just make sure you-all don't waste a morsel," Emilie said.

Poll said, "Spread it wide and thin, boys."

"We'll do that, ma'am."

Bryce frowned at the cheerful squad, watched in sullen silence as Alex turned the team. He kicked his horse to a walk, annoyed that the girl was holding in the spirited Kittering grays. He wasn't used to keeping pace with a carriage because the lady driving was tactful.

"Whose kind thought was that?" he asked.

"What?"

"The delicate repast."

"Alex thought of it," Emilie said, "but we all contributed."

"It's little enough to do," Poll said.

Alex hadn't missed Bryce's heavy sarcasm. She sounded defensive. "I figured they'd be hungry."

"I hope it chokes them!"

"Bryce Furlong!" Emilie was shocked.

"They ran at the Big Black River!" Bryce's pent-up anger, accumulated for several days, exploded. He felt he'd been badly used in the battle around Baker's Creek, riding back and forth with orders, a dangerous, unglamorous duty. They'd given him this sad, slow-footed nag, and a brigadier's aide had cursed him for tardiness. The cursing still rankled, festered by the sorry figure he'd made plodding through the retreat. "Turned and ran! They burned the bridge, but they didn't hold the crossing worth a damn!"

"Our army?" Poll's face and voice showed disbelief.

"Some army!" In Bryce Furlong's estimation an army without cavalry was totally unfit for combat. He had no patience with defeat, nor sympathy for the beaten. "A rabble that look like scarecrows, and fight the same way!"

"Oh, come, Bryce."

"That's not fair," Emilie said, pouting.

Alex kept her tone mild, trying to pacify. She said, "Just because they lost a battle against odds is—"

"They lost more than the battle!" Bryce interrupted with an impatient sneer. "They lost Loring's whole division!" He saw consternation widen six eyes, realized the girls hadn't heard. "That's right. Only a handful of companies came back here with the others."

"Were they—wiped out?" Emilie's whisper was almost tearful. There were a lot of Mississippi boys in General Loring's command.

"Hell, no!" said Bryce, with relish. "They just slipped away in the dark. Got past the Yankee left flank and wandered off somewheres." He scowled, thinking that Loring was probably marching to join Joe Johnston. "I only wish to the living God I'd gone with them!"

"Why, Bryce?" asked Alex. "Don't you think our army can hold the town without those troops?"

"Oh, sure," Bryce said, shrugging. "They'll hold it all right. At least long enough."

"Long enough?"

"Till Johnston gets here, Poll. But I don't like being cooped up in Vicksburg for a week or ten days. Not under a nincompoop like Pemberton."

"Oh?"

"You know what he said as he rode in. I heard him myself." Bryce tried to imitate Northern speech, and failed. " 'Just thirty years ago,' says Pemberton, 'I began my military career by receiving a cadetship at the United States Military Academy—and today—the same date, my career is ended in disaster and disgrace.' "

Alex bit her lip. The statement certainly didn't sound very confident. She didn't doubt Bryce's veracity. It wasn't his language, and he wouldn't have known the date of Pemberton's appointment either.

"But it isn't ended," Poll said.

"Not while he holds Vicksburg," said Emilie.

"I know," Bryce said. "I know. He was just moaning low." Even a major soon learned that the West Pointers took care of each other no matter how the fortunes of war veered. Pemberton, decided Bryce, would probably be promoted for sitting on his backside until Johnston's army relieved him.

"Our boys won't run this time," Alex said.

"They've no damn place to go." Bryce's grin was malicious. He didn't care if he was being unjust to exhausted troops. "But they sure went away from the Big Black like rabbits. Bowen and Vaughan had the rearguard, and their men just wilted when the blue-bellies attacked."

The three girls were silent. Bravery was the South's proudest boast; cowardice under fire was unthinkable. They all believed those editorial axioms, wondered why Bryce insisted on relating a shameful incident.

"I saw your friend Dixon bolt with the rest, Alex."

The taunt was soft, but barbed. Alex felt her heart leap, the blush mount. At least he's alive, she thought.

"Who?" asked Emilie.

"You know," said Poll. "The soldier Alex nursed through malaria. The one that stayed at her house."

"Oh. Him."

Bryce Furlong turned in the saddle. He stared at Alex, eyes narrowed and cold. He said, "Now, *that's* news."

"I wrote you about it," Alex said. She didn't look at him, but she sensed his suppressed fury. Surely, she thought, he'll not show jealousy in front of our friends.

"You mentioned a soldier. You didn't name him."

"Tempe Dixon," said Alex. She spoke casually, without heat. "He was sick and we took him home."

"Cozy," Bryce said. "Very, very cozy."

Emilie glanced sideways at him, nudged Poll. They were, after all, Alex's friends. The blonde girl recognized the distress signal, was aware of tension. Every girl, Poll thought, has her troubles with masculine moods. She spoke with hearty cheerfulness.

"Your family's at the town house, Bryce. The plantation must be in Yankee hands, but they all got out in time."

"They'll loot Tonica Hill, too, Alex."

"Yes, Emilie. I'm afraid so." Alex was grateful for the conversational efforts. She knew that Bryce was smoldering, but she didn't want a public scene. "Do you think they'll really free the slaves?"

"Our slaves?" Emilie uttered a hoot of laughter. "Huh! You should hear Maurice talk about Yankee trash!"

"That's right, Bryce," said Poll, chattering desperately. "Both Big Jules and Little Jules insisted on coming in from your plantation. Your father told me. They wanted no truck with those nigra-loving abolitionists. Soon as they heard the bluecoats were getting close, they just begged your pa to take them along."

"Your boy, Zack, brought in the horses," Emilie said. Mention of the Furlong jockey reminded her of something that should pleasure Bryce. "Saladin's safe in his stall."

"Saladin," repeated Bryce. His interest was stirred enough for speech. He would thrash out the Dixon business with Alex later. "How's he look?"

"Fit as ever," Emilie said. "You can swap him for Rosinante there."

"Rosin—who?"

"Rosinante," said Alex. "Don Quixote's horse." She knew that Bryce hadn't read a book since his school days, barely bothered to scan the newspapers. "Emilie was referring to your remount."

The cavalry major glared, affronted. He missed the literary comparison, but was sure it was an uncomplimentary jest. They were poking fun at him! To mention Saladin in the same breath with this plug was an insult.

"I would hardly," he said, coldly, "risk a thoroughbred racer in the cavalry. Saladin was not bred for warfare."

"How unlike some men," said Alex. She had had enough of Bryce for the moment. Slapping the long reins she sent the team racing into Vicksburg.

Bryce Furlong, left behind, cursed long and loudly.

· 18 ·

TEMPE DIXON rolled out of his blanket when the enemy cannonade began. He sat a moment, blinking, letting his eyes adjust to the darkness. As he lit a cheroot the match flame showed the yellow clay walls of the trench, the shadowy movement of other awakened soldiers.

"Damn and blast!" Lack Norris cursed through a yawn. "Can't them Yankees let a feller sleep!"

"If they can't sleep," Tazewell's voice said, "nobody sleeps."

Grinning, Tempe puffed his cigar, deliberately using tobacco smoke to chase drowsiness. The grouchiness, he thought, was normal. The boys sure didn't sound whipped or scared. Maybe they were as glad as he was to get back to high ground, to lie snug in Vicksburg's fortifications. Baker's Creek, flood-swollen, had seemed like another bayou, and the Big Black River, a wide, sullen stream, had been well named. He'd been dragging tired at the river even before the bluecoat charges broke them. But this was another place, another day.

It was, Tempe guessed, the pitch-black hours of early morning. He recalled the date. Tuesday, May 19th. The Yankee cannon thunder rumbled from the east; the whining shells arched directly overhead to burst behind them. Besides, the Confederate batteries were silent, holding their fire until the last moment in order to hide their positions.

Sergeant Tazewell's bellow seemed louder in the narrow earthwork. "Everybody! On your feet!"

"Aw, Sarge," Lack said. "Be-cripes sake! What's the all-fired hustle?" He sounded close in the blackness. "The blue-bellies won't attack in the dark!"

"It's only three o'clock," moaned another voice.

"How do you know?"

"'Lonzo, here, has a watch, Sarge."

"You just wear it over your heart, 'Lonzo," said Lack. "It's better than a pack of cards for stopping minnies. Near as good as a Bible."

The remark brought cynical laughter. Veterans like the sharpshooters had long since discarded such popular folk superstitions. Those who carried Bibles put their faith in prayer, not thickness; the gamblers trusted to luck. Neither Minié balls nor shell fragments showed discrimination.

Tempe blew a smoke-ring, wondered at its shape in the darkness. The rustle around him as men rose was proof that their mettle had been restored. There were the usual soft curses, the familiar metallic clinking of weapons. He knew better than to expect horseplay or hilarity before a fight, but the words and noises expressed readiness.

They're all right again, Tempe decided. They'd been beaten twice on successive days, but that could be forgotten. All these veterans needed was a few hours' rest, a respite from marching, a chance to judge the strength of the defenses they occupied. Burning the bridge over the Big Black had given them that, delayed the enemy just long enough. It had been a tight squeeze, but they'd made it.

"Tempe?"

"Right here, Sarge."

"We're moving up to the pits."

"I know. Let me finish my smoke."

"Give me a puff," Lack said.

Tempe passed the cigar, rose and stretched. He checked his rifle, frowning to remember their position in detail. The sharpshooters were still attached to Bowen's infantry, Pemberton's reserve, in the center of the entrenchments, reinforcements for any threatened place in the lines. But the unit, as crack shots, was embedded in rifle-pits in the front of S. D. Lee's command.

They had filed into that post yesterday, been snug by noon, admiring the high breastwork, the firing-step, the battery on the bluff above them. To their right they could see the labyrinthine network of trenches around the railroad cut, and the solid mass of the strong point called the Square Fort.

The first Yankee skirmishers had appeared about four in the afternoon. Tempe smiled grimly now, recalling the cocky, overconfident advance of the blue infantry. Before sunset the sharpshooters had made them pay for that carelessness, and the Yanks had dug in on the flat ground about three hundred yards away. They had even managed to emplace a field gun.

"Three furlongs off," Lack had said, "to the left."

Tempe shared Tazewell's opinion that the howitzer was one of their own, captured at Champion's Hill. The gray ranks knew they'd lost a passel of cannon in that battle, and talk exaggerated the number. They welcomed the inflated estimate. If the blue-bellies figured they faced a lightly gunned foe they were in for a surprise.

"Come on," Tazewell said. "Come on."

"Here, Tempe." Lack returned the glowing cheroot.

Taking a last inhale, Tempe dropped the butt, stepped on it. He moved out of the twist in the trench where they'd slept, twenty yards behind the pits. Now, he could see the cannon flash all along the Yankee lines. It was a cloudy night and the barrage made its own flickering horizon.

"Lot of them," Lack said.

"The Army of Tennessee. Grant's whole menagerie."

Tazewell said, "Three corps."

"Our pickets are back," Tempe said, seeing the crouched figures in a sudden glare of shellburst.

"Well, hell," Lack said, "it's noisy out there."

They followed a sloping ditch into the rifle-pits, scattered as each rifleman sought a previously chosen loophole. These were deep entrenchments, with clay-smooth walls and sandbag-topped ramparts, that snaked across a jutting spur of hill. They had been carefully designed for maximum defense with minimum exposure.

Recalling the shallow mud holes before Chickasaw Bluffs, Tempe approved this protected position. Assaulting troops would be slowed by the inclined approach, raked by commanding fire.

He made himself comfortable, sitting cross-legged on the firing-step. There was no need for the sentries to keep more than a desultory watch. The Yank cannonade was heavy, but it was exploratory, without specific targets. A night bombardment against unknown fortifications could only wreak haphazard damage while it tried to draw an answer. Unless the Confederate guns replied the enemy artillery was wasting its ammunition.

The Vicksburg works, Tempe figured, were built to withstand an even heavier pounding. But while it shook the earth and lit the sky the blue infantry wouldn't charge.

"General order from headquarters," the sergeant announced. "The general wants every man to fire low and carefully so as not to waste ammunition."

"Now just what in God's name," drawled a sharpshooter, "does he reckon we've been doing?"

"Sarge," said Lack, "if ole pimply Pemberton doesn't cotton to the way I handle this here Enafield, tell him to come on down and show me."

"There was some pretty high-falutin' blazing away yesterday," Tazewell said. "Just burning powder. You must have squeezed off a couple dozen shots yourself, Lack."

"Twenty-one exactly. And a Billy Yank chawed dust every time."

"Come off it. At three hundred yards or better?"

"I just said they chawed dust, Sarge. I ain't claiming I hit them, but I sure discouraged them."

Tempe chuckled at the exchange. He had done his share of fancy shooting whenever a distant bluecoat made an attractive target. It was another thing that helped restore the marksmen's morale. They could wait in safety, draw bead by choice, fire from a rest.

The sergeant said: "It's a good order. You-all be sparing at long range. But when they start a-coming, let her rip!" He moved away, big frame folding into the shadows down the trench.

Settling his back against the wall, Tempe tried to doze. Neither roaring cannon nor screeching shell bothered him, but he nodded and woke a dozen times before he quit. Lack was standing beside him, peering over the parapet. Tempe reached, plucked a butternut trouser leg.

"See anything?"

"Dawn," Lack said.

Tempe rose, stood beside his friend, gazed eastward. Above and behind the flashing guns the sky was paling with a slow grandeur that mocked the enemy's spasms of flame. Gray changed to a faded blue that deepened as it was tinted with pink and gold. The sun inched upward, a scarlet disk festooned with brilliant streamers. Then, while they watched, it was day.

"Going to be a scorcher," Lack said.

"More ways than one, Lack."

An early-morning breeze riffled through the canefield below them, stirring the green stalks. The Yankee howitzer, over six-hundred yards to their left, blazed, and the light wind vanished as if blown away.

They could see movement, now, in the enemy lines, the smoke-wisps of breakfast fires. At the far edge of the cane a blue-clad picket suddenly stood up, turned as he shifted his rifle to his shoulder. The foreshortened, distant figure started to saunter back to his comrades.

"Well, well," said Lack. His indrawn breath was audible as he stiffened to aim.

The rifle cracked. The Yankee soldier jumped as his slouch hat flew off, swirling. He dropped his gun, snatched for it. Hatless, bent double, he scurried for safety.

"A miss," Tempe said, hiding his pleasure at the man's escape. It was too lovely a sunrise to be spoiled by an unnecessary kill. One Yank would make no difference, this early.

Lack, reloading, shrugged. He started to speak, ducked as enemy muskets flared. Dust spurted from the parapet's rim. There were sharpshooters in blue awake, over there, too, eager to greet the morning.

"Jump Jim Crow," said Tempe. He thrust his rifle across a sandbag, cocked it, and waited, gazing down the barrel. Beyond the cornfield sunlit metal winked. He fired at the reflection.

The morning hours passed in this long-range marksmen's duel, though the Yankee cannonade continued. Occasionally a Confederate howitzer snorted in reply, but the battery behind Tempe's outfit remained silent. At noon the trench was crowded by an entire company of gray infantry that marched in to support the sharpshooters.

"Who you?" asked Lack.

"37th Mississippi." The gaunt corporal who answered had an Alabama accent.

"We left you birds at Haines Bluff."

"Oh, we pulled out of there night before last. We been here in the works since yesterday morn."

"Glad to have you along," Tempe said, and meant it. The reinforcement showed that the trench was to be held, in force, when the bluecoats charged. There could be no more falling back.

He was sound asleep, curled on the firing-step, when the sudden quiet jerked him awake. Tempe was on his feet, raising his gun, before his brain registered the reason. The Yankee cannonade had stopped.

"What time is it?" he asked, thickly.

"About two," Sergeant Tazewell said.

Tempe gazed down the slope to the brakes that bordered the ditch at the bottom. He raised his glance, head turning, to scan the canefield. There was no doubt that the enemy was forming for attack. He could see the dark blue mass, the cold shine of bayonets.

Cannon boomed through the stillness. Single guns fired at intervals. One. Another. A third.

"Their signal," Lack said.

"You wait for ours," said the sergeant.

The Yankee shout, the deeper, hoarser bellow they used, rose as the bluecoats charged. Leaping forward they became a line, successive waves of racing soldiers. To left and right, as far as Tempe could see, the Federal infantry swept toward the Vicksburg bluffs like a flash-flood, an unleashed blue torrent.

"Here they come," Lack said.

"Lord Jesus," said another voice, prayerfully.

Beside Tempe, the Alabaman in the Mississippi regiment, began to recite softly. The low cadence had a familiar swing and Tempe recognized a broken version of the 91st Psalm.

". . . He is my refuge and my fortress: my God; in Him will I trust . . . He shall cover thee with His feathers . . . His truth shall be thy shield and buckler . . . not be afraid for the terror by night; nor for the arrow that flyeth by day . . ."

The seventh verse rang in Tempe's memory. *A thousand shall fall at thy side, and ten thousand at thy right hand; but it shall not come nigh thee.*

"Hold it," Tazewell said. "Hold it now. Wait for our cannon."

The Yankees trampled through the cane, reached the brakes that edged the ditch.

"Now!"

As Tempe fired the blast shook the breastwork; its roar was deafening, stunning. The entire semi-circle of Vicksburg's defenses erupted in one, thunderous volley of smoke and flame.

He saw the Yankee attack below him shatter like broken glass. The bluecoat lines disintegrated into fragments. Soldiers reeled, tumbled, crumpled in that deadly, leaden sleet. A handful jumped into the ditch, fired back; most dropped, cowering, into the cover of the cane.

There were no more charges. The Yanks clung where they'd been stopped, trying to answer the withering fire that poured down on them. The battery atop the hill slashed them with canister; the incessant rifles cut the tops from the cane that hid them. When night fell the blue soldiers raced back to safety, leaving many dead.

"Stopped them," Lack Norris said.

It was, Tempe thought, not a boast, but a simple statement of fact. The entrenchments had proven their worth.

Vicksburg could not be taken by assault.

All day Vicksburg's houses trembled, and while the battle raged on its outskirts its people listened. The surrounding fortifications, the protective barricade whose armed heights formed a hooked thumb-and-forefinger, were only two miles from town. A dark cloud of smoke, ominous as a thunderhead, hung over the rim of those encircling ridges, a more nebulous, more changeable semi-circle than the solid hills it shadowed.

Cannon vibrations quivered down every street. The inhabitants tried to judge the fortunes of war by the changing sounds of conflict. Out yonder, down around the railroad cut, up near Shirley's white house, the brave men in gray were fighting to keep Vicksburg safe.

Most of the white civilians were anxious, but confident; the slaves, natural diplomats, reflected their owners' moods. Neither race attempted to do business as usual. The town's fate was being decided in a hitherto unusual way.

The more curious, black and white, clustered around the Cowan house, watching the couriers go in and out of General Pemberton's headquarters. Others climbed Sky Parlor Hill to gaze south, downriver, to where the Yankee admiral, Porter, was massing another enemy fleet in threatening numbers. Some went to the churches to pray, some to the taverns to drink. These were nearly all men. The women who had no errands of mercy in the hospitals stayed home, in parlor or hut, and pretended that household chores occupied their time.

Alex Kittering was too restless to pretend. Awakened by the opening cannonade, she had spent the rest of the night listening, vainly trying to control a fear that mounted with the passing minutes. Beneath the filmy mosquito netting that shrouded her bed, the constant iron rumble seemed as oppressively enclosed as the heat.

Rising at daybreak brought no surcease. The girl wondered how the gray soldiers could stand the sustained bombardment, the nerve-wracking noise. Imagination pictured havoc and carnage, made her meager breakfast tasteless.

She knew Bryce Furlong had planted the seeds of her worry. His contempt for Pemberton's beaten Army of Defense had shaken her confidence. Whipped men who had run once, might run again. Poll had claimed that Bryce was prejudiced, made blind angry by his sorry remount. Emilie had simply refused to believe that any Southerner could show cowardice.

Both explanations, Alex thought, were wishful thinking. Bryce was a major, a veteran; he knew a rout when he saw one. She was almost sorry he hadn't called to quarrel about her nursing Tempe Dixon. A good angry argument might lessen her trust in his opinion.

At the hospital Alex found her own uneasiness magnified in every ward. The bed-ridden soldiers, sick or wounded, were troubled by the guns. A few shivered; more tossed with feverish restlessness. Many stared listlessly, plucked at covers, as they listened. The talk was subdued and sporadic, with long pauses.

"Ain't getting closer," a soldier said.

"You hope," said the man in the next bed.

Alex, passing among them, smiled until her lips ached. She came from outside, and every inmate who could talk greeted her with a question.

"Any news, ma'am?"

"Not yet," Alex said.

"How's it going, ma'am?"

"We don't know yet."

"Is us winning or losing, miss?"

"All we know is that there's a battle."

"Hell! Begging your pardon, but there ain't no missing *that* sound."

A shellburst victim, an amputee, broke into a peal of shrieked hysteria. "Oh, God damn them, God damn them, God damn them, why don't they stop?"

It took several minutes for Alex and Doctor Randall to quiet the man while the other patients watched with shocked and silent disapproval.

Turning away, sickened more by the gangrenous odor than the violent outburst, Alex hurried from the room. A cheerful voice near the doorway checked her departure.

"Hit's all right, Miss Kittering. The blooming barrage takes some poor blighters that way."

She stopped to stare, piqued by the strange, high-pitched voice. This patient was a round-faced man, not tall, with a ruddy complexion hardly faded by hospital pallor. He was sitting up, fully dressed, with a bandaged leg propped on a stool.

"You know my name, soldier?"

"That's right. It ain't—isn't—likely I'd forget."

"I'm afraid you have the advantage."

"Christmas Eve, Miss. I was with Tempe Dixon shepherding blacks for labor. Name of Jollibee. Cedric Walter Jollibee."

"You're a friend of Tempe's, then?"

"The same squad," Jollibee said, "till I took a ruddy minnie ball in the calf. 'Amstrung me, it did, but it didn't break no bones and it's healing proper."

"Were you—at the Big Black River, Mister Jollibee?"

Jollibee grinned and shrugged. "Big and little. Black, green, yellow and chocolate. If you ask me I've been at every stinking stream in the state of Mississippi."

"No, I mean at the battle. Two days ago."

"I was here then. Why?"

"Well," said Alex, "somebody told me that our boys—Tempe, too—ran." She flushed slightly under Jollibee's gaze. "I—you—do you believe it?"

"I believe it. But it's nothing to fret about, Miss Kittering. We skipped away from Shiloh, and Corinth, too. If Tempe Dixon ran he had a good reason."

Alex glanced toward the distant thunder. She said, "There's good enough reason out there now."

"No," Jollibee said, shaking his head. "That's not the same pot of tea. Not quite. I came past those bluffs the other day. Stout as the Tower of London, those works. Tempe and Taze and Lack and the others can hold there till doomsday."

"You sound very sure, Mister Jollibee."

"That's my considered professional opinion, and I've been soldiering for donkey's years." Jollibee nodded gravely. "I intend to rejoin my fellows at the first possible instance."

Alex was warmed by his calm definiteness. For the first time that day victory seemed more probable than defeat. She said, "You're English, aren't you?"

"Cor!" said Jollibee, exaggerating his Cockney speech. "Now, 'owever did you guess?" He joined her laughter, added a farewell piece of advice. "Ease your mind, miss. Our side ain't—isn't—exactly as safe as churches, but we'll win today hands down."

The girl felt much better after her meeting with the Englishman. She returned home to find her grandfather clumping through the downstairs rooms. As his crutches thudded more loudly, Alex realized that the cannonade had stopped.

"Listen, Grandpa."

Joab's unlit cigar twitched between his teeth as he cocked his head. He stared at his granddaughter, nodded. The French clock on the parlor mantel chimed twice.

"The cannon have stopped."

The old man removed his cigar, glared at its frayed end, tossed it into the empty fireplace. He didn't think that one battle, a half-century ago, made him a military expert, but he knew that an artillery lull was a prelude to a charge. He said, merely, "Yes, Alex."

"Does—does that mean it's over?"

"No, Alex."

"But—"

"It's only beginning. I'm afraid it will not end for a long time." Weeks, Joab thought, or months. Those who spoke confidently of Joe Johnston threatening Grant's rear forgot about the Union strength along the Memphis-Charleston Railroad.

The old man and his granddaughter did not hear the Yankee signal guns, but nobody in Vicksburg missed the crashing explosion of the Confederate army's initial volley. In the Cherry Street house the crystal chandelier tinkled wildly, Mimosa dropped a tray, and Epie Mae Kittering stifled a scream.

Neither Alex nor Joab noticed these minor, closer noises. They concentrated on the distant turmoil, gazing at each other in sorrowful distress. With unspoken understanding they knew they were both thinking the same thing. That was death out there, two miles away, where men were locked in clamorous struggle for the once friendly, walnut-shaded hills.

The girl prayed for a Southern victory that would save her town from capture. Joab, with weary disillusion, didn't bother to pray.

I tried to tell them, he thought, I talked myself blue but nobody listened. He groped for a chair, slumped into it. Nobody had listened and now the war, no longer confined to the river, was around them all.

"Alex."

"Yes, Grandpa?"

"Would you pour me a drink, please?"

She fetched the decanter, filled a glass, watched him gulp the liquor.

Her voice seemed like a thin, young echo of the old man's strained tones.

"Does it help, Grandpa?"

"What?"

"The whisky."

"Not really," he said. "Not really, Alex."

They sat for a long time in silence, drained of emotion, in an apathy that accepted the distant gun-roll as a familiar, ever-present sound. Epie joined them, very pale but working embroidery with agile, steady fingers. Mimosa and Andrew hovered and vanished, moving on tiptoe like attendants at a funeral. As the shadows in the room thickened, predicting the end of an endless afternoon, Epie Mae spoke with quiet petulance.

"I do wish Stephen would get here."

"He will when he can, Ma."

"He didn't come home at all last night, Alex."

"I'm sure he couldn't help it."

Joab stirred, glanced at his daughter-in-law. He said, "Stephen's a staff officer, Epie, and they all must have had other things on their mind last night."

"Other things than what, Father?"

"Why—other than domestic duties." The old man was a trifle surprised at Epie's tone. The question had been almost sharp.

"A man's first duty," Epie said, "is to his family."

"But, Ma, they knew there'd be a battle today." Alex was startled out of her lethargy by her mother's cold, flat statement. What had disturbed that usually calm manner? Then, thinking she knew, Alex felt a rush of affection. The battle's nearness set everybody's teeth on edge. "You needn't worry, Ma."

"Worry?"

"Yes. Pa's at Headquarters."

"I know that, child."

"I mean, he's safe. He won't be in any danger."

"Well, I should hope not," said Epie, looking at her daughter as at a complete stranger. "Wherever did you get such a ridiculous notion?"

"Epie," said Joab, "it isn't so ridiculous. In case you haven't noticed there's one hell of a fight—"

"That will do, Father. I declare your language is deplorable."

Alex gasped at the brusque interruption. She saw Joab's openmouthed amazement. Her mother scowled at them both, flushed, and sprang to her feet, spilling her needlework. She kicked the cloth aside as her voice rose, thick with fury.

"Why are you both staring at me?"

Alex, frozen, thought of the hysterical soldier. She had never heard her mother speak like that, never seen her teeth bared. She seemed an entirely different person.

"We're not staring, Epie."

"No, Ma."

"You are! You are!" Epie pressed both palms to her cheeks, rolled her eyes. "He told you, didn't he? He told you!"

"Who?"

"Your fine son! Stephen!" She spat the name. "He promised not to tell. He swore he'd take me away to Mobile or Biloxi so that nobody'd know till it was all over!"

"Stephen hasn't told me anything."

"Ma, you'd better let me—"

"Lies! Lies!" Epie stamped, beside herself. "He kept me here for his pleasure! And now—those guns—it's too late! The Yankees are all around us, all around us, and I'm trapped here! Trapped!"

"Ma, please calm yourself." Alex reached out to comfort her mother.

Epie slapped her daughter's hand away. "Don't touch me! A grown daughter. You're all alike! *Kitterings!* At my age. You've made me a laughing stock! My friends."

"Epie, you can't blame Stephen if the Union army—"

"Not blame him?" Epie's mirthless laughter made her listeners wince. "I *do* blame him! The blame is Stephen's, the shame mine! Him, and his lustful, sinful—" She choked on the words, burst into tears, turned to run from the room. One last, sob-broken sentence trailed after her. "I hope—I hope he burns in hell!"

Joab, watching Epie's ungainliness as she ran, suddenly realized her predicament. Poor Epie, he thought, and cursed himself for not noticing. She had hidden her condition with wide-skirted, loosely fitted dresses, but Stephen should have spoken. His son's recent apologetic subservience to Epie had seemed his normal manner.

"Grandpa," said Alex, stunned and bewildered. Her mind guessed at the reason for Epie's outburst, shied away from it.

The old man didn't hear his granddaughter. Mimosa appeared in the doorway, and her impassiveness betrayed knowledge. Joab wasn't surprised. No mistress could hide morning-sickness from a slave-maid. He was the product of a frontier Mississippi, belonged to an earlier, more outspoken generation. His question ignored Alex's presence with hoarse bluntness.

"How long, Mimosa?"

"Four, five months. Maybe more." Mimosa shrugged, shook her head. "I ain't exactly sure, Mister Joab." She had kept Epie's secret, would keep those that involved turpentine treatments and peppery concoctions that failed to induce miscarriage. Mimosa, in such matters, considered all males as enemies.

"Sweet-living Jehovah," said Joab. "That's all we needed!"

Alex's slow nod agreed, sharing his distress. The girl was not upset by her mother's pregnancy, realized its abrupt disclosure was cannonade-inspired. But she was deeply shocked by Epie's bitterness, the violently expressed hatred for Stephen.

"Poor Ma," she said, thinking of her father.

Joab's glance showed scowling admiration. Never, he thought, in this house or at Tonica Hill, had an expected offspring been announced in such virago terms, but Alex was taking it well. Knowing health and age were important, he said, "She'll be all right, Alex."

You ain't doing the birthing, old man, Mimosa argued silently. She cleared her throat to recall them to normal matters.

"Major Bryce is a-calling, Miss Alex."

Bryce Furlong glowed with news of the victory. Vicksburg's defenders had repulsed the Yankees with heavy losses. They could easily stand firm until Joe Johnston relieved the town. The major was not surprised that Joab nodded abstractedly, and clumped out; he was delighted by Alex's warm greeting.

The girl obviously wished to please him. He forgot past differences and hurt feelings. Tempe Dixon's name was not mentioned, but Bryce, magnanimously, dismissed that incident as unimportant. By her behavior Alex apologized for her former willfulness.

It was a feat worthy a skilled actress. She was trying to be very nice to her fiancé, because she had just discovered that her mother hated her father.

BOOK THREE

The Bluffs

· *19* ·

The lovely, rolling countryside that separated the two capitals, at Washington and Richmond, had become the great duelling ground of the war. To the majority of stay-at-home spectators, Northerners or Southerners, this was the center ring that held the main attraction.

Even when the arena was quiet, the great army antagonists resting, it did not lose its magnetism. The Federal Government, as if stunned stupid by the defeat at Chancellorsville, worried itself sleepless over the Army of the Potomac, but failed to remove the discredited Hooker from its command.

A jubilant Confederacy waited for its General Lee to invade the North, settle all doubts about independence. The Army of Northern Virginia, gray veterans sassy with victory, expected it. Everybody, on both sides, expected the invasion. The only questions were "when" and "how."

In that tense atmosphere the other theaters of war were afterthoughts. President Lincoln, who knew better, was advised that Vicksburg, 'way down in Mississippi, was less important than the closer, immediate threat.

President Davis, who lived there, hoped that Lee would scare the North into panic that would take pressure off his home state. He still thought Pemberton and Joe Johnston could handle U. S. Grant.

In spite of a brilliant campaign Grant had failed to capture Vicksburg. His cocksure Army of Tennessee had been smashed back from its defenses.

This Yankee army, with justice, was proud of its record. In the twenty days after they crossed the Mississippi River the bluecoats marched one hundred and eighty miles, won five battles, captured the state capital and 6,000 prisoners, seized 88 enemy cannon. They had inflicted heavier casualties than they suffered. They had also eaten everything edible in their path, and one repulse was as easily swallowed.

At ten o'clock on the morning of May 22nd, 1863, Grant let them try again. The three corps stormed the Vicksburg defenses all along the line. Fighting with reckless courage the Yankees took a few, un-

important outer-works, planted several flags. The Confederates fought
with murderous efficiency. The attack ended in failure.

Grant sent north for siege guns.

"Truce!" shouted the small officer. "You hear now, you-all? There's been
a truce arranged between us and the Yanks, a-starting at three o'clock
this afternoon!"

Tempe Dixon turned to stare at the messenger. Other riflemen in the
trench were more vocal. A chorus of catcalls and derisive whistles saluted the announcement.

"Truce?"

"Who says?"

"Truce, my flea-bitten foot!"

"It's some damn snide Yankee trick."

"Sure it is!"

"Reckon the Yanks've had a belly full."

"A blue-belly full! Haw!"

"What for a truce, Lieutenant-boy?"

The courier, a boy Lieutenant certainly to judge by the down on his
pink cheeks, glared at the veterans. He never quite believed these hard-
shell Mississippi foot soldiers recognized his commission. Back home
in Charleston it was understood that two years' study at The Citadel
certainly qualified a gentleman, of any age, for a volunteer second-
lieutenancy.

"I'll tell you what for," he yelled. He was young enough to think ungrammatical speech indicated toughness, that loudness exerted authority.
"I'll tell you, you cotton-picking heathen. The Yanks want to bury their
dead!" In the sudden quiet the lieutenant visibly swelled his chest. He
knew how to handle these oafs, after all.

"All right, Lieutenant," said Sergeant Tazewell. "We won't interfere
with that. How many hours?"

"Eh?"

"The truce, son. How long does it last?"

"Oh. Five hours. From three till eight." Like a ruffled South Carolina
gamecock the youngster strutted off down the trench.

The dusty infantry, tattered and clay-smeared to a monochrome sepia
that blended gray and butternut, reacted to the message with an almost
ludicrous solemnity. Men spoke in subdued tones, climbed onto the
firing-step with the elaborate casualness of drunkards. They gazed over
the parapet at the twice-contested battlefield, the ground between the
armies. Standing together, a packed, silent rank, the riflemen looked
down and across that shadeless, bullet-desolated strip where no man
walked and lived.

It was high noon, and mid-summer hot. The sun overhead was a round, yellow-white blister on a cloudless blue sky. With pitiless clarity the sunshine's brightness exposed every detail, pebble and weed, in the baked plot of earth.

But the shimmerings above the enemy dead were not heat waves. The murmuring flies, blue-black and glistening, clustered in flickering masses.

Their perpetual buzz emphasized the noon-day quiet. At intervals a cannon clanged, but the rival batteries were only trying to keep each other honest. Few rifles were fired once the truce was announced.

Lack Norris mopped his brow, and spat. He said: "The poor bastards. Three days in the sun. Time they was put away decent."

"More than time," Tempe said. He swallowed hard, fighting nausea. The stench that rose from the bloated corpses was sickening. Tempe thought the odor part of the stifling, breathless heat.

The Yankee bodies were strewn like jetsam left by a careless tide. They lay as they'd fallen, with their arms, blue clumps huddled in the cane, crumpled among the brakes, sprawled in the ditch. Men's limbs were as lifeless as the rifles, useless debris left by the receding waves of two assaults.

Lack softly whistled a snatch of tune. "Well, Father Abraham," he said, "I reckon this is as far as they come."

"Seems as if," Tempe said sadly. They all knew the Northern rallying song, had parodied it obscenely around campfires. But no one was joking now. The dead were soldiers like themselves, and there but for the grace of God—

"I wish they'd get at it," Tazewell said.

"Yes," said Tempe. At least the field was deathly still now except for the flies. The night after the assault had been noisy with moaning wounded, pain-twisted voices clearly audible through the gunfire. Some had even called out intelligibly; others had blubbered, whimpered, shrieked. In the warm darkness it had been worse than the first night at Shiloh, where thunder and lightning drowned the wailing chorus.

One cried 'God bless us,' Tempe thought, recalling a quotation. Wasn't that *Macbeth*? Like the murderer in the play he had been unable to say, 'Amen.'

There were other cries that were welded into his memory. The unseen Yankee who called for his mother, a plaintive, puzzled query repeated over and over. The other poor soul who went to his Maker in screaming blasphemy. But the worst had been the Yank who asked for water.

There had probably been scores of such requests from thirst-tormented wounded. The men in Tempe's trench would remember a single voice. The same voice endlessly speaking the same two words. *Water, please.*

The man had begged through the night. *Water, please.* It had an unchanging insistence that was easily identifiable. *Water, please*. Moonlight and gunfire made compliance impossible. To move out between the lines was plain suicide.

By sunrise death had silenced the others, but the quavering plea continued. *Water, please*. The Confederates heard it whenever there was a lull in the fighting, imagined it when musketry crackle and shell-screech made hearing impossible. Growing fainter, the voice ticked away the hours of a long day; it was only a weak croak in the late afternoon.

Through some trick of acoustics the gray sharpshooters couldn't place the sound. They riddled the cane with futile mercy shots, waited tensely, cursed as the cry came again.

He died in the dusk, Tempe recalled, God rest his soul and give him drink. He wondered if the bluecoat realized he had a passel of rebel mourners.

"Eating time," cried a voice now.

"Such as it is," Lack said.

The rations, cooked behind the lines and brought forward during the night, were guarded by a captain, with detail, from the 37th Mississippi. This officer carefully measured out each man's share—a small pound of hard bread, a half-pound of stringy, overcooked beef.

Canteens rattled as soldiers prepared to wash down the meal with water. Every squad debated the question that Lack Norris now asked his messmates. "Sarge. Tempe. Shall we eat it all now or save some for later?"

"Well," Tempe said, "I'm hungry."

"Shucks, man," said Lack, "that ain't an answer. That ain't even a reasonable argument. Everybody in this whole damn army is hungry, and this here mouthful won't do a hell of a lot about it!"

Tazewell placed beef on bread, hefted it. "It's all we get for twenty-four hours, Lack."

"Now, there's an unnecessary reminder."

Tempe rasped a thumbnail through the stubble on his chin. "Let's eat," he said. "That new lieutenant says we'll be relieved tonight. Maybe we can rustle up a decent meal."

"And shave," Tazewell said. "And bathe."

"My lice get nervous at the words." Lack scratched inside his shirt. "All right. We feast now, and gamble on later. Did I say feast? That sun must be getting to me."

They dawdled over the food, trying to multiply the skimpy bites by chewing slowly. Tempe, gnawing beef and sipping tepid, metallic-tasting water, realized they really hadn't eaten a full, satisfactory meal since Champion's Hill. He hoped the quartermaster general, whoever he was, was being extra careful with supplies. It was too damn soon to be scraping the bottom of any barrels.

He noticed that neither of his friends, in fact none of the men within earshot, uttered many complaints. Veterans didn't expect to feed sumptuously in the front lines, but grousing was their normal recreation.

Golly, Tempe decided, we're all too scared to contemplate what a shortage in victuals would mean.

Shrugging the thought away, Tempe deliberately rejected whatever he'd read about the great sieges in history. Sufficient unto the day was the truce. He was aware that the cannon had stopped, that a crow, streaking past overhead, cawed with raucous loudness.

The sergeant licked his fingers, glanced up at the sky, down over the parapet. His casualness failed to conceal relief.

"Here comes their burying party."

Tempe turned to watch. All along the fresh, dark furrow that marked the newly dug Yankee entrenchments, blue figures were crossing into the open. They waded into the cane slowly, not hurrying. Sunlight winked on the shovels and picks they carried; the black slouch hats looked very dark, their bare arms and galluses very light. A few were stripped to the waist, but none wore jackets.

They came forward in groups until the field was thronged with moving men, and the uneven tread of laggard steps shook the earth. Tempe saw a man stumble, the clash of his dropped spade sounded like a struck anvil.

Lack put his rifle aside, started to scramble over the rampart. He said, "I'm going down there."

"Why not?" Tazewell said. "It's a truce."

Glancing left and right, Tempe could see that singly, in pairs and squads, weaponless soldiers were climbing out of the works, strolling down the slopes. The sepia-tinted gray dribble swelled to a slow, human landslide.

"Let's go," the sergeant said.

They clambered from the trench, ambled after Lack. Tempe found the air outside the close clay walls a trifle cooler. By the time he reached the ditch at the bluff's foot a hedge of Confederates bordered the battlefield. The Yankees were already digging graves.

For a few minutes the gray infantry stood in respectful silence, watching the enemy work. There were no offers to help, not from unwillingness, but out of politeness. The Yanks were good soldiers, entitled to bury their own dead. And the toiling bluecoats understood.

Then, the talk began, friendly banter in the soft, Southern voices and the flat mid-Western tones.

"Hello, Reb."

"Hi, you, Yank."

"Howdy, Johnny."

"Afternoon, bluecoat."

"Hot, ain't it?"

"This, Yank? This ain't hot."

"Always like this in May, Johnny?"

"Naw. Sometimes it gets real uncomfortable."

"You Johnny Rebs all talk tall."

"Why, on a real hot day you can fry fish just by setting the skillet in the sun."

Tempe, edging closer, listened with mixed feelings. This morning these men had been trying to kill each other; now they were as neighborly as mammies in the laundry. The Yanks were muscular veterans, sunburned and rawboned, with callused hands. They were mostly young, and he guessed that the majority were farm boys from the prairie states, the Northwest Territory. They had been weathered by service to the tough pliancy of old leather.

He wasn't surprised at the lack of animosity. The bluecoats, too, had learned to respect their enemy, to forget hate when the fighting ended. Only politicians and civilians drew bitter, wordy caricatures that depicted soldiers on the other side as monsters.

Given another time, Tempe decided, and we'd all go off fishing together. He wished it would happen.

Lack was talking now to a lanky, straw-haired Union corporal. The Yank seemed about nineteen, if you looked close.

"Who you?" asked Lack.

"Joe Williams, Johnny."

"No." Lack's gesture included a group. "I mean, which crop of Billy Yanks?"

"Twenty-second Iowa. Thirteenth Corps."

"McClernand's?"

"Yep. We was off on your right three days back."

"Picking berries?"

"Skim it, Johnny. We give you what for over there."

"And got paid back with interest."

"Oh, I dunno. We pretty near took your Square Fort."

"Pretty near is second best."

"One of our boys—alone—captured fourteen of you rebels. Feller named Griffith."

"I heard something about that. Had a repeating rifle, didn't he?"

"Yep. A Colt's repeater. Some officer dropped it when they tried to take that gun emplacement. Griffith picked it up just in time to catch your boys with empty muskets."

"Well, we've still got the cannon."

"True. What else've you got?"

"We've got Vicksburg, Yank, and we aim to hold it." Lack took out a cigar, bit off its end.

The lanky corporal licked his lips. He said, "I was speaking in the trading sense. That cheroot now. You got more of them?"

"Tobacco? We got more tobacco than bullets."

"You wouldn't care to swap?"

"Depends."

"We ain't had a smoke for days. And few chaws."

"Make an offer."

"Well." The bluecoat reached inside his shirt. "I got me a little sack of coffee beans I could spare."

Tempe and Sergeant Tazewell stiffened. Lack, lighting his cigar, used cupped palms to hide his eagerness. They had not tasted any coffee for weeks, nor real coffee since God knew when. The last brew they'd made had contained a select blend of ground acorns.

"Coffee?" said Lack.

"Yep."

"In the bean?"

"We put it in a bucket and pound it fine with rifle butts."

"I reckon it skins the cat."

Glancing cautiously about, Tempe smiled and relaxed. Similar transactions were taking place all around them. The field was rapidly assuming the aspect of an open market-place. Trading was brisk, business-like. He saw a butternut-clad private offer to exchange a bowie knife for something; a bandy-legged Yank hastily patted the last earth on a grave, turned to haggle.

"You willing to swap, Johnny?"

"How much for how much?" asked Lack.

"This sack for say-maybe a dozen of them stogies."

"Well—"

"It's a fair barter."

"Middling fair."

"I'll throw in these newspapers." The corporal brandished a folded wad of pages. "We've read them, but they ain't so old."

"I reckon you've made a deal."

Tempe moved forward to join in the negotiations. He contributed more cigars, and let Tazewell bargain with an enemy sergeant. While he thumbed through the Yankee newspapers, Tempe listened, grinning, to two Irishmen who had forgotten they belonged to opposing armies.

The one in blue was a stalwart redhead; the other, slim in patched butternut, had a shock of raven-black hair. Both spoke with a heavy brogue that thickened as the conversation waxed.

"And what name would you be having, Yank?"

"O'Connell, it is. Michael Joseph O'Connell."

"A relation of himself? The Liberator?"

"Sure, I'm thinking we were once."

"Then, shake hands with Peter Whelan."

They pumped hands solemnly, touched by the chance meeting on this new sod. Whelan, the Confederate, shared his plug of chewing tobacco without hint of trade.

"I'm from the west," he said. "County Mayo."

"I'm from Armagh myself."

"Armagh! God help you! No wonder you're fighting for the naygur-lovers."

"That I am not. But didn't the ship land me in Boston-Mass, and my pickax take me far out to Iowa?"

"Sure, that's the way of it. We shipped to Biloxi after the famine. And me standing no higher than my da's boot top."

Tempe turned away, wondering what beside the small army pay made immigrants like these join a war that didn't concern them. A wish to conform to new neighbors? A hope to win place fast? Sheer zest for fighting and adventure? Whelan, for example, must have lived poorly competing with slave labor, but risked his life daily to perpetuate it.

Then, staring at the stained newsprint, Tempe forgot the Irishmen. He held three papers, the Cincinnati *Commercial*, the Missouri *Democrat*, and the Chicago *Tribune*. Their front pages showed different advertisements and local items, but all had columns and comment on the same story under type heads of mourning black.

"Listen, boys," cried Tempe, reading. "Lee whipped the Yanks to a frazzle at a place called Chancellorsville in Virginia."

It was the first the gray ranks had heard of the recent Confederate victory. Lack Norris grabbed one sheet; Tazewell took another. Others crowded around, the literate craning to catch a glimpse, the illiterate waiting to hear. Nobody was surprised to get the information from Yankee newspapers. They told as many lies as their own journals, but they were the Southerners' best source of Northern feelings.

"That ain't news," said the bluecoat corporal.

"It is to us," Lack said.

"Sure," O'Connell said, "them Easterners can't fight."

"Can't or won't." The corporal sounded definite.

"If you Yanks," Lack said, "would be a mite sprier about delivering the papers, we might learn these things a lot sooner."

"Sorry, Johnny. We been busy."

Tempe, tightly gripping the crumpled sheets, was envious of the triumphant Army of Northern Virginia. It must be fine to win more often than you lost, to make enemy editors howl and complain the way these were doing. But he had a vague feeling of neglect and was startled to hear a Yankee voice put it into words.

"Them paper-collar dudes back East think they got a mortgage on this whole damn war!"

"Virginia's a long way off," said Corporal Williams. "'Bout as far as Iowa, I guess. What happens up there ain't going to change nothing around here."

"Well, now, it might," Tazewell said. "It just might." He beamed at the newspaper, folded it carefully. "You never can tell."

He's all cheered up, thought Tempe, but he won't spill a professional opinion in front of the enemy. It was easy to follow the big sergeant's thinking. If General Lee was as powerful and rampageous as the Cincinnati *Commercial* seemed to fear, he might be able to spare some troops to help Joe Johnston. That would surely end the siege.

The good news, the successful trading, the friendly talk, sent the sharpshooters back to their lines with renewed spirits. Relief made the day perfect. They were lounging in a glen, sniffing the aroma of boiling coffee when the truce ended. The first enemy shell that whined through the dusk made them dive for cover.

"For cripe's sake!" Lack Norris said. "Don't spill the coffee."

· 20 ·

VICKSBURG had always been a river town. The traffic and commerce, the steamboats, barges and skiffs, the very level of the water, made the Mississippi a fascinating spectacle for slave and free. Not even the pressing Federal army, spread around them to the east, could change the habits of a lifetime.

The inhabitants still looked riverward for entertainment, for meditation, for reassurance, like gallery gods who preferred to gaze down on pageantry from the heights. Their preference was not entirely a free choice. Only the defending soldiers were allowed into the network of trenches on the landward bluffs that surrounded the town. The sound of gunfire across two intervening miles whetted curiosity without appeasing it. A listener could only guess when battle raged or slackened, how the gallant gray troops fared, whether the Yankee besiegers were making progress. From the other bluffs, the high ridges above the Mississippi River, a spectator could see what was happening.

If this waterfront panorama displayed a formidable enemy threat, it

[215]

was also familiar and unfrightening. There, on the wide, unchanging, twisted stream, was a fleet of enemy gunboats, but once before the towns-folk had gazed down on the like. Farragut's warships had come, and shelled, and gone. The damage had been unimportant. This flotilla, un-der Admiral Porter, numbered more vessels, eighty-one by actual count, but that fact was calmly dismissed.

The mighty Father of Waters was Vicksburg's moat. Guarding it were the batteries whose heavy cannon had earned the term—Gibraltar of the Confederacy. The U. S. Navy, in ironclads or wooden hulls, couldn't possibly silence those big, shore-based guns. Q.E.D., as the scholars said, the town was safe from assault on its river-bank side.

Alex Kittering was not deceived by this common conclusion. It was, she thought, like boasting about the back door's locks while an axe ham-mered on the front one. The girl was convinced that Vicksburg's fate was being decided on land, in the eastern defenses, by the stubborn men in gray. If Grant's army broke through, the river batteries were use-less, and the river itself made flight or retreat impossible. That was ob-vious from Sky Parlor Hill. The enemy gunboats weren't active, but their patrols commanded the river. Bryce Furlong, gazing through bin-oculars, reported another detail.

"The bluecoats seem to be building a gun emplacement over there in DeSoto."

"That's ill planned," Poll Randall said. "What good can a cannon do 'way across the river?"

"They can shoot at the courthouse," Alex said, not sure that so distant a gun could reach that conspicuous, white target. Only politeness kept her boredom hidden.

She had climbed to the town's favorite view-point with only mild pro-tests. The blonde girl's presence made pleasing Bryce easier; a threesome offered protection from any intimate discussion.

From dawn to dusk, these days, Sky Parlor Hill was never completely deserted. The idle, the indolent, the curious and the concerned flocked there at all hours. The crowd changed, increased or diminished, but never vanished. Some slaves spent hours staring vacantly at the enemy fleet; some citizens, with nothing better to do, followed every ship move-ment like diligent commodores.

Now, early on an uncomfortably hot morning, under a brassy sun that was burning the haze from the river, the hilltop held about three-score spectators. Invalid soldiers were sprinkled like grit among the so-ber civilian coats and the few more colorful dresses. There was the ever-present wolf-pack of small boys, the white leaders noisier than the dark-skinned followers. The adult slaves, as usual, were the more notori-ous work-dodgers, a lazy black fringe sprawled on the edge of the bluff.

Alex decided the motley gathering was a miniature reflection of Vicksburg itself. She couldn't remember when the town had been so crowded, not in flood time, or holiday; there were actually as many strangers on the streets as familiar faces.

The girl was counting civilian refugees, not soldiers. Not even the heated oratory and the wild torchlight parades that urged and welcomed secession had attracted such an influx of visitors.

"More mouths to feed," muttered Alex.

"What's that?" asked Poll.

"Nothing important," Alex said, and bit her tongue. Food, she thought, in another week or so, would be the most important topic in town. Epie Mae's petulance at the breakfast table had made that very apparent.

"Andrew," she had said, shoving her cup away, "this is not coffee, but slop! And my eye-opener tasted worse!"

"I'm sorry, Miz Epie, but—"

"But, what?"

"There isn't much left and—"

"Well, get some more!"

Her mother, Alex realized, was using her delicate condition as an excuse to tyrannize the household. There wasn't any real shortage in the Kittering larder as yet, but there was no way to replenish dwindling supplies from empty markets. Stephen acted as cowed as the servants, and even Joab refused to argue with his daughter-in-law. If Epie demanded special dishes life would be hectic as long as the siege lasted.

Alex shrugged away these speculations. "Bryce," she said, "has there been any news from General Johnston?"

"Not to my knowledge," Bryce said. "Not yet."

"He is coming, isn't he?"

"Of course he is!" Poll Randall said, with childish faith. "As soon as his army is ready."

Dismay clouded Bryce's face. He said, "Don't even *think* anything else, Alex."

We are all, Alex thought wearily, refusing to face the harsh fact that relief may be late in coming.

Even Poll's cheerful confidence sounded false. "Joseph E. Johnston is a Virginia gentleman. He'd never leave us in distress!"

Bryce had seen Johnston's army, knew its numbers. The slight Virginian had a great military reputation, but nobody could manipulate divisions that he didn't have. Yet surely, by this time, Johnston had been reinforced by troops from Forrest, from Bragg, maybe even from Robert E. Lee.

"Unless the siege is raised soon," Bryce said, "we're in trouble. We've hardly enough horse fodder for another ten days."

Alex considered the remark typical. Bryce would show concern for horses before it entered his mind that people could go hungry. She knew he was serving as volunteer aide to General Forney, and that the duty irked him. Her father had told her how Bryce carried dispatches to the lines with reckless speed, riding his own gray gelding, Cloudy, down the Graveyard Road as if enemy shellfire didn't exist.

She said, "Your own regiment is probably galloping toward us this minute, Bryce." As soon as she'd spoken she regretted it. His lips twisted in a grimace very like the soldiers she dosed with quinine. He spoke with bitterness.

"And I should be leading them! This is no place for a cavalry officer!"

Poll clutched Alex's arm, pointed. "Look, there," she cried. "What's that Yankee gunboat trying to do?"

Bryce turned, raising the field glasses. Alex shaded her eyes with her hand. A stir swept through the people around them. The laziest slave condescended to rise and stare. In the sudden tense hush a boy's shrill, changing voice rose and cracked. "That there's the U.S.S. *Cincinnati!*"

The enemy ironclad, a long, squat shape with ugly humps of armor over her paddle-wheels, had come tearing out from behind the hairpin bend. The black smoke pouring from her funnels left no doubt she was under forced draft, at full, pitch-pine-and-tallow speed. Her wake boiled; her prow knifed tall, white furrows from the muddy water. The ship's swift dart from behind the curve of the opposite shore, her straight, undeviating course for the near, Vicksburg bank, gave her a look of deadly purpose.

"She means business," Bryce said.

"She's heading for Fort Hill," said Poll.

Alex nodded in silent agreement. They were all river-town natives, too wise in the ways of steamboats to mistake the *Cincinnati's* intent and direction. She was charging in to challenge the Confederate battery in Fort Hill.

"Them Yankees must be daft," said a portly civilian.

"No." A fever-wasted soldier disagreed. "No, it's got plan. If they can silence Hill's guns the bluecoat infantry will attack from the north."

Alex saw the smoke-puff an instant before she heard the cannon. The gunners in Fort Hill had decided that the *Cincinnati* was close enough.

That first shot struck the gunboat's flagstaff. The wind-taut candy-striped Yankee banner crumpled as it was swept away, fluttered through the air, twirling like a gust-driven sheet torn from a clothesline.

The spectators cheered; Alex clapped her hands. The hit was more symbolic than vital, but it touched Southern pride to see the hated flag humbled. Every watcher had a momentary thrill at the visual image of Northern power overthrown. It seemed to capture, in one fleeting glimpse, all that the Confederacy was trying to do!

Before the cheer died the battery's second shot crashed. It was a direct hit that smashed into the ironclad squarely amidships. Metallic dust flew, speckled in the sunlight. The *Cincinnati* shuddered and swerved, knocked off course.

Again, the fort's cannon slammed. The third shell plowed into the gunboat at the water line. Spray spurted like a stabbed artery. The *Cincinnati,* her armor pierced, staggered from the blow, and didn't recover.

On Sky Parlor Hill even the whooping small boys knew the Yankee ironclad was mortally wounded. That was apparent in her list, in the limping way she struggled through a slow turn. The *Cincinnati,* filling fast, could only flee. Already her trailing escort of smaller ships was scattering like disturbed water-bugs.

"By God," said Bryce, "that's damn fine shooting!"

"It's Henri," Poll said.

"Who?"

"Henri Duchesneau, Alex."

"What are you talking about?" Bryce asked.

"That third gun," Poll said patiently. "The Brooks. The shot that hulled the Yankee. Henri's in charge of that cannon."

"How do you know?" Bryce had no wish to applaud Henri Duchesneau. The Creole lieutenant was too damned superior as it was. Whenever they met Bryce was reminded of racecourse and gambling house where he had tasted defeat.

"He told me," Poll said. "When the telegraph wires were cut Henri asked for artillery duty. He was assigned to Fort Hill. And I know the sound of his gun."

Alex, noting Bryce's frown, made no comment. She didn't like his envy of others' achievements, but recognized its roots. He was eager for glory, avidly desired military fame, and the very nature of the siege hobbled him. In the old days she had teased Bryce when he sulked, but Epie's diatribe against Stephen was too fresh in her memory. We must keep our relationship pleasant, Alex silently repeated. She was not aware that she sighed.

They watched the stricken *Cincinnati* wallow in clumsy flight. Fort Hill was silent; the gunners evidently disdained to waste powder on a finished foe. The battered gunboat barely edged around the shield of the west bank's bend when the spectators saw her funnels settle with a tell-tale tremble.

"Sunk her!" shouted a slave.

"That'll learn them!" cried an invalid soldier.

Cheers rose above the riverfront bluffs, rolled from hill to hill. The artillerymen in every battery danced around their guns. An unknown civilian leaned from the courthouse cupola to wave his hat. The crowd atop Sky Parlor Hill yelled itself hoarse. Poll embraced Alex while Bryce, grinning, nodded approval.

You'd think, thought Alex, that we'd lifted the siege. She straightened her bonnet after Poll's impulsive hug. The girl was pleased by the battery's success, but one sunken enemy ironclad didn't really change anything. Alex realized that most of Vicksburg would take it as another proof of the town's invulnerability. She could hear the initial comments around her now.

"Let Porter chaw on that!"

"Damn near blew her out of the river!"

"Never saw such shooting, sir! Never in my born days!"

"The Yankees won't try that again!"

"Ole Grant'll get drunk tonight!"

We make too much, Alex decided, of small victories, grasping at straws to bolster hopes. Her grandfather, Joab, had called such volatile enthusiasm a loser's trait, likened it to the gambler who crowed on winning a small pot with the false premise that it changed bad luck to good. Alex didn't believe that the South was so deluded, for not even the great victories in the east, joyously celebrated, had altered the Federals' slow conquest of the Mississippi Valley.

She could list all the bright names. First Manassas. The Shenandoah Valley. The Seven Days. Hampton Roads, and the flash-in-the-pan success of the *Merrimac*. Second Manassas. Fredericksburg. Chancellorsville. But Grant's growing army was outside Vicksburg.

"Miss Alex! Miss Alex!"

Runcey Carr's bellow interrupted Alex's summary. She turned to watch the boy bound toward her, face flushed almost as red as his hair. Alex smiled, ignoring Bryce's annoyed glance.

"Did you see it, Miss Alex?"

"You mean the *Cincinnati?*"

"Sure! Did we really sink her?"

"We sunk her," Bryce said.

"With three shots," said Poll.

Like a one-man hound Runcey waited for Alex to nod confirmation. Then, hopping from bare foot to bare foot he danced between glee and disappointment. His voice tried to make the same quick shifts.

"Wow! Gol-darn! What a rip-snorting jim-dandy! Wish we'd seen it!"

"How'd you ever miss it, Runcey?" asked Alex.

"We was down street in town," Runcey said, "when we heard the guns. Argufying over the price of biscuits. By the time we climbed up here it was all over. Drat, drat, and double drat!"

"Watch your tongue," Bryce said. He flushed when Poll giggled at Runcey's amazed stare. The Kitterings allowed the boy too much familiarity. Runcey, after all, was only an urchin hireling.

"That's all right, Bryce," said Alex. "We all know Runcey's vocabulary." She glanced past the boy, and her gaze locked with Tempe Dixon's.

Recognition and reaction were simultaneous. Her stomach quivered as her mind registered his identity. Tempe, thought Alex, and her heart jumped. He was standing ten feet away. He looked fit, a little tired, tanned, very ragged. Tempe's gray eyes seemed as keen and clear as ever; his gaze was warm, searching.

Alex realized he needed a haircut. The irrelevant notion made her feel like crying, but she smiled instead. She forgot that Bryce Furlong stood at her elbow.

At that radiant smile Tempe raised his hat, and stepped forward. He had not missed the major's presence, but he would have brushed past Pemberton himself to get closer to Alex's smile. His greeting betrayed his feelings.

"Hello, Alex."

"Hello, Tempe. How're you?"

"Fine, thank you. And you?"

"Just fine."

They made the trite words sound fresh and intimate.

Poll Randall gulped, and glanced at Bryce. His face looked grayer than his uniform. The cold glitter of the glare he fixed on Tempe frightened the blonde girl. It made Runcey Carr's skin prickle with goose flesh.

"Tempe and me," the boy said, "have been a-hunting down grub for his squad."

"Well, I declare," said Poll in loud desperation, "doesn't your ex-patient seem right pert, Alex?"

Neither Tempe nor Alex paid the slightest attention. They continued to speak conventional phrases in a manner that excluded their companions, the hilltop, the world.

"Your family is well?"

"Quite well, thank you."

"Mister Joab?"

"Grandpa flourishes."

Bryce, listening, let his rage mount. This Dixon upstart had been a bother from the beginning. Now his quiet conversation with Alex was intolerable.

"We couldn't find any flour," Runcey said, "and the baker wanted a dollar and a half—U.S.—for one crumby gingercake."

"Is it just stifling in the trenches?" asked Poll.

"Please convey my respects to your grandfather."

"Of course," said Alex.

"Corporal!"

There was a metallic snap in Bryce Furlong's tone that ended friendliness. He pitched it low, but that merely emphasized the hostility.

The effect was electrifying. Poll Randall froze; Alex and Tempe blinked in startled awakening. Runcey, wincing, blurted a correction. "He's a sergeant now."

Tempe silenced the boy with a glance. If Furlong intended to force a quarrel, rank only weighted the odds. This time, Tempe thought, I won't let him make a private matter a military argument.

"Sir?" he said, standing at attention.

"Why aren't you in the lines?"

"Like yourself, Major. I'm off duty."

"You have a pass?" asked Bryce, infuriated by the comparison. Like himself, indeed! This fellow had the gall to set himself up as an equal.

"In my pocket." Tempe did not reach for the pass. He was daring the officer to make an issue of it, before Alex and the other girl, before a dozen curious bystanders.

"Tempe and me," Runcey interjected, "was foraging extra food for the boys in the trenches."

"Did you have any success?" asked Alex. She spoke calmly, in a deliberate attempt to take the initiative from Bryce. Her eyebrows signalled Poll to follow suit.

"With the refugees and all," Poll said, instantly, "the shops are nearly bare." She was thrilled by the tense situation, relished her role in controlling it. "I just wager you had the hardest time."

Runcey said, "We managed to find about three dozen biscuits."

The two soldiers, facing like pugilists at the scratch, heard this flowing chatter with different feelings. Tempe was amused, recognized the trio as peacemakers. Bryce Furlong, momentarily checked by the prattle, felt impotent fury.

"Oh," said Alex, "we can do better than that. You come along to Cherry Street, Tempe. There's half a ham we can spare, and some sugar and—"

"Alex." Bryce's interruption was low but sharp. He spoke behind clenched teeth.

"Yes, Bryce?"

"This invitation. You know my feelings."

"I think so." Alex was tired of pampering Bryce, didn't care if he made a scene. His attitude toward Tempe had made her angry but she showed no temper. "The brave fighting men protecting the town must be fed."

"Damn all that!" Bryce pointed his finger at Tempe. "I'm talking about him! Dixon! I'll not have my fiancée lallygagging through the entire town with this fellow!"

"Mister Furlong," said Tempe, coldly, "your choice of words is offensive."

"And I," Bryce said, "find your manners even more so. I was speaking to the lady."

Poll Randall gasped. This was getting out of hand. A blow swung atop Sky Parlor Hill would be a town scandal in a matter of minutes. Runcey's grin indicated that such talk might explode into action.

Alex, outwardly unperturbed, raised a hand. She said, "Gentlemen, that will do."

Both men looked baffled. Tempe wondered which side the girl was on; he had spoken in her defense. Bryce felt baited beyond endurance, but knew Alex would never forgive a public scene.

The girl gave them no chance to argue. "You are both behaving like children," she said, "and I find it a very distasteful exhibition." As she continued Alex began to enjoy her own phrase-making, the feeling of power over two men. "This is hardly the time for Confederate soldiers to quarrel among themselves. The enemy is at the gates. We all must stand united in defense of our homes."

"Bravo," said Tempe, and laughed.

Bryce glared at him, stared when Alex giggled. The major had been mesmerized by his fiancée's oratory, impressed by her patriotic ardor. Now, she was sharing some obscure joke with Dixon.

"You minx," Poll said. Trust Alex to get one belligerent laughing, and the other tongue-tied with the same speech.

The joshing epithet did more to establish peace than Alex's flowery platitudes. Bryce Furlong visibly relaxed. He trusted Poll's judgment. The blonde girl was right; Alex was playing the coquette, leading Dixon down the garden path.

Bryce had never really understood the feminine game that teased suitors to fluster, but its practice, among belles, was a part of the Southern tradition. A gentleman did not make an issue of so unimportant a gambol.

"I accept the rebuke, Alex," he said, with dignity. His smile was a polite lip movement. He was hoping that Dixon, like a boor, would make a crass remark.

Tempe's bow was carefully correct. "Oh, so do I," he said, gravely. "So do I." He was not going to let Furlong out-do him in courtly manners, though the major had missed the point. The gray-eyed twinkle was for Alex alone, and it shared a secret.

Oh, dear, thought Alex, I wish my knees didn't go limp when Tempe looked at me like that. Bryce was her fiancé. She was promised to Bryce. But, at the moment, the important thing was to keep both men civil. She didn't want to hurt either. They were risking their lives every day.

Refusing to admit that this rivalry flattered her, Alex said, "I meant every word of that speech."

Runcey Carr was slightly disappointed that there wouldn't be a fight, but he took Alex's remarks literally.

"It," he said, "was right fine, Miss Alex. Every bit as good as what General Pemberton said."

"General Pemberton?"

"When?"

"The other day," Bryce said, pleased at the blank expression on Tempe's face. "Right after we threw the Yankees back the second time. It was an address to the troops."

"Never reached us," Tempe said. "Not my company."

Alex grabbed at the chance to keep an impersonal topic going. She appealed to Bryce's vanity, his love of show. He couldn't resist displaying his superior knowledge. The girl coaxed with smile, and voice.

"Tell us what the general said, Bryce."

"Well," said Bryce, "he mentioned that they—the men—had heard he was incompetent and a traitor. That he intended to sell Vicksburg." The major glanced at Tempe. "It seems that there was such talk among certain soldiers."

"All soldiers talk," Tempe said.

"Treasonous slander?"

"Please go on, Bryce," said Alex.

"Yes," Poll said. "Do."

" 'Follow me,' " cried Runcey, quoting, " 'and you will see the cost at which I will sell Vicksburg. When the last pound of beef, bacon and flour, the last grain of corn, the last cow and hog and horse and dog shall have been consumed, and the last man shall have perished in the trenches, then, and only then, will I sell Vicksburg.' "

The boy brandished his fist as he finished, then stood, arm raised, as if fixed by Bryce Furlong's glare. Runcey looked sheepish, aware that he'd stolen the major's thunder.

"How come you memorized it, Runcey?" asked Poll.

"I happened to be down to the *Daily Citizen* when Editor Swords was setting it in type. He was worried about not having enough paper to print many copies, and he asked me, and a couple others, to learn it off by heart."

As if it was Shakespeare, thought Tempe, which it isn't. He didn't care much for the general's conclusion. From the way Runcey and he had tramped the town in vain search for foodstuffs most of the items mentioned were damn near down to last.

Alex was thinking along the same lines. There was no need to stress hunger pangs until they griped. Poor General Pemberton, goaded by unjust accusations, had managed to make defiance depressing.

"To the last man," Poll Randall said.

"Of course it won't come to that," said Bryce. "That's just a figure of speech."

Tempe looked at the major. The man wasn't out there in the works at night, hearing the noises that meant moving supply trains, fresh troops, picks digging emplacements for big rifled cannon. Unless Joe Johnston's boys came a-running to the rescue pretty soon there were going to be more damn-Yankees around Vicksburg than they had in Philadelphia.

"We're getting rid of more'n a hundred prisoners tomorrow," Runcey said. "Ferrying them across to DeSoto on parole. At least we won't have to waste food on greedy bluecoats!"

Alex was reminded that Tempe's problem wasn't solved with a few biscuits. She spoke with brisk efficiency, quelling any objections by imperious assurance.

"Tempe, we'd better get you that half ham right away. Bryce, your arm, please. Runcey, go find our carriage. Scoot, now! Martin's probably dozing in the shade. I'd take it kindly, Tempe, if you'd escort Poll ahead of us."

Runcey scampered away, and the men obeyed Alex meekly. Bryce was scowling, but he was quiet. Tempe Dixon listened to Poll's chatter. They left Sky Parlor Hill with well-bred decorum.

If only it lasts, Alex prayed. Just for a few hours. She knew that she had postponed decision, settled nothing. Inevitable choice was closing in on her like the Federal army around the town. The warm glow she'd felt at seeing Tempe had shaken her resolution to honor her pledge to Bryce.

The distant cannon-rumble reminded her that for the besieged there was always more hope than certainty.

'Twas at the siege of Vicksburg,
Of Vicksburg—of Vicksburg!
'Twas at the siege of Vicksburg,
When the Parrott shells were whistling through the air!
Listen to the Parrott shells!
Listen to the Parrott shells!
The Parrott shells awhistling through the air!

ALEX KITTERING, hammering on the piano's keyboard, sang the parody as loudly as she could, but failed to drown out the noises that inspired it. The whine of arching shells, the tearing bursts that sent down spatters of shrapnel, made an accompaniment that dwarfed the music.

"Please, dear," said Epie Mae in a tone of patient suffering. "My head is just splitting."

"Alex," Stephen Kittering said, "you hear your mother?" He stopped pacing to glance nervously from wife to daughter.

"Yes, Pa." With elaborate care Alex lowered the keyboard cover. It might have been foolishly defiant to play while the shelling shook the house, but at least it was something to do. She had felt an irresistible impulse to fight sound with sound, to show courage through song. Tonight the Yankee siege guns were welcoming June with a barrage that seemed to rain down on the town with cloudburst ferocity.

At three o'clock in the morning, the Federal artillery's favorite hour, the opening thunderclap had routed the family from bed, sent them all scurrying downstairs to comparative safety. The hour accounted for the candlelight, the absence of house servants, their very informal attire.

Stephen paced in a brocaded maroon robe that shimmered as he moved. Epie wore a lavender silk wrapper that made her skin look sallow. Alex had a checked cotton peignoir over her lawn nightdress. In spite of the heat her grandfather was swathed in a quilted, faded dressing gown that overflowed the armchair where he sat reading.

Old Joab glanced up from his book, winked at Alex, licked his thumb and turned a page. Even when a close explosion outside the open windows made the candleflames flicker, he refused to be disturbed.

Trust the Ancient, thought Alex fondly, not to panic. There was probably more frightening noise than real danger. The enemy gunners, army and navy, were forced to shoot high over Vicksburg's bluffs at random, unseen targets.

"Maybe," Stephen said, "they need me down at Crawford Street." He referred to Headquarters in the Cowan house, but he sounded uncertain.

"Don't you dare leave me!" Epie Mae said. She drew the wrapper more tightly around her swollen figure, and sniffed. Her voice became demanding. "Where's Andrew? Where's Mimosa, Benjie, Big Sarah? Those lazy good-for-nothings should be here attending to their duties."

"It's not even four o'clock, Ma."

"Really, Alex, you can't think they're sleeping through all this racket!"

Joab spoke to his book, without turning. "Be reasonable, Epie. There's a scrap-iron hailstorm out there. Worth a body's life to go traipsing around in it. Just pray our people are safe."

"Why shouldn't they be safe, Father?"

"The slave-quarters are wood shacks, flimsy as cigar-boxes. One hit would smash a hut to flinders."

"They were never hit before."

"The Yanks didn't have Parrotts before."

"That's right, dear," Stephen said. "They have big rifled cannon now—siege guns—like those on our riverfront. And Porter's fleet has a great many mortar vessels."

Alex saw her mother's shrug, and bit her lip. There was no use telling Epie these military details. She neither listened nor understood, but blamed others for every inconvenience, discomfort, or moment of fear. With pregnancy her quiet composure had changed to sullen distrust.

"I think it's slackening," Stephen said.

They all listened in tense concentration. Joab closed his first edition of *Little Dorrit* on a crooked forefinger, cupped the other hand behind an ear. Stephen stood very erect, head back, his eyes closed and his mouth open.

Alex, watching them both, believed that their faces displayed an essential difference in their characters. The old man waited, with intelligent patience, for a fact to register; her father seemed to be praying for a miracle.

Poor father, she thought, and glanced at her mother. Epie, lips pursed, was gazing at the carpet. Her whole attitude portrayed resignation.

The cannonade lessened like drums raggedly withdrawing from a parade. There seemed to be no more close shellbursts, and Alex could hear the reports of single guns. In those first moments of comparative quiet she was unable to distinguish between friendly or unfriendly fire.

"Yes," Joab said, "they've definitely diminished in volume."

"Thank God," said Stephen.

"Perhaps now," Epie said, "we all can get some sleep. As usual the

Yankees were just being persnickety. Disturbing folks without harming much of anything. Well, it's over for a while."

A short while, Alex decided, while the over-heated guns cooled. She hoped the men in the trenches had suffered as little harm as her mother believed.

Then, they heard the bell.

It rang with a brazen clang-clang that all Vicksburg knew, a double-note tolling that carried clearly, but seemed a tinkle after the uproar from the cannon. Whoever was pulling the bell rope was hurried and frantic.

"That," said Stephen, "that's the Constitution firehouse."

"Yes," Joab said.

"You mean there's a fire?"

"Yes, Ma." Alex strangely recalled the days of peace when this same tocsin, at night, had been a major event, a dread alarm signal of catastrophe. In her childhood fire was the great enemy that could destroy the whole town overnight. That hazard, like flood and hurricane, was now less frightening than war.

"They hit something," Joab said, "which ain't any wonder. They sure did enough shooting. Thank the Lord there seems to be no wind. Alex, take a look outside and—" He stopped, knuckles whitening as his grip tightened on his book.

Footsteps, running, scraped on the gravel walk, pounded up the front steps. The doorknocker clapped once, and then somebody hammered on the panel. Runcey Carr's voice, muffled and panting, kept time with his beating fist. "Mister Joab! Miss Alex! Everybody!"

"That's Runcey," Joab said, needlessly.

"At this hour," Epie complained.

Alex raced to the door, yanked it open. The boy nearly tumbled into her arms. His eyes were wild; sweat ran in streaks down his smudged face.

"Miss Alex," he said, fighting for breath, "there's—there's a fire!"

"Yes, Runcey. We guessed."

"I—I ran all the way—"

"*Runcey!*" Joab was struggling out of the armchair, pawing for his crutches. "Come in here, boy! What is it?" He ignored his son and daughter-in-law, stood waiting.

"Mister Joab," Runcey said. "Mister Joab, sir. It's—it's the warehouse."

"Our warehouse?"

Runcey nodded, doleful and miserable. He said, "Them Goddam Yankee bastards put a couple shells right into her, Mister Joab."

"Is it bad, Runcey?"

"Burning. The blaze got a headstart before anybody noticed. I come as quick as I could. One gable end is all flame."

"Alex," said Joab, "fetch my clothes. Stephen, you tell Martin to ready the carriage."

"Now, Father," said Epie Mae, "you can't do anything." As if soothed by another's misfortune, she was quietly composed, not snappish now, the matron taking charge of excited children. "I'm sure it's not as serious as Runcey thinks. We'll just send a slave to see. The fire laddies are very efficient."

Stephen, white-faced, said: "Epie's right, Pa. Besides—you might get hurt. The—the Yankees may bombard again with—with renewed vigor."

Skirts hiked to her knees, Alex was already scrambling up the stairway. She heard her grandfather's grim rejoinder. He spoke without bluster, bluntly crisp. "There's no time to argue. Do as you're told, Stephen. Get cracking. The fire laddies don't own that warehouse. I watched it being built. I aim to watch it now."

The girl hastily pulled a dress on over her nightgown, grabbed a cloak, thrust bare feet into shoes. She couldn't waste precious seconds fussing with petticoats, stockings, her hair. Darting into her grandfather's room she snatched clothing from his wardrobe, taking the first suit that came to hand. The warehouse, the family business, had never been Alex's main interest, but she knew what they meant to Joab.

Descending the staircase Alex found the house servants, informed by some mysterious process, had not needed Stephen's summons. They had appeared, fully dressed, with ghost-like suddenness. Andrew took the bundle from her, beckoned Benjie's aid, proceeded to dress Joab quickly and neatly. Mimosa was pouring drinks.

It was only minutes—an interminable, endless delay—before the carriage rattled into the driveway. Alex saw that her father had detached himself from the bustle. Stephen was sipping whisky with dilettante precision. Joab scowled, but made no comment. The younger man, apologetically, stammered an excuse.

"Pa, I—I'd better stay—stay here with Epie."

"Of course," said Epie. "I'm not even sure it's seemly for Alex to—"

"I'm going with Grandpa."

"Come on!" Joab said. He crammed on his hat, clumped to the door. Andrew helped him down the steps and into the vehicle, but none of the slaves spoke. The grave dark faces expressed silent sympathy.

Alex sat beside her grandfather, Runcey on the box with Martin. As soon as the gray team turned toward the center of town they could see the glow, a garish orange that silhouetted billows of thick, black smoke. The girl and the old man sucked in audible breaths.

"There it is," Runcey said.

"Lord, Lord," said the coachman. "That's sure brimstone enough to suit the preacher." Martin, without orders, urged the grays to faster speed. The horses gave him trouble; they were still nervous from the shelling.

The Kittering warehouse, two storied and deep, covered most of a town square on the south side of Washington Street. By the time its owner reached the scene the whole structure was ablaze. Flames licked and darted along the eaves, gleamed through already gaping clapboards. The street entrance, where the office with door and windows formed a drafty box, held the roaring red inferno of a furnace. The heat was intense; it blistered the paint on houses across the road.

Martin, half-standing with taut reins, fought to hold the grays. He said, "The team won't go no closer, Mister Joab."

"This is close enough," Joab said. He spoke very softly as if talking was painful.

Alex wanted to cry, found no consoling words. She touched one of the old man's crippled hands. He turned it, gripped her fingers. The girl could smell the choking fumes from flaming cotton bales, the sharper odor of burned sugar.

"Gone," said Joab. "All gone."

"Nobody could get near it," Runcey said, sadly.

"Two hundred hogsheads of sugar, Alex. I was saving the sugar to pass out when victuals got really scarce."

"Yes, Grandpa." She knew that he meant *give*, not *sell*. Food had supplanted King Cotton as the town's most precious commodity.

Armed soldiers held back the spectators, and others helped the helmeted volunteer firemen. There were two hoses throwing water; men in rows bent and straightened, bent and straightened, as they worked both the town's pumpers. The newer "Big Six" Americus engine shot a stronger stream than the old Southwark, but both looked puny against the conflagration.

Alex saw that these fire-fighters were trying to save the adjacent buildings, realized they could do nothing for the warehouse. The spectators stood in awed silence, black faces and white turned to the flames with rapt fascination. A great many men and boys had risked death by wounds to watch the fire.

She felt her grandfather's clasp slacken, but clung to his hand. Even with the false ruddiness cast by the firelight the old man's cheeks had a chalky pallor.

"Gone," he said, again.

"We still have the steamboats," Alex said.

"Southern ships," Joab muttered, "in a Yankee river."

With a roar that sent a shower of sparks upward into the coiling smoke the warehouse roof collapsed. The flames leaped higher, unleashed, rapidly eating away what structural shape remained. Firemen hastily pushed and pulled the Southwark pumper to a safer place.

"Take me home, Martin," said Joab.

Runcey jumped down from the carriage. He said, "I'll wait here. I'll come around when it's over."

"It's over now, Runcey," the old man whispered.

As they drove back through the empty streets the Yankee cannon started to shell again. Martin let the team run, anxious to get out of the open.

The girl didn't think her grandfather even heard the guns.

Out of a murky sky cluttered with dark, angry clouds, the rain poured down on the trenches, drenching the soldiers in both armies. The storm forced a respite in the daily exchange of gunfire, stopped the eternal digging by which the Yankees inched closer to the bluffs. But the discomfort seeped into men's spirits as the wetness soaked through their clothes.

Tempe Dixon, ankle deep in the dirty yellow water that filled the bottom of the rifle-pit, cursed the bad luck that made him stand sentry on such a day. The squad had cut cards and he'd drawn a trey.

"You must be lucky in love," Lack Norris had said.

Not even that, Tempe thought sadly. He was in love with a girl who was going to marry a wealthy officer. For her to marry anybody was bad enough, but to pick the likes of Bryce Furlong was almost unbearable. Furlong had made no threats when they left the Kittering house after Alex donated that basket of food. The major had merely looked down his nose, and sneered.

"You want a bite?" Tempe had asked, stung.

"No, Dixon. *I* don't beg."

Turning on his heel, Furlong had walked away with an arrogant swagger that made Tempe want to throw the basket at him.

The impulse, Tempe recalled grinning, had been brief, and quickly restrained. Food was not to be wasted on gestures these days, nor for any other reason. Not when this morning's rations consisted of a "large" pound of soggy peas-mixed-with-flour, bread, the same amount of beef, a sprinkle of sugar and a few drops of vinegar.

It sure wasn't much to keep a soldier going for twenty-four hours, even if enemy action was restricted by rain. Tempe had swallowed the vinegar dutifully, but the tart taste contained a more bitter warning.

"Scurvy," he muttered, "is damn near all this army needs!" He had no trust in less than an ounce of prevention, but its very presence worried him. When a commissary officer started thinking about scurvy he was apt to be counting future supplies on his fingers.

He cast a routine glance over the parapet now, noted that the distant Yankee picket, a vague bulk in the slanting gray downpour, was trying to keep warm by walking his post in a military manner. The bluecoat, several yards in front of the nearest Federal breastwork, looked lonely and miserable.

"Just relax, Soldier," Tempe said. "We aren't coming out, and you're not getting in. Not today. Not soon either."

The enemy picket was probably talking to himself, too. Maybe counting his steps—ten paces north, ten paces south. Or northeast and southwest. The direction didn't matter. Like the siege itself the solitary figure was engaged in a routine military operation that wasn't going anywhere.

Tempe had lost the elation won by the two smashing repulses inflicted on the Yankees. He would hold, like his comrades, until hell froze, but with dogged stubbornness that blazed into savagery only when provoked.

It was provoked every day by a few fierce minutes of cannonade, or a sudden flurry of riflefire. The Yank artillery hammered at them; their own guns hammered back. A man had to be careful or an enemy sharpshooter would put a hole in his head. You paid that back in kind.

The rest, Tempe decided, was boredom. Even off duty, behind the lines, the shelling and the noise had become commonplace. There'd been some damage, some good men killed, in places the blue-bellies had managed to dig themselves too damn close, but the siege was now a slow, wearisome contest between havoc and survival.

"*In the morning,*" quoted Tempe, "*thou shalt say, Would God it were even! and at even thou shalt say, Would God it were morning!*" He smiled, recalling that they all seemed to invoke the Bible more frequently now as the siege continued.

A hubbub of voices rose behind him from the dug-out alcove they had roofed with two filched planks. For a moment Tempe thought it was a squabble over the interminable game of Old Sledge, another dispute about faded pips on greasy, tattered cards. Then he realized that these were cheerful greetings.

"Look what the rain brought back!"

"Hail the wounded he-ro!"

"He-ass for coming back."

"Hi, you, English?"

"I'm fine," said Jollibee, "and I rather guessed you gentlemen needed a spot of reinforcement."

"Well, you ain't exactly Johnston's army, Jollibee."

"You're welcome anyway," Tazewell said. "What's that you're toting?"

"That, Sergeant, is my new gun. The marksman's delight."

"Listen at him," said Lack Norris.

They came tumbling into the trench, splashing through the dirty water. Taze and Lack were grinning; the others looked as pleased. Jollibee, limping a little, was as sodden but a trifle cleaner than the rest. He was carrying a rag-wrapped rifle, and he saluted Tempe with exaggerated precision.

"God rest you merry, Tempe."

"Hi, Jollibee," said Tempe. The little Englishman was a real professional. He was well out of it with an honorable wound, but he'd returned as soon as he could walk. "How's the leg?"

"Feeling the weather at the moment," Jollibee said, "but otherwise jolly well healed."

"You picked a fine day to come back," Lack said.

"Self preservation, Lack. Strike me if it ain't a lot safer up here than it is in the town."

"You mean it?" asked Tempe, startled.

"Every blooming word. What Grant's gunners miss, Porter's practice on. Night and day. The streets ain't safe, and there must be a dozen houses pounded to kindling. Folks have their blacks out digging caves to shelter in."

"Bad as that, eh?"

"Right, Sarge. The shells don't make any distinctions, and I'd say the civilian casualties are as high as the army's."

"Anybody we know?" Tempe said, trying to sound casual.

Jollibee was unwrapping the rifle, but he paused to answer. "Not as I heard. The Kittering warehouse burned to the ground—shellfire—but the family is all right." The Englishman chuckled. "It's all a matter of chance. The ruddy courthouse stands out like a Rajah's white elephant and the Yanks can't seem to hit it."

Tempe gazed westward, peering into the rain curtain as if he could see the town. He thought of Alex, her grandfather, Runcey Carr. Any chance shell that dropped into Vicksburg—! He shook away the fear. There was nothing he could do except pray it didn't happen.

"What do you think of this?" asked Jollibee. He stripped the last rag from the rifle, held it out for inspection. The sharpshooters crowded around.

"What's special about it?"

"It's a Sharps .58 caliber carbine made by S. C. Robinson in Richmond. Some call it the Confederate Sharps. It's a breech-loader, but the important thing is this." Jollibee tapped a finger on a long cylinder attached to the top of the barrel by a metal clamp.

"Looks like a spyglass," Lack said.

"Right-oh! It's a telescope to sight through. You remember Mike Tansey, the big Mick from the Paxton Machine Shop who worked on the torpedoes in the Yazoo? Well, he figured this out, and made it. He came visiting me in hospital, and we tried it, and you can draw a bead on a fly at a thousand yards!"

Lack snorted in disgust. "Another new-fangled weapon that's a-going to win the war!"

"You're full of axle-grease, Jollibee."

"Spyglass shooting! In a pig's eye!"

Tazewell took the carbine, examined it. He said, "I've heard these guns leak bad at the breech."

"Not this one, Sarge. Mike reinforced it. Here, Tempe, you try it."

Hefting the gun, Tempe snapped open the breech, made sure it was unloaded. Then he rested it across the parapet, snuggled the butt against his shoulder, tried to sight. It took a moment to adjust to the strange feel of the telescope's eyepiece.

Through the glass, in spite of wet blur from the steady rainfall, the Yankee picket leaped into magnified focus. Tempe was surprised by the clarity; he could see the glisten on the man's rubberized black cape, the shine of his face. It would be easy, Tempe decided, to put a bullet any spot you wished.

"How about it, Tempe?" asked Sergeant Tazewell.

"Should work," Tempe said, "if a feller knows how to shoot. Aiming's a mite tricky, is all." He tossed the carbine back to Jollibee. "It brings them up real close, but they're close enough as it is."

"Sure thing!" Lack agreed. "That dingus ain't no good now, Jollibee. There's places along the lines where you can practically spit on the Yankees."

"When they got into the ditch last time," another sharpshooter said, "we just rolled the grenades down on them."

Jollibee, scowling, was busily loading his new gun. He said, "Some people can't stomach improving themselves."

"My stomach," Lack said, "could stand improvement, but we can't eat your fancy firearm."

Tempe knew they were teasing the Britisher, knew too that the device was practical. The telescope made long-distance marksmanship much easier, deadly in skilled hands. In that lens any enemy within a gun's range was a bull's-eye target. He didn't like the idea. If Mike Tansey could rig such a thing you could bet your bottom dollar, gold coin, that Yankee mechanics had done the same.

"If you fellows just got to be shown," Jollibee said, "I'm the man can do it." He scrambled up on the firing-step. "Stand aside, Tempe." There was a sharp click as he cocked the Sharps.

"Hold it," cried Tazewell.

"Stop him!"

"Watch it, you idiot!" Lack Norris cried.

Tempe moved, cupped his hand over the carbine's telescope. "Easy, Jollibee," he said. "Just what do you think you're doing?"

"Why," said Jollibee, spluttering, "why, I—I'm going to prove that this gun—"

"Oh, no, you ain't," Lack said. "That's a picket out there."

"I know what a Yankee looks like, you damn fool!" Jollibee was almost purple with exasperation.

"So does Lack," Tempe said. "That's a Yankee picket all right. But we don't shoot at pickets."

"Who don't?"

"We don't, and they don't," Tazewell said. "It's against the rules."

"What rules?"

"Well," said Tempe, "we sort of made them up between us. The Yanks and us. Mutual like. As long as a picket on either side just stands around minding his own business nobody takes pot shots at him."

Jollibee glanced around, saw all the sharpshooters nodding agreement. He said, hesitantly, "I don't believe it."

"Gospel," Tempe said. "It saves a lot of wear and tear on pickets and it doesn't harm anybody."

"T'other night," Lack said, "when I was out there, me and the Yank had to settle our territories by pow-wow. His damn-fool officer had him way over near us."

"That," said Jollibee, "is a hell of a way to fight a war!"

He stiffened as a Yankee cannon boomed, ducked as the shell whistled overhead. The others waited, not moving, for the projectile's noise to pass.

"There isn't any good way, Jollibee," said Tempe. "But you just heard another."

Lack Norris laughed. He said: "The Yankee schoolbell. Recess is over."

· *22* ·

As June's bright sunshine grew warmer, ripening toward summer, the citizens in the warring states spoke more of cannon than of crops. Both North and South expected a bloody harvest. Both governments seemed willing to expend lives and treasure to reap it, in the search for victory.

The sixteenth President of the United States called for a hundred thousand more soldiers. Abraham Lincoln thus showed his faith in his country's future. Those new recruits could not allay any immediate danger.

The first President of the Confederate States placed his trust in God and Robert E. Lee. With thin-lipped calm Jefferson Davis watched his brilliant general muster an army of seventy-four thousand. Those ragged veterans carried the South's highest hopes.

Newspapers, everywhere, mentioned the siege at Vicksburg with the bored repetition of a dateline. It lacked a battle's climactic drama.

Nobody, outside its neighborhood, had heard of Gettysburg, Pennsylvania.

In the West, as well as the East, armies were preparing to move. The Northern General Rosecrans readied his troops at Tullahoma, Tennessee, to search out Braxton Bragg. Across the Mississippi, in Arkansas, under-manned Confederate forces made vain forays to draw Union soldiers away from Vicksburg.

Grant refused to be diverted by these attacks. He let the Federal gunboats handle them, though he kept a wary eye on his rear where Joe Johnston had twenty-thousand rebels. With Vicksburg completely encircled Grant made plans to detach Sherman's Fifteenth Corps to keep Johnston occupied.

The stocky Yankee general was riding a new horse, a handsome spoil of war. Since it had been taken from Brierfield, the mount was named "Jeff Davis" for its former owner. A crack rider as a cadet, Grant still liked fine horses. They gave him more genuine pleasure than commanding a hundred thousand bluecoats. He intended to ride "Jeff Davis" into Vicksburg.

Grant, in the saddle, had everything under control.

VICKSBURG, under the changing schedules that fired the Federal cannon, was a place of hourly hazard. No one knew when the next barrage would begin, or who would fall victim to a shell fragment this time. Every day saw more houses reduced to rubble that made the escape of the white courthouse a recurring miracle. In their extremity, as always, the inhabitants turned toward their hundred hills. They burrowed into the familiar, friendly clay bluffs that stretched between the town's outskirts and its network of defenses.

The male slaves dug the cave-shelters on the landward slopes, away from the river with its pounding gunboats. The women of both races furnished them, even tried to decorate them. Some of these caves had patches of spare wallpaper. Most were overcrowded. Not one was bomb-proof enough to withstand a direct hit.

Around these warrens, in the gullies and ravines, the shaded glens, the raw diggings, the refugees lived a pioneer existence. There were the usual hardships of unplanned camping—mosquitoes, bad water, primitive sanitation. In necessity, scrambling for safety, owner and slave forgot respective positions. Mothers snatched up their own children first, the nearest others next. Black skin or white made no difference when the indiscriminate shells came searching.

The Kittering house on Cherry Street was struck by enemy gunfire on the night of June tenth, the twenty-second day of the siege. Though many nearby homes were desolate and abandoned, the flower gardens sere with yellowing weeds, the Kitterings were still in residence when the first shell hit.

Fortunately no one was asleep in the upstairs rooms. It was a wild, stormy night, slashed with wind-whipped rain, shaken by natural thunder, lit by quick glares of occasional lightning. In that turmoil the sudden, rending crash that tore into the roof brought the shock of terror.

Alex Kittering jerked out of her chair with a startled cry. There was no mistaking that impact, the immediate explosion. The ormolu French clock on the parlor mantel skittered; the chandelier danced to a high, harsh tinkle of clashing crystal.

"Oh, my God," whispered Epie Mae. Then, she screamed, a frenzied, throat-tearing shriek that seemed to last a minute.

"Stop that!" Alex shouted. "Stop that right now, you hear?" Anger helped control the girl's own fright. Her thinking was suddenly clear-headed and practical. There was a cave ready and waiting, dug by the combined efforts of Andrew, Benjie and Martin. They were all dressed, needed only coats and umbrellas. "We'll have to leave here, run for the cave."

Joab sighed; he sounded as if he had expected this final blow.

"Run?" Epie said. "Run? In *my* condition?"

"It's only beyond the next hill," Alex said. "About half a mile." She calmly lied about the distance. Epie's stubborn refusal to display her pregnant figure had kept them in the house until now. The Ancient was no longer a reliable ally. Joab had been sunk in lethargy since the warehouse fire. "We'll all help you, Ma."

"Your father isn't even here!" Epie made it an accusation.

Thank God, thought Alex. At least they would not have that to contend with in this emergency. Stephen was on duty, safe from the ranting that made him a flustered, useless penitent.

"Andrew," the girl called. "Mimosa. Benjie." She used a normal household-summons tone. Neither the old butler nor Mimosa would panic, and Benjie, in his wife's presence, was almost as reliable.

"We is right here, Miss Alex," said Andrew. The trio stood in the hall doorway, waiting. Benjie's eyes bulged whitely, but that was the only sign of emotion.

"Are there blankets in the cave?"

"Yes, Miss."

"Put them there myself," Mimosa said.

"Food, Mimosa?"

"Some. Not much. What we could spare."

"All right," Alex said. "One of you tell Big Sarah to take the children there." The others, too, were Kittering people, entitled to protection. She wanted them all safely out of danger.

"My wife," said the butler, "has already done that. She has been spending the nights there."

"Nobody," Mimosa said, with a tight smile, "steals food on Big Sarah."

Alex's nod gave full approval. She said, "Well, then, fetch wraps and overshoes for yourselves and—" She stopped, listening, and her attitude froze all the rest.

The enemy shell screeched closer, closer, and slammed directly overhead. This time windows crashed, shattering, and the carpet underfoot seemed to shake.

"I thought so," Alex said. "We mustn't wait any longer."

"Just a minute!" Epie Mae glared at her daughter. "If you're giving the orders, Miss Overseer, I demand that you call for the carriage! I cannot possibly travel on foot—"

"You'll have to," Alex said. "Not even Martin can handle horses with bombs bursting so close."

"But, the storm—"

"I'm sorry, Ma. The rain can't kill you, but the Yankees can!" Alex made the statement flatly, gestured the slaves into movement. Her mother stared, open-mouthed, but Joab's wide shoulders straightened.

The old man's voice was alert, gruffly itself again. "You'll do, Alex," he said. "I never had much doubt, but it's good to be sure. Whatever happens, you'll be all right, girl."

"Thank you, Grandpa," Alex said, abstractedly. Martin had appeared in the hall, twisting a dripping hat in his coachman's hands. The girl turned to handle this new problem. "Yes, Martin?"

"Miss Alex, I sure can't harness the team. They is a-kicking their stalls to pieces. But they is safer there than busting through the streets."

"We can't leave them locked up, Martin. If the stable should catch fire—"

"Miss Alex!" The coachman sounded reproachful. "I ain't aiming to leave them. Not the grays!"

"You can't stay. You might be hurt."

"I'll be all right, Miss Alex."

There was no time for lengthy argument. As she took the hooded cloak Andrew brought, Alex said, "Bless you, Martin." The scrawny driver grinned, knuckled his forehead, and disappeared.

"Here's your umbrella, Miss Alex."

The article Andrew offered was a gaudy yellow sunshade. Alex took it without question, glad that the butler was too hurried to be choosy. She watched Mimosa, shawl over her turban, bundle Epie into another cloak, produce a wide-brimmed bonnet.

"I don't want that," Epie said.

"Take it," Alex said, with brusque impatience. She turned to the butler. "Andrew, we must blow out all the lights."

"All out 'cept in here, Miss."

"Good. Mimosa, you take care of Mother. I'll see to the lights, Andrew. You and Benjie make an arm-carry for Grandpa."

"No," Joab said. "No, I can go it on crutches."

"Don't argue, Grandpa!" She stamped her foot. "That would just delay us! We must get away from here fast." Alex saw that her mother, impressed, yielded to Mimosa's ministrations.

The old man crashed the crutches together. "Hold the ends, boys," he said, "and I'll ride in the middle." That was how the slaves carried him.

Alex was blowing out the last candle when she heard the warning whistle. She called out to the others. "Stop! Don't step outside till it explodes!"

The third shell missed the house, burst high to scatter metal on the gravel driveway. Thunder, rolling, drowned the spattering sound, and the noisy wind.

Alex frowned, shook her head. The storm made it impossible to hear the cannon, judge the time between shellbursts. Was it one gun driving them from the house, or more? Was it a navy mortar, or a giant army rifle?

"Come on," she said. "Now! Don't try to run, but don't dawdle." She led the way into the blustery night.

At the foot of the steps a gust of wind turned the yellow parasol inside out. Alex let go of the handle, watched it twist away over the flower garden. The others were made of sturdier silk. Mimosa held one above Epie; the old man on his perch had the third. Alex moved to her mother's other side, took her arm.

They had not gone twenty yards before Epie Mae balked. "Alex," she yelled, shouting over the gale. "Alex, my jewels!"

"What?"

"I forgot my jewels!"

"I got your case under my arm, Miz Epie," said Mimosa. "Don't you fret, now."

Come on, Ma!

"These weren't in the case! My pendant! The ruby ring! My shirt-waist watch on the diamond bar! I left them in my nightrobe pocket!"

The girl could picture her mother, in dishabille, preening before a mirror in a pathetic effort to disguise her shape with baubles. Alex felt both sympathy and exasperation. "Mimosa found them," she said, firmly, "and brought them along."

The wind whipped the lie away, unheard. Mimosa, fighting to retain the swaying umbrella, gave a dismayed grunt. The maid knew how her mistress prized possessions. Without thinking, Mimosa said, "Oh, Miz Epie, you didn't!"

That confirmed Epie's fears. Her voice rose, cold and determined; it was a tone that brooked no argument. "I will not stir another step without those jewels! This is ridiculous! You can't make me, Alex! Not one step!"

They were standing at the edge of the road beside a tall hedge that bordered someone's deserted terrace. The hedge shielded them a little from the driving rain, but the wind lashed its leafy twigs to a frantic rustle. There was no sign of life anywhere.

"Put me down, boys," Joab said. "No sense breaking your backs just standing here." He stood, clutching Andrew's shoulder. The old butler held the crutches with one hand, his master with the other.

"You hear me, Alex?"

"I hear, Ma."

Alex wiped rain from her eyes, stared back at the lightless house. She was trying to orient herself in the noisy darkness. The downpour drummed on the roadbed; the wind howled through foliage. There was thunder from clouds or cannon. The girl saw the flash from the nearest riverfront battery as it fired back at the enemy. To the north against the black sky a Yankee shell exploded over the town, in sudden blossom like a fireworks rocket.

"Do something, Alex!"

"Be quiet, Ma."

"Girl," said Joab, "the trinkets ain't worth the risk."

A flash of lightning, white tendrils streaking, lit the landscape for a lurid instant. Alex saw the familiar, wide shape of the house in the background, its closed shutters like neat, black patches. Closer, under mushroom-curved umbrellas, were her mother and Mimosa, Joab and Andrew, white faces next to dark. Benjie stood in the rain, a step apart.

Here was a slave idle while an errand waited. Epie, noticing, snapped her command. "Benjie! Run fetch those jewels. My robe's on my bed."

"Yes, ma'am!" Benjie had an old habit of obedience. When the mistress spoke like that he jumped.

Even as he turned Benjie started to run. A crash of thunder erased Alex's cry and Mimosa's moan.

"Benjie, wait!"

"Oh, Lord, no."

Rain and darkness swallowed Benjie before he crossed the road. The others could neither see him, nor hear his footsteps. The wind drew a swirling curtain between the group and the racing slave. There was no chance of catching him. The distance was only twenty yards, and Benjie ran fast.

Lightning cracked, illuminated everything in blue-white glare.

Alex, throat dry, saw Benjie's form on the steps, dark against the door panel. The whole façade was sharply detailed by the vivid flash. Dropping across the front of the house, directly above Benjie, was a blurred smoke-trail.

"*Down!*"

As she yelled, Alex hurled herself forward, dragging mother and slave-maid with her. They plunged into the hedge, crushing through the thick brush, heedless of tearing twig or whipping switch. There was only an instant of wet, leaf-scented darkness.

Then, the hedge seemed to tilt, ripped across by a blinding explosion.

It left Alex stunned, ears ringing. She forced herself to rise, scrabbling at the slippery bushes. There was smoke in the rain now, and the odor of gunpowder.

Mimosa gripped her arm. They stared into the storm, toward the house, together. The girl was dimly aware that Joab had struggled to his knees, that Andrew, crouched, held a torn umbrella.

The next lightning flash revealed the damage. There was no doorway left on the Kittering house, most of the front wall was a jagged, gaping hole. There were few signs of Benjie—a handful of discarded rags on the shattered steps, some horrible stains.

"Benjie," whispered Mimosa, and choked. They had sent her husband into danger once too often. *They*. The white folks. The masters.

"I—I'm sorry, Mimosa."

"It wasn't your fault, Miss Alex." The girl spoke in a dull monotone. She felt no personal hatred, but a growing rebellion against slavery.

"Andrew. I'm sorry." Alex repeated the inadequate words. Benjie was, *had been*, the butler's son.

"The Lord gives, Miss Alex," said Andrew, "and the Lord takes."

The Lord maybe, thought Mimosa, has the right. But not humans!

Not owners because they're white. She was going to be free. *Free!* Whichever side won this here fool war!

Joab Kittering, on his knees, raised his face to the rain, and spoke. The old man intoned the psalm like a tired preacher. *" 'They walk on in darkness: all the foundations of the earth are out of course. But ye shall die like men, and fall like one of the princes.' "*

Appropriate, decided Alex. Let them chisel it in stone as an epitaph for Vicksburg if there's enough town left to hold a monument when the siege ends. The girl felt a deep sense of failure. She had taken charge, accepted the responsibility of the household's safety, but she'd let a nerve-ridden woman send Benjie to a needless death.

Then Epie Mae's groan brought them all back to present danger, exposed position, the necessity for action.

"Ma!" cried Alex. "Are you all right, Ma?"

Her mother was lying face down, crumpled and half-conscious, at the foot of the ragged hedge. She was not wounded, but her face was very pale. Epie's mumblings were a strange, incoherent mixture of whimpers, wails, and baleful hisses.

Mimosa took one look, raised frightened eyes. "We got to get her out of here, Miss Alex."

"We all better get out of here," Joab said.

"Yes," said Alex. "Yes. We must reach the cave. You take her other arm, Mimosa."

The maid nodded, braced herself. Blaming Miz Epie Mae could wait. This was woman-stuff now, and that came first. It wouldn't help Benjie none to let an innocent babe get born in a ditch.

Their walk to the cave was a long nightmare of struggle. Alex and Mimosa half-carried, half-dragged, the fainting woman. They slipped, floundered, pushed, pulled, and stumbled. Sometimes by urgent pleas they persuaded Epie to stagger a few steps, sometimes she was a dead weight. Alex thought only of her mother's need for help and shelter. She wasn't even aware that Joab, though aided by Andrew, was slogging along on his crutches in grim silence, and had fallen far behind.

When they reached the Kittering cave Epie returned to full consciousness with a shriek. Big Sarah, a veteran midwife, gravely confirmed the diagnosis. "It's her time."

"Too soon," Mimosa said. "Too soon."

"I'm telling you it's her time!" Big Sarah was definite. "Those is the pains."

"She had a shock," Alex said, "a fall. We'd better send Andrew for Doctor Randall—" She glanced around, noticed the butler was missing. "Where is Andrew?"

"Still coming along with Mister Joab."

"We can't wait," Big Sarah said. "Not now. You can send if you want, but the doctor won't be in time. Not on this night." She chewed her lip, broad, black face worried. "Baby this early ain't good."

Mimosa said, "I know."

"You-all will have to help me."

"All right."

"You, too, Miss Alex."

Alex nodded; she had heard the plural "you-all." In the candlelit cavern her mother's screams of pain had a hollow ring. The girl fought down rising nausea. She was more fatigued than frightened. Drawing a deep breath Alex started to roll up her sleeves. "You'll have to tell me what to do," she said.

It was not a particularly long labor, but it outlasted the storm and the cannonade. Epie's baby was born in the blue-gray quiet before dawn. The tiny boy was perfectly formed. He lived about five minutes.

When she was sure her mother would survive, Alex went outside into the cool, wet-fresh smell of morning. Benjie, she thought, and my little brother! The Yankee gunners should feel real proud. The phrases Joab had spoken kept returning to her weary mind. *Die like men, and fall like one of the princes.*

That wasn't how it happened in a siege.

· 23 ·

TEMPE DIXON, standing in the creek, splashed water on his chest. The narrow stream wasn't deep, but it ran tumbling clear. There was no soap, of course. He scrubbed with plain, cool water. It felt good, refreshing after days in the trenches. There was one disadvantage. A clean body made a man hungry.

Or rather, *more* hungry, Tempe thought. None of them now ever quite lost the dull emptiness in the pit of the stomach. Meals were stop-gap affairs, even if a man wolfed a whole day's ration at a sitting.

The items in the last meager issue, carefully portioned to each soldier, was typical. A half pound of cornmeal, three strips of bacon, a half pound of suspect beef, a thumb-length chunk of sugar cane was supposed to last three days. No wonder most of the company had colic, or dysentery. Tempe figured his lucky discovery of a ripening blueberry patch had saved him from the latter, weakening malady.

Now, it was a warm Sunday morning, and they had found a pleasant place to bivouac. The tree-shaded creek that twisted through a protected hollow made it an almost perfect rest camp. He hoped the artillerymen on both sides remembered the Sabbath, and kept it holy. Both sides were firing only an occasional gun.

Sergeant Tazewell was off somewhere reading a borrowed Bible, but most of the other sharpshooters preferred cleanliness to godliness. Jollibee, sitting naked on the bank, was now running a lit cigar along the seams in his pants in search of vermin. Tempe could hear Lack Norris, farther upstream, singing as he washed.

The tune was a pre-war air, but the words were siege inspired.

> *A life on the Vicksburg hills*
> *A home in the trenches deep*
> *A dodge from the Yankee shells,*
> *And the old pea-bread won't keep*
> *—the bread—the bread—*
> *The old pea-bread won't keep!*

"Lack," said Jollibee, "would never shine at Canterbury Hall, and I can't bear to think of his fate in any penny-gaff place in London." He sighed in reminiscence. "Now, this—outdoors and all—is like Vauxhall in the old days."

"It's Vicksburg now," Tempe said, wading from the water. "He's warbling about our two eternal worries. Food and shells. My pa would call it doggerel, but it sounds right cheerful."

He borrowed a light from Jollibee's cigar-end, and sat on the bank, smoking, while the sunshine dried his skin. His clothes were draped over bushes, and his ragged drawers didn't look as if they'd stand another cleansing.

Tempe didn't want to think about that. That, or hunger, or lice, or any of their daily risks and hardships. These pleasant moments, basking in the sun, tasting strong tobacco smoke, scrubbed and shaven, were too rare and precious to be spoiled.

"Me and Lack," said Jollibee, "worked a nice spot of hocus-pocus on the ruddy Yanks yesterday."

"Mmmm," murmured Tempe, not really listening. The warmth sinking into his body made his mind happily blank. The sporadic reports of distant cannon were too normal to notice.

"You know how sassy their sharpshooters act?" Jollibee chuckled through a puff of smoke. "Same as our boys do. Draw a shot, then pop up when it misses to shout insults. Sporting flash, and safe as Rothschild's because the fellow shooting can't reload in under thirty seconds."

"Pudding-head trick," muttered Tempe.

"It passes the time," Jollibee said, "and gingers the long, dull hours.

[244]

Anyway, this Yank was a blooming pest. He was a big, yellow-haired hulk, likely a Dutchman, and he thumbed his nose at us whenever a bullet passed."

"Mmmmmm." Into Tempe's dreamy contemplation came an image of Alex Kittering. He wondered how the girl was faring. Jollibee's voice began to fade. . . . "This blue-belly's language was gutter-low. So me and Lack got together. Me with the telescope Sharps and Lack with his Enfield. We snuggled into the same loophole like peas in a pod."

First, Tempe thought, Alex seemed to be dressed in green, then in blue, then in mulberry. The changes were not abrupt; his sleepy brain accepted them placidly. She was smiling and lovely, held out her hands to him.

"The Yank fired," Jollibee was saying. "Lack shot back at the smoke. I drew a bead on the same spot. And the blighter jerks up over their sandbags like Punch in the show. He's cocking a snoot, as usual, and his mouth is open to bawl curses."

Dozing, Tempe knew that all was well between himself and Alex. Somebody nearby chuckled with satisfaction.

"I drilled the beggar clean in the collar-bone!" Jollibee inhaled deeply, exhaled gustily. "But we only worked it once more before some son-of-a-bitch bluecoat slicker got fancy with a repeating rifle. Must have held six shots."

At this point Lack Norris's noisy approach scared away Alex's image, returned Tempe to wakefulness. He raised drowsy eyelids to scowl at the intruder. Lack was singing lustily as he marched, splashing, down the creek-bed.

> Do they miss me in the trench, do they miss me?
> When the shells fly so thickly around?
> Do they know I've run down the hillside
> To look for my hole in the ground?
> But the shells exploded so near me,
> It seemed best for me to run;
> And though some laughed when I craw-fished
> I could not discover the fun.

"The Louisiana boy who made that up," Tempe said, bleakly, "was killed three days later. I understand why."

Lack said, "He couldn't sing as good as me."

"Then," Jollibee said, "he's better off dead."

Tempe rose, stretching. Dreams were nebulous things better left alone. They raised false hopes, sowed discontent. In the harsher, real world neither the siege, nor his love, seemed to have much chance of reaching a successful conclusion.

[245]

As he dressed in slightly damp garments he worried about Alex. What was really happening in Vicksburg? The rumors that came out from town to the army were as upsetting as the rations, and a damn sight more plentiful. Every trench and rifle-pit was a hotbed of gossip; every squad inflated and distorted each tale before it passed to the next. The town was a shambles. It was as unscratched as the courthouse. Civilians were starving or feasting on secret luxuries. The riverfront batteries sank a Federal gunboat a day. The riverfront batteries couldn't hit the side of a barn.

Joe had it from Charlie, thought Tempe, who got it straight from the darky sweeper at Headquarters. Pemberton had a new plan to save the army. Pemberton had shot himself in despair.

"You pays your money," muttered Tempe, "and you takes your choice."

"What's that, Tempe?"

"Nothing, Lack. I was just thinking."

"Jeez! On an off-duty Sunday?"

He grinned, without mirth, wishing he knew Alex Kittering's true condition. No day passed without that worry. Fortunately, like most veterans, he'd stopped believing a tenth of what he heard. Rumor mongering was the army's favorite pastime.

"Tempe Dixon! Anybody around here named Tempe Dixon?"

"Somebody's calling for you, Tempe," said Jollibee.

"So I hear."

The shouting came from a grove of trees to the rear. Sergeant Tazewell appeared on its fringe. The big man was gazing back over his shoulder. He cupped hands to mouth and yelled.

"This way for Tempe Dixon!"

"This way!" bawled Lack and Jollibee in unison.

The unseen shouter had sounded adult, but a boy trudged out of the woods. Swinging a straw hat in one hand he walked with a steady stride gaited to cover mileage. The sunshine touched his hair with torch-red brightness. "Hi, you, Tempe!" called Runcey Carr.

"Hi, Runcey! What are you doing out here?"

"Looking for you."

"I heard," Tazewell said. "I was over yonder chawing the gristle with the 46th Alabama, and I heard tell some youngster was a-hunting you, Tempe."

"Since daybreak," Runcey said. He was barefoot, and he stepped into the creek with a pleased grunt. "That sure feels good. I reckon I've hoofed over half these hills. You fancy sharpshooters are hard to find."

"How'd you get by the provost guard?" asked Lack.

Runcey's gaze was blandly innocent. "What provost guard?"

"The question," said Jollibee, "is withdrawn."

The boy accepted the foursome's laughter as earned applause. These soldiers were Tempe's friends, but he didn't aim to tell his methods of avoiding restrictions. He said, very gravely, "You fellers got anything to eat?"

Embarrassment showed on every face. Lack and Jollibee looked at each other; the sergeant gazed up at the sky. Tempe swallowed, said, "Well, now, Runcey, you see—"

"'Cause I," said Runcey, unsmiling, "am a mite tired of toting these here little old yellow June apples." He had been holding his hat like a straw purse, the brim crushed together in one fist. Now, he opened it to display pale gold spheres nestling inside the crown.

"Apples!" said Lack.

"Young man," Jollibee said, "you are doubly welcome."

Tazewell, leaning forward, started to count. "One, two, three—"

"Four," said Runcey. "One each." He tossed the apples, flicking them from the hat, to each soldier in turn. "Go ahead. I already et my share."

"You're sure?" asked Tempe. If they were real white gold, he thought, they'd be worth less. Without waiting for Runcey's answer, he bit into the fruit, shutting his eyes as he tasted the tangy juice. His stomach twitched at this unexpected treat.

"Ripe," mumbled Lack, mouth full.

"Tasty," Jollibee said.

The sergeant nodded agreement as he chewed.

Runcey, watching them eat, thought they looked hungrier than some of the stubble-bearded soldiers he'd run across while searching for Tempe. Somehow, the shaved faces and clean shirts made privation more apparent. The others had been ragged scarecrows; this quartet, as threadbare, were famished men.

"What's the news from town?" Tempe asked. He betrayed his concern by speaking about another topic before he finished his apple.

"I fetched a paper," Runcey said. He took a stiff, folded sheet from the hat. "*Daily Citizen.* Come out several days back. First since the middle of May." Cocking the hat on his head he unfolded a single-page newspaper printed on the blank side of a piece of wallpaper.

Tempe took it, glanced curiously at the curlicue pattern, a dark-green design on paler background, passed it to the sergeant. The news I'm interested in, he thought, won't be set in type.

"Wallpaper," Runcey said, "was all Editor Swords could find, and he ain't got much of that."

Tazewell, munching apple core and spitting seeds, held the newspaper high so the others could peer over his shoulder. Jollibee was the first to comment.

"I say! Look, there!" He stabbed the sheet with a finger. "This says that Joe Johnston has an army at Canton, and is coming to help us."

"Coming, hell!" Lack said. "Canton's north of Jackson. He's going backwards."

Tazewell, reading, said, "General Loring with ten thousand troops is reported to have crossed the Big Black River."

"I'll believe that when I see them!"

"Me, too," Jollibee said. "Besides, ten thousand won't do more than pester all the bluecoats Grant has out there. That's neither a threat nor a promise."

"Tempe," said Runcey, lowering his voice, "can I talk to you alone for a couple minutes?"

"Sure, Runcey."

They moved aside from the discussion, strolled along the creek's bank. Tempe lit a fresh cheroot, sat down on a rock. Runcey, squatting beside him, gnawed a chew from his tobacco plug.

"How is—how are all the Kitterings, Runcey?"

"If you mean Miss Alex, she's all right." The boy spat, not looking at Tempe. "I was talking to her last evening. She ain't got enough to eat, and she's got too much to do, but she bears up. You needn't fret about Miss Alex's health none. She's fixed that cave like a top-deck stateroom."

"Cave?" Tempe said. "What cave?"

Runcey told him how most of Vicksburg's population had sought shelter underground. Then the boy plunged into his problem.

"I couldn't go troubling Miss Alex with what's bothering me. She's got more'n enough trouble in her sack. Missus Epie's sick from losing her baby. Mister Joab ain't well either."

"Mister Joab?"

"Tempe, I went out to that cave to tell Mister Joab that the grays were safe. The carriage team. That me and Martin had snaked them out of the stable, and had them safe hid on board the *Tonica*. Mister Joab didn't even know me."

"What's the matter with him?"

"I reckon he just got old all of a sudden, Tempe. Overnight like." Runcey aimed a jet of tobacco juice at a crawling fly to hide emotion. He was very fond of the old man. "Anyways, he didn't care about the team, nor Martin, who's been his coachman for years and years, or nothing. And that team is worth plenty, and Martin hisself ain't no cheap field hand."

"Maybe—maybe they don't have enough to eat?"

"Who has?" Runcey shrugged away that problem. "But I took Miss Alex some of them apples, and old Andrew, the butler, had found him a fresh sassafrass stump for making tea. Him and Mimosa is almost as handy as me at scaring up eatables."

So it was true, then, Tempe thought, the town was as poorly fed as the army. Alex, forced to subsist on scraps, might fall victim to some disease. He expressed his personal worry in a generalization.

"That's damnably hard on women and children."

"Sure is. But I come out here to ask you what I should do."

"Do?"

"About the team, Tempe. The horses."

"I—I don't understand." Tempe had lost the boy's discourse somewhere. "There was an order restricting each regiment to three teams of mules but—"

"That's just army," Runcey said. "That ain't nothing to do with folks. Mules *or* horses. But somebody's got to guard those grays, and there's only me and Martin."

"Guard them from what?"

"Jump MacGregor."

"The gambler?"

"Jump's waterfront place got burned down the same night we set fire to DeSoto. But he hung around, trying to get damages out of the general, or somebody. Well, he hung around too long. He got hisself caught in this here siege like a hound dog in a bear trap. So, being Jump, he ferreted out a way to make a pile. There ain't anybody betting now, except maybe which way the next shell drops, but Jump got him a new gamble."

"A new gamble?"

"Him and the Smasher has been a-swiping mules and horses."

"But—who'd buy them with the town so—"

"They butcher them. What in blazes do you think we all been eating?"

"We guessed about our own rations," Tempe said, "because the so-called beef was sweet and stringy. Taze said 'mule' and Jollibee 'horse.' But—"

"Jump doesn't sell to the army. He wants no truck with the quartermaster or Confederate dollars. Civilians pay more in hard cash or barter. Silver candlesticks and such." Runcey snorted in disgust. "Most folks is suffering, but Jump MacGregor's getting rich."

"Are you sure, Runcey?"

"Floyd told me. He was Jump's mulatto cash man, remember? Well, he was in on it, but he got scared when they stole Saladin."

"Saladin?" Tempe nearly dropped his cigar. "Bryce Furlong's race horse?"

"Yes, sir!" Runcey swore with sudden violence. "Ain't that the limit? The finest thoroughbred ever run in these parts, and he ends up in the stew-pot. That Jump ain't got a decent bone. He won plenty on Saladin in his day!"

"Furlong must be furious."

"He don't know. None of the Furlongs know yet. Zack, their jockey, had charge of Saladin while the family went off to live in a cave. It wasn't his fault—the Smasher laid him out—but the little nigra's too scared to tell a soul. He reckons Bryce will have his hide."

"But, Runcey, everybody in town knew that horse!"

"Not as cold meat. You just don't get the way things are, Tempe. There's livestock wandering loose all over town—mules, horses, cattle. Left behind when folks took off, or got killed. The Yank shrapnel gets at least one dumb beast a day. They's a dead mule collecting flies at the head of Main Street, and I seen a cow grazing in the Kittering flower garden."

Tempe nodded; he knew that garden. He could see the animal among the magnolias and myrtle, nibbling along the passion vine.

"She was dry," Runcey said. "I couldn't get a drop of milk out of her. The shelling drove me off, and she was gone when I come back. Otherwise I'd have taken her out to Miss Alex. Poor Bossy was so scrawny her ribs showed, but there were a couple of meals still on her."

"That's what Jump MacGregor's doing!"

"Now, listen here, Tempe! There's a Mississippi-wide difference between folks helping theirselves to stay alive, and Jump making a greedy profit! Most everybody in town is sharing what they have! Gladly! Even the slaves ain't complaining. Jump is the miserable rotten apple in the barrel."

"He's not alone," said Tempe. "The shopkeepers raised the prices as soon as the siege started."

"Some, not all. And they can raise them to the moon now, because their cupboards are bare. Jump makes the meanest, price-jumping grocer you ever saw look like the Angel Gabriel."

"How does he get away with it?"

"Same as he did playing cards. A fast shuffle and a slick deal. He only works at night, and he don't waste time hunting for strays. Not Jump. He hits places he knows stock is still kept. Generally him and the Smasher settle for one animal a night, never more than two. They sell it right away. Meat won't keep in this weather."

"Why doesn't somebody shoot him?"

"Jump MacGregor? The Smasher does the slaughtering, and peddles the pieces. Jump is just the go-between, the man who knows a man. He's doing the customers a hush-hush favor. He strikes the bargains, and he never bilks the same folks too often. Oh, he's got the deck stacked his way, Tempe."

"*You* know what he's doing."

"Well, sure. Ain't I been telling you?"

"Then, report him to Headquarters."

Runcey looked as if his chew suddenly tasted sour. He did not hold with tale-bearing. Riverboat people settled their own scores without running to the authorities. In this case he had an even stronger reason to avoid such unethical behavior. "That's what Floyd aimed to do, Tempe. Yesterday morning they found him floating in the river."

"Oh?"

"Of course, he could have cut his own throat from ear to ear." Runcey paused to let his listener reach his own conclusions. "Besides, the Smasher's a friend of mine. I wouldn't want to get him in any trouble."

"Runcey, if he's in cahoots with Jump—"

"The Smasher just does as he's told. There's no real harm in the Smasher. It's Jump I'm worried about."

"You think he knows you have the Kittering team?"

"He don't miss much. That's why I come out here to see you. I can't trouble Miss Alex. I can't talk to Mister Joab. And Mister Stephen— well—even if he was handy, a thing like this ain't exactly his kind of fish-bait."

Tempe smiled at the boy with affection, recognizing a more youthful reason for this meeting. Runcey, for all his precocious self-sufficiency, was only a lad; he had wanted to unburden himself to someone. Such dark, criminal secrets were too heavy for a boy to carry around, single-handed.

"Runcey," he said, "I'll do anything, but unless I get leave I'm stuck out here. There's plenty of soldiers in town would be delighted to help you take Jump MacGregor into custody, and if you can catch him in the act—"

"Hell," said Runcey, "I'm not afraid of Jump. I can handle him by myself."

"Why, then, what—?"

"What I need is permission."

"Permission?" Tempe blinked, completely at a loss.

"Sure. I got me old Mister Joab's Springfield fowling piece on board the *Tonica,* and a single-shot horse pistol. There's plenty of weapons and ammunition in town. Plenty of percussion caps too, now that the feller floated through the whole Yank army, down the Yazoo and the Mississippi, with two hundred thousand new ones."

"We heard about that. We weren't sure it was true."

"True for sure. He's supposed to be some scout from Virginia named Fontaine. Anyways, with those weapons nobody's going to fool around the *Tonica* or the *Chickasaw*. Not while I'm there. Trouble is I'm off a lot, fishing or hunting for food."

"Where are the guns now?"

"Hidden in the *Tonica's* boiler. Martin's safe enough by daylight."

"But Jump and Smasher will come by night."

"That's the point. If I ain't there—and sometimes I ain't—Martin, unarmed, wouldn't stand a chance. He's a nice old codger, but he couldn't fight a school girl."

"If you have two guns, why not—"

"Jerusalem God!" Runcey said, in horror. "You don't think I'd give a nigra slave a loaded firearm without asking somebody if it was all right?"

"I beg your pardon," said Tempe, humbly. He kept his face grave, aware that the boy considered the dilemma an important one. "Of course not. I take it you're asking me for permission?"

"Yes, Tempe. By law I'm under age, and Martin belongs to the Kitterings. If he has to go shooting a white man, even trash like Jump MacGregor, there'd better be somebody full grown who can stand up and vouch for him."

"I'll do that," Tempe said. He was far from sure his promise had any legal status, but Runcey needed reassurance. "Under the circumstances Martin is only defending his master's property."

"Well," said Runcey, with a satisfied grin, "that's a load off my mind." He spat with double force and volume. "All I wanted was permission."

"Tempe!" Tazewell's voice interrupted their talk. "Get your rifle. We're moving out." The big sergeant sauntered toward them. "Word just come. We're changing our position, going north a ways to the fort on the Jackson Road."

"Now?"

"Now. Seems the Yanks are digging a mine under the fort, and they might find it harder work with sharpshooters pecking at them."

"A mine?" asked Runcey. "A blow-up mine?"

"I reckon so, Runcey," the sergeant said. "Some engineer officer claims he can hear their pick-axes underground."

"Wowie!" Runcey said. "That makes my troubles little bits of nothing. You go take care of them Yankees, Tempe. I'm all right, now."

Tempe started toward the stacked rifles, stopped, spoke over his shoulder. "Runcey, why didn't you go to Major Furlong?"

"Him?" Runcey said, spitting. "I wouldn't tell *him* whether the fish was biting!"

THE CONFEDERATE redan defending the Jackson Road was blown sky-high by a Federal mine at four o'clock on the afternoon of June twenty-fifth.

The explosion shook the surrounding hills, sent debris rocketing upward through a sudden billow of thick, black smoke. As a sound, this was the loudest, single blast of the siege. People two miles away in Vicksburg stopped in mid-stride, startled by the extraordinary, tremendous power of the report. But, except for the nervous skeleton force in the little fort itself, no soldiers in the vicinity were surprised.

Everybody on both sides knew that the weeks of digging had stopped, and knew why. The bluecoat regiments that had done the spade work were confident of success. The gray veterans, waiting at a safe distance behind the undermined salient, were equally confident they could plug any gap torn in their defenses. Only the handful of men directly above the sputtering fuse had any cause to worry, and they may not have realized they were expendable.

Tempe Dixon's sharpshooter company had a front-row view of the eruption. The riflemen were waiting on the dusty, sun-baked roadbed, assigned to raise the effective strength of some battered Missouri infantry. There was no shade on that stretch of road and the sweating soldiers were beginning to feel neglected when the spark hit the powder.

"God Almighty!" cried Tempe Dixon as the flash ripped from earth to sky with a roar. For a moment he was blinded, then he couldn't believe his eyes. A caisson wheel rose, spinning, into the sunshine. Through the geyser of smoke a man's figure, completely whole, seemed to fly straight up, turn in the air, and dive down toward the Yankee lines.

"Did you see that?" asked Lack Norris.

"I shut my eyes," Tazewell said.

Jollibee sounded impressed, said, "Guy Fawkes must have descendants."

"Come on," yelled the Missouri captain. "Let's get up there before the Yanks do!"

They went forward with a rush, following the road uphill toward the near edge of the smoking crater where the redan had been. Tempe, racing near the head of the column, saw no sign of dead or wounded, only the jagged black rim of a gigantic ash excavation. To his right a gun crew, cursing, pushed a howitzer into position.

The shrill battle cry rose as they flung themselves down on the lip of the huge hole. It was a victory scream. They had beaten the Yankees to the vulnerable ground; the massed bluecoats, lined bayonets aglitter, were still coming, in the open, across the narrow strip of withered grass between their trenches and the bluffs. After long days of laborious tunneling the mine had ripped a pathway through Vicksburg's defenses, but the gray soldiers closed the gate before the dust settled.

Below Tempe, the whole hillside looked as if it had been turned into a cavernous hollow by a giant hand wielding an enormous scoop. This yawning socket, wide and deep, formed a scorched, blackened chasm more formidable than the fort it replaced. The steep sides offered no foothold; the bottom of the pit was a sunken trap.

"Fish in a barrel," said Lack Norris, chortling.

Jollibee said, "The Black Hole of Calcutta."

"It'll be a tomb," Tazewell said.

The Yankees, thought Tempe, know it, too. He could see the almost imperceptible shudder ripple through the charging blue lines as they neared the waiting crater. No soldiers in the world wanted to rush into an abyss rimmed with enemy guns.

He judged from the new blue of uniforms that this was a fresh Yankee division, chosen for the task. They were good troops. They must have realized the assault was hopeless, but they made their try. With a shout they plunged forward.

Then, the guns were hammering, and all was noise. Tempe fired as fast as he could reload. The bluecoats were so jam-packed there was no need to aim.

Around him, the clanging howitzers, the deeper roar from bigger cannon, beat through the continuous sharp rattle of small-arms. The crater's bottom filled with weird seepage, smoke, gunflashes, writhing men. This seething mixture was torn with explosions as the gray infantry dropped lit grenades on the hapless, struggling Yankees.

The advance was checked, and beaten, pounded to pulp in the mine-made mortar by a fiery pestle. Recoiling to the hole's far edge the blue-clad soldiers tried to stand, broke, and ran. They stumbled back to shelter, pursued by artillery fire and the wild triumphant screeching of the defenders.

Tempe fired a final shot, mopped his sooty face, and reached for a fresh cartridge. He didn't know how long the fight had lasted, but it had ended as abruptly as it began. Sudden quiet, too, could smite the ears with explosive violence.

"They won't try that again," Tazewell said, grimly.

"Not today anyway," agreed Lack.

"No," Jollibee said. "There go their cannon. The infantry won't be coming back." He twisted to watch a shell streak overhead. "Same old blooming stalemate."

"How long, oh Lord," Tempe said, "how long?" He finished reloading, clumsily fitting the percussion cap with damp fingers. Heat and thirst swept through him like a fever attack. He wanted to get away from the stench of blood, burned flesh and gunpowder, from the sight of the Yankee dead. Licking caked lips with a swollen tongue, he said, "I'll go back for water, Sarge."

"All right, Tempe."

Weariness and revulsion made Tempe careless. The sharpshooters had been under steady, relentless shellfire for thirty-six days. Most of that time Tempe had spent fighting in the lines. The lulls in the siege had become routine procedure, and a habit is hard to break. Now, he forgot he was not behind a parapet in a well-dug trench, where a crouch brought full protection from enemy rifles.

He stood up, crouching as he turned, on the hilltop edge of the crater. It never occurred to him that he was outlined against the sky.

Tempe drew a deep breath, and started down the slope. His step was slow; he was too tired to hurry.

The bullet hit with the impact of a vicious punch. It was a stunning blow, sharp and solid, that spun him from his feet, knocked him sprawling down the hillside. The grating jar of his fall seemed part of the same disaster.

Jesus, thought Tempe in dazed prayer, I'm hit. There was grit in his face, in his mouth.

The pain came with the warm, wet flow of blood. Tempe twisted under the sudden torture, felt it gush from his left shoulder, pour down side and arm. He could not distinguish between the blood and the pain, but the spreading agony left him breathless.

"Give me a hand here," said Tazewell from far away.

Lack's voice sounded even more distant. "Tempe. Tempe. Ah, Jeez, Tempe."

"My gun," said Tempe, from the depths of shock. "I dropped my gun." Speaking was very difficult, but he did not know he was whispering.

As they lifted him the pain receded and by the time he was sitting up he could think clearly. The faces around him swam back into focus. He was propped against Lack's chest; Taze was baring the wound; Jollibee was hovering. Tempe managed a smile, summoned strength for clear utterance.

"How bad is it, Taze?"

"You'll live," said the sergeant. He tore off Tempe's shirt sleeve, balled it into a pad to press against the wound.

"Those minnies," Jollibee said, "make a nice, neat hole."

"Did it break anything, Sarge?" asked Lack.

"I can't tell."

Tazewell's big fingers caused a pang that brought cold sweat to Tempe's forehead. He chewed his lip until the pain passed. It's bearable, he decided, and that's a good deal. The thing to watch was giddiness; he mustn't go fainting like a girl with the vapors.

"Some blue-belly son-of-a-bitch," Tempe said, with deliberate belligerence, "is a damned fine shot!"

"I'll get the bastard," Lack said.

"Do tell," said Tempe, giving Lack an affectionate wink. It was a heartfelt, worthless promise, impossible of fulfillment. They all knew that, but vowed vengeance was an automatic reaction.

"That's the best I can do," Tazewell said, sitting back on his heels. "There ain't enough whole cloth between us for a decent bandage. You'll have to hold it in place, Tempe."

"All right." Tempe reached for his shoulder tentatively, applied pressure. The wadded homespun under his hand seemed very bulky, but it didn't feel wet. "Thanks, Taze."

"Get along to the field hospital," the sergeant said. "That needs proper care, clean bandaging, a surgeon. I don't think anything's broken, but gun-shot wounds are tricky."

"Help me up."

They helped him to his feet, stood watching anxiously as he swayed. Tempe braced his legs, found them firm. He was surprised to discover he was fairly strong, capable of careful movement. One of the walking wounded, he thought. Things could have been plenty worse.

"It's a good thing," Jollibee said, "you left your jacket in camp. That shirt has come to the end of its days."

Tempe glanced down at his bare left arm, streaked with dried blood, grimy with dirt. Well, he thought, remembering not to shrug, that's the least of my worries. He said, "I'll have to borrow me another shirt somewheres."

Lack retrieved his hat from the road, dusted it on a thigh, offered it. "Here," he said. "You need any help walking?"

"No, thanks. I can make it, Lack." Tempe pulled the battered slouch hat low over his eyes.

The Yankee gunners, as if infuriated that the mine had proved a fiasco, were beginning to shoot in rapid-fire sequence. Their thunder increased, rose to cannonade proportions. Shells, whistling through their arcs, started to burst over the defenses at more frequent intervals.

"Let's not stand here," Jollibee said.

"No," said Tempe. "Go on back. I'll be all right."

"You know where the field hospital is?"

"Sure, Sarge. I saw it when we moved up. It's just beyond our camp."

An enemy shell came whining above them. As usual they stopped talking, judged the sound of passage without looking up, waited for it to pass. Most soldiers said that you never heard the one that hit you.

"I'll take care of your gun," Lack said.

Jollibee said, "You're well out of it, Tempe."

Tempe looked at him, glanced skyward. "This is a siege, English. Nobody's out of it. Those damn Parrotts aren't a bit choosy." He turned away to start the long walk. "You-all take care. See you soon."

"Good luck," called Tazewell.

Tempe did not look back. He knew they wouldn't waste moments gazing after him. Not in the open where a chance shell might find them. He would have to move from cover to cover himself. The Yankee siege guns sowed their deadly seeds like a drunken farmer, here, there, high, low, anywhere.

With that in mind, he left the road, climbing among trees. The Yankee artillery astride the Jackson Road was good enough to figure the track it took toward Vicksburg, and cover it with shrapnel.

It was a trifle cooler in the shade, but Tempe didn't hurry. Walking wasn't painful unless he stumbled but all the terrain around the town was hilly; any stroll, away from the highways, was a succession of ascents and descents. Tempe stepped gingerly, as if carrying eggs, stopped frequently to rest. The battle sounds behind him had the familiar steady rumble he knew so well.

"Another day," he muttered, "another stand-off."

The mine, and the fierce fight after it, had been a change, but the successful repulse had left him depressed, not exhilarated. Maybe that was the wound, gnawing at spirit as well as flesh. Grant had inched his lines as close as he could without taking the Confederate breastworks. Today they had trumped the latest Yankee trick.

"And the siege goes on, and on, and on."

That was the bullet that choked. Today's victory only meant tomorrow's doling out of shrinking rations. A few more men died; there was a little less food.

He stopped in the trampled glen, last night's bivouac, where they had left their few possessions. The camp was deserted, littered with bundles, the ground scarred with ashes from the several fires. The bleak look of the place added to his depression. Over there, he recalled, was where the two Mexican boys from Waul's Texas Legion tried to teach them how to make jerky out of mule meat. Later, in the glow from the same campfire, somebody insisted he'd eaten fried rat recently, and found it tasty.

Even the lies we swap now, Tempe thought, are about food.

The uniform jacket was where he'd left it. Bending to pick it up, he removed his hand from the rude bandage. A spasm of acute pain made him stagger. He had to stand for a minute, breathing deep between clenched teeth, until that sharp grinding stab diminished. Then, he hung the jacket on his good shoulder, and went on, treading even more carefully.

Tempe found the field hospital just outside the town's suburbs, in a little narrow twist of bottom between two hills. Since the grass-green strip ran roughly parallel to the river the hills gave it fine protection. Now, in the late afternoon the westerly hill cast a shadow. Half in that shade, half in sunshine were two tents and the suspended fly of a third. The canvas was patched and faded.

There was a soldier with a bandaged leg drowsing under the fly. Tempe could hear running water, snores from one tent, murmuring voices in the other. In spite of their clear sounds the guns seemed very far away from this peaceful spot.

"Doctor around?" Tempe asked the soldier.

Blinking awake, the man nodded. He was very thin, with a pale stubble of beard, and dark-ringed eyes. Through a yawn he said, "Where'd you get it, feller?"

"Can't you see?"

"No, I mean what spot in the lines."

"Jackson Road."

"Kee-ripes!" He stiffened with interest. "Where the damn-Yanks blew the mine? Kee-ripes! We heard that bang way down here! You wasn't blown up in that, was you?"

"I wouldn't be here if I had," Tempe said. "I got hit afterwards."

"Kee-ripes! I served in that there fort. How many was inside when she went?"

"Some say less than a hundred."

"I hope to spit. Kee-ripes!" He shook his head, slumped back into listlessness. "Doc Jones is in the bigger tent."

"Thanks."

As Tempe trudged toward the tent, a man emerged from it. He was a giant, balding, with a sandy mustache on a florid youthful face. He stood, holding the tent-flap open, talking to someone inside as he watched Tempe approach.

This, Tempe decided, is the cleanest person I've seen in weeks. Everything about the big man seemed to shine, his skin, the long hands, his unbuttoned uniform coat, the white ruffled shirt and black broadcloth trousers. You had to get real close to notice that the clothing was threadbare.

"You looking for a surgeon, soldier?" called the young giant in a melodious Carolina bass. When Tempe nodded in reply, the broad shoulders bent toward the tent, the voice lowered to sympathetic regret. "You see how it is, Miss. Just like I said. The wounded are my responsibility."

"I can wait my turn, Doctor," said Tempe.

The sentence was barely finished when Alex Kittering thrust the doctor aside, and stepped into the sunshine. "Tempe!" she cried. "Oh, Tempe!"

Tempe stared as at a miracle. She was wearing something green, and the sunlight brightened the color of her chestnut hair.

"Alex," he said. His smile was joyously grateful.

Alex knew she'd never forget Tempe as he was at that moment in the sun-lit bottom. His face was black with smeared soot, his ragged clothes were filthy. The dangling arm, blood crusted, seemed as limp as the gray jacket.

He was smiling, and he was wounded. All the love she'd kept back welled up at sight of that clumsy bandage. It swept through her with a surge that made her dizzy. There was no room left inside her for doubt or question, no room for anything but the pounding of her heart as it beat out the essential, important facts. This was Tempe, and he was hurt, and she loved him. That love made her voice as weak as her knees.

"Oh, my dear," she said, "you're wounded."

"It's nothing, Alex," said Tempe. He realized that the wound had moved this girl in a way that words never could. The realization brought a dazzling happiness that made even the pain a blessing. "Nothing much at all."

"Well," said the doctor, "we'd better take a look at it anyway."

"Yes," Alex said. "Yes." She wasn't really addressing the surgeon. Tears, warm and stinging, blurred her vision. She moved toward Tempe through mistiness. This was her love, for now and forever, and he was hurt.

Tempe took two steps to meet her.

Slowly, being very careful of his shoulder, Alex placed one hand over his on the bandage, cupped the other around Tempe's chin. Leaning forward, she raised her face and kissed him. It was a long, very gentle, tender kiss, a pledge and a promise.

With that soft mouth against his own Tempe would not have stirred if a shell burst above his hat. He was so conscious of her lips, her touching hands, her nearness, that he probably would not have heard it.

"Kee-ripes!" said a voice.

The surgeon noisily cleared his throat. He was young and sensitive;

embarrassment made him feel even bigger than usual, a mountain of intrusion. This couple, obviously, should be alone.

Alex sighed, and stepped back. She was rosy, but unflustered. When Tempe started to speak, she placed a fingertip on his lips. Then, she removed his hat, stroked the damp hair back from his forehead, slipped the jacket from his good shoulder. Holding the garments she turned to the surgeon; her voice was low, but happily proud.

"Tempe, this is Doctor Jones. Doctor, Templeton Dixon."

"Taliaferro Jones, sir," said the surgeon with a bow. "At your service. Delighted to meet Miss Kittering's fiancé." Under the circumstances it was a natural mistake. Jones had noticed the diamond ring, had learned never to judge a soldier's fortune by his ragged uniform.

Before Tempe could say anything, Alex chuckled. "He will not be much of a fiancé," she said calmly, "if we don't get him patched."

"Of course," Taliaferro Jones said drily. Woman's logic, he thought, as if it was *my* canoodling kept him waiting. "Of course. Won't you step inside, Mister—er—"

"Sergeant," said Alex.

"Sergeant Dixon."

"Alex—"

"Come along, dear. We can talk later."

Like a sleepwalker Tempe followed her into the tent. Except for the real pain in his wound he would have been sure he was dreaming. Everything seemed crazily out of proportion. The size of this Taliaferro Jones, Alex's kiss, her acceptance of the surgeon's mistake, the number of shining steel instruments laid out on a cloth-covered table. Even the sunlight, filtering through tent canvas, had a different, unnatural quality.

Alex glanced at him sideways. Tempe caught the twinkle in her eyes. By God, he thought, if she says I'm her fiancé, then I am!

"I'll fetch water, Doctor," said Alex.

"Good. You sit there, Sergeant." There was nothing ponderous about Taliaferro Jones. For all his bulk he moved with grace and speed. "Who put on this butternut bandage?"

"Another sergeant."

"Not bad, considering. Had to make do with what he had, eh?"

"Yes, sir."

"The trouble with us all." A long hand gestured toward the row of bright surgical knives. "Look at those. Came out of a completely fitted medical chest found floating after we sunk the *Cincinnati*. Salvage, Dixon. Brace, now. The cloth's sticking, and it's going to hurt."

"Yes." Tempe tensed, trembling as the bandage was pulled away from the raw wound. He had to fight to keep from yowling at the pain.

Alex, returning with a kettle, winced when she saw his shoulder. She turned very white, but didn't spill a drop of water. Her voice was steady, without tremor. "It's started bleeding again."

"Yes," said Taliaferro Jones, bathing the wound with an incredibly gentle touch, "but I can stop that." He was chattering to divert the patient. "Now, you take those scalpels, lancets, *et al.* The Yankees probably have such kits by the hundreds, but a Confederate army surgeon has to find one in the bulrushes floating like Moses."

Alex, watching the big young man work, recognized his skill. Jones reached under the table, brought up a whisky bottle, pulled the cork with his teeth. The girl knew what to expect; she put her weight on Tempe's good shoulder, holding him down as the surgeon poured liquor into the open wound.

Tempe twisted, choked back an oath. His shoulder seemed to be on fire, seared from front to back. When the pain lessened, he said, gasping, "Why don't you use a red-hot poker?"

"Sorry," Taliaferro Jones said, "but that should clean it." He applied pads, began to bandage, handling the linen strips with dexterity. "I've only one good dose of chloroform left, a gill of laudanum, and exactly sixty-three morphine pills. There you are. You're lucky."

"Lucky?" Tempe and Alex spoke in unison.

"Sure are. You can thank M'sieu Minié that his nasty little invention went straight through without touching bone. There was no need to probe for lead or splinters. Here. Have a drink."

Tempe tilted the bottle, gulped whisky while Alex stripped off the rest of his shirt and washed him thoroughly. He was glowing, inside and out, by the time she had finished. He didn't even protest when she threw the remnants of his only shirt into a corner.

"You can't put that back on," Alex said. She turned to the doctor, smiling. The siege had taught her to wheedle food or favor without scruple. "Do you suppose you could lend him a clean shirt, Doctor Jones?"

"I suppose I could," Taliaferro Jones said, "if I had one." He was neither flattered nor annoyed by her request. Girls as lovely as this one were born to coax gifts from men. "It is a question of purely academic interest."

"Oh, well. Grandpa has spares a-plenty, Tempe. You can—" Alex stopped with a gasp. Her hand flew to her mouth. "Grandpa! I forgot!"

"Forgot? Forgot what?" Tempe rose at the horrified look on her face.

"Grandpa—seeing you—I—I forgot all about him!" The girl sounded ashamed, guilty, close to tears. "How could I?"

"It was natural enough," Taliaferro Jones said. "First things first."

"What about Mister Joab?"

"Oh, Tempe, I—I think he's dying."

"Now," said Tempe, trying to forestall her weeping. "Now, Alex." He reached, drew her close, holding her with his good arm.

Alex, face against his bare chest, let the tears overflow. She cried noiselessly for a few moments. Then, hearing Tempe's heartbeat, feeling the smooth, hairless skin under her forehead, she recovered enough to murmur a muffled explanation. "We—we sent Andrew for Doctor Randall. But he didn't come, and didn't come. Mimosa told me about—about Doctor Jones being here. He—he set her little boy's wrist when a shell fragment broke it. I—I thought maybe he'd come see Grandpa."

Tempe, stroking her hair, gazed over the bowed head at the big surgeon. Taliaferro Jones raised his hands in a gesture of helplessness indicating his surroundings.

"But—but he says he can't come, can't leave here. And Grandpa—oh, Tempe, we can't just let him die!"

"Hush, girl," Tempe said. "Hush. The doctor's a soldier under orders. Your grandfather would understand that."

"But how could I just clean forget—"

"That was my fault." Tempe stilled her wail by holding her tighter. "Seeing me wounded drove it out of your head." He tried not to sound boastful. If he came before Joab as Alex's worry, she had really forsaken all others.

"You mustn't blame yourself, Miss Kittering," said Taliaferro Jones. From what the girl had said, there wasn't much anyone could do for the old man.

"No, darling, you mustn't."

"Darling," thought Alex, has such meaning when Tempe says it. She was conscious of his warmth and smoothness, of the comfort in his embrace. I am glad, she decided, that he isn't hairy-chested.

"Tempe," she said, tilting her head back to gaze at him, "will you come back with me?" Her eyes, still wet, were shining, very blue. "Grandpa's asked for you. Twice."

"For me?"

"Yes, first he said 'that boy,' and we all thought he meant Clay, or even Runcey. But then he spoke your name."

"Of course, I'll come," Tempe said.

"You want a sling for that left arm, Sergeant?" asked the doctor.

"Do I need one?"

"Not really. Just don't go flinging it around. Tuck it up like Napoleon now and then." The surgeon imitated the famous portrait of Bonaparte as First Consul. "The old emperor, not this present fellow."

Alex helped Tempe into his uniform jacket. She carefully draped it over the bandaged shoulder, leaving that sleeve empty. Tempe tucked his left thumb into a belt-loop on his trousers.

"How about that, Doctor?"

"If it feels right, it's all right. Coddle that shoulder, but watch it for stiffening. Can you change a dressing, Miss Kittering?"

"Yes."

"Do so in about five days. Please use clean linen, and if there is any pus, laudable or otherwise, bring the sergeant back here." Taliaferro Jones drew himself up to his considerable height. "I do not hold with re-using bandages until they fall apart, or that a discharge means a healthy wound."

"Thank you for everything, Doctor," she cried. Impulsively, with gay gratitude, Alex rose on tiptoe to kiss the surgeon's cheek.

"You are most welcome." The big man's florid face turned scarlet. He considered it the finest fee he'd received in army surgery.

Tempe, grinning, recognized a fellow being. He, too, he remembered, had once been startled by Alex's impulsive kiss. Now, secure in her love, he found the practice engaging.

"We both thank you, Doctor Jones," he said.

Following Alex from the tent, Tempe first noticed her slimness. The skirt of her simple green linen dress fell straight to her ankles, swayed with the hip movement as she walked. He realized she had discarded hoops or crinoline for freedom and convenience during the siege. Tempe, who had sisters, knew that fashion was clumsy and cumbersome for out-door tasks.

"This way," Alex said. She took his arm to guide him, swinging his dented slouch hat in her other hand.

"Get fixed up, bub?" called the thin soldier from under the tent fly.

Tempe answered without turning. "Yes, thanks. I'm fine."

"Kee-ripes!" the other said. "I'll say!"

They walked south through the narrow bottom, conscious of the soldier's curious gaze. Once they moved out of sight, in among the cooler shadows of the trees, they relaxed. Alex gave a contented chirp, half-snort, half-sigh; she slid her hand down his wrist until their fingers met and linked. They went on like that, through the woods, hand in hand.

There was a slight awkwardness between them, a shyness that kept them silent, but it was a warm, tender feeling without anxiety. Tempe was content not to break the spell. Alex, enjoying his nearness, was even more lighthearted. She had made her choice, at long last, and the act had freed her from the hobbles of convention, the rigid bonds of etiquette.

Both knew they had much to discuss, but that could wait. They loved each other. That was enough for the moment. That, and the sure knowledge that nobody or nothing would change them.

Considering where they were, and when, such supreme confidence was touching and ridiculous. Neither gave that a thought.

The roar of cannon, the drone and crump of shells, even the crashes that signalled hits, made no impression. They might have been taking a peacetime stroll in an enchanted forest. Tempe, who was trained to know better, didn't bother to estimate the nearness or distance of any battle sounds. The fact that he was walking with Alex, in mutual love, had him enthralled. Surely, the turn of her head, the flash of her smile, was more important than these noisy distractions.

The girl recovered first from this false, romantic sense of security. She was mindful of his wound, watching for signs of fever or weakness. He mustn't overdo, and she tried to slow him with talk.

"Tempe."

"Yes, Alex?"

"You're out of it, aren't you?"

"The war?"

"The siege."

"Nobody's out of it, Alex," he said, as he had to Jollibee. "But I won't be fighting again until the wound is healed."

"It'll be over by then. One way or the other." Alex didn't believe that the siege would be raised, but she didn't want to sound defeatist.

"Probably," Tempe said. He had his own theory about how the siege would end. Some afternoon the Yankees would simply walk over an army too weak from starving to reload its guns. Yet he didn't want to disillusion Alex.

They walked on, but the silence was broken. Now they were both eager to talk as they sauntered. Tempe wanted to hear Alex put their understanding into words. That would be balm for his pain, tonic for his growing weakness.

"Alex."

"Yes, Tempe?"

"You will really marry me?"

"Yes. Oh, my dear. Yes, yes, yes!"

Stopping, they kissed with slow enjoyment. Again they were careful not to press close, to avoid any contact with the wound. Alex held his face between her hands. Tempe placed his palm on the back of her head, on the silky round knot into which she pinned her hair. But there was fire in the kiss, a passion made stronger because it was controlled.

"Darling."

"Tempe. My Tempe."

"When?"

"As soon as we can. As soon as you're well."

"I'm well enough."

"Ah, no," she said, twinkling. "I want a whole man. It would be different if the pain was mine to take, to share."

They reached a shallow, clay-brown rivulet, and its gurgle told them that a twilight hush lay on the land. The guns had fallen silent as day drew near its end. No bird flew; the insects still slumbered.

As they forded the little stream, splashing through two inches of water, Alex, skirts hiked in one fist, tried to help Tempe with a firm grip on his bicep. And Tempe, who had waded half the bayous in the delta country, was enormously pleased by her solicitude.

"It's not far now," Alex said.

"Your cave?"

"Yes, it's just beyond the next clearing."

"I'm sorry."

"Are you getting tired?"

The clearing was a walnut-bordered patch of high grass on the westerly slope of a hill. They paused to gaze across the surf-like rolling landscape to where the setting sun hung in the sky, beyond the hidden town, beyond the mighty river. The sun was bright ember-red gilding the smoke-haze left by the cannon with lines of gold and pink and scarlet.

Alex looked at its beauty, felt the sadness of the hour and the quiet. Another day was dying. The Ancient, her beloved grandfather, was dying, too. Suddenly, without warning, she was crying.

"Alex!"

"Oh, Tempe. Poor Grandpa."

"I know," he said, inadequately. What else was there to say? Tempe believed the girl had kept this sorrow stifled for his sake. Down under my happiness, he thought, I have been expecting these tears.

"Why Grandpa? Why *him*, Tempe?"

"There is never any answer to that."

"Oh, Tempe!" Weeping, Alex turned to him, buried her face against his breast, crushing his hat between them.

"Let go, Alex. Cry it out."

"Hold me, Tempe. Hold me." She slid a hand under his coat, hugging him. The smooth flesh seemed to warm her; the back muscles under her fingers seemed to give her strength.

"Alex. Darling." Tempe held her as tightly as he dared. His one-armed grip was fiercely protective. He patted her head, made inarticulate murmurs intended to comfort.

"I—I can't help it."

"Don't try, Alex."

Tempe's clumsy caressing loosened the knot in her hair. The chestnut tresses came tumbling in waves about her shoulders. Alex felt the weight, the disarray. She shook her head, sniffled, raised her face.

[265]

He kissed her gently, tasting the salt tang of tears, feeling the tremulous lips. Tempe put his cheek against the girl's, and whispered, "It comes to us all, Alex."

That was how Bryce Furlong found them.

Bryce had climbed through the walnut grove with annoyed briskness. He had a horseman's distaste for walking, but his mount was tired; he had left it hitched in front of the Kitterings' cave. Mimosa had told him where Alex had gone. He was too impatient to await the girl's return. The major knew the direction of the field hospital. He had pressing plans that sent him hurrying to intercept Alex.

In his wildest imaginings, his most jealous broodings, Bryce Furlong had never expected to discover his fiancée in Tempe Dixon's arms. The clearing seemed to jump around the entwined figures. White rage rose in Bryce's throat. It blurred the background; he saw only the couple.

The man was shirtless, naked under his coat. The girl looked flushed and tousled, with disheveled hair. General Van Dorn had been shot on less evidence.

In flagrante delicto! The only Latin phrase he knew blazed in Bryce Furlong's brain. He was too worldly, too suspicious, to reach any other conclusion.

With an inarticulate cry of fury, he plunged forward to rend and kill.

Tempe heard him coming, but had no time to meet the attack. He was turning when the fist smashed from nowhere, sent blinding rockets jolting through his head. Sky and earth tilted as he fell. He hit the ground hard and his wound exploded with pain.

"Bryce!" Alex screamed the name.

"Yes, Bryce!" He spoke in a tight, tense voice, chill with hate. "You wanton bitch."

"Bryce, he's wounded!"

"I'll kill him," Bryce said, not hearing. He was rigid with deadly purpose, fumbled at the fastening on the flap of his holstered revolver.

Alex saw he meant it. She flung herself on him, clawing, kicking, beating with Tempe's hat.

The flailing onslaught staggered Bryce momentarily. He fended her off with a push, but she swarmed back.

"No, Bryce! No!"

The girl's shriek cleared Tempe's stunned head like a dash of cold water. He came up into a crouch, balanced on a stiffly extended right arm, poised as a runner at the starting mark. He saw Alex slapping at Bryce Furlong the way a frightened bird tries to protect its young.

Bryce caught the girl's wrist, hurled her from him. She went down, sprawling, and the tumble tossed her skirts high to expose bare thighs.

The sight lashed Bryce's fury. "Strumpet," he said. "Whore!" He stepped back, and drew his pistol.

Tempe, watching the long Colt slide from its holster, felt the cold sweat of fear. Furlong was only three yards away. Three yards! Too close for him to miss. Too far to cross before he fired.

Everything in Tempe's vision seemed to move with incredible slowness. He saw Furlong's mouth working in a livid face, the narrow insane eyes, the rising gun muzzle. Alex was struggling to her knees. Every sound was magnified. Tempe heard a rustle in the grass, Alex's heavy breathing, the loud metallic click as Furlong's thumb cocked the hammer on the revolver.

The major took deliberate aim. He sighted down the long barrel, drawing a bead on Tempe Dixon's forehead.

Then, Tempe moved in a desperate lunge. He did not think it would succeed, but he couldn't just wait to be killed. Even as he dived for Furlong's knees, heedless of pain, thrusting his body with all the power in his legs, his stomach cringed in anticipation.

First would come the searing blast, then pain and death. Nobody could miss at such short range.

Alex was still holding Tempe's hat. Without thinking she threw it at Bryce, flipping it backhand with a flick of her wrist. It scaled through the air. The brim struck Bryce on the nose. It had no more force than a fluttering moth, but it spoiled his aim.

The shot crashed out with thunderclap loudness.

Tempe, deafened, felt the Colt's hot breath. The flame singed his hair, but the bullet missed, plowed into the ground. Driving forward, Tempe's good shoulder slammed into Bryce Furlong's shins.

Bryce, upended, pitched across his enemy. They rolled together for an instant, thrashing in a tangle of arms and legs. Tempe kicked free, whirled to attack. He was eager, ready to seize this chance to stay alive.

His thinking was faster than he could move. He was skilled at rough-and-tumble; the planter-bred major was not. But the wound was a crippling handicap and Bryce was armed. The odds favored Furlong.

Bryce's fury aided Tempe. The fall, the missed shot, had added the final indignity to pride already wounded. Berserk, in blind, unthinking rage, he swung the heavy revolver at Tempe's head, using it as a club.

It was a wild, wide swing. Tempe, fighting for his life, twisted inside it with a quick blur of motion. He butted Furlong under the chin, drove a knee into his stomach, grabbed for the weapon. His fingers clamped on the other's wrist, wrenched.

Cursing, Bryce hammered his free fist into Tempe's face.

Like a striking snake, Tempe jerked his head down, sank his teeth in

Furlong's hand. The Colt dropped to the ground. He tried to reach it, but Furlong hurled him away with a convulsive heave.

Tempe fell on his back, striking his wounded shoulder. Pain rocked through him, made him giddy. He knew he was beaten, spent by the brief fight. Furlong knew it, too. With a savage grin he scrambled after Tempe, fingers curved and ready to strangle.

Alex had stood, staring, frozen by their violence. She had never seen grown men fight to kill, with murderous, primitive blood-lust. Now, galvanized by Tempe's danger, she leaped to snatch up the revolver.

She cocked the gun, and fired. The Colt, roaring, nearly bucked out of her grasp.

Bryce and Tempe heard the bullet whine between them. They were both soldiers and the loud report, the closeness of the missile startled them to wary immobility.

"Don't move," Alex said. "Don't move, Bryce. Next time I'll aim." She held the pistol in both hands; the barrel was steadier than her voice.

Slowly, Bryce Furlong rose. The rage ebbed, leaving a strange emptiness. He did not know this girl, with the rumpled hair and torn dress, threatening him behind a deadly weapon. He was not afraid, but he no longer cared enough to risk his life.

"I mean it," Alex said.

"Yes," said Bryce. He wondered why he had ever wanted to marry her. The situation lacked honor, romance, chivalry, all the bright beliefs he cherished. It was a tawdry affair involving some strange slut and her paramour.

"You leave Tempe alone!"

Tempe, watching in silence, saw Furlong's lips curl in disgust.

"Gladly," Bryce said. He brushed his hands together, straightened his cuffs. He felt the need to explain, spoke with cool aloofness, attempting to detach himself from a sordid mess. "I only came here because I'm leaving Vicksburg tonight. If that scout with the percussion caps could float in on a log, I can float away on one. I didn't know you were—busy."

Tempe stirred, but held his tongue. He could hardly make a fist, much less fight.

"I—I wish you success," said Alex, flushed by his insulting tone. Let Bryce think what he wants, she decided, as long as Tempe is safe.

"Well, I found you," Bryce said. "And—thank God—I found you out before I left." His contemptuous glance raked them both in turn. "You deserve each other."

"We—we are going to be married."

"I'm sure it's necessary," Bryce said. He picked up his hat, held out his hand. "I'll need my revolver."

Alex stared at him. Then, she pointed the gun at the sky, and fired.

She kept cocking the hammer and pulling the trigger until a click told her the gun was empty.

Bryce Furlong waited, sneering at the gesture.

Removing her engagement ring, Alex offered it with the gun. She said, "I—I'm sorry, Bryce."

"I'm not." He put the ring in a pocket, slid the Colt into its holster. Then, he turned on his heel, and walked away.

Alex waited, not moving, until Bryce's footsteps could no longer be heard. She was weak with relief, didn't know whether to laugh or cry. Nobody had ever spoken to her like that, but it seemed a small price to pay for a peaceful, happy future.

"Tempe," she cried, turning to him, "he thought that we—that we—" The hesitant speech made her blush furiously; she stamped a foot in anger. "He dared think that—that you and I—"

Then, she ceased to care what Bryce thought because Tempe fainted.

· 25 ·

VICKSBURG, during the worst of the siege, remained a church-going community. On the last Sunday in June, after six weeks of bombardment and slow starvation, the number of devout seemed to have increased. They came from caves and damaged homes to attend services.

There were different denominations, but each congregation prayed for deliverance. Some of the slaves shouted this request vociferously; a few of the shrewder planters tried to bargain silently with the Almighty. The Lord's Prayer, too, had universal appeal, was recited with fervor. *Give us this day our daily bread* had a practical meaning for these besieged suppliants.

The various churches were crowded with civilians and off-duty soldiers. St. Paul's, the Catholic Cathedral, was no exception. Those who had attended the parish Mass left as part of a slow-moving throng. It flowed sluggishly down the church steps, clogged into groups in the open square. The parishioners stood about in friendly chat. They were mostly of Irish and French extraction. Both countries produce a gregarious people.

Across the river, from the big Parrott rifle's emplacement, the Yankee gunners could see this gathering, a dark mass sprinkled with gray uniforms. Maybe the bluecoat soldiers were eager, experimenting with the range, or merely bored. Whatever the reason, the target proved too inviting. They elevated the cannon, and fired.

The long gun crashed and recoiled. A shell, trailing its smoke-wisp, lofted high over the Mississippi's waters.

It burst directly among the crowd, exploding into deadly fragments. Concussion and scattering metal knocked the bystanders down with the haphazard brute force of a tornado. Women screamed and scurried; strong men cowered. Some of the fallen rose, stunned by the blast but unharmed. Other people stayed crumpled, bleeding into the dust. One man's arm simply disappeared. The stricken, wounded and dead, made the least noise. They were past panic.

Henri Duchesneau had been talking to Emilie Verrier when he heard the dropping projectile. He shoved the girl down, fell on her, trying to shield her with his body. The Creole lieutenant was badly wounded; Emilie was merely scratched. Both were unconscious, sprawled together on the ground, the man still protecting his companion.

A priest, wearing alb and stole, came out of the church, walked among his scattered flock. The quietly moving white figure seemed to calm the most hysterical. Those who had started to run came back to tend the wounded, to cover the dead. The priest stopped to kneel for a moment beside every outstretched form. His hand moved continually through the gesture of blessing. His murmured Latin words of absolution were repeated over and over, a droned litany asking pardon for each of the afflicted in turn.

The priest made no distinction, in this hour of death, between his faithful and others of different folds. He even recited the Latin over the corpse on the outskirts of the crowd, farthest away from the exploding point. Perhaps the curate thought this particular dead man needed a prayer, for he had fallen on his back and his upturned face was easily recognized.

Anyone familiar with Vicksburg could have identified the body. His name was Jump MacGregor.

The gambler was not a member of any church. He had come in search of a customer, a pious pew-holder who was not averse to paying profiteer prices for horse meat without asking questions. Jump was, as always, playing the percentages. What place was less suspicious, more ideal for a shady transaction, than the sunny square in front of the cathedral?

Jump had timed his arrival so that he could mingle with the crowd. He had a lucrative deal brewing that involved a certain hidden team of matched grays. He had just spotted his prospective buyer when the shell swooped out of the sky.

The blast changed the odds. Although the rotund sharper was farthest away, shielded by dozens, the flying steel splinter found him. It was no bigger than a pencil point, and it smashed through the square right glass of Jump's rimless spectacles without ruffling his white mustache, but it served. Jump MacGregor never knew what killed him.

The dead were carried away; the wounded were hurried to homes and hospitals. Doctor George Randall, early on the scene, patched Emilie Verrier easily enough, but Henri Duchesneau's condition was critical. He needed surgery and constant post-operative care. Poll Randall, highly excited, offered her own bedroom and volunteered to act as nurse.

By the time the free Negro who acted as bell-ringer for the cathedral pulled his rope to greet the noon-hour, the square was deserted and empty. But to all Vicksburg within earshot the solemnly tolled twelve strokes sounded like a death knell.

They could not be heard in the cave where Joab Kittering was dying.

The old man was sitting in his favorite armchair, salvaged from Cherry Street. In his lucid moments he had insisted on this posture, and not even Alex could persuade him to lie down. Now, as he came out of coma to clarity, Joab knew that death was very near. That strange last-gasp spurt of sensibility that nature sometimes gives a dying body restored Joab's faculties. He could listen to his own dirge with grim pleasure.

Big Sarah, at the cave's entrance, was singing her favorite spiritual for the master's passing, and she sang it well.

> Swing low, sweet chariot,
> Comin' for to carry me home.
> Swing low, sweet chariot,
> Comin' for to carry me home.
>
> I looked over Jordan, and what did I see,
> Comin' for to carry me home;
> A band of angels comin' after me.
> Comin' for to carry me home . . .

"It will take," said Joab Kittering, "a pretty sturdy chariot, and some muscular angels." His voice was quavery, but it was clear. There was even a touch of his old growl, and its strength surprised those waiting around his chair.

All the family, except young Clay, was present. Andrew, black face glistening with tears, stood near his master; Mimosa kept in the background. The aged butler had been Joab's first slave; he knew he was losing a friend whose will would grant a few years of unsought freedom. The copper-skinned maid was genuinely sorry Joab was dying, but figured it meant one less tie to bondage.

Epie Mae, reclining on a pallet, sighed as she misjudged her father-in-law's vigor. He had been dying for days and now he sounded stronger than before. Epie didn't really want to hurry this demise. She just liked things orderly.

Joab heard the sigh, but ignored it. He had better things to do with his last minutes than waste them on that worn-out resentment. Epie, too, had known hardship and suffering. They had left her sickly, but essentially unchanged.

The old man gazed at his son, Stephen, at Alex holding Tempe Dixon's hand. He had recognized Tempe several times in the recent, misty past, though he wasn't sure when. Day and night were much alike in the dim, candle-lit cave. Joab couldn't recall if he'd spoken to the young soldier.

"Hello, Tempe," he said.

"Hello, Mister Joab." Tempe felt Alex's fingers tighten on his. It was the first time her grandfather had addressed anyone clearly in several days.

"You hurt bad, son?"

"No, sir. Not too bad."

"It's a clean wound, Grandpa," said Alex, "and it's mending." She was trying not to weep. The Ancient sat slumped instead of upright, and his skin was the color of wax.

"You two?"

The girl knew what he meant. She said, "Yes, Grandpa. We—we're going to be married."

"I'm glad," Joab said. He closed his eyes for a moment to cherish the thought. He'd never liked Bryce Furlong; this boy would be much better for Alex. The Furlong world, the planter aristocracy, the old South, would be gone forever when the war ended. Tempe had the quality to build a new world for Alex. With faint amusement Joab wondered if the sons of poets were always practical. His own son—

"Stephen."

"Yes, Pa?"

"The lawyer has my will."

Stephen shifted his feet uneasily. He didn't know how they would manage without his father. Joab had always seemed indestructible; the broad shoulders still looked capable of many burdens. Expressing a futile wish, he said, "You'll be around for a long time, Pa."

"You were never," Joab said, "very good at futures. Cotton or otherwise." The remark was wearily patient, without sting. "There won't be much coming, Stephen. Between them, the fire-eaters and patriots have about done for Kittering and Son."

"We'll make out, Grandpa," said Alex. She couldn't bear him worrying at the very end.

"Of course we will," Epie Mae said.

"Gone," the old man said. "All gone."

"Don't, Grandpa."

"You'll have to start over." Joab's speech was slower now, labored. He stared at Alex, trying to impart his meaning to the girl who held his largest stake in the future. "The—the siege won't last much longer."

"We know, Pa."

"Oh, Grandpa!" Alex felt the tears overflow. Tempe put his arm around her.

"Don't cry," Joab said. "No need. I'm not—I ain't—sorry to miss the finish." He managed a wry smile. "I—I always said they'd win, but—least—won't have to watch them marching in."

"We may beat them yet, Pa."

The big head turned toward Tempe; the bushy eyebrows asked the question.

Tempe couldn't lie to a dying man. Here, he thought, is a patriarch who sat up to greet death; he wouldn't flinch from the truth. Stephen Kittering was a staff officer, and maybe at Headquarters they still reckoned on plentiful ammunition, but Tempe knew that the fighting men were starving.

Slowly, he shook his head.

"Thought not," Joab said, with a sigh. "Stephen."

"Yes, Pa."

"Find—a place for Tempe."

"Mister Joab," said Tempe, "that isn't at all—"

"My wish. You hear, Stephen?"

The old man was deliberately making it a dying request. Stephen was no businessman. The firm would need young blood and strength in the days to come. Joab believed the Yankee conquerors would seize the two little steamboats, but Northern mills would eventually buy cotton.

"I hear, Pa."

Joab wanted Tempe under obligation, in Vicksburg, not taking Alex off into the piny woods somewhere. The broad chest heaved as Joab struggled for breath, but he gathered all his strength for one last dicker.

"Promise me, Tempe."

"Mister Joab, I'm in the army."

"Armies disband," Joab said. "Afterwards, then. Give it a try. Alex—Alex's share will need—" Agony contorted his face, and he gasped for air.

"Promise him, Tempe," whispered Alex. "Please."

Good girl, thought Joab, clinging to his purpose. Alex was a true Kittering, knew how to strike a bargain. He tried to summon another argument in the growing dimness. His lips moved, but the words came out as unintelligible puffs of breath.

"All right, Mister Joab," said Tempe, to ease that straining body. "I promise. Whatever you say."

"Tempe promised, Grandpa."

Joab Kittering nodded, and relaxed. Done, he thought. Sealed and delivered. Tempe would keep his word. It was the best a dying man could do leaving an uncertain, war-torn world. Vicksburg, and the country—the somehow re-United States—would need the likes of Tempe and Alex. Strange that he couldn't see them standing so close. Everything seemed to be blurring together.

"Swing low," sang Big Sarah, "sweet chariot."

Joab shuddered, and closed his eyes.

"He's gone," Epie Mae said.

"No, ma'am!" said the butler. "No, ma'am. He's breathing."

He was asleep, but it didn't last long. The rasping breaths slowed, and finally stopped.

Alex hid her face in Tempe's good shoulder.

In peacetime half of Vicksburg, slave and free, would have attended Joab Kittering's funeral. He had been an early settler, a prominent citizen, a man with many friends. His age had diluted most of the hatred aroused by his stubborn opposition to secession, and the Confederate States. Even his enemies now admitted that the gloomy old cuss had hit the nail on the head. He had predicted disaster, and—by God!—it had sure come home to roost.

As it was, the town had seen enough of death. Not many cared to brave the Graveyard Road to the little cemetery so close behind the northern defenses, in range of the Yankee cannon. The small procession consisted of family, including slaves, Runcey Carr and Tempe Dixon, and a few friends. Mister Verrier brought Emilie's excuses. Franklin Furlong came with his wife, and Clara. The Anglican minister read from the Book of Common Prayer. There was no eulogy.

But the coffin rode behind the Kittering grays. Martin had the team groomed to shining elegance, and he kept them stepping smartly.

The Furlongs did not speak to Alex. She was too overwhelmed by genuine grief to resent the snub. Bryce's parents and sister would hardly forgive her for choosing Tempe instead of the idolized family hero.

It was Runcey Carr who told the girl and Tempe that the major had escaped from the town. "Floated down the river on a log."

"He told us he would," Alex said.

Tempe nodded; he had never doubted Bryce Furlong's courage. The man was a spoiled, arrogant snob, but he was brave enough to scare the foolhardy. In Tempe's opinion he was too rash to make a good soldier, too emotional for sound judgment. Bryce had been killing-mad in the clearing, and he had botched the job.

"He'll make it, too, Alex," said Tempe. "He'll get through the Yankee lines somehow, join up with Johnston or maybe Braxton Bragg. You know, Bryce and fellers like him will keep this war going for a long time."

"Yes," Alex said. "Bryce, and my brother, Clay, and a whole passel of men as brave, and even smarter."

"You reckon it should end here, Tempe?" asked Runcey. "Iffen we lose Vicksburg."

Tempe said: "I reckon it makes sense. If the Yankees take this town —which looks likely—Port Hudson, downriver, is sure to fall. They'll hold the whole Mississippi valley, then. We haven't a prayer of winning it back."

"What about Robert E. Lee?"

"Nothing Lee's army can do up north will change things along the river. Nothing he could do, or Joe Johnston, or Bragg made much difference to this here siege, did it? Maybe, as some say, too many big guns were sent to Charleston. Maybe, as others claim, Grant out-smarted Pemberton. The reasons don't matter once the river's lost."

"You sound like Grandpa," said Alex.

"You do at that," Runcey said.

"He was a pretty clear-headed man."

"What you're saying," Alex said, frowning, "is that the Confederacy can't win. That the war is lost."

"Is that it, Tempe? Are we whupped?"

"Shucks, Runcey, I'm not a statesman or a general. I'm not saying we've lost yet, or that we're bound to be beaten. The fighting can drag on for a year or more, and things can change in a twinkling. But, from where I sit, the Yankees can't lose unless they get plumb tired and give up. They're stronger all the time. We get weaker."

Runcey cocked his head, listening to the rumbling guns. "They sure are persistent, ain't they?"

"You come eat with us, Runcey," said Alex. She didn't want to think about the aftermath of defeat, how the Yankees would treat their prisoners, what a conquered, ruined South might face. "Those same bluecoat gunners, for once, have made sure we'll have enough."

The funeral meal was ample. An enemy shell had conveniently slaughtered a stray cow grazing on a hillside about a hundred yards from the Kittering cave. Mimosa had dug a mess of collard greens from somebody's forgotten garden. Lack Norris, who arrived bearing Tempe's rifle, sniffed the aroma of broiling steak with wide-eyed appreciation.

"Stay and share," Alex said.

"Well, now—"

"Please do. My—my grandfather would have wished it."

"It's right nice of you, ma'am," Lack said, without further argument.

"How'd you find me?" Tempe asked when they were alone.

"Asked around," Lack said. "Should have followed my nose. Jerusalem! That sure smells good. Our last ration was mostly dirty, unsifted corn meal, crawling with weevils, and about four ounces of pickled pork."

"High living."

"Ain't it the truth?" Lack glanced around cautiously, took a crumpled paper from his tunic. "Have you seen this?"

"No, what—"

"Watch it! I wouldn't want Major Kittering to catch us reading it. Somebody's supposed to make sure a copy gets tossed into Pemberton's Headquarters, but I'm not the mailman!"

Tempe read the scrawled letter. He skipped passages, but the meaning was perfectly clear. The paper was titled "Appeal for Help."

We as an army have as much confidence in you as a commanding general as perhaps we ought to have. . . . We give you great credit for the stern patriotism you have evinced in the defense of Vicksburg. . . .

Men don't want to starve, and don't intend to. . . .

If you can't feed us, you had better surrender us. . . . This army is ripe for mutiny, unless it can be fed.

Just think of one small biscuit and one or two mouthfuls of bacon per day. General, please direct your inquiries in the proper channel. . . .

The signature said, "Many Soldiers." Tempe folded the paper, handed it back. So, he thought, it has come.

"This has Jollibee's high-faluting style," he said.

"I ain't saying," Lack said, grinning, "he mightn't have had a hand in it. Soldiering is Jollibee's business. He can't see fighting on and on for no pay and poor food."

"Tazewell never agreed to that."

"Taze wasn't needed," Lack said. "Neither was I. There's plenty of others feel like they wrote it down, Tempe. They're starving hungry and bone weary. They want to quit."

"How many?"

"Too many. Hell, Tempe, it's just a question of time. In places the Yankees are only about five yards from our lines! When they ain't shooting, they keep digging, pushing forward behind cotton bales that the Sarge calls sap-rollers. We burned a couple by soaking wads in turpentine and shooting them out of smooth-bore muskets. They had more the next day!"

"More and more," Tempe said, "against less and less."

"The Yanks don't have to rush us again. Another week and they can just walk on in nice as do-se-do at a barn dance!"

"Don't let Alex hear you," said Tempe, glancing at the fire where the food was cooking.

"All right, but you can't tell me that the folks in Vicksburg want to hold out much longer either. Jollibee was telling me about the famous sieges in history. People eating all kinds of truck, and never giving in, and ended up famous. Well, they can have it! The next siege the Yankees decide to stage, I'm going to be somewheres else!"

"Tempe," called Alex, "things are about ready!"

"You know," Lack said, rising, "if there was more of beef like that, we could keep them out forever."

Tempe knew he meant it, knew, too, that it was true. Vicksburg's Army of Defense had withstood every Yankee attack, had thrown the bluecoats back from the fortified bluffs again and again. The tattered gray soldiers had fought, and died, and clung, undismayed by superior enemy numbers, or by the relentless artillery that pounded them, from land and river, at all hours of the day and night.

Even the unhappy, anonymous band, he decided, who composed that appeal to Pemberton would fight tomorrow, and God knows how much longer at the mere promise of food. But the general was too honorable a commander to make a promise to his troops that he could not possibly keep.

"Do you need help cutting the meat, Tempe?"

Alex's question brought him back from reverie to gaze down at his untouched plate. His smile thanked the girl. "No, thanks," he said. "I can manage."

"You learn," said Stephen Kittering, touching his own black silk sling. "You're lucky you won't have to fumble for the rest of your life." He felt a kinship with Tempe, with all other Confederate wounded. A tie of blood, Stephen thought, pleased with the cliché. Maybe Alex had done well, after all. Bryce Furlong was a greater catch, but the fellow never seemed to get scratched.

"Eat," Alex said. "You can talk later." She had no appetite herself, but food was too precious to be wasted. No sorrow, however deep, was worth a spurned meal. Not after so long a siege. She forced herself to swallow mouthful after tasteless mouthful. They had enough left for maybe two more skimpy meals, though Mimosa had carried shares to the neighboring cave-dwellers. Meat didn't keep for long in the hot summer weather.

Epie Mae looked askance at Lack Norris's table manners; he had no more social graces than the boy, Runcey. She supposed she should be grateful that Tempe Dixon was more presentable. *Mésalliance* or not, it would do no good to argue with Alex. The girl was as self-willed as old Joab.

"I'd better get back to Headquarters," said Stephen, rising. He glanced at his wife as if seeking permission.

"Must you," said Epie, listlessly. She made the remark automatically, without really caring. It would be a long time before she decided that her husband had been adequately punished.

"Yes." Stephen regarded the two younger soldiers, hesitated, and said, "I suppose I shouldn't discuss it, but there's some talk of a truce."

Lack looked up with a frowning seriousness that masked levity. He was always amused at the way staff officers took it for granted that the ranks only knew what they were told. His voice was smoothly interested.

"You mean the Yanks want to negotiate?"

"Well, not exactly."

Tempe shook his head at the sharpshooter. He would not have Alex's father baited. The poor man might be as ineffectual as he seemed, but that could be an asset in a father-in-law.

Runcey Carr, chewing, wiped grease from his mouth, and waited for Tempe to speak. The boy's chipmunk-bright eyes darted back and forth, watching the uniformed men.

"Any truce would be welcome, sir," Tempe said. "We don't seem to have much choice left."

"My feeling exactly," Stephen said. "Of course these aren't my decisions to make." He sounded wistful. Those guns, now rumbling beyond the bluffs to the east made Stephen's sleep a hectic tussle of fits and starts. Even his wife's attitude would be more bearable if the cannon stopped firing.

Poor father, Alex thought, catching the tone. If the decision was his, he wouldn't know how to make it. She kissed him farewell, frowned when she saw Epie turn her cheek.

"I'll go along to town with you, Mister Stephen," said Runcey. "I want to make sure Martin gets the team safe under cover."

Lack left with the others. Life around the Kittering cave settled into a humdrum, stay-alive passage of hours that bewildered Tempe Dixon. Without the tragedy of imminent death to keep time dramatic these refugees seemed absorbed with mere existence. Old Joab had left an emptiness in more than his big armchair.

No Yankee shells came close enough to disturb Epie Mae's afternoon nap. Mimosa and Andrew went out foraging. Big Sarah herded the young slaves away from the cave, hushed their play to a respectful mourning tempo.

Tempe realized that Alex had disappeared into the cavern's depths on purpose, that she wished to be alone. He understood; he would be around when she wanted him. When Ma died, he remembered, I crept off alone, and Pa had to come hunting for me.

That night, under a star-flecked cloudless sky, Tempe was smoking as he listened to the cannon growl. He did not bed down in the cave, among the women and children, where the air was stifling. During the death watch for the old man Tempe had slept in snatches, outdoors. It was too warm for the thinnest covering, and he found a hollow that made safe cover. Tobacco helped keep the mosquitoes away. He trusted that God would take care of the Yankee shells.

They are not trying too hard now, anyway, Tempe decided, judging by the sounds. The bluecoats burned powder by the numbers, from habit, and our gunners fired back to show they still could. Both sides were muttering to prove they hadn't dropped out of the game.

He heard a rustle in the grass, close, and turned.

"Alex?"

"Yes. I—I couldn't sleep."

She's been crying, he thought. She sounded very subdued and woe-begone, and Tempe felt a rush of tenderness.

"Neither can I," he said, snubbing out the cigar.

Alex slipped in beside him. He slid his arm around her shoulders, and she snuggled against him.

"Feel better now?"

"Yes, Tempe." Alex was strangely at peace. Her fingers found the inert wrist folded across his chest, and she held that hand in both her own. His lean, hard frame was stretched beside her; the heat of the touching bodies pressed through their clothes.

"Comfortable?"

"Yes, Tempe."

Even the masculine odor of tobacco, Alex thought, is comforting. This was how Tempe would be through the years, a refuge when she was hurt, a place of homecoming in sorrow as well as joy. He turned his head, and his lips kissed the thin flesh at her temple.

"Ah, Tempe."

"Shh, darling. Rest."

Alex's breasts tingled, and her loins seemed all warm softness. If that was desire, she decided, mixed with the backlash of too much emotion, it was welcome. Let it swell my tenderest places as grief's tears left my eyelids swollen. Let it soothe, and heal, excite and restore. It was good to know that Tempe would be there for that, too.

After a while she fell asleep in his arms. Tempe held her quietly through most of the night.

General Robert E. Lee had spoken the word in mid-June. He sent Jeb Stuart's cavalry to mask his advance, moved the Army of Northern Virginia behind the screening mountains. The gray legions, ragged veterans with speckless guns, poured north across the Potomac, spread into Pennsylvania. There were almost 75,000 men in that invasion force, a confident host, proudly bearing its many victories on the bright red battle flags.

The Army of the Potomac hurriedly turned in pursuit of its old rival. Blue-clad Northern troops were strung out along the roads on June twenty-seventh, when the Confederate invaders reached Chambersburg, Pennsylvania, and seized a hundred thousand dollars worth of supplies.

On the next day, President Lincoln appointed a new U.S. commander named George Gordon Meade. Unless this general did something the rebels might race through the soft, rolling harvest land like conquerors. Harrisburg seemed certain of capture. Philadelphia, Baltimore or even Washington could be next.

Rattling over the telegraph wires came wild reports and wilder rumors. Lee's army was loose and ravaging. The North was swept with panic, and the South got drunk on dreams.

Then, on July first, searching Federal cavalry under General Buford bumped into Confederate skirmishers. Fame came to Gettysburg with those opening gun-shots.

The most furious open battle this continent ever witnessed raged for three days. Valor made bucolic place-names like Little Round Top unforgettable, and carnage littered a cemetery whose sign prohibited firearms. With two great armies locked in a death-grapple nobody gave much thought to a distant siege. But, on July third, while the Southern General Pickett massed his troops for the final charge that left him an immortal failure, the white flags of truce came out from Vicksburg's defenses.

Under the hot Mississippi sky, beneath a scrawny oak tree, the commanding generals conferred. The Confederate, Pemberton, in his neat gray, moodily plucked at the grass. His opponent wore rumpled, unbuttoned blue, chewed a cigar, and resembled a uniformed farmer.

Grant was a laconic man, but kindly. They talked for almost two hours.

Always a good winner, Grant's terms were generous.

THE SILENCE of cannon and coehorn made the day seem unnaturally quiet. It had a different feel than the uneasy lulls that had been so like the tense pause between thunder and lightning. This stillness wasn't shattered by rattling small-arms, nor even the lone crack of a sharpshooter's rifle. This was finish, surrender. The muffled tread of marching men had a solemn cadence that seemed to emphasize the occasion.

Tempe Dixon marched with his comrades. He planned to join Alex later, after they'd gone back into the town to sign their paroles. But, now, this was where he belonged, among the silent defeated who had fought beside him so long, in the straggling gray ranks winding out of the breastworks to lay down their arms.

It was, ironically, a beautiful summer morning. The fair blue sky was dotted with lazily moving fluffy clouds, and the heat was less intense. The kind of day when you sang on rising, and went fishing. Nobody around him was singing, or even talking much. They needed no commands for what they had to do. Their cussing had been done, and they didn't feel like banter.

The sharpshooters had never been noted for their drill on parade, but they kept step, at a funeral pace, carried the rifles at right-shoulder shift, in line. Sunlight flashed on the bobbing bayonets.

Good thing, thought Tempe, they got me in the left shoulder. It had been a long time since he'd toted an empty Enfield for pure show, but he wouldn't have wanted to spoil this correct military formation. Not before all those watching Yankees.

"Come to crow," Lack Norris had growled when they first sighted the massed regiments of bluecoats.

That had proved false. The Yankee regiments stood in proper ranks alongside the road, formed square around the disarming field, at respectful attention. There were no jeers or catcalls. A few gunners climbed on their pieces for a better view of the proceedings, but they, too, watched quietly.

They cheered only once, Tempe recalled, in barked salute for the first surrendering contingent. The Yanks were good soldiers, recognized their beaten enemies as equals.

The sharpshooters shuffled to a halt now, and the front file peeled off to ground arms. When his turn came, Tempe lowered the rifle carefully, moving with one-handed awkwardness.

He felt a pang at parting with the Enfield. Someday he would own another like it. Jollibee, he noticed, had removed the telescope from his Sharps.

They waited until the regimental color-bearer placed the swathed flag on the pile. The torn red-and-white banner looked vivid against the stacked guns. A faint sigh, quickly suppressed, stirred the sharpshooters. Then, without command, they wheeled into column for the march back.

"You know what day this is?" asked Sergeant Tazewell.

"The Fourth of July," Tempe said.

"Uh-uh. Independence Day."

"Theirs," Lack Norris said, "not ours!"

"It's ours, too, Lack."

Jollibee said, "Well, it's jolly well not mine!"

"Just be glad the fireworks are over," Lack said.

"Paroled," Tazewell said gloomily. "Not to bear arms until exchanged."

"You going home, Sarge?"

"Where's home, Tempe? I've been in the army—theirs or this one— since I was younger than you. I ain't rightly got any place to call home."

"Well, I'm going to mine," Jollibee said, "by the first ship I can catch. I've had enough of your blooming country, and your private war."

"There'll be more fighting," Lack said.

"Not for me."

"You're quitting cold?"

"Lack, we've just been sacked." Jollibee shook his head. "It's London for me, and a long holiday. I may take the Queen's shilling again, but I'm not in any ruddy hurry."

"How about you, Tempe?"

"I've surrendered for keeps," Tempe said, choosing the words carefully. After they were married he would take Alex to Noxubee County for a visit. She'd like Pa, and the girls. The rest of his plans were vague, except that they'd live in Vicksburg. "I don't think we can win, Lack."

"We lost plenty today," Tazewell said.

"How much do you think?" asked Lack.

"Somebody told me," Tempe said, "we had about a hundred and seventy-two cannon."

"Thirty thousand men," said the sergeant, "and about twice that many muskets."

"Thirty thousand?"

"Give a few, take a few, Lack."

"Well, where the hell were they? I never saw any thirty thousand at Champion's Hill, or here in the works either!" Lack sounded indignant.

Tazewell shrugged his big shoulders. "They wasn't all effectives."

Neither were we, Tempe thought, at the finish. They had reached the outskirts of the town, and he could see the white courthouse shining on its eminence. It still looked remarkably new and unscratched. As he gazed a flag fluttered up on the tall pole. He was too far away to distinguish colors, but he knew it would be candy-striped, the old Star-Spangled Banner. The Yankees were already taking possession.

"When do you think we can leave?" Lack asked.

"It'll take a while to parole that many men," Taze said.

Tempe realized they would be parting in a few days, might never meet again. The thought depressed him. He would stay in Vicksburg, try to straighten out Alex's wrecked inheritance, house and business. Jollibee would go home to London; Taze would probably wait to be exchanged. Lack sounded ready to fight again, but he was just as likely to change his mind, go seeking adventure.

I will miss them, Tempe thought. There'd be other, new friends in the future, of course, but none would be close in exactly the same way these three comrades had been.

They met further evidence of the Yankee occupation at the first cross-street. A bluecoat company, bayonets in line, swung out to precede them. Another was making camp by the roadside. Several slave children trailed after the marching strangers. Behind them came a dusty mule dragging a sutler's wagon.

"I say, my good man," Jollibee called to the driver. "If you'd driven that poor beast down here yesterday, we'd have eaten him."

The blue-clad soldiers laughed. A portly mess-sergeant, ladle in hand, turned from the campfire.

"Hi, Rebs," he said. "Speaking of eating, how about joining us?"

None of the sharpshooters moved. Tempe wondered if the hunger showed on his face as it did on the others. Lack wet his lips; Jollibee's Adam's apple jounced as his throat worked. Tazewell found speech first.

"You ain't joking, Yank?"

"Hell, no! Come and get it."

Other Yanks were quick to second the invitation. The twangy Northern voices were eager and friendly.

"Step right up!"

"Come on, take pot-luck!"

"Help yourselves."

"We got plenty."

There was plenty, and the Yankee infantrymen, flocking around, pressed generous portions on their former enemies. Tempe's nostrils quivered as he relished the variety of aromas. There was a cauldron of baked beans with thick slabs of salt pork. There were skillets in which bacon strips sizzled. There seemed to be buckets of fresh coffee.

That smells best, Tempe decided. But even the hard crackers the bluecoats passed around tasted wonderful.

The starving Confederates ate ravenously, trying not to wolf the food. No meal had ever matched this feast. They licked fingers, burned their mouths with too-hot coffee. The considerate enemy looked away whenever a rebel seemed near to tears.

"Damn nice of you," Tempe told the mess-sergeant.

"Bushwah," he said.

"Buncombe," said another.

A third avoided thanks by handing Tempe a copy of the Vicksburg *Daily Citizen*. This sheet, too, had been printed on wallpaper.

"It's dated Thursday, July second," the Yankee said, "but it just come out today. The note at the bottom of the last column says we found the type set up. You can see it's the only place that mentions the surrender."

Tempe nodded, as he glanced through the newspaper. It seemed to be full of quips about the siege, gaily optimistic about its ending.

"According to that," said the bluecoat soldier, "your man, Lee, is chasing them paper-collar Easterners in the Potomac Army all over God-help-us."

"Sure," Tempe said, with a shrug, "and according to the same source you Yanks haven't a chance of getting here where you are!"

The other man laughed, folded the paper carefully. "Well, it still makes a good souvenir."

Tempe hesitated, but real need came before courtesy. The Yanks had been so friendly, he hated to ask an additional favor. Alex and her family would be at Cherry Street. Nobody had stayed in the caves after yesterday's truce. There wasn't anything, he decided, he wouldn't beg for to help Alex.

"I was wondering," he said, "if you could spare some of this food for a few friends of mine in Vicksburg?"

"Sure, Reb," said the mess-sergeant. "Take all you want. You needn't even bring back the buckets."

Lack would help him with the hauling. Alex would be mighty pleased with the gift. Coffee and beans were a sight more precious than pearls.

"You know, Tempe," said Alex, "I never thought to see them on our streets, but they're right friendly."

"The damn-Yankees?" Tempe chuckled at her expression.

"Don't tease," Alex said. "I mean it." The bluecoat soldiers were everywhere, clustered on corners, crowding the roads, but their behavior had surprised her. They acted like rescuers instead of hated foes.

"Five days," Tempe said, "and you're reconverted." He smiled at her fondly, knowing how she felt. The occupation troops had been careful not to rub their enemies' noses in the town's fall. He hadn't heard any crowing when the news came through about Gettysburg.

They were standing on the courthouse steps. Tempe had come out of the building to join Alex after signing his parole. The Federal officer in charge, a captain, had been more than courteous. He knew Tempe's name and rank. Major Stephen Kittering, who had signed at the Cowan house, had mentioned both, and the captain seemed pleased to oblige. Tempe had permission to stay in Vicksburg, or leave at will.

Alex was wearing bombazine, mourning black, but her skirts were fashionably wide again, and the flat oval bonnet had a perky tilt. When she wrinkled her nose at him, Tempe's muscles melted. Even with the lack of privacy, he thought, in that battered shell of a house, we'd better get married fairly soon or there'll be a scandal.

"Maybe," she said, "I was only half-converted all the time. Grandpa made a pretty good devil's advocate."

"You're talking heresy."

"Well," said Alex, "they don't seem to hate us, and that makes it hard to hate them." A passing lieutenant in blue tipped his black slouch hat. Alex bowed, stared after him. "You see?"

"He might even be a gentleman, Alex."

"Oh, stop. You know I've met Northern gentlemen. But I'll admit I expected a few at least to treat us like criminals. No Yankee I've met seems to be a dirty abolitionist!" All the slaves in town, she recalled, were now free, and Mimosa had simply vanished.

"Most of them aren't. These soldiers are from the prairie states." Tempe had told her about seeing Grant at close quarters. The stocky Union general was as different from the natty Southern officers as a man could be. He didn't even look like a West Pointer. Grant had the air of a sturdy mechanic who knew his job, and intended to do it right.

"It's very confusing." Alex watched a squad of bluecoats march around the nearest corner. The Yankees, she decided, had brought a briskness of stride and speech to Vicksburg that was as refreshing as cool weather. Shops were re-opening as fast as the owners could stock them.

"Some of them think the war's over, Alex. Port Hudson surrendered yesterday. Now, they control the entire length of the Mississippi."

"It's only over for us, Tempe. The folks along the river. There are too many others who do hate the Yankees. Bitterly, without knowing any. In places that haven't seen a blue uniform since their state seceded. Those people will fight on, and on."

"After Lee failed, as we failed here?"

"After a dozen more failures, Tempe. I know! I've the same violent dislike for coercion, the same stubborn streak."

"Don't worry, I'll beat it out of you."

"That," she said, with a gamin grin, "should provide an entertaining evening." She saw the look in his eyes, and blushed. It seemed highly improper and daringly pleasant to be thinking such thoughts on the most prominent front steps in town.

"Tempe! Tempe! Miss Alex!"

Runcey Carr's excited yell made passers-by stop to stare. The boy came racing down the middle of the road, heedless of horse traffic or pedestrians, bare feet kicking dust as he ran. Runcey had lost his hat somewhere; the wind-rumpled red hair was a flickering torch.

A Yankee carter cursed as Runcey ducked under his team's muzzles. The horses whinnied, tossed their heads.

"What's got into Runcey?"

"I'm sure he'll tell us, Tempe."

Runcey skittered to a stop in front of them. He was panting, so pale with excitement that his freckles seemed huge. "Tempe. Miss Alex. I've been looking for you all over!"

"Get your breath," Tempe said. "You found us."

"They want to hire the steamboats!"

"Please, Runcey," said Alex, wincing. "You don't have to shriek."

"But—but—"

"Back up, and start over," Tempe said. "Who wants to hire what steamboats?"

"Yankee traders. Our steamboats."

"You mean the *Tonica?*"

"The *Chickasaw,* too, Miss Alex. Both of them!" The boy fumbled inside his shirt, drew out a sheaf of greenbacks. "Look-a-here!"

"Runcey!"

"Where'd you get all that money?"

"This? This ain't nothing. It's just a—a binder so's I'd go straight to the owners without listening to any other traders. These here fellers are buying cotton. They've got United States government permits, and everything. They've got the cargo. They want us to ship it North."

"But, Runcey, those ships have been tied up, out of commission for—"

"There ain't nothing wrong with them, Miss Alex, that steam in the boilers won't fix."

"You're sure?"

"Tempe. Of course I'm sure." Runcey sounded annoyed.

Tempe felt something of the boy's excitement. The Kittering vessels were private property, had done no fighting. The Federal authorities were generously letting Vicksburg's merchants trade with anyone who wasn't an active enemy.

"If we can get the ships released—"

"We can! Others are doing it! But, we don't want to get left behind. I reckon cotton's fetching high prices in the North, and my Yankees are in a rush." Runcey gulped a deep breath, spoke more calmly. "They'll pay plenty, but they wouldn't do business with anybody my age. I ran all the way out to Cherry Street. Both Mister Stephen and Missus Epie said it was up to you two."

"My parents said that?"

"Yes, Miss Alex. Your ma said to tell you Mister Stephen would sign any papers you needed." The boy looked puzzled. "And that she wanted passage on the first boat to Memphis."

Alex gave a slow nod. Her mother was very anxious to get away from Vicksburg. Every damaged house reminded Epie Mae of the siege. She would be very comfortable as a martyr among her kin in occupied, but unscarred Memphis.

"What about crews, captains, pilots?"

"We can find plenty willing to jump aboard right here in Vicksburg, Tempe. Good rivermen, too. Sid Auter should be around. Other pilots. I already sent Smasher for Mike Tansey to look over the engines."

"The Smasher? But—"

"Aw," said Runcey, sheepishly, "there ain't any harm in him now, Tempe. It's like I told you. He's steady as a ship's clock as long as somebody tells him to do right instead of wrong."

"Will Mike and the crews trust us until we can pay them?"

"Why not? Everybody's in the same fix. But we get paid, and pay, in Yankee dollars, greenbacks."

"Runcey," said Tempe, "you'll own the firm before you're through."

"Not me! But I'll be its best pilot." The boy laughed, did a jig step. "Now, listen, Tempe. You go in the *Tonica*, I'll ship on the *Chickasaw*. Supercargo, purser, overseer—the feller looking out for the firm's interests."

Alex, listening to the two males make plans, was amused. Tempe was every bit as absorbed as Runcey, and both had half-forgotten her. That was all right. The Ancient had told her she could trust the boy's river lore, and she'd be along to guide Tempe's judgment in this first venture.

He wasn't, she thought, going off on any steamboat trip alone. Not on *my* honeymoon! Alex smiled, thinking how Poll Randall had finally gotten the elusive Creole, wounded Henri Duchesneau, under her care.

"We had better," she said, "hustle down to the riverfront and sign those cotton traders firmly to Kittering and Dixon."

Tempe blinked, stammered. "What—what did you say?"

"You heard me."

"Sure," Runcey said. "Sure! Kittering and Dixon. Sounds fine!"

That it does, agreed Alex silently. It sounds like a future, a bright, rosy future that would live through the war into the days of peace. Tempe took her arm, and, as they headed for the waterfront, the girl looked down on the wide, unchanging river, at the dark Yankee gunboats now nestling close under the bluffs. There would be steamboats whistling, churning in and out of Vicksburg again, and soon.

Then, she turned and gazed up at the hills.

Someday she must count them, see if there really were a hundred.